THE TOBY MYE
BC

Saving
Benito

Andy Hughes

ISBN 979-8-862679-24-3

This book is a work of fiction and any resemblance to
actual events or persons is entirely coincidental

Cover design by Leah Hughes

CHAPTER 1

Birmingham, England
Monday 5th August

Benito held his breath as he tiptoed across the creaky wooden floor, pausing every time it made a sound. Even though it was still August, he shivered in the night air as a cool breeze blew in through the broken window pane above the brown leather two-seater couch. The first quarter moon shone through the glass, lighting up the room just enough for him to see his way around without tripping on anything. He jumped as something rubbed against his left leg and he looked down to see a cat meowing softly up at him. His uncle had said no one was living in the house at the moment – maybe the cat had climbed in through the hole in the glass.

He said a prayer to his friend Toby's God, wondering once again if He would ever one day be his own God. Turning right, he crept up the hallway and counted the doors on the left and when he reached the third one he stopped as he placed his hand on the door handle. Benito's ears were straining to hear any movement in the bungalow – he wouldn't put it past his uncle to lie to him. Tadeo knew that Benito would not have gone into the house if he knew someone was living there. Benito jumped a second time, catching his breath as the cat rubbed up against his leg again, meowing pitifully. Despite his circumstances, he leaned down and gave the small soft animal a stroke on his head and the cat purred in response.

Shaking his head at his foolishness for wasting time, Benito turned the handle and walked in the large bathroom to the toilet where he put his backpack on the floor before gently lifting the cistern lid. His heart pounded at the scraping sound as it rubbed against the side. He placed the lid on the seat then he reached in and grabbed the package. He lifted it out, removing the heavy item wrapped in a thick cloth. He took out the bundle of money from his bag and put it in the plastic bag making sure it was firmly sealed before placing it back in the cistern. He replaced the lid then put the small bundle in his backpack. He wiped his damp hands on his jeans then slung the pack on his back before he began his slow retreat out the way he had come, still treading quietly, even though he was sure now that there was no one in the house.

When he reached the back door, he clicked the latch so it would lock as he shut it behind him and walked out, but just as he pulled the door shut behind him, the cat dashed out and caused him to stumble down the step. He only just managed to stop himself from falling over as he got his balance at the last second. He stood for a moment as the cool breeze brushed his face and he steadied his breath before walking quietly across the long grass and out the tall wooden back gate, not noticing the small furry creature scurry through just before he clicked it shut behind him.

Benito quickly walked down the overgrown path between the backs of the houses, looking over his shoulder now and then, even though someone could be hiding in any one of the myriad of shadows that were cast from the fences and sheds. Someone's back door slammed and an owl hooted, unsettling Benito further as he broke into a jog. Reaching the end of the lane, he ran across the dimly lit street and into the empty park. Well, thought Benito, he hoped it was empty. He glanced over and saw a couple of teenage figures sitting on the swings and drinking. Benito saw the orange glow of a cigarette and, as the boy exhaled, the smoke made its own eerie shadow against the concrete wall that lined the one side of the park. The two figures stopped and appeared to look in Benito's direction, pausing from their banter and he tried his best to keep his pace steady so he did not appear frightened. One thing he had learned, it was best that people did not know when you were scared. Many people saw this as an opportunity to cause him even more trouble than he usually was already in when he was working for his uncle.

Finally, Benito reached the other end of the park and turned left on the path, now slowing to a brisk walk as he saw his uncle's car in the distance. His uncle would be angry if he knew Benito had been running. "Boy! You'll draw attention to yourself! Only guilty people run!" Tadeo's angry voice rang through head, and Benito blew a slow breath through pursed lips, trying to calm his breathing. The back of Tadeo's hand was very hard when it clipped the side of Benito's face. Instinctively, Benito rubbed his left cheek that still held a faint bruise from the last time.

When he was within thirty metres of the BMW saloon, Benito slowed his pace even more and attempted a casual stroll. The blue car looked black in the dark and Benito checked the number plate just in case. A lot of criminals seemed to like the BMWs, so it wouldn't surprise him if some other dubious character was parked on the side of the road in the middle of the night.

Opening the rear door, Benito climbed in and unzipped his backpack, while his uncle's impatient hand was thrust back towards him. He grabbed it out of Benito's hand as he retrieved it from the bag.

"Shut the door, you idiot!" growled Tadeo, and Benito jumped to obedience, slamming the door hard. Benito cringed in anticipation of his uncle's next harsh words, "Stop making so much noise and stop trying to wreck my car!"

The man who was sat in the passenger seat chuckled softly as Tadeo handed him the package. "Just can't get the staff these days, huh?"

Tadeo started the car and headed off down the road as Benito leaned back and put on his seat belt. He put his bag on the seat beside him and as he did, a soft weight landed on his thighs and his heart jumped in panic as he let out a squeal. Just then a street light flashed in the car and he was shocked to see the cat sat crouched comfortably on his lap.

"What's the matter with you, boy?" Tadeo glance over his shoulder as he turned a corner, nearly hitting the curb. He let out a loud curse. "Look what you made me do! We nearly had an accident! What's the matter? You find a spider back there?!" He laughed gruffly and the man beside him chortled.

"Uh, no, Uncle!" His uncle would be furious if he knew there was a cat in the car. He hated animals. Especially ones that would leave hair on the seat. "Uh, I mean, yes, Uncle ... I mean I thought it was a spider – a huge one! – but it was only a shadow." He took a deep breath. "Sorry Uncle." Benito stroked the cat's head and the animal began to purr softly. Benito hoped that his uncle would not hear the noise above the engine as he drove through the streets of Birmingham.

Ten minutes later, he pulled over by a long row of brick houses that all looked the same. Benito wondered how people knew which house was theirs. A low privet hedge ran along the front of the garden with a broken gate hanging on one hinge. Benito could not quite see on the other side, but by the shadows it looked like an unkempt garden with a child's toy ride-on car on the front path. Poor kid, thought Benito. What chance did the child have with a father – he assumed it was his father – like that?

The man unwrapped the gun and looked it over in the moonlight. "It looks good." He paused for effect, "But if it isn't exactly what I asked for, there'll be trouble!" He had an even deeper, meaner growl than his uncle and Benito shivered in the back seat as he ran his fingers along the cat's soft fur for comfort.

Tadeo turned in his seat, and spoke in a slow, firm voice, "Rodriguez has always been meticulous in the past – he has been paid well." He looked over at the man who held the gun and squinted his evil eyes with meaning, "And so have you. So we are even. I don't want to hear from you again." The two men stared at each other, each trying to assert their own dominance. "Are we clear?"

The man started to speak then, deciding that silence was more intimidating, he said nothing and opened the door. Climbing out of the car and shutting the door quietly, he turned and sauntered through the gate and along the path like he had just been for a night out with the boys, instead of buying an illegal gun with which he would probably injure or kill someone.

Tadeo drove off without saying a word and remained silent the rest of the journey back to his house. Despite the fact that his very presence was putting Benito in harm's way, Benito felt comforted by the soft warm bundle curled up on his lap. He tried to imagine how the cat had kept up with him when he had hurried from the house where he had picked up the gun. Or why? Didn't the little creature have a home? He had looked healthy in the house; but then it had been dark. Benito sighed. What was he going to do with the innocent animal once they arrived home? If his mom was at home he could give the cat to her, but she was still in hospital. There had been complications from the pneumonia that had put her there in the first place, and she was now in intensive care. No one was allowed to visit her for fear of further infection. A tear rolled down Benito's cheek and he quickly wiped it away. Tears made his uncle very angry.

7

Tadeo pulled up on his drive and looked in the rear view mirror just as Benito wiped his tear. "Are you crying?!" He snarled.

"No, Uncle, I have some dust in my eye." Benito took some tissue from his pocket and wiped his nose.

"Why is your nose running?" Tadeo turned around and looked straight at Benito.

Benito's heart starting banging against his chest, hoping Tadeo could not see the cat in the darkness. "Uh … maybe … uh … maybe I'm allergic to dust … or something." Benito offered feebly.

Tadeo scrunched up his face and stared at Benito, making Benito's ears begin ringing from the blood that was racing around his body as his heart pumped ever faster. "I ought to give you a clip around the ear, because I know you deserve it for something!"

A wet scratchy tongue licked Benito's thumb that was conveniently by the little mouth. Benito just looked down, saying nothing, and Tadeo took it as an apology for being pathetic – *and so he should*, thought Tadeo. He twisted his mouth as he looked at his nephew. It wouldn't be long before he would look too much like a man to be used as an innocent looking youth. He was eighteen, but he had still been useful because he was skinny and looked very young for his age, but he was beginning to fill out – despite Tadeo under-feeding him to keep him small. And he was actually starting to get a bit of teenage stubble. Maybe he could still use him. He *was* proving to be more intelligent than Tadeo had given him credit for – and braver. Getting that VIN number from the car in Louisiana had showed initiative. He'd have to decide what he was going to do. But not tonight. He was tired tonight and his bed was calling him.

Tadeo opened the car door and climbed out. He shut the door and stood, waiting for Benito who was trying desperately to think of what he was going to do with the cat. Suddenly, he realised that Tadeo was watching him, so he opened the door and leaned out, dislodging the cat who jumped silently to the ground and trotted across the grass to the edge of the hedge that bordered the two semi-detached houses. The movement caught Tadeo's eye.

"What's that?" He walked around the car as Benito shut his door carefully, watching the cat sit unperturbed on the grass, looking back at Tadeo. "Shoo! Shoo! You stupid animal! You are probably the one that has been leaving your mess behind! Go on, shoo or I'll deal with you permanently!" Tadeo whispered loudly so he would not arouse the neighbours. The cat crept under the hedge out of Tadeo's sight and Benito let out a deep breath. Tadeo shot a glance over at him. "He a friend of yours?" He accused Benito who shook his head vehemently.

"No, Uncle, no! Of course not. I know you do not like animals – I would never encourage a cat to come into the garden." Benito stood with his backpack hanging in his hand, not wanting to move until his uncle did.

Tadeo faced Benito, and although it was dark Benito knew Tadeo was glaring at him, trying to intimidate him. Benito remained silent and finally Tadeo turned and walked up to the front door of the semi-detached house, turning the key in the lock and stepping inside. Benito waited only a moment before following Tadeo into the small hallway. Tadeo was already in the kitchen, getting a beer out of the fridge, so Benito trotted up the stairs and into his bedroom, shutting the door so he would hopefully not have to speak to Tadeo again.

Benito sat on the bed and listened to the movements of his uncle downstairs, and when he turned on the television,

Benito dared to open his bedroom window and look down to see if he could find his new friend. The cat was sat on Tadeo's front lawn, looking around, and Benito wondered if he was looking for him, so he called out in a whisper. "Hello there!"

The cat looked up, and when he saw Benito he immediately stood and began scouting around. Benito wondered what he was doing, and then slowly shook his head in wonderment as the cat scooted through the hedge, expertly climbed the adjoining neighbour's tree, across a branch that overhung the roof and onto the gutter of the house. Trotting across to Tadeo's property, he stopped when he was directly above Benito and meowed before jumping down to the top of his open window and inside Benito's room, landing on his bed. Giving a satisfied meow, he looked at Benito and meowed again, as the teenager stood staring in disbelief at the grey and white cat. Now that he saw him in the light, he could see what a lovely coloured cat he was, mostly light grey with white from his chin down along his stomach, and two uneven front white socks. His dark blue eyes blinked at Benito slowly.

Finally, after several minutes, Benito sat down on the bed beside the cat and began stroking his back thoughtfully. "You must be thirsty. I'll find something to put some water in for you to drink." Benito stood, and bit his lip looking at the intriguing animal, and shook his head again, wondering why the furry creature had chosen to befriend him.

Standing up, Benito walked to his bedroom door, opening it then shutting it directly behind him. He began to tiptoe down the stairs, then thought the better of it since his uncle would still hear him, and if he was trying to be quiet, Benito would raise Tadeo's suspicions. So for the last few steps the teenager trod heavier and Tadeo shouted at him from the living room.

"What are you doing?!" he growled at his nephew. Benito stopped by the doorway into the living room and saw his uncle leaning back on his chair with his feet on a stool, beer in one hand and a large bag of crisps in the other. Benito's stomach growled and Tadeo sneered.

"I was just getting a glass of water, Uncle," said Benito slowly, looking hungrily at the salty snack in the man's large hand.

Tadeo squinted his eyes, and an unpleasant smile stretched across his face. "As a reward for doing the job tonight..." he paused and Benito grew hopeful, thinking he would get something to eat. However, Tadeo laughed and continued, "I'll pay another month of your mother's rent on her flat! She may yet live to go back to it, more's the pity. She's costing me money. I wish she would either die or get well and go back to work. She always was an indecisive woman!" He put a handful of salt and vinegar crisps in his mouth, looking at his nephew tauntingly before turning back to his television programme.

Benito was distraught. His uncle's callous attitude towards his mom and his spite towards him threatened to bring tears to his eyes, so he quickly turned and walked into the kitchen, wondering how he was going to get his new friend some water.

"And wash the dishes while you are in there, you lazy boy!" Tadeo chortled from the living room at the comedy he was watching on the large screen.

Benito sighed, then perked up. That would give him time to figure out what he would do. He smiled as he looked at the clutter on the kitchen table. Two take-away containers were there from earlier, and one had a little bit of left-over chicken, and black bean sauce and rice in the other. He quickly put the two together and put the lid on, placing it on the side before quickly washing the dishes, including the one now empty

11

container. He rinsed out the sink, grabbed the containers and turned off the kitchen light, walking steadily towards the stairs, hoping – praying – that Tadeo would not stop him. Another guffaw came from the living room and the teenager trotted up the steps and into the bathroom where he filled the empty container with water before returning to his bedroom.

The cat was now curled up asleep, but he opened his eyes as Benito entered the room then shut the door behind him. He put the container of water on the floor and slid it under his bed, then opened the other container of Tadeo's leftovers, and slid that under too. The cat immediately jumped off the bed and drank thirstily, before tucking into the food and quickly finishing off Benito's meagre offering. Benito changed into his pyjama shorts and t-shirt and turned off the light, waiting for his eyes to adjust to the darkness before he walked over to his bed and lay down on his side on top of the covers. The cat leaped up and snuggled into the crook of his arm and promptly began purring.

He didn't know how he was going to secretly take care of a cat, but Benito was adamant he would do whatever he needed to take the best care of this little creature who had attached himself to him. He gently stroked the soft head and smiled to himself, despite how much trouble he would be in if Tadeo found out.

Benito had been missing his new friends that he had met in Nicaragua and then in America, and since his uncle had taken away his phone he had no way of contacting them. He doubted he would ever see them again. He sighed, saddened at the thought. He had never really thought much about friends before – he had mostly just thought of survival. It had felt good to have friends; people he felt who actually cared about him. He just wasn't sure they cared enough to try and find him.

Benito pressed his face into the top of the cat's head and the soft animal nuzzled him gently. He would have to think of a name. But what, he wondered? Then it came to him: he had been reading in his Bible about a man from Israel who had gone out to fight some other people and God had told him he had too many men. Benito got up carefully, trying not to disturb the cat and switched the light on. He went to the drawer by his bed and took out the little red book and found his place, Judges 6, and began to read. Gideon! Yes, He had started out with 32,000 men and God had him whittle his army down to 300 men to fight the thousands of Midianites and Amalekites because He did not want the Israelites to think they had won the battle themselves. God wanted them to know that He had fought for them. In the end, God indeed did conqueror Israel's enemies.

Benito spoke softly to the cat, "I think I will call you Gideon." As the teenager closed the Bible, he noticed what it said on the front: placed here by the Gideons. How had he not noticed that before? Yes, of course, they were the group of people who placed Bibles in motels — one such room in Louisiana was where he had taken this from. He still felt slightly guilty, but decided God would probably understand that he had no money to buy one, and he felt that the Gideons would have given him one for free anyway, had he ever met one!

Feeling happier now that his little friend had a name, Benito shut off the light and crawled back down on the bed beside Gideon, pressing his face again into the soft fur and sighing contentedly. He still wasn't sure how he was going to feed the little animal, but the teenager closed his eyes and with determination in his heart, he thanked God for sending him this new friend, quickly falling asleep to the purring in his ear.

CHAPTER 2

Tuesday 16th August

"**B**enito! Get up, boy!"

Benito sat bolt upright in bed, his heart hammering against his chest, as he tried to shake the fog of sleep from his brain. The cat! He looked around, but his little grey friend was nowhere to be seen. Benito silently thanked God as he blinked a few times and looked up at his uncle standing menacingly in the doorway.

"Yes, Uncle?" He answered with a croaky voice.

"What are you doing still in bed, boy? It's nine o'clock! We've got work to do!"

Benito blinked again slowly, thinking to himself that being up until nearly three o'clock in the morning doing the gun run, his uncle would have allowed him to sleep until at least ten. He shook his head; what was he thinking? Of course his uncle would not allow him any leniency.

"Sorry Uncle, I'll get up straight away." Benito pulled the duvet off of him and swung his feet down onto the floor, trying desperately to remember what it was they were supposed to be doing. Maybe it was better not knowing.

"You can have some breakfast when we get back with the parts. I want to get going because I don't know how long it is going to take me." He growled for effect before shutting the door behind him firmly as he left.

Oh, yes, thought Benito. There was something wrong with his car and he wanted to fix it. The exhaust, that was it. Benito's stomach grumbled loudly at him, and as he quickly got dressed he looked down at his skinny frame. He remembered Caleb and Joe comparing themselves and he thought about how tall and well-built they both were.

Benito's body still looked like a twelve-year-old. Another sigh escaped him before he remembered to thank God again for his friend and wondered when Gideon would return. He left his room and shut the door gently behind him, hoping that the little creature would, in fact, return.

When they came back from the store, Tadeo took the parts out of the back of his car and turned to Benito. "You have ten minutes to have some cereal and a small glass of juice, then I want you to get back out here to help me." He squinted his piercing blue eyes at Benito then looked down at his watch. The teenager didn't need to be told twice and he dashed into the house and into the kitchen where he grabbed a bowl and filled it up before pouring over some milk, then quickly getting a glass of juice, he took a quick look into the fridge to see if there was anything his uncle would not miss, that he could give to his cat. He spotted a pack of loose ham and he took two slices and placed them on top of his cereal before hurrying up the stairs to his bedroom.

A big smile spread across Benito's face as he saw the little animal curled up on his pillow, and he put his cereal and glass on his bedside cupboard. Gideon opened his eyes and yawned as he saw Benito, blinking at him slowly. Benito took the ham and tore into several small pieces and put them into the bowl that was just under his bed. He gave the cat a scratch on his head as he jumped off the pillow and began eating the ham. Benito sat on his bed and gulped down half the juice before grabbing his cereal and shovelling it in his mouth, nearly choking as he tried to swallow as he chewed. He didn't want his uncle coming in the room and finding his new friend.

Five minutes later, Benito stroked Gideon's head as he again curled up on the teenager's pillow, grabbed his dishes and hurried downstairs, quickly washing them and leaving them on the draining board before hurrying out the front door where his uncle was just sliding himself out from under the car.

"I said ten minutes boy, not eleven!" The large man grumbled at his nephew quietly. He wanted the boy to know his disapproval, but he did not want to get the attention of his nosy neighbours. Tadeo had only lived there for a few months, but he felt like they were watching him. He would have to move again soon. He smiled to himself. If this job he was planning worked out well, he would be able to start looking for a private house out in the country somewhere, away from prying eyes. Maybe even in another country.

"I'm sorry, Uncle, I washed up my dishes because I thought you wouldn't like the mess." Then to divert any more anger towards him, he added, "What do you want me to do?"

"Get under here with me and hold up this up."

Benito obeyed and slid under the car beside his uncle to hold up the part that Tadeo was working on. His uncle said no more to him except for instructions of getting tools, where to aim the flash light and what to hold on to. And for the next couple of hours, Benito obediently did as he was told while his uncle worked on his car.

It was after 1:00 by the time Tadeo finished fixing his car and he ordered Benito, "Make us a couple of sandwiches! You can have one and I will have two. I'll be in as soon as I've put my tools away."

Benito responded immediately and scurried into the house to make some sandwiches. He put three slices of ham in his uncle's sandwiches and put one in his, then hesitated. Perhaps he could get away with two, and not have his uncle find out, if he let the lettuce hang out and hide the meat. He sliced a tomato, added some lettuce and mayonnaise before putting them on plates which he placed on the kitchen table. Sitting down in front of his sandwich, he bowed his head and thanked God for the food – and once again for Gideon, and began eating.

When Benito had finished the first half of his sandwich, Tadeo came in and poked his head into the kitchen to have a look at what Benito was eating. Then he looked at the sandwiches that were waiting for him. "You know I like cheese in there as well, boy! I've worked hard this morning! And you may have half a glass of milk. I'm going up to have a quick shower and then we will go see your *mother*." He said the word with disdain. "The hospital called to say we could have a short visit with her today." He paused as he scowled, "Though of course, *I* don't want to, but I thought you would like to." He turned and Benito listened to him walk heavily up the stairs.

Tadeo chuckled to himself as he got in the shower and turned it on. It was important the boy had a continued incentive to obey him. If Benito saw his mom, he would remember how important it was to obey his uncle Tadeo who was paying her rent while she couldn't work, and also gave her money for food sometimes when she was struggling. He wouldn't bother with his weak-minded sister at all if it wasn't for the boy's usefulness. To make matters worse, Gabriella had started going to church a few months ago. Tadeo involuntarily snarled out a chuckle. *God*, he thought to himself; the idea of such a Being was a crutch for all weak-minded people. Well, see how her God would protect her from him, Tadeo, in the near future. Benito was eighteen years old – an adult – and this big job Tadeo had planned would involve Benito in such a way that would put him in prison for a very long time if he was caught. That would be incentive enough! Then Tadeo could tell Gabriella's landlord she no longer needed the place. Tadeo could stop paying rent and stop giving her money for groceries. His sister would be out on the street where she belonged, and would no longer be a problem for him.

Benito finished his sandwich and his half glass of milk while Tadeo was still showering. He put his dishes in the sink then hurried upstairs to check on Gideon. He was disappointed to find that his little friend had once more disappeared, but he felt confident that he would return later.

Taking his Bible from the drawer, he positioned the pillow behind his back as he sat back to continue reading. He was disappointed to find that when Gideon died, the Israelites again turned their backs on God. It seemed that when they had a godly leader, they were godly, but when their leader wasn't, neither were they. In fact, sometimes they did quite evil things. He put the book on his lap and thought to himself. It didn't seem that their love for God was very sincere, if they could be swayed by their leader. God must have been very disappointed in them. Did He appreciate their devotion under a good leader, or did God feel sad knowing, as He must, that it was not genuine? But then, was he, Benito, any different? He could behave 'godly' when he was with his friends in Louisiana, but here with his uncle, he was doing all kinds of crimes. Yes, it was out of fear for his mother, and himself – but he felt certain that did not make it all right. How many people were being hurt by the guns and other things he was helping to supply people?

A tear trickled down his face, and as he heard his uncle stomp up the stairs he quickly wiped it away and put his Bible back in the drawer. Tadeo burst through the door without knocking and scowled at his nephew.

"Let's go, boy, I don't have all day!"

Benito jumped off the bed and grabbed his trainers, quickly putting them on and tying them up, before grabbing his hoodie from the bottom of his bed, and hurried out after his uncle who was already down the stairs and out of the front door. Benito clicked the door shut behind him and hurried to the back door on the passenger side. Out of the corner of his eye, he saw Gideon, curled up in a little spot of sunshine, under the hedge that divided the Tadeo's house from the neighbour's, and he smiled happily to himself.

"You afraid of me, boy?" Tadeo chortled gruffly as he started the engine, and looked over his shoulder at Benito who was quickly putting on his seatbelt. "You always sit in the back!" He laughed again, but the teenager said nothing as the BMW backed out of the drive and headed towards the hospital.

Tadeo pulled into the hospital car park and pulled into one of the last spots available, then the two of them walked over to the large building and through the automatic doors. Tadeo walked up to the desk and, conjuring up an ingratiating smile and an east London accent, leaned down towards the pretty young auburn haired lady that sat behind it. "Hello, darlin' I wonder if you would mind directing a poor lost man. We are here to see this young lad's mother, Gabriella Demara."

The young woman duly succumbed to his charm and smiled flirtatiously back. Benito was shocked as he looked at his uncle, whose face actually seemed to transform into the attractive man he was aiming to portray. The teenager remained silent as he observed the teasing banter between the two of them, amazed that he was still looking at the same man who was actually his nefarious uncle. He should have been an actor, Benito thought to himself. He could probably have made lots of money and had lots of women falling for him.

Five minutes later, they were walking down the hallway towards the intensive care ward. A waiting room was just outside, and Tadeo sat down. His face had turned back to his normal expression as he scowled at Benito and nodded his head towards the door. "What are you waiting for? Go on in.

I'll wait out here. Don't be long." He leaned over to pick up a magazine from the table in front of him, and Benito walked over to the double doors. Immediately through them there were another set of double doors, and on the other side was a curved desk with an older lady and a young man sat behind it. The man carried on with his paperwork, but the woman looked up at Benito and smiled compassionately.

"Are you here to see your mother, sweetheart?" Benito looked confused, but nodded as she continued, "The receptionist phoned up to say you were coming. If you just have a seat over there, one of the nurses will come out and take you to her." She gave him another warm smile before returning to her work, and Benito sat in a chair nearest the door that he assumed went into the actual ward. He looked up as the doors from the hallway opened and a kind-looking black-haired man carrying a black book, approached the desk. Again, the woman looked up and spoke. "Hello, pastor Frank, how are you today?"

"Afternoon, Margaret! I wanted to see Gabriella for ten minutes, if I may." He beamed at her, the corners of his mouth stretching across his face, and Benito instantly liked him.

"Oh, I'm sorry. Her son is here," She nodded to Benito who smiled faintly at the amiable man who seemed the complete opposite of his uncle.

"That's all right!" He looked over at Benito, nodding, and back at Margaret as he held up his book: "I can do some reading while I wait, if that's okay?"

"Of course! Would you like a cup of coffee?" she asked as she stood up and headed into a back room before he could answer.

"Yes please," answered the man behind the desk speaking for the first time without raising his head. "I thought you would never ask!"

Pastor Frank chuckled as he sat down beside Benito, and they heard Margaret call out laughingly, "You *are* idle, Tim!"

Frank turned to Benito and offered his hand, "Hello, son. My name is Frank," he said unnecessarily. Benito took the man's warm hand and looked up at him slowly.

"I'm Benito," he replied as the warmth from the man's hand and face seemed to envelope the teenager like a soft thick blanket.

"How are you, son?" Frank asked softly.

"I'm okay, thank you," lied Benito underneath the blanket.

Frank tilted his head and he squinted his dark brown eyes thoughtfully. "I have spoken a little with your mom," he began. "Since she has been in here, some days she has been able to talk and we have had good conversations. She tells me you are staying with your uncle, her brother."

The blanket began to slide off and Benito lowered his eyes. "Yes, sir."

There was silence for a moment, then Frank spoke. "Benito," he said in such a way that compelled the teenager to look back up into the man's searching eyes: "And he treats you kindly?"

Benito involuntarily shivered as the warm covering now lay in a pile by his feet. He felt hypnotised by the man's gaze, and opened his mouth to speak, but nothing came out. His heart started pounding and his feet began tapping, Just then, a nurse came through the ward doors and looked down at him.

"Benito?" He looked up and nodded. Another kind smile greeted him. "Come with me, darling, I'll take you to your mom." Benito stood, and without looking back at Frank, followed the nurse into the ward that held six beds. Someone lay on each bed, eyes closed and arms attached to various machines. Benito sucked in a deep breath and the nurse, the same height as him, put her arm around his shoulder and patted him gently as she guided him to a chair beside his mom's bed. He flopped into it and grabbed her hand, and tears welled up in his eyes as he saw her pale skin and the oxygen mask over her face. She opened her gentle brown eyes at his touch and they widened with delight as she pulled the mask down and smiled at her son, squeezing his hand. Tears flowed down his cheeks at her reaction, and he stood.

"Is it okay if I give you a hug?" he asked, worried he would hurt her.

She nodded fervently and leaned forward as she pulled him towards her. He he kissed her cheek and they embraced, mother and son both crying.

"I've missed you so much, Benny!"

"Me too, Mom!" Benito stood up and wiped his nose with his shirt sleeve. The nurse came over with a box of tissues and they each took one to dry their tears. Gabriella clung tightly to her son's hand as she lay her head back on the pillow and closed her eyes, breathing deeply. Benito watched her, saying nothing, lost in his own thoughts. They sat in silence for a while, and Benito was just about to stand up when his mom opened her eyes again and looked directly at him.

"You're all right with your Uncle Tadeo, honey, aren't you?" There was a desperation in her eyes for him to be happy, and he could not disappoint her.

"Of course, Mom! Terrific!" He forced a smile that he hoped looked natural, but the faintest glimmer of understanding entered her face and he felt compelled to dispel her fears. "I'm just fine, Mom, don't worry! You just concentrate on getting better!" He sat back down, but she continued to hang on to his hand. Gabriella pursed her lips and tilted her head, analysing her son.

"I got myself a Bible, and I am reading it every day." He spoked animatedly and was rewarded with a broad smile he knew she would give in response. "I don't understand a lot, but I am trying."

"That's great, Benny." She lay back on her bed and closed her eyes, taking in a deep breath and releasing her tight grip on Benito. He took her hand and placed it carefully on her stomach as he stood up and kissed her cheek again and whispered softly. "I'll let you rest, Mom. There's a Pastor out there that wants to see you. Shall I tell him to come another time?"

Her head moved slowly back and forth on the pillow. "He comes every day to read to me and pray. I can listen while my eyes are closed."

Benito nodded and turned to leave as he gave his nose another wipe before stuffing the tissue in his pocket. Tadeo would be annoyed if he saw evidence of him crying. He would have to find somewhere to wash his face before he went out into the hall. As he walked into the ICU reception area, Pastor Frank motioned for him to sit down beside him and Benito inadvertently glanced towards the double doors that led out to the hall where Tadeo was probably slowly growing impatient.

Frank noted his look and whispered, "It will only take a moment, Benito, please, sit down for a moment." Benito reluctantly obeyed and sat with his hands folded on his lap, not wanting to look into the man's face. "Are you a Christian, son?"

Benito shrugged his shoulders. "I don't know, sir. I don't think so – I do too many things wrong – I am not sure God likes me."

The pastor smiled warmly, even though Benito was not looking up at him. "We *all* do too many things wrong, Benito. That's why we need Jesus. It is the gift of His life on the cross that takes away our sins and presents us clean before God."

Benito started to stand, anxious about Tadeo's response to his delay in returning. Frank put his hand on Benito's shoulder to stop him, and continued quickly. "Have you got a Bible?" Benito nodded. "Read Ephesians. Ephesians 2, verses 8-10." Benito tried to put the verse in his memory, as he finally managed to stand and without saying goodbye or looking at the man, walked over to the desk to ask the woman if there was a toilet he could use. She pointed him to a door in the corner that he had not noticed, and hurried over to it, washing his face and drying it with a paper towel. When he came out, the pastor was gone, and Benito hurried out into the corridor where Tadeo was sat scowling.

"What took you so long boy?" He scolded him quietly as he stood, quickly glancing around, and seeing no one, smacked Benito on the side of the head with the back of his hand, his ring catching Benito's ear. A sharp pain caused Benito to gasp as his ear began to ring, and his hand automatically reached up to cover his ear. "That didn't hurt! Stop being such a wimp! Come on! I've got some things to do." He growled, and marched down the hall, with Benito trotting to keep up with him.

⸺⸺⸺⸻●●⸺⸺⸺

BIRMINGHAM AIRPORT

"Toby! Toby!"

Toby and Rebeca turned as they walked out of the double doors with their bags and headed towards the medium height, dark-haired woman with feminine curves, waving frantically at them. Toby strode towards her open arms with a wide grin, while Rebeca held back, walking slowly behind him, unsure of how to greet Toby's mom. She needn't have worried though, for as soon as she had given her tall son a huge hug, she turned to Rebeca and embraced her enthusiastically as well.

"You must be Rebeca! How wonderful to finally meet you!" She gave her son another huge squeeze and kissed his cheek before she stood back, smiling happily at them both, holding a hand of each of them tightly. "The girls wanted to come into the airport with me to meet you, but they were too wound up about your return and meeting Rebeca, and I didn't think I would be able to keep track of them!" She laughed as she continued. "I left them in the car with your dad – I am sure he is going crazy by now!" She stopped suddenly and Toby nearly walked into her. "I guess I'd better let him know relief is on the way!" She tapped on her phone quickly, then put it in her bag, before charging happily through the crowded Birmingham airport and out of the automatic doors with Rebeca and Toby following behind with their bags.

They walked through the car park and Toby spotted their car in the distance just as the passenger doors flew open and two similar looking girls with chestnut hair jumped out and ran towards them squealing.

"Toby! Rebeca!"

Not knowing who to hug first, the girls pulled the two teenagers into a group hug and Rebeca laughed. Toby gasped as he smiled, "I can't breath!" Then added, "I think this is mostly for you, Rebeca, they don't normally want to hug me!"

The girls broke into fits of giggles as they released their hold and bounced in front of Toby and Rebeca, "But you have been gone for sooooo long, Toby!"

Toby cocked his head as he looked at them and then Rebeca – they were nearly the same height as her. "I think you girls have grown!"

Thrilled at the comment, they shrieked excitedly, saying in unison, "We *knew* it! We told Mom we had! But she hasn't had time to measure us! Will you measure us when we get home?!" There was a measuring tape stuck to the wall in the corner of the kitchen at the entrance into the house, that had been there since Joe was a toddler.

"Sure!" Toby grinned as he ruffled their short curly hair simultaneously, shaking his head instantly as he recognised the same action that so irritated him with Joe. However, it didn't seem to bother the girls at all and they leaped into the back seats of the silver seven-seater VW Touran as his dad got out of the driver's seat and came around to give his son a great bear hug. Dave Myers was a couple of inches taller than Toby and built solidly like his other son, Joe, with the chestnut hair of his daughters. However, there was no mistaking the fact that they were father and son.

"It's great to see you again, son. We are so glad that you are back safely home with us!" He turned to Rebeca and held out his hand warmly, placing his other hand on top of hers when she reached out. "And you too, Rebeca. We are grateful for all you have done for Toby!"

"Come on!" screeched the twins from the back of the car, "We want to get measured!"

"There isn't a lot of room for your bags with the twins in the back," apologised Toby's mom, "I probably should have left the girls behind with Joe."

"That is fine, Mrs Myers, we can put our things on the seat and floor between us," said Rebeca as she climbed in first, placing her bags on the floor. Then Toby tossed his on the seat between them and jumped in as well.

"Oh, my dear! Please call me Emily!" She climbed in her seat and looked over her shoulder at Rebeca with a wide grin as Dave slowly backed out of the parking space. She nodded towards Toby's dad, "And please call Toby's dad Dave!" Rebeca grinned in response as she put on her seatbelt.

It was over an hour's drive to the village where the Myers lived, but the time passed quickly with lively chatter from Samantha and Alexandra, interspersed with Emily's interjections of, "Girls! Let someone else have a chance to talk!"

Rebeca, who was twisted around in her seat listening to the twins, laughed in response, "That is all right Mrs – Emily – it gives me a chance to get to know each of them, and now I can tell the two apart quite well."

Emily raised an eyebrow, "I'm impressed! They really are quite similar and most people take a long time to get to know the difference."

"Well for one thing, their eyes are shaped a little differently. Also, Alexandra lifts both her eyebrows a little when she is excited, and although Samantha does the same, she lifts her left eyebrow ever so slightly higher than her right."

This made the girls burst out in fits of giggles as they raised their eyebrows in an exaggerated fashion at each other. Toby looked at Rebeca and shook his head slightly: "I never cease to be impressed by your powers of observation! I have never noticed that before!" He paused, thinking it over. "I mean, I know which is Sam and which is Alex, but I have never thought about *why* I know which is which."

"And that is why I am a better tracker than you!" She smiled, pleased with herself.

"Rebeca!" chided Toby, "You do have a fault, after all!" Rebeca's face scrunched in confusion, as Toby continued, "Pride!" He paused and added, "And here I thought you were perfect, but I guess you are not after all; how disappointing!" Toby laughed heartily, but Rebeca's face fell and he was immediately sorry for his teasing.

"Toby, how rude!" His mom was turned in her seat and saw Rebeca's face. "Rebeca is only speaking the truth –

she *is* a better tracker than you! In fact, from what I have heard about your ventures, I don't know anyone who could find their way – and others – better than Rebeca!" Emily reached back and patted Rebeca on the knee. "Don't you worry about Toby's comments, dear! God has blessed you with an amazing gift, and there is nothing wrong with acknowledging the gifts He has given you!" She smiled encouragingly at Rebeca.

Rebeca managed a weak smile back, but she felt disappointed with herself. Although she was hurt by what Toby had said, she realised it hurt because it was true. She *did* have pride in her tracking abilities. It was the one thing she had that Gwen did not have – Gwen, the beautiful rich girl who had been kidnapped and held by Tadeo in Rebeca's village in exchange for some diamonds. Toby had inadvertently gotten himself involved as well, and Rebeca had helped the two of them escape. Despite having had self-confidence and the assurance of her worth in God's eyes her whole life, since she met these teenagers, her view of herself had become skewed.

The two young girls did not notice the atmosphere had changed, and continued to chatter away happily, then began firing questions at Rebeca about life in a jungle.

"What kind of food do you eat?" asked Samantha.

"Well," started Rebeca, "we live by a river, so we eat lots of fish." Then began a detailed explanation of all the food they ate, interjected by the twins' various questions of catching, preparation, and also washing up without a kitchen sink!

Soon Dave Myers pulled up on the gravel drive of their detached house and everyone piled out of the car, with the twins hanging on to each of Rebeca's arms as they walked up to the house, still chattering and asking Rebeca questions about life in a jungle.

28

"I thought the twins could move into your room, Toby. And you move in with Joe, since he has a king size bed. Then Rebeca and Gwen, when she arrives tomorrow, can have the girls' room since they have bunk beds. I thought it best that the guests have their own beds."

"Yes, that's fine," said Toby as he waited for the twins and Rebeca to go inside first.

"Oh, no!" said Rebeca, "I don't want to push you out of your room, Toby. I can sleep on the floor somewhere."

Toby laughed. "You are in civilisation now, Rebeca, everyone gets a bed! I'll just get a few of my things out before the twins get in there, and you make yourself at home in their room!"

Joe walked into the kitchen when they entered the house and a wide smile spread across his face as he opened his arms to give Rebeca a hug which she happily returned. He held on for a little too long, before stepping back and looking down at her as he fought the urge to kiss her cheek. Emily Myers raised an eyebrow as she briefly caught the deeply wistful look in Joe's eyes before he turned away to welcome his brother as well.

"I've given my room a clean and changed the sheets, you'll be pleased to know, little brother!" Joe laughed as he ruffled Toby's head, waiting for a rebuttal and surprised to get none. He cocked his head curiously, but said nothing as Toby, Rebeca and the twins took the bags upstairs to their bedrooms.

"I've got a chicken curry in the slow cooker for tea, and only need to make some rice which will take about twenty minutes," Emily called up the stairs after them.

"Tea?" Rebeca looked at Toby curiously as he rummaged through some drawers deciding what he would need.

"Our evening meal," Toby explained, grinning.

"Did you think we grind it all up and drink it?" Alexandra asked, and both twins chuckled.

Rebeca placed her bag on the carpet and sat on the bed frowning as she asked, "What do you call the drink you make with herbs and hot water then?"

"Tea!" the twins shouted gleefully, and Rebeca looked thoughtful.

"Then how do you know what you will receive when someone offers you some tea?"

This time Samantha spoke up, "Usually if someone is going to give you a drinking tea, they ask if you want a cup of tea. If it is something to eat, they ask if you want tea." She tittered, "Get it?"

Rebeca nodded and smiled, "I think I understand."

When Rebeca and Toby had unpacked their things, they all went downstairs and enjoyed a delicious meal of chicken curry and rice with apple crumble and custard for afters. Then they spent the evening in the living room drinking cups of tea while Toby, Rebeca and Joe recounted all their adventures.

CHAPTER 3

Tadeo and Benito walked into the living room of the small flat on the 14th floor. The tall block of flats was one of two buildings side by side, and the large window on the far side of the room looked out at someone else's living room. The short, fat greasy-haired man closed the curtains and then turned the light on. There was a wooden table in the middle of the room with four rickety chairs surrounding it. On the table was a deck of cards. Tadeo went into the small kitchen off to the side and put the cans of beer he was carrying on the counter, before helping himself to a beer from the collection of drinks on the counter. Benito knew they were going to be there a while, and made himself comfortable on the dirty grey couch.

"You've got loads of beer there, Rodriguez! What did you want me to bring some for?" Tadeo scowled good humouredly and punched the man in the arm.

"Because, you never bring any beer unless I say! You haven't brought beer the last three times!"

Before Tadeo could respond, the door buzzer rang and Rodriguez pressed the button. "Who is that?!" he growled.

"It's us, you idiot, let us in!" Benito recognised the voice of Phil, a medium height, grey-haired man with a pot belly who was a doctor. He sometimes prescribed things for Tadeo, like sleeping tablets for Benito. The teenager thought about the man's patients and wondered if they had any idea what kind of man their GP was? Tadeo had to pay a reasonable amount of money for the pills and Benito guessed that the doctor made a lot of money that way, since he drove a brand new Porsche Panamera.

Five minutes later, there was a short knock on the door and Phil walked in. Behind him was a medium height stocky man with dark red hair and gold/green eyes that reminded

Benito of a snake. The man's snake eyes darted around the room nervously and as he turned and shut the door behind him, Benito saw the gold watch and the large diamond ring on his left hand.

"Who is that?" He squinted his eyes at Benito suspiciously and Tadeo laughed.

"It's Benito, my nephew. Don't worry, Keegan, he's good." Keegan continued to stare at the teenager and Benito felt his skin crawl and his heart began to palpitate. A cold air seemed to descend on him. Benito had met many of Tadeo's 'friends', but none had had this affect on him, and he shivered involuntarily, unable to divert his eyes from the hypnotic gaze of the reptile man.

"Keegan! Chill!" Tadeo slapped the man on the back in a friendly manner and ushered him to the table where Phil and Rodriguez were already sat with their beers. "You're wasting time, man!"

Rodriguez began dealing the cards and Keegan finally sat down.

"I'm a bit skint this week, so let's start off with £10 a bid," said Tadeo as he picked up his cards, "And we'll play deuces wild."

"No way, man!" grumbled Keegan, "You've already picked up your cards. I'll call wild – two-eyed jacks." He picked up his cards and put them in order.

"Ten pounds is low," complained Phil, "I've only brought twenties." He placed a thick wad on the table in front of him.

Tadeo nodded towards Benito, "He costs me a lot to feed! And I had to pay his old girl's rent this week. Give me a break!"

Benito cringed at the slang for his mom, and he thought to himself that the amount of food he had eaten this week probably barely cost ten pounds. His uncle glared at him, daring him to challenge his claim, but the teenager said nothing.

Rodriguez stood up and went into the kitchen, opening up a cupboard, then coming out with a stack of tens. He handed them over to Phil. "Here's four hundred – that should be enough to start with. Phil counted the notes, then counted out the equivalent in twenties, placing them on Rodriguez's hand as he did so.

Turning to the pile of magazines on the table beside him, Benito picked up the top one, immediately putting it back down as he saw the scantily clad woman on the front. The top three magazines were all of that nature and Benito quickly scanned down the pile until he found an *Angling Times*. He wasn't interested in fishing, but there was nothing else to do. He wished he had brought his Bible, though he doubted Tadeo would have let him.

A raucous laugh made Benito glance up at the table. Rodriguez had a cigar hanging from the side of his mouth. He took it out as he spoke, "I think you'll find the top ones the most interesting, boy!" Benito blushed, making all the men roar with laughter, and he looked back down at the magazine he was holding, trying his best to make it appear that life cycle of a salmon was the most interesting thing he could be reading.

"I saw that!" accused Keegan angrily as he pointed at Rodriguez's hand. You cheated! I saw you swap cards!" He threw his own hand on the table and the other two men stared at Rodriguez, waiting for a reply. A string of cuss words flew from the man's mouth denying the claim, before he took another deep drag on his cigar. He looked at each of the men staring back at him, then finally threw his own hand on the table.

"Fine! If you don't believe me, we'll start again!"

Tadeo groaned loudly, "I had a good hand!" He swore vehemently as he threw in his hand as well. Benito tried not to listen as he turned back to the salmon article. Rodriguez gathered the cards and began to shuffle, but Phil grabbed the cards out of his hand.

"*I'll* shuffle this time, I think!"

A few hands later, Tadeo grumbled as he threw in his last tenner. "I've got nothing left!" The other men laughed, then Keegan spoke as he looked over at Benito.

"How 'bout the boy? He's worth a couple of tenners!" Perfect white teeth glared at Benito behind the man's sinister smile, and Benito looked up from his magazine, panic spread across his face. He looked at his uncle who was rubbing his chin contemplatively. Benito's heart began banging at his rib cage – surely his uncle would not agree to that! The magazine slipped from his hands as Tadeo pondered, then finally answered.

"Not permanently, but I am willing to bet two weeks of his pathetic life!" He laughed heartily and the other men joined in like he had just told the funniest joke. "But you have to give him back … with no broken bones!" They all laughed again, and Benito squeezed his eyes tightly, hoping that he was having a terrible nightmare; he didn't want to imagine what the reptile man would make him do for two weeks. This only served to draw more chortles and guffaws from the men as they continued the game and Benito silently prayed.

A few minutes later, Tadeo shouted, "Gotcha!" and threw his hand down, "Full house, kings high!" He glanced over at Benito as he gathered his money, and laughed, "Sorry, boy! No holiday with Keegan for you this time!" This brought raucous laughter from the others and Benito started to breath again, quietly thanking God. How ironic that he was now thanking God that he could stay with his uncle.

"I'm hungry," stated Rodriguez, "let's get some Chinese."

Phil moaned, "We had Chinese last time. I want a pizza."

Keegan and Tadeo piped up together, "You *always* want pizza!" Then Tadeo continued, "We want Chinese," and Keegan nodded in agreement.

Before Phil could reply, Rodriguez had his phone out and was dialling the restaurant. He looked around at the other men as they gave their orders, and Phil reluctantly gave his. He ordered the food and then got up to get another beer as Tadeo dealt the next round.

Benito could no longer concentrate on the magazine, but watched the next few games, praying that God would increase Tadeo's pile of winnings. The teenager was not sure that God would help someone win at gambling – he felt that gambling was probably something He did not approve of, so maybe He would not get involved in such a thing. Whether by God's help or not, Tadeo's pile of cash did indeed increase considerably – so much so that by the time the buzzer rang to advise the men that the Chinese food had arrived in the lobby downstairs, Tadeo felt generous enough to pay for the whole lot, and waved some notes at Benito.

"Go down and get our food, boy! Chop! Chop!" Benito jumped up and took the money then scurried out the door before his uncle could get angry at him. He stood in front of the elevator for a minute, then opened the door to the right of it and trotted down the fourteen floors. The elevator was old and Benito was not keen to get in it by himself. He'd have to take it to go up though, otherwise he would take too long. Benito's stomach growled at the thought of the food and wondered if his uncle had bought any for him. They hadn't eaten anything since his sandwich at lunch time, but he couldn't always guarantee on getting three meals a day – his uncle often said he didn't believe in the traditional three meals a day, even though he always managed to have three himself. Tadeo said you should get food when you worked, and since Benito had only visited his mom in the afternoon and had not done any work for his uncle, he doubted he would be entitled to anything to eat. He had hoped they would stop at his uncle's before coming here, as he thought he might be able to at least get a couple of slices of bread without his uncle knowing, but they had driven around to a couple of car dealers, looking at expensive cars. Benito was not sure why they were looking at cars that he felt sure his uncle could not afford, but he did not question it. Finally he was in the lobby and he handed the money over to the young, blond delivery boy who swapped him for the large bag of hot food. He had an extra small paper bag that he thrust at Benito.

"This was left from my last delivery – they said they didn't order it. Would you like it?"

Benito nodded vigorously, not caring what was in the bag, only that it was edible. "Yes, please, thank you very much!" He took the small bag and the boy turned and left before Benito could ask for change, and the teenager's heart began racing, wondering how much money his uncle was meant to receive back. The smell of the food brought his attention back to the extra package and he looked inside; it was eight chicken nuggets! He started to pop one in his mouth when he thought of Gideon. The cat would surely need something to eat when Benito got back. The teenager promptly put the nugget back and rolled up the top of the bag, then stuffed it down his shirt. He zipped up his hoodie and pulled it out so the precious bag would not be noticeable, then hurriedly turned and pressed the button on the elevator which promptly dinged open as though it had been expecting him.

Back at the flat, Benito shut the door behind him and brought the food over to his uncle who growled at him, "Not on our cards, you idiot! Put the bags on the kitchen counter and we'll be in there when we are finished this hand!" Benito obediently went into the kitchen and pushed the beer to the side to fit the large bag of food on the counter. Suddenly he remembered the change and he swallowed hard as he walked back into the living room and stood between his uncle and Keegan, unsure of what to say.

Keegan, glared up at Benito and grumbled, "What are you doing standing there? You doin' some cheatin' for your uncle, boy?!"

Benito jumped to the side closer to Tadeo so he could not see Keegan's cards, "No sir! I … uh … I…"

"Spit it out, you blockhead!" Tadeo pressed his cards to his chest and scowled at his nephew.

"I … uh … he … uh … the boy … he didn't give me any … change …", stumbled Benito, whose stomach began growling loudly just then.

Tadeo leaned forward as he burst out laughing, "He can keep the twenty-five pence – that's probably the best tip he is going to get around this neighbourhood!" The other men roared in response, and Benito sighed with relief as he sat back down on the couch.

Five minutes later, they cleared away the cards and put the food on the table, then each of the men grabbed their boxes and emptied the food on their plates. Benito unconsciously licked his lips as he watched them, and Phil scowled at him.

"Stop that!" commanded Phil, and the others looked at Benito who promptly sucked his tongue back into his mouth and closed his lips tightly. "It's like having a begging dog at the table!" Phil looked at Tadeo, "Don't you feed the kid?"

Tadeo broke into a wide grin as he emptied a container of sweet and sour pork onto some fried rice, "Like a good dog, he eats when he works!" He stuffed a forkful of food in his mouth and before he finished chewing, continued, "and he ain't done any work this afternoon!" Again the men all chortled at this apparently hilarious joke and they all tucked into their food while Benito picked up another magazine and tried to focus on the newest camping gear for people who wanted to hike in the wildest areas of the world.

When the food was mostly consumed, it was gathered up and put into the kitchen and Rodriguez got a cloth and wiped the table, then dried it with a towel before they all sat down and continued to play.

"Oi! Dog in the corner!" Tadeo shouted at Benito who looked up from the magazine, his heart pounding as it always did when his uncle shouted at him. "Wash up the dishes for Rodriguez, we don't want to be unhelpful guests, now do we? And you can eat any of the leftovers!" He guffawed as he picked up his cards and the teenager jumped to his feet, trying not to look like he was in a hurry to see what was left.

He found his uncle had left little of his pork and rice, but Benito grabbed a fork and scraped it to the side of the plate, managing to get three mouthfuls. He got another three off of Rodriguez plate of chicken chow mein, and was delighted to get several more from each of Phil and Keegan's plates. He was almost beginning to feel satisfied with the amount that was in his shrunken stomach; then, as he was throwing away the boxes and lids, he found a small paper bag of fortune cookies. He bit the end off of one and took out the little piece of paper that he did not bother to read, then put the rest in his mouth, but then grew worried as it was so loud, and he was afraid one of the men would complain or want their cookies back. Just then a loud chorus of 'You cheated!' filled the air and Benito happily and quickly finished the rest, before he filled the sink with warm water and Fairy Liquid and washed up the few dishes that get used for a Chinese takeaway.

After he wiped down the surfaces, he emptied the water from the sink and made sure everything in the kitchen was tidy before heading back to his perch on the couch. He picked up the magazine again, but with some food in his stomach and feeling relaxed after a stress filled day seeing his mom, Benito's eyelids grew heavy and he was soon asleep.

"Wake up, boy!"

Benito's eyes shot open and his heart rate instantly doubled as he sat bolt upright. When he looked up he was greeted by his uncle's beer breath inches from his face. "Wwwhat, Uncle?!" he questioned loudly in a panic.

Tadeo guffawed and said in a quiet voice, "It's time to go home, boy."

Benito shook his head as though he could clear his brain fog with the action, and struggled to get to his feet quickly to follow his uncle out of the flat. He certainly did not want to be left behind on his own with Rodriguez. His magazine selection told Benito all he wanted to know about the kind of man he was, as if Benito didn't already know, what with the guns he supplied Tadeo.

The two did not speak in the elevator, and Benito wondered if Tadeo was fit to drive. The teenager's shirt had come untucked and he felt the bag of chicken nuggets hanging down slightly. He looked over at Tadeo who was busy with something on his phone, and tucked in his shirt as he shifted the nuggets upward and then quickly pulled down his hoodie. Tadeo glanced at him, but immediately returned to his phone. The doors opened and Benito followed Tadeo out of the building and across the car park to his car, the cool air clearing his head. He wondered if Gideon would be waiting for him, or if he had given up?

Twenty minutes later, they walked into Tadeo's house and Benito started up the the stairs, but Tadeo tapped his shoulder. "Where do you think you're going? I want a coffee before you go to bed. And bring me a doughnut — I think there is one left. I'm feeling a bit peckish!" The large man strolled into the living room and turned on the TV before sitting heavily in his chair then kicking off his shoes as the recliner stretched back. Benito quickly made the coffee and put the doughnut on a plate, then took it to his uncle who was already laughing at the sitcom. He grabbed the items from Benito who started to turn away then stopped.

"Was there anything else you wanted before I go to bed, Uncle?"

Tadeo looked over at him, struggling to focus, and Benito knew it would not be long before he was snoring. The man squinted hard, then slowly shook his head from side to side, and Benito quickly left and trotted up the stairs before he could change his mind. He paused outside his bedroom door, then slowly opened it and walked in before turning on the light. He smiled. Gideon was curled in a tight ball next to the teenager's pillow. He opened his eyes and slowly blinked at Benito as he yawned and stretched. Benito took out the chicken nuggets and broke them into pieces in the container, then grabbed the other tub and quickly dashed out of his room to refresh it with water from the bathroom sink.

When he got back, the nuggets were half gone, but Gideon stopped for a moment to look up to the teenager and meow a quiet 'thank you' before turning back to the chicken and finishing it all off. Benito bent down and gave the soft creature a stroke. He closed the window and curtain while he changed, then sat on the bed. He pulled open the drawer beside the bed and got out his Bible. He was too exhausted to read it tonight, but he wanted to mark the verses in the Bible that Frank had mentioned. He found Ephesians, but could not remember the verses, so he took a scrap of paper and just marked the beginning. It wasn't a long book, so he would read the whole thing in the morning. He put the Bible back in the drawer, got up and turned the light out, opening the window in case Gideon wanted to go out early, and crawled under the blankets. A few moments later the cat had snuggled in next to Benito and the teenager pressed his face into the soft fur, thanking God yet again for his lovely friend. And as he did, added a belated thanks for the food he had eaten at Rodriguez's flat. Somewhere in the distance an owl hooted and Benito closed his eyes, disappearing into the Nicaraguan jungle.

———◦———

Wednesday 17th August

Rebeca sat on the wooden bench in the back garden in the early morning sun, watching a woodpecker pecking in a tall red oak tree in the Myers' large back garden. She sipped the glass of water and closed her eyes, listening to the chatter and whistles of the various birds. The sounds were different from her village in Nicaragua, yet they made her feel at home and she smiled contentedly.

"Rebeca! Rebeca!" The bird song was interrupted by the calls of Samantha and Alexandra, and Rebeca opened her eyes to see the girls running towards her full of excitement. "Will you take us fishing? You can show us how you do it in the jungle! Please?!" When they reached her, they each grabbed a hand and pulled her to her feet. "Pleeeeease?"

Rebeca laughed: "How can I refuse such an enthusiastic request?" She was delighted that the girls liked her and she was pleased that she could teach them something they were so keen to learn.

Alexandra gleefully held out a Swiss army knife, "I've brought this, so you can sharpen some branches to use as spears!"

Samantha was already at the back gate, unlocking the latch. Rebeca and Alexandra followed her out of the garden and down the side of the wheat field until they reached the footpath that took them towards the small river that flowed quietly past the village. The sun was growing warm in the clear blue sky and the piercing call of a buzzard made the three of them stop and look up to see the great bird gliding high in the air.

When they neared the edge of the river, Samantha stopped and turned towards Rebeca and her sister. "Can we go to the lake, instead? Daddy says the fish in the river aren't for eating – barbel and carp – you have to throw them back. There are trout in the lake. I want to eat fish for breakfast!"

Rebeca cocked her head at this information. "Why would you catch a fish and throw it back?"

The twins giggled as they looked at each other and shrugged their shoulders. "I think Daddy says it is 'sport'!" Rebeca frowned and the girls laughed at her confusion, even though they did not completely understand the idea either.

"Well, of course we want to catch fish we can eat. Besides, if we spear the fish, there would be no point in throwing them back anyway, as they will be dead!" said Rebeca matter of factly.

"Yay!" The girls cheered and Samantha pointed in the distance. "There is a bridge over there where the road crosses the river, and the lake is not far past that!"

Soon the three reached the lake. It was a curved oblong lake, about 70 metres wide and 100 metres long with various trees along the edge and several small wooden docks jutting out onto the water. There were two people on the far side, each sitting perched on a stool on their own dock with all their gear piled behind them. Rebeca scouted around until she found a suitable tree to make some spears. She finally found one with straight, strong branches that were just the right thickness, so she broke off three of them and gave one to each of the girls.

"Clean off all the leaves and any little side branches and I will show you how to sharpen the end," Rebeca said as she quickly began to clean off her own branch. The girls eyes were glued to Rebeca as she knelt down, placed the branch near its end, firmly on the end of her knees, and quickly carved a razor sharp point to the end. She then helped each of them do the same. When they each had a sharp spear, she instructed, "When the fish are near, watch them for a while until you are sure which direction they are going. Then when you are sure, bring down your spear just in front of them. In the few seconds that this will take you, the fish will have swum directly under your spear." When they looked at her bemused, she added, "Here, let us have a little practice."

Rebeca took a vine and tied it to a lump of soil, then dragged it back and forth in front of Samantha who took several stabs before she finally stabbed the lump of soil. "Well done, Samantha!" cheered Rebeca, who then did the same for Alexandra to practice.

Finally, they were at the water's edge, unaware that the two men on the far side were now watching them intently as they walked along, while Rebeca looked for the best place for them to wade into the water. Finally, she was satisfied she had found the perfect spot, and the twins, who were dressed in t-shirts, shorts and trainers – as was Rebeca – followed her in.

"You must each find a spot and stand perfectly still and be perfectly silent," said Rebeca quietly, "Sometimes you must wait a long time before the fish are comfortable with you in the water and come near."

Despite their excitement, the twins obeyed completely, and stood mesmerised as the water that they had disturbed slowly cleared, and they could see the trout swimming a little distance away. The sunlight glistened on the surface of the water, occasionally blocking their vision of the bottom and Samantha let out a soft yelp as a trout brushed past her ankle. She immediately covered her mouth as Rebeca shook her head and placed her finger over her mouth, still holding the spear completely still at a forty five degree angle. Two seconds later, Rebeca's spear sliced through the water, barely making a ripple on the surface, and she pulled up a twelve inch trout that wriggled for a brief moment before it became motionless. Alexandra's face lit up and she started to move, but Rebeca stood still and ever so slightly shook her head.

The time was ticking by and Rebeca was just about to say that they could go home and just cook the one fish when Samantha's arm shot down with the spear piercing the water, and when she brought it back out again with a large trout on the end, both girls screamed with excitement. Rebeca smiled, happy that at least one of the girls had got a fish, and the three of them waded out of the water onto the shore.

Both Samantha and Alexandra were thrilled; it did not seem to matter which of them speared the trout, and Rebeca was glad. The sun was even hotter now, and by the time they got home, their clothes had begun to dry.

Samantha locked the gate behind them and Alexandra trotted towards the house. "I'll get some matches and we'll make a fire to cook the fish!"

Samantha handed her spear and trout to Rebeca to hold while she got wood ready in the fire pit that the family had in their garden. Between them, they soon had a good fire blazing. Rebeca gutted the fish and threw the insides on the fire where they soon were burnt to ashes. She then skewered the two fish together with the two spears so they could be held over the fire.

"What are you waiting for?" asked Alexandra.

"The fire is still a little too hot. We need it to go down a bit so we can cook the fish slower," answered Rebeca. The twins brought some chairs closer to the fire and the three sat down to wait for the fire to cool enough to cook their breakfast.

"That's where you are! I was looking all around the house for you girls!" They turned around and saw Emily coming out of the back door and walk across the lawn towards them. "Why are you having a fire n..." Emily stopped when she saw the fish on the end of Rebeca's spears. "Where did you get the fish?"

Dave stepped outside just as the twins jumped up and excitedly recounted their fishing adventure, squealing with delight as they told with enthusiastic narration how Rebeca and Samantha speared their breakfast.

Dave and Emily raised their eyebrows and looked at each other, both with mouths open. Finally Dave spoke, "You got trout ... from the lake?"

Rebeca suddenly realised there was something wrong and her happy contented face grew worried. "What is the matter? Are the fish not good from the lake?"

By this time, Joe and Toby had come outside to see why the twins were making such a commotion. They looked at each other and started chuckling.

"We're not members at the lake. You need a permit," said Dave finally.

"A ... permit?" queried Rebeca, "What is a permit?"

"It is written permission, that you have to pay for. It is someone's lake and they put trout in it and charge people to fish there," piped up Toby through his laughter.

"It is someone's lake and they put fish in it to catch? I did not know you could own a lake! And why would you buy trout, then charge people to catch them? Why would you not eat the fish you bought? That is strange."

Alexandra and Samantha's faces fell and they started snivelling. Samantha blubbered through tears, "Do ... do we have to give the fish back, Daddy? We were going to cook them for breakfast!"

As it began to dawn on Rebeca that they had in effect, stolen the fish, she grew concerned. Toby immediately stopped laughing and hurried over to Rebeca, putting his arm around her shoulder to comfort her. He fought the urge to kiss her ruffled hair as a picture of Rebeca spearing fish in Nicaragua popped in his mind and he said affectionately, "It's all right, Rebeca, you didn't know."

Emily smiled at Rebeca and then looked at the girls, "No, you do not have to give the fish back. Daddy will call Mr Jones and explain everything." She opened her arms to envelop the twins in a hug as she looked over at Dave. "Won't you, honey?"

"Uh ... yes, of course! I'll do that straight away!" And he hurried into the house as the girls cried out in delight.

"Is it time to start cooking the trout?" Alexandra asked hopefully.

Rebeca looked over at the fire, feeling pride had gotten her again, and said quietly, "It is a little hot, but I will just hold them higher."

Toby couldn't help himself, and he touched her cheek gently, "It really is okay, Rebeca. It is wonderful that the girls could have this experience." He grinned, looking her in the eyes until she smiled weakly back. "And I am very much looking forward to our breakfast!" They walked over to the fire, and as they sat down and Rebeca lowered the fish over the fire, Emily raised an eyebrow at the exchange between them, then looked over at her other son, whose face had grown sad.

Oh, oh, thought Emily. *Two brothers in love with the same girl. This surely could not end well.*

With that thought, she turned into the house to prepare some hash browns and fried tomatoes, mushrooms and onions to go with the fish.

When breakfast was cooked, they gathered around the kitchen table, and as they all tucked in Dave told them about his conversation with Mr Jones.

"Evidently he and a buddy were out fishing on the lake and saw the whole thing. He was going to come over and tell them it was private fishing, but he said he grew curious as they made themselves spears and could not help being impressed by how they caught their trout!" He chuckled as he looked over at Rebeca who was now blushing as he added, "He said there was no need to pay for the fish, but could Rebeca teach him how to do that as well?" Everyone at the table laughed as they continued their breakfast and conversation turned to Gwen's imminent arrival.

CHAPTER 4

"Benito!"

Benito's eyes flung open and he sat bolt upright in his bed. Gideon jumped to the window ledge and was on the roof mere seconds before the door burst open. The teenager's heart was pounding so hard his ears were ringing. He felt certain that years were being taken off of his life by these shock awakenings.

"Get out of bed, it's eight o'clock! I got some work for you to do and I need to go over some things before we head off. Get dressed and go downstairs and have some breakfast!"

Rubbing his eyes, Benito threw the covers off and swung his feet down on the floor. "What can I have, Uncle?"

Tadeo grumbled, "Have what you want, boy! Today we are going to do some practising and make some good money while we are at it!"

The pleasure that had arisen at the first statement was destroyed immediately by the sinking feeling caused by the second. Making good money, and certainly whatever he had to 'practise' to make the money, was not going to be enjoyable for the teenager, but when Tadeo shut the door behind him, he hurriedly put on his clothes and then went down the hall to have a quick wash in the bathroom sink. His stomach gurgled loudly, his hunger competing with the gnawing feeling of foreboding of what his uncle would make him do.

As Benito sat at the table with a huge bowl of cereal and poured himself a large glass of orange juice, Tadeo sat opposite him drinking his coffee.

"I want us to do some practising today. I can't decide if it is better for you to be the distraction or me. It will probably be better if you do the nicking and I do the distracting, since you would be less suspicious, but if you get nervous, you might not be able to get the goods."

Eating his cereal quickly, so he could hopefully get some toast in him as well, Benito listened to his uncle. Benito looked up at Tadeo's words. "Steal stuff ... in the day time?" he asked incredulously.

Tadeo shook his head and frowned. "This is exactly why I am not sure how we should do it. You look jumpy already!" He pursed his lips and squinted his eyes, as he put down his coffee and leaned forward to get his face closer to Benito. His deep voice grew even deeper as he spoke slowly, "You better get calm, boy! You need to do this well, 'cause I ain't paying for your mom's rent out of my own pocket! She's got some extra bills that came in that have to be paid as well!"

The food in Benito's stomach began to turn sour and he dismissed the thought of the toast. He swallowed hard and his hand shook as he put down the glass a little too loudly on the table. Tadeo's hand shot across the table and grabbed the collar of Benito's t-shirt and gathered it tightly in his strong hand, squeezing Benito's throat until he started coughing.

"Don't mess with me, boy! You get your act together, or I'll go pull the plug from your mama's bedside instead! Then she won't need no rent money!" He let go of Benito's shirt, giving the teenager a thrust and as he did, the chair wobbled back on two legs and Benito had to grab the table to right himself. He gasped, then looked at the bowl of cereal, only half finished, and started to stand as he picked it off the table.

"Don't you dare, boy!" Shouted Tadeo angrily, "I paid good money for that food – you are going to eat every mouthful of it!"

Benito grew pale as he struggled to swallow another mouthful of cereal and his stomach twisted. He felt the acid inch its way up his throat and he covered his mouth, panic filling his eyes as he felt his stomach begin to reject what he had eaten.

Tadeo jolted to his feet and grabbed Benito by the shoulders, shaking him violently. "If that food ends up in the toilet you are going to get such a beating you'll be wishing you never been born!"

Benito's eyes welled with tears and he squeezed them shut as he swallowed firmly and willed himself to keep his breakfast where it was. The sight of the tears made Tadeo slam his hands down on the table before storming out of the kitchen yelling as he left, "You make my blood boil, boy! I'm going upstairs to brush my teeth and you better be finished your breakfast before I come back down!"

The oddity of Tadeo's need to brush his teeth triggered an unexpected snigger in the teenager's head, and it was just enough to cause his stomach muscles to relax. He breathed in deeply, praying for God to help him finish before his uncle came back. In through his nose, out through his pursed lips. He repeated it a few times, then opened his eyes and looked down at the bowl. Slowly, he picked up his spoon and lifted some cereal to his mouth. He breathed out through his nose and concentrated on relaxing every muscle in his body as he chewed.

Amazingly, Benito finished his cereal and juice, and had washed up the dishes before Tadeo's heavy steps came back down the stairs. He turned as his uncle entered the kitchen.

"I'm ready, Uncle," he said quietly.

Tadeo scowled, "You get up there and brush your teeth! You don't want no rotten teeth now, boy do you?!"

The irony of his uncle wanting him to brush his teeth while he was happy to beat him always struck him as borderline psychotic, but Benito was not about to argue as he trotted up the stairs to obey. When he was finished, he took a quick peek in his bedroom to see if Gideon had returned, and was disappointed that he could not have a little snuggle with the comforting creature before he went off with his uncle. He clicked the door shut and walked slowly down the stairs with a heavy heart, to his uncle who was waiting in the living room. He pointed to a chair.

"Sit down while I explain what we are going to do. I want your full attention because I don't want you messin' things up!" Benito nodded and sat down, looking directly at Tadeo's evil blue eyes which were wide with anticipation. "I want you to pretend to have some kind of fit." He paused, squinting his eyes, "I don't mean no tantrum, kid, I mean like a seizure!"

Benito sputtered in protest, "B-bb ... but ... I don't know how to have a ... a ... f-fit, Uncle!"

"You watch the telly, don't you boy?! Do like what they do on the telly!" He smiled evilly, "Show me now, how you are gonna to pretend you are fittin'," Tadeo ordered. When Benito hesitated, Tadeo's face began to turn purple, "Get fittin'! Now!"

Benito jumped up, then threw himself on the floor, thrashing about wildly.

"No! You idiot! You look like you are possessed or something!" Benito instantly stopped and opened his eyes, looking up at his uncle who was hovering over him angrily. "Be more like your muscles are contracting, like this." He got on the carpet beside Benito and showed him how he wanted him to pretend to 'fit'.

Finally, after much coaching, Benito's acting was up to Tadeo's standards and he told him to get up off the floor. Benito sat back on the chair and asked hesitantly, "How will I know when you want me to do it?" He still was not sure he could do this in public, but the fear of a serious beating from

51

his uncle, coupled with the financial needs of his mom, made the frightened teenager determined to get it right.

"Well," began Tadeo, "we are going to start in an antique shop I went in the other day. They have an antique perfume bottle they're selling for £800 – probably not worth more than £400, but it will be a good practice run. There is a grandfather clock near the bottle. I'll ask the guy if the clock keeps good time – that'll be your cue to start your seizure. Just make sure that he is standing between us, so he will have to turn his back on me to look at you." He paused for a moment. "Got it?"

Benito did not trust his voice, so he nodded vigorously, pretending he was confident, and his uncle's evil grin spread across his face happily as he slapped his knees and stood.

"Let's get on, then!"

The teenager jumped to his feet and followed Tadeo out of the front door and into the car, climbing as usual into the back, causing his uncle to shake his head. Benito smiled as he spotted Gideon in his little spot under the hedge and wished he could give him a little cuddle. Instead, he strapped himself in, and silently looked out the window as his uncle drove for just a few minutes, then stopped outside a corner shop. He turned around to Benito and gave him a couple of coins.

"Go buy some of those mints you eat, they seem to settle your stomach." Tadeo didn't care about Benito's stomach, but if the kid was more settled, he would perform better.

Benito took the money in his sweaty hand and stepped out of the car. The plump cashier looked up and smiled at him as he walked through the dinging door.

"Your regular Murray Mints, love?"

Benito smiled weakly back speaking softly. "Yes, Maggie, thank you."

She was a kind elderly woman and had a relaxing way about her. He gave her the coins and she gave him a penny change with his receipt, which he stuffed in his pocket. He thanked her quietly as she waved him goodbye and he got back in his uncle's car. He sat down, then reached in his pocket to pull out the penny to give back to his uncle. Tadeo laughed and grabbed the penny, tossing it in the little space in the console that held spare change.

Benito pulled open the pack, and as he did, it ripped awkwardly and a large amount of the sweets landed on his lap and around him. Tadeo sighed deeply, but said nothing as he looked forward, waiting for his nephew to pick them all up and pop one into his mouth. He gave him another couple of minutes before turning around again to look Benito in the face.

"Better?" He asked, his blue eyes piercing at him, insisting that his nephew say 'yes'.

Benito nodded despite his nervousness as he sucked the mint hard, willing his stomach to settle. His heart was still dancing in his chest, but his stomach actually did feel a little better, though for how long Benito was unsure.

Tadeo pulled away from the kerb and drove another ten minutes before heading down a quiet street then turning at the first junction, heading towards the antique shop.

It was a small shop on a quiet road and Tadeo pulled up right in front. Tadeo turned in his seat to look back at his nephew. The kid looked terrified and the large man had second thoughts. They had never done day work before. This was branching out for them. But they had to practise if they were going to get the big prize. Benito looked up as he realised his uncle was staring at him, and he sat straighter, giving an air of confidence.

"Any questions?" Tadeo asked, his piercing eyes trying to determine if his nephew was going to be able to pull it off.

Benito took a deep breath and nodded, saying with much more confidence than he felt, "No, Uncle."

"You're not going to let me down?"

"No, Uncle."

A little bell on the door dinged as they walked into the little shop. An elderly couple were inside looking at a rocking chair, so Tadeo pretended he was browsing while he waited for them to leave.

Finally, the man turned to the small, slight gentleman who owned the shop, "It's a bit more than I wanted to pay." The woman frowned and opened her mouth to voice her opinion, but the man continued, "If you come down fifty pounds, we'll have it."

The shop owner smiled and said nothing for a moment, then finally spoke, "I'll knock off thirty, and that's it."

The woman looked at her husband expectantly and he grinned, shaking the other man's hand, "Deal!" The woman's face lit up and she sat in the chair happily rocking back and forth slowly while her husband paid for it. Shortly, the two of them left with the chair as the shopkeeper held the door open for them. He stepped back inside and turned to Tadeo who had positioned himself in front of the mahogany grandfather clock. Benito took his cue and walked casually behind the man pretending to look at the wooden toys in the window display.

"That is a mighty fine clock! Immaculate," said the shopkeeper coming up beside Tadeo, "1700's," he added with pride, as he ran his hand down the side of the smooth polished wood.

Benito's heart began pounding hard and he grew light-headed as his breaths became quick. His teeth began to chatter and he started shaking as he waited for his uncle's words. By the time Tadeo spoke, Benito felt close to fainting, "Does it keep good time?"

Benito collapsed on the floor, only half acting, and closed his eyes as he pretended to have a seizure. The shopkeeper turned around at the sound of Benito hitting the floor, and at that moment, Tadeo stepped sideways closer to the perfume bottle and only just managed to get it to his jacket pocket before the man turned back around.

"What's the matter with your son? Why are you just standing there? Aren't you going to help him?"

Tadeo put on a slightly concerned face and walked over to Benito, bending down as he spoke. "He has epilepsy. He has seizures sometimes; I just need to make sure he is comfortable." Speaking to Benito, he hinted to him, "It's okay son, I know you can hear me. It will be over in a minute."

Benito was only too glad to comply and within seconds, relaxed into a motionless pose partly curled up on his side. He took a few real shaky breaths and opened his eyes, looking up at Tadeo expressionless. Tadeo helped him to his feet and held him up by his shoulders. "If you open the door, sir, I'll take him out to the car where he can sit down."

The gentleman scurried to the door and stood outside while he held it open, watching Tadeo get Benito into the back seat of the BMW. Fortunately, just then, a well dressed woman in high heels wearing an expensive looking dress walked in as the man held the door, and he turned his attention to his next customer.

Tadeo shut the door and jumped in the front seat, starting the motor and slowly driving away down the road. He looked in the rear view mirror at his nephew and grinned, "Well done, boy!"

He looked at him for a moment, then frowned, "You don't have to keep up the act, you know! You still look sick."

Benito *felt* sick. It was one thing being a go-between for Tadeo and his nefarious acquaintances in the cover of darkness. It was quite another helping his uncle steal from an innocent shopkeeper in broad daylight. He wasn't sure he could do it again.

"I think in the next shop, I'll have the fit."

Benito's head began to buzz and he could actually hear his heart pounding in his head and his blood racing around his body as he strained to listen to his uncle's next words.

"It was quite a close call. I nearly didn't get the bottle. I should have foreseen that as the adult, the guy would expect me to deal with you. If I have a fit, it would be more natural for you to just stand frightened and let the sales clerk help me." He nodded slowly as he agreed with himself, tapping the steering wheel as he thought about their next stop.

Fifteen minutes later, he pulled into a side road and parked. The next shop had security cameras and he didn't want his car on camera. He turned around to look at his nephew and had second thoughts. If Benito messed this up, it could get him in trouble too. But if Tadeo could get him to cooperate, it could be just the leverage he needed to keep the boy under his control – at least until the big job, and then, well … .

"Okay, kid, the bottle covered the rent for a month, now we need to pay the bills. The hospital said your mom could go home soon," he lied, "and you want her going home to a nice warm flat, don't you?"

Benito looked up at his uncle's sick grin and felt his breakfast begin to rebel. He thought of his mom in the hospital bed and tears threatened to surface, so he took a deep breath. He wanted to help his mom. But surely he was going beyond what God could ever forgive him for. He breathed in deeply and let it out slowly through his lips. Who was he kidding? He'd already gone beyond that, and his mom needed the money, especially if she was going to go home. He faked a smile and nodded at his uncle.

"Now, this place specialises in engagement and wedding rings, so there will be people looking at trays of diamond rings and …".

"P-p-people? There'll be people there?"

Tadeo growled, "Of course there will be people there! I took you to the quiet shop first to try out our plan, but shops usually have people in them, you idiot!" He glared at his nephew, what little patience he had disappearing quickly. "So I want you to get beside a nice tray of diamonds and decide which you are going to take when I have my fit. Remember to be on the opposite side to me, so when everyone turns to watch me, no one will be watching you!"

Benito tried desperately to calm himself, "O ... kay, Uncle."

"You're sure you're ready?" he asked slowly.

Not daring to speak again, Benito nodded, and they got out of the car. They rounded the corner and walked down the busy street a few paces until Tadeo stopped outside the jewellery shop and pulled the door open, walking confidently in. He stopped as he came to a counter displaying a selection of men's rings and Benito walked further in, and, as his uncle had said, a young couple were looking at a tray of diamond rings. He saw some watches on the other side of them, and made his way towards them. He'd only just reached them when he heard his uncle collapse to the floor and cause his 'scene'. As predicted, everyone turned to look at Tadeo, and Benito reached over and grabbed a ring with the largest diamond, stuffing it in his jeans pocket before rushing over to Tadeo's side. By the time he got there, Tadeo's 'episode' was finished, and he was supposedly recovering.

"It's okay, Dad, I'm here,"

Tadeo gave a little moan as he lay on his side with people gathering around. Benito rubbed his back and repeated, "It's okay, Dad." Someone asked if they should call an ambulance and Benito shook his head, "It's okay, this happens sometimes, he'll be all right in a bit." Shortly, Benito helped him to sit up and Tadeo breathed in deeply. Finally, as Tadeo appeared to be recovering, people began to grow disinterested and return to what they were doing.

Benito panicked and quickly helped Tadeo to his feet, then slowly they made their way out the door. As soon as they were around the corner they ran to the car, where they jumped in and Tadeo was shortly racing down the quiet street and out onto a busy road where they soon blended in with the traffic.

"Did you get anything?" Tadeo asked expectantly as he looked in the rear view mirror. Benito nodded and dug in his pocket to find the diamond ring, holding it up for his uncle to see.

Tadeo grinned widely, "That's a huge diamond – great work, boy!" Then he laughed wickedly, "You can now consider yourself a thief! I hope you kept your head down so that they couldn't see your face on the security cameras!"

"W-w-what? You never told me to do that!" Benito grew terrified. Everything else he had done for his uncle had been in places without security cameras – just dark dealings with dark people in dark places. No one saw.

"Yup!" Tadeo indicated a right hand turn and waited until it was clear. "The police will be after you now. You're eighteen – you'd go to adult prison if they caught you!" He chortled, "And a skinny whipper-snapper like you would get eaten alive in prison!"

Suddenly, it was no longer just about his mom. Benito realised what his uncle had done. He was now a wanted adult criminal who could go to prison. He looked down at the beautiful diamond that glistened in the sunlight as it shone through the car window. What had he done? Who could help him now? There was silence in his head, then a quiet voice filtered through – *no one*.

The doorbell rang and Emily went to answer it. When she opened the door, for one fleeting moment she was speechless as she saw the beautiful girl in front of her. Her sons had told her of her stunning, natural beauty, but she was not prepared for the young woman who stood at her doorstep. Gwen was wearing beige capris, a silk top the colour of her emerald eyes, and a cream cashmere cardigan and was just putting her sunglasses in her brown leather tote bag. She had a couple of bags by her feet, and the taxi driver who had carried them to the door was heading down the front path.

"Hello, you must be Gwen!" she smiled warmly.

It had only been a brief second or two, but Gwen caught the look – and once again Gwen was amazed that she had even better first time reactions from people when she was wearing no make up – something Toby had helped her discover when she first met him in Nicaragua. Her shoulder-length blond hair had been hacked off by a sukia in a savage tribe, but Toby said it had given her an even more natural beauty.

Joe hurried to the door to grab her bags, and Toby was close behind him. Emily again raised an eyebrow at the similar reactions of her sons. Maybe this relationship thing would pan out between the two of them after all.

After everyone hugged Gwen, including Rebeca who had now arrived at the door, they showed Gwen to her room.

Rebeca stopped at the doorway of the bedroom as Gwen followed Joe and Toby into the room and placed her bags on the floor.

"I was not sure which bed you would like, so I took the top, since I thought perhaps you would not like to climb up and down the ladder." Rebeca spoke quietly, unsure of how Gwen would react to her. Things were very different from when she'd first met Gwen as Tadeo's kidnapped victim being kept in Rebeca's village. Rebeca knew who she was in the

59

jungle – here in the western world, everything was confusing to her.

Gwen's friendly smile caught her off guard, "I've never slept in a bunk bed before – the top might have been fun!" When she saw Rebeca's face grow concerned, she added, "but the bottom is fine! Either way, I've never slept in a single bed before, so I hope I don't fall out!" She laughed coyly as she glanced over her shoulder at the boys.

Just then, the twins burst through the doorway into the now crowded room and Rebeca smiled saying, "I will go and help your mother prepare the meal and make some room for the girls!"

Alexandra spoke first as they rushed up to Gwen, "Wow! You are beautiful, just like Toby said!"

Gwen grinned and winked at Toby who duly blushed.

Then Samantha reached out and put her hand gently on Gwen's wrist. Gwen half smiled at her, puzzled.

"But you feel the same temperature as Alex and I!" Samantha burst out, and Alexandra copied her sister and put her hand on Gwen's other wrist, nodding her head vigorously. "We heard Joe telling Toby how hot you were – but you just feel normal!"

Gwen cocked her head and raised her eyebrows, smiling as she looked over at Joe who stood silently with his mouth open and his face red. Toby doubled over as he burst out laughing.

"Were you sick or something?" asked Alexandra. "Once Samantha and I were sick and we got really hot! Mom said it was 'cause we had high temperatures!" She turned to Joe who still could not speak: "Was Gwen sick when you said that?"

Gwen was thoroughly enjoying seeing Joe squirm, so she asked innocently, "I don't know, was I sick when you said that, Joe?" She stepped forward and stood directly in front of him, looking up into his eyes that were now transfixed to hers, and

Toby laughed even more hysterically – he had never seen his brother look so uncomfortable. Alexandra and Samantha just looked at each other bemused.

"Uh … uh …" Joe sputtered.

"Why do you look sunburnt?" asked Samantha.

"Are you all right, Joe? How come you can't speak?" added Alexandra.

That just made Joe irritated. He didn't want to be the butt of the twins' unintentional joke. He turned to Alexandra, annoyed, "Of course I can speak, you little twerps! Why don't you just get out of here before I throttle you!" He stepped towards them with his hands outstretched and the girls screamed, running from the room. Joe pretended he was chasing them, but as soon as he got to the bottom of the stairs, he stormed through the kitchen, out of the back door and across the garden where he let himself out through the back gate heading towards the river to let off steam.

Gwen and Toby were left alone in the bedroom and Gwen's face turned serious. "He has a temper," she said quietly, disappointment in her voice.

"Well, it *was* rather embarrassing!" Toby chuckled, trying to lighten the mood. He was only too glad that the twins had not heard him agree with Joe.

Gwen nodded absent mindedly. "I must call Mummy." She looked around the room. "I think I will go out in the garden. I'm not sure she would approve of …". She didn't finish her sentence as she headed out of the room, phone in hand.

Toby raised an eyebrow at her comment and watched her leave, wondering how a girl could invoke such opposite feelings in a guy within minutes. Girls were hard to figure out sometimes.

A short time later, they all gathered at the kitchen table for lunch. Joe, who had returned subdued, decided it was safest to sit between his mom and Rebeca. Toby sat down beside Gwen and looked at the empty chair on the end.

"Where's Dad?" he asked his mom.

"He went over to ... he had to pop out to see someone. He should be back any minute," she answered evasively. Dave had felt compelled to pay for the trout and had gone over with some money to pay Mr Jones, and Emily did not want to embarrass Rebeca any further.

Just then, Dave stepped into the kitchen from the back door. As he sat down, Toby introduced Gwen, and he smiled to himself as he saw his dad recover quickly from seeing her for the first time. It really was impossible not to react to such a stunning girl. Toby looked over at his mom who was also smiling as she watched her husband nearly miss his chair as he sat down.

"It's lovely to meet you, Gwen, did you have a nice journey?" he asked politely.

"I expect she flew first class, so she probably had a nicer journey than Rebeca and I!" chuckled Toby as he buttered a cheese roll.

"Oh, my goodness!" exclaimed Gwen with a look of horror, as she ladled out some of the soup into the bowl in front of her. "Daddy and Mummy would never let me fly *commercial*! I took one of Daddy's jets. It is very comfortable, so I had a very relaxing journey, thank you."

"Uh ... *one* of them? How many jets does your father have?" asked Emily incredulously.

"Only three," Gwen replied, as though she was talking about bicycles. She smiled. "He has a thing about jets, but Mummy made him sell two just recently. She said we really only needed one each, in case we all needed to go somewhere at once." Gwen continued, oblivious to the shock of her friends, "Living in America, it is *so* far to get anywhere!"

"Indeed!" said Dave, chuckling to himself as he dipped a piece of his roll into his soup.

Toby's phone beeped in his pocket, and as he took it out to look at it his mother frowned at him. He looked at the name T-Rex on his screen, waiting for him to answer. "It's Pamela!" he said, surprised. "Please may I just answer it quickly? It might be important."

Emily sighed and nodded, "Take it into the living room, please Toby, you know how I feel about phones at the table."

Toby jumped up and hurried into the other room as he clicked the green square. Pamela was a girl they had met in America when they were looking for Emmie, his little capuchin friend. Her huge, brace filled grin appeared on the screen and Toby couldn't help but smile back. "Hey Pamela! How's it going?"

"Hi Toby! It seems like ages since you were here and we were having that amazing adventure looking for your monkey! When I went back to the shop it seemed so boring but I got a raise, so that is good, even though I do still have to put up with my manager, Mr Flatley. Can you believe it, we had three returning customers yesterday who all asked for me personally to help them, and he *still* got mad at me for giving their dog some treats! He actually threatened to remove my pay rise, although it isn't really his decision, but it was *his* boss's decision – you know, the guy who owns the store. Though I don't know if he actually owns the store, since it is a franchise, and I don't know if you own a store or just rent it or …".

Toby's eyes began to glaze over and he shook himself, snickering as he realised he had forgotten how difficult it was to keep Pamela's conversations short. "Sorry to butt in," he paused, then added quickly before she could take a breath and continue, "but we are just having lunch so I need to keep this short!"

"Oh, sure!" giggled Pamela, "You are probably wondering why I am calling, though of course, I could be calling just to say 'Hi, how are you?', though that would be boring. But I actually do have some information that you are going to want to know about. My dad came home from work last night and told me, but I had to go out to watch a band concert that my sister was in – which was okay. She plays the flute and is not bad at it, though the flute isn't a very exciting instrument, but it did sound pretty, and then we had to go out for a meal. When we finally got home, my phone was dead so I had to charge it and then while I was waiting for it to charge, I fell asleep and ...".

Toby sighed and rubbed his temple with his right hand, finally managing to interject, "Pamela!"

"Oh, yes, sorry! I got side tracked!" She tittered, shaking her head so her ponytail swung back and forth, "You know I really think I ...".

"You said you had some information?" Toby interrupted, trying desperately to get the information from her.

"Yes, yes, yes!" she smacked forehead with the palm of her hand, then squinted her eyes at Toby in a concentrated look. "Yes, right, Dad said they had tracked Benito down to Birmingham. I know it isn't that great, since if your cities are as big as ours it ...".

"Benito?" asked Toby questioningly. "Not Tadeo?"

"Well, it seems that Benito was caught on a security camera stealing a diamond ring. There was a man having a seizure on the floor – they think it was Tadeo pretending so he could distract everyone while Benito took the ring – but they didn't see the man's face."

Toby's face fell, "They caught Benito stealing a diamond ring? Was it very valuable?"

"He didn't say," replied Pamela, scrunching up her face, "but it sounds like it was valuable enough to get him into big trouble."

"Poor Benito," sighed Toby. "Thanks for that, Pamela." He paused for a moment then asked, "Oh, Pamela! Would you send us the address of the jewellery store?"

"Sure!" nodded Pamela vigorously.

"I've got to go, but I'll …".

"Keep me informed?" asked Pamela hopefully, with a closed mouth smile and raised eyebrows.

"Of course!" He smiled at the friendly girl. "Bye." Toby clicked off before she could begin speaking again, and returned to the kitchen. Everyone turned to him as he sat back down in his chair.

"Pamela said Benito is in Birmingham. She has an address where he was seen on a security camera," he said simply. He didn't want his parents to have any more information than was necessary, as he didn't want to worry them.

"Well then," said Gwen with a grin, "I guess we will be heading off to Birmingham tomorrow!" Rebeca, Joe and Toby all nodded in agreement, but the twins pouted.

"Awww, tomorrow? You guys just got here!" said Alexandra.

"And Rebeca was going to teach us how to catch and skin a rabbit!" piped up Samantha, and Alexandra nodded vigorously in agreement.

"Oh," said Emily trying to smile. "I'm sure there will be time for that later," she added, hoping that there would actually *not* be enough time for her little girls to learn this gruesome sounding skill.

CHAPTER 5

Tadeo pulled up outside Peking House takeaway and turned around to face Benito. "Since you did some work this morning, you can have a Chinese – what do you want?"

Benito still felt sick from his 'work' earlier, but his stomach rumbled. "Uh, I don't know what there is to have."

Tadeo rolled his eyes and shook his head. "Never mind, I'll just get you something." He climbed out of the car and Benito sat lost in thought looking out of the window and watching the people walk by. His thoughts drifted to his friends from Nicaragua and he wondered what they were doing. *Definitely not robbing stores*, he thought to himself. What would they think of him now? He sighed. What would they have thought of him before, if they had known the things he had done for his uncle? Another, deep sigh reverberated through his chest. What did it matter? He would never see them again.

He wiped a tear from his eye as he thought about the direction his life had taken. He had thought that maybe his friends' God would give some meaning and hope to his life – hope for this life and the one to come when he died. If nothing else, Benito felt certain there was a Heaven and a hell. A holy and righteous God would certainly have a final judgement on all the evil in the world. But what did Benito have to do to gain meaning in his life and have the hope of Heaven? How could he ever do enough good to make up for all the wrong he had done?

The car door opened and slammed and Tadeo slid in behind the steering wheel, putting the bag of food on the seat beside him before doing up his seat belt. He looked at Benito sat in the back and smiled a sinister smile.

"Off to Keegan's now."

Panic filled Benito's entire being and he felt faint, now only vaguely conscious of the inviting smell of the hot food that was drifting towards him and dancing up through his nostrils. He wanted to ask why, but he did not want to know the answer. Whatever reason Tadeo was going to Keegan's, it was not going to be good.

A short while later, Benito noticed the houses had gotten larger with bigger gardens. Large trees lined the sides of the roads. Tadeo slowed down and turned left into a drive, stopping at the gate and rolling down his window so he could press the buzzer on the keypad. The gates soon clicked and slowly opened wide so Tadeo could enter, the BMW's wheels crunching on the drive as he rolled towards the large house.

The front door opened as Tadeo stopped the car and opened his door. He climbed out and then bent back inside to grab the food, growling at Benito who was sat cowering in the back. "Get out, boy! You're not eating Chinese in my car!" He smiled slyly as he added, "Besides, you are going to stay here a day – Keegan wants to try you out to see if you are worth a bet in our next poker game!" He guffawed loudly and Benito felt his stomach turn and he nearly retched. "Get out of my car before you make a mess, you idiot!"

Benito opened the door and leaned out, but the rush of cool air revived him and he breathed in slowly, calming himself as he got out of the car and shut the door quietly. Keegan's snake eyes squinted at the teenager from the step and scowled.

"He ain't gonna make a mess in my house, is he? Marlene will skin my hide!"

"Keep 'im in a shed tonight, if you like!" Tadeo laughed as he held up the bag of food and walked towards the house. Benito trailed behind, a desperate urge to run entering him, but knowing he was no match for either of the men.

They stepped inside the immaculate house and Keegan shut the door behind them. Tadeo kicked off his shoes and, opening a door in the entrance, slid them in under the shoe rack, above which were several jackets that hung neatly on the rail. He turned to Benito, "Take off your shoes kid, Marlene don't like no shoes in the house."

Benito looked down at the lush cream carpet and untied his trainers, placing them beside Tadeo's before he shut the door. When he turned around, the two men were already across the spacious living room and entering the archway into the kitchen. He walked in their direction, between the beige leather sofa and glass coffee table that held a vase of tulips, thinking how comfortable the carpet was on his feet. He almost laughed at the thought that had entered his mind as he made his way towards where two nefarious men were laughingly deciding his fate like he was a lawnmower that one man was loaning to another.

The bright kitchen had large windows that looked out into the well-kept garden that was mostly grass with colourful shrubs and mature trees lining the edges. The walls of the kitchen were lined with oak cupboards and granite counters with a large granite covered island in the middle and an oak table on the left with eight chairs around it. The two men were sat on either side the table, helping themselves to the food and Benito gently pulled out a chair beside Tadeo, scraping it on the stone floor. Tadeo shot him a glare as he put two containers of food in front of the wary teenager. As Keegan slid some cutlery and a plate across to them, his gold bracelet clinked on the table. Benito avoided the man's eyes as he opened the container and tipped the food onto his plate, then carefully put the empty box back into the bag that was still on the table.

Despite himself, the egg fried rice and sweet and sour chicken made the teenager's stomach rumble. He paused a moment as he silently thanked God for the feast before him and prayed for help and strength in what he would have to face.

Just then, the front door opened, and they all turned to see a well dressed, beautiful auburn-haired woman enter. She took off her bright blue wool jacket and hung it in the cupboard, then unzipped her leather boots and exchanged them for some gold shoes that Benito thought his mother would wear to a fancy party.

"Hello, Tad," she greeted Benito's uncle as she came into the kitchen, then looked over at Benito, smiling down at him with compassion in her eyes. "Hello, darling, you must be Tad's nephew." She touched his face with her smooth fingers and as her long, freshly polished red finger nails caught the teenager's eyes, he flinched. "Oh, hon!" she smiled at him, wiggling her fingernails in the air, "You needn't be worried about these! They are perfectly harmless, sweetie!"

Benito caught an anxiousness in her eyes as she shot a glance at Keegan, then, walking around the table to him, she leaned over, carefully drawing her fingernails across the man's chin as she leaned down and kissed him on his cheek. Then Marlene clicked across the stone floor, her hips swinging the short flowing skirt that matched the colour of her nails. She got herself a glass from a cupboard and filled it with cold water from the tap.

"Hey, babe, put on some coffee, will you?" Keegan winked at her and she nodded silently, looking over at Benito who was now staring at this woman who purveyed a kindness tinged with a hint of guardedness.

"What would you like to drink, sweetheart?" Marlene smiled again at Benito and he marvelled at how calm she made him feel. It was almost hypnotic.

The two men looked at Benito as he continued to be transfixed by the woman, and Tadeo gave him a hard jab in the ribs: "What's wrong with you, boy? Marlene asked you a question!"

"Uh … oh … uh … water will be fine, ma'am."

"Just water, are you sure? I have some blackcurrant squash."

"Uh … okay … yes please, thank you," he stumbled. Another harsh glare from Tadeo turned the teenager's focus back to his food and he began to eat, while Marlene put some squash into a large glass before taking out a bottle of sparkling water from the fridge and filling the glass to the top. She brought it over to him, and he didn't dare look up again as she placed it on the table. She gently stroked the top of his head before clicking across the kitchen and starting the coffee maker.

Benito heard a couple more clicks and then there was silence as he assumed she walked out of the kitchen onto the soft carpet. When he looked over his shoulder, she was gone.

"Well, then, you haven't said how much you want for his services?" Keegan nodded over to Benito as he scooped up the last mouthful of his food. Benito closed his eyes and tried to focus on the extra food that his body so badly craved.

"Five hundred," Tadeo said.

"Five hundred?! That's a lot." Keegan glanced over at Benito and his snake eyes flashed. A chill ran through the teenager's body.

"Look, you're earning a large amount tonight. If he doesn't meet your requirements, I'll give you a reduction of two hundred quid." He put a forkful of food in his mouth and chewed as Keegan mulled it over. After a minute, Tadeo added, "And I want two hundred up front."

Keegan put his fork down and wiped his mouth with the linen serviette by his plate. "I'm only getting three thousand." He twisted his mouth and breathed through his nose heavily. After a moment, he agreed. "All right. You've got a deal."

The machine across the room beeped and Keegan got up, walked across the room and opened a cupboard where he got out a metal cash box. He took a key from his pocket, opened it up and counted out the notes. After he put the box back in the cupboard, he poured two cups of coffee. He brought them over and placed one in front of Tadeo. He placed two hundred pounds down beside it, then turned to Benito.

"Right, here's what I want you to do." Benito continued to eat as he listened to Keegan's plans for the evening. "I've got some new buyers and I don't trust them yet. So, we'll go to one of my lock-ups, pick up a car and drive it to their site. You'll follow me, then I want you to drive it in and collect the money. Simple. Think you can do this simple task for me?"

Benito almost sighed with relief. It would be dark. One criminal to another. No innocent people. A thought entered his mind at Keegan's comment, *new buyers*. He knew what that could mean – cops. Tadeo had run into that problem several years ago, when Benito was only thirteen. Tadeo was selling some guns. It was in a small, dark abandoned warehouse and there were three men. One of the men stepped forward and handed over the money to Benito and as the teenager held out the sports bag, he caught a look between the other two men who happened to be standing where a dim light shone on them. Suspicion immediately entered the teenager and he turned so he was ready. As soon as the first man zipped open the bag, Benito caught the nod and he propelled himself out of the warehouse and around the back down the dark lane. He wasn't good at much else, but he could run fast. He knew the area well – Tadeo had used it a few times – and soon lost the undercover police, winding back to jump into the then Volkswagen Tiguan that was waiting for him, only managing to say 'cops!' as he gasped for air. Tadeo put his foot down and they sped off down the street. Benito was glad later. It had spooked Tadeo for several weeks and the teenager didn't have to do any 'work' while the man reformulated his plans.

"Well?" Keegan was staring at him and Benito realised the man was waiting for an answer. The teenager nodded slowly.

"Yes, sir," he managed quietly.

Keegan turned to look at Tadeo. "I could drop him back off tonight."

Tadeo shook his head and winked at the other man. "No. I've got plans and I don't want him disturbing me."

Keegan smiled knowingly and said nothing as he watched Tadeo slurp back the rest of his coffee and stand up. "Right. I'm off then. I don't want him back before noon." He turned to leave and Benito's heart rate increased as he watched his uncle slip on his shoes and head out the door. The click of the lock as he shut the door made Benito feel like he'd been locked in a prison. He turned to Keegan who was staring at him and smiling a horrible smile.

Benito panicked and blurted out loudly, "My uncle said you couldn't hurt me!"

Keegan leaned back in the chair and laughed wickedly. "He said I couldn't break any bones!" Fear filled Benito and he began to shake. Keegan snarled and leaned forward into the teenager's face. "Your uncle's right. You ARE pathetic!" He pushed his chair away from the table and stood up suddenly, nearly knocking it over, then strode out of the kitchen, across the living room and up a staircase on the far side.

Benito sat still, listening to the rhythmic ticking of a clock on the wall. Tick tick tick. Like his life, it kept going forward. Tick tick tick. He had no control of its direction. Tick tick tick. He folded his arms on the table, and leaning his head forward, silent tears streamed.

Toby, Rebeca, Joe and Gwen sat under the large oak tree at the back of the garden to discuss their plans. Emily had taken the twins to swimming lessons and David was in his office at the front of the house.

"I'm thinking we should stay somewhere central. I know there is a Travel Lodge in the centre of Birmingham," Toby put his thoughts forward to the others.

Gwen raised her eyebrows as she looked down at her phone, swiping and tapping as she spoke, "I totally agree that central is best – since we don't know which direction we will be going. We have the address where Ben …". She smiled and interrupted herself, looking up at the others. "But Mummy would not approve of the Travel Lodge. We will stay at the Hyatt Regency. Do we all want separate rooms?"

Joe and Toby sat with mouths open, still amazed at how money was of no consequence to Gwen and her family. Rebeca did not know the difference between a Travel Lodge and the Hyatt, so she just waited for the others to decide, oblivious to the query.

Joe spoke first. "Uh … I think … are you sure? It is an expensive hotel." He felt foolish saying it to a girl who had flown over on a private jet, but he felt somehow he ought to.

Gwen tilted her head and smiled at him, "Hon, don't you know it is crass to discuss money?" She looked over at Rebeca and then back at him. "We're in *my* world now." Joe gave her a funny look and she immediately chided herself for sounding rude. Despite his temper, she was growing fond of Joe. She softened her tone and spoke gently, "Look, my parents will always be grateful for the three of you rescuing me in the jungle. This is their way of thanking you all. Please just see it as a gift. A gift that we won't worry about discussing again, okay?" She stroked his arm with her fingertips and looked meaningfully into Joe's dark chocolate eyes.

Joe tried not to get distracted by her touch. He cleared his throat and broke away from her gaze, looking at the others. "Two adjoining rooms will be fine, don't you think?" Toby and Rebeca nodded.

Gwen looked back down at her phone and tapped. "I think a suite would be good, but there is only one bedroom in a suite, so we'll have to have a twin room as well. It is on a different floor, but that is fine if we have the suite as well." She looked back up at the others and added, "Do you think a week will be all right? Best to book longer than we need. We can always leave early if we like, but in August, you can't always be guaranteed that we could stay longer than we planned."

"While Gwen is …," Toby started.

Gwen looked up and smiled, "Done!"

Toby continued, "Okay – Pamela sent me the address of the place where Benito took the ring. I think we should go around and see the place as soon as we've dropped our stuff off at the hotel. We can talk to the owner."

Rebeca grinned, remembering a previous time they had made enquiries, when they were looking for Emmie in Florida. She and Toby pretended they were students researching monkeys. "What is your plan this time?"

Toby sighed deeply through his closed lips, "This time, Rebeca, I think we need to speak the truth."

"Good!" She responded, her grin growing wide. "I much prefer the truth!"

"The train to Birmingham leaves every hour in the morning," Joe turned to Gwen and teased, "unless you want to hire a helicopter?"

Gwen cocked her head, a closed-mouth grin stretching across her face as she raised her eyebrows, "We can take a train if we can go first class!"

They all laughed, though Rebeca was not sure what they were laughing at. The phrase 'first class' was as mystifying as the idea of buying fish, putting them in a lake, and making people pay to catch them.

A short time later, Emily returned with the girls and a collection of ice creams, and the afternoon was spent entertaining the twins – or perhaps the twins entertaining the others!

———>●<———

Benito awoke with a start as a gentle hand rested on his back. He lifted his head off his arms that were now aching, having been in the same position for a couple of hours, and he looked up into the kind face of Marlene who was bending down beside him. He noticed a deep fatigue in her blue-green eyes.

"Are you all right, sweetheart?"

"Y-y-yes, ma'am. Thank you."

Marlene pulled out the chair beside him and, sitting down, smiled compassionately. "Don't lie to your aunty Marlene now," she spoke quietly.

The kindness in her voice compelled him to speak truthfully, "My mom is very sick in the hospital and I'm worried about her. My uncle said ...". Benito's gaze went back to the table as the desire to burst into weeping enveloped him.

Marlene continued for him, "Your uncle said you were keen to learn more about 'the trade', but you aren't, are you? You're not just frightened of the men. You don't *want* to do what they do; but your uncle makes you feel like you have to." Her gaze drifted off as she added even quieter, "Like me."

Benito sat silently, gazing at her with a deep sadness. He wanted to ask why she stayed if she didn't like it, but he said nothing.

Finally, she turned back to him and stroked his head, like his mom always did, and tears threatened to surface but he managed to hold them back. Years of practice taught him how.

"It's too late for me," she spoke, looking directly at him. "I've burned my bridges and I can't go back." She half smiled at Benito. "But you … I could help …".

"Hey babe! What's for tea?" reptile man called out as he walked down the stairs. He looked at the two of them suspiciously and frowned as he walked into the kitchen. "You two look like you are conspiring. What were you discussing?"

Marlene gave Benito another gentle touch on his head as she stood. "Benito was just telling me about his mama. How sick she is." Then she added, "I thought we'd order in."

"I had a takeaway for lunch," Keegan grumbled.

Marlene waved her nails in front of him, "I can't cook when I've just had my nails done!"

Keegan guffawed, then grabbed her and pulled her towards him, kissing her forcefully. "You can't cook when you *haven't* had your nails done!" He whispered in her ear, "Remember, I own you, …". Benito heard the cruel words, and frowned involuntarily. Keegan turned on him, "What's the matter with you, kid?!"

"N-n-nothing, sir."

"Leave the boy alone, he ain't done nothin' to you," Marlene defended Benito.

SMACK!! The back of Keegan's hand hit hard against her cheek and one of his rings slashed her skin. Marlene's hand automatically reached up but Benito saw the cut before she covered it.

"Look what you made me do!" Keegan yelled at Marlene who stood shaking, but staring him down. "I was going to take you out to dinner tonight, and now I can't! You stupid woman! I don't know why I put up with you. Maybe I should swap with Tadeo – I'll have the kid for a few weeks and he can have you! Then you'll appreciate me when you see what a pig *that* man is!" He stormed out and sat on a beige leather chair that matched the sofa, phone in his hand. "I'm going to order from that new Korean place down the road." He looked up at Marlene who was still stood in the same place, blood now seeping through her fingers. "And don't come in here and bleed on the carpet!"

Marlene walked over to the sink and leaned over, turning on the tap and splashing the water on the side of her face. "Benito, sweetheart, will you go upstairs to the bathroom at the top of the landing? In the little cupboard under the sink, there is a black first-aid box. Will you bring it down for me?" Benito jumped to attention at her quiet words and hurried across the room and up the stairs. He was soon back with the box.

"Would you like me to help you?" he offered, as he looked around and could not see a mirror.

"Sit back down, boy! She can sort herself out."

For one brief moment, Benito stood in defiance, but he darted back to the table when Keegan stood up. Marlene shot the teenager a faint smile to thank him, then turned her attention to dress her wound.

Forty-five minutes later, they were sat at the table and despite the tantalising smell drifting up their nostrils, two of the three had little interest in the food that sat in front of them. Marlene and Benito sat in silence opposite each other as Keegan, positioned beside Marlene, spoke about a local politician who had been discovered doing something fraudulent.

Suddenly, Keegan slammed his fork on the table. "You two better start eating and not waste my money!" He looked over at Benito who quickly began eating. "You're more trouble than you are worth, boy! Don't think you'll get a holiday with me again – Marlene has been a good girl lately, and look what you turned her into!"

Immediately, Marlene faked a smile and leaned over to Keegan, kissing him on his cheek. "Sorry, honey, I don't know what got into me earlier. Forgive me?"

"Hmmmm," Keegan looked at her and she touched his cheek gently with her fingertips, "I don't know … you were pretty disrespectful to me, babe. You might have to go in your room tonight."

Marlene said nothing, and focused on her food, while Benito wondered what he meant and thought if the 'punishment' was making her spend a night in a room on her own, it sounded more enjoyable than spending time with snake eyes.

After they finished eating and Marlene had cleared the dishes away, the three of them sat in the living room on the comfortable sofas. Keegan and Marlene each had a glass of wine and were sat on the sofa, while Benito sat on one of the chairs with a cup of hot cocoa that Marlene had quickly made for him before Keegan could think of a reason to complain about it.

Keegan picked up a remote control beside the tulips and pointed it opposite the sofa, towards the large television that was recessed in the bookcase covering the wall. Immediately, a football game appeared and Keegan put his arm around Marlene, who leaned into him as though they were lovers; and Benito wondered in amazement of how deceiving appearances could actually be.

Suddenly, Benito thought of Gideon. He had left his window open. There was water in the dish, but no food. And what if Tadeo went in his room and found the gentle tenacious creature? He said a little prayer for God's protection on the animal – a prayer which God had already answered, as Tadeo was otherwise occupied with a young lady in an expensive restaurant.

The teenager was not very interested in football, and since the chair he was sitting in was extremely comfortable, once he finished his hot drink and put it in the dishwasher, he came back to it, pulled the recliner mechanism and lay back. Despite the situation – or perhaps because of it – he was soon sound asleep dreaming that he was on a football pitch playing with Toby and the rest of his new friends.

"How do you become a Christian, Joe?"

The two brothers were lying in the dark in Joe's king size bed, and Joe had just been about to drift into unconscious when his brother's unexpected question jarred him awake.

"You want to become a Christian?" Joe turned over and looked at his brother in the dark, thrilled that his little brother was finally interested in learning how to be saved.

"Well," Toby began slowly. "I finally confessed my feelings to myself, and Rebeca, and after all my thinking and deliberating she said she couldn't have a relationship with me because I wasn't a Christian."

"Oh," said Joe, disappointed that his brother was not approaching the matter of faith with the right heart. However, unwelcome feelings of hope made him wonder if Rebeca could now turn her attention towards himself. Being second place wasn't ideal. But he could live with it if it meant being with Rebeca.

What was he thinking?? How could he be so hateful as to not be more focused on helping his brother learn how to be assured a place in Heaven?

"Well?"

"It doesn't work like that. You can't become a Christian for someone else." Joe answered finally.

"Rebeca said the same thing."

Joe couldn't help smiling. "That must mean it is true!" He chuckled.

"That doesn't help."

"No. Sorry," Joe sighed, thinking about what to say.

"So, how *does* it work?"

"Toby. How many church services and Sunday School classes have you gone to and you don't know the answer to that?"

"I haven't been for several years, so I guess I forgot about anything I actually listened to – which wasn't much. My mind wandered a lot because I didn't want to be there. I remember Noah built an ark and Jonah was eaten by a whale." He paused for a moment, thinking things over. "I mean, supposedly you are a Christian, yet you have a bad temper and you don't really look any different from anyone who is not a Christian."

Toby's words pierced Joe to the core of his soul. He wanted to lash out, but was immediately convicted of their truth. *He didn't really look any different from anyone who was not a Christian.* Joe sighed so deeply that he had to gasp to inhale.

"Are you all right?" Toby asked.

"No … I mean yes … I …"

"Are you mad because I said you had a temper?" Toby asked, oblivious to the awakening he had initiated in Joe's heart.

"No."

Silence.

"So, are you going to answer my question?" Toby persisted.

"I … don't know, Toby. I thought I knew." Joe struggled to finish his thoughts out loud. "But if I don't look any different … then maybe I don't."

Toby couldn't see his brother's face, but he could hear it in his voice. Self confident, self assured Joe was struggling with what made him a Christian. Toby turned over and closed his eyes, disappointment weighing heavy on his heart.

———◦———

"Please don't lock the door!"

Benito's eye's shot open at the raised voices. He looked over to the sofa, but Keegan and Marlene were gone.

"You've made me doubt you, babe. I can't trust you to stay put and not cause trouble."

Benito looked towards the stairs from where the voices were coming down. He crept to the bottom and looked up. He could see the two of them stood outside a door – Marlene was clinging to Keegan and crying.

"It's so small and dark, Keegan, please, I'll be good, I promise!"

She tried to put her arms around his neck but he pushed her back, and shoved her inside, clicking the door locked with a key. She screamed, pounding on the door with her fists and snake-eyes swore, unlocking the door and swinging it open angrily. Benito heard a loud smack, and Marlene went quiet. Benito felt sick. Keegan locked the door again, and Benito darted back to his seat and lay back, closing his eyes just as reptile man came around the bottom into the living room.

"Get up!" Keegan's angry voice increased the teenager's heart even more but he opened them slowly, pretending that he was just waking from a sleep. Sitting up properly, he pushed the foot rest back into place and stood up. Keegan was inches away from his face, his gold/green snake-eyes flashing like they were electric. Benito was sure he saw faint lines on the man's face that looked like scales under a thin layer of skin, and a chill raced down the teenager's spine. "Put your shoes on!"

Benito jumped up and dashed over to the front door cupboard, finding his shoes and tying them up quickly. By the time he was done, Keegan was stood ready, with his hand impatiently on the front door. They walked across the crunchy gravel toward the double garage that was attached at a right-angle to the house. Keegan pressed the remote on his key chain and the door slowly went up. Keegan had a black BMW, the next model up from Tadeo. Benito opened the back door and slid onto the seat, quietly shutting the door and putting on his seat belt. Keegan climbed behind the steering wheel and minutes later they were making their way down the road.

The new LED street lights flashed through the window as they drove along in the dark on the quiet street. Benito closed his eyes. It was probably best if he did not know where they were going. The less he knew the better.

He must have drifted off, as it seemed only seconds later when Keegan stopped the car in front of a row of garages. He got out and walked towards one, opening it and stepping into the darkness. Lights turned on and a brand new Land Rover Discovery rolled out. Keegan jumped out and shut the door behind him. Walking over to his BMW, he opened the back door and stood waiting like a chauffeur while Benito got out.

"Right," said Keegan, "follow me. It is about fifteen minutes away. I'll stop just short of the place – its a wooden building and there's a sign on the front that says: Reg's Auto Body Repairs. Once I've pulled over, go just past me and turn onto the parking area. They'll be watching for us, so the doors should open as you approach it. Drive in. Get out, but hold onto the keys until they give you the money. I've got a gun, so tell them I'll use it if there is any funny business."

Benito nervously looked at the vehicle, nodding his head. He had never driven anything like that before. He looked sideways at Keegan who was waiting for him to get in. The teenager slowly walked towards the vehicle and climbed up and slid onto the leather seat. It almost made him feel like a child. Keegan was already in his car and driving off, so Benito quickly put the Discovery into gear and pulled out onto the street to follow, his heart beating heavily against his chest.

Halfway through the journey, he passed a police car that was parked on the side by a late night convenience store. Two officers were stood by the car talking to a couple of teenagers. He held his breath, thankful for the darkness – he was sure he did not look like the kind of person who would own an expensive vehicle like this – and did not breath again until they were well out of sight in his rear view mirror. When he looked forward, he panicked as he saw that he had let a considerable distance get between him and the BMW. He put his foot down a little and slowly crept forward until he was a reasonable distance behind.

Finally, Keegan pulled over and Benito looked ahead at the buildings. He spotted the sign, indicated, and pulled onto the gravel car park. As he did, sure enough, the large sliding doors opened. He drove slowly into the dimly lit, near empty building, and stopped. As he got out, two men were just shutting the doors. One man walked toward him with a holdall. When he reached Benito, he opened the zip and the teenager looked inside at the money. He picked up one of the bundles that was bound by a thick elastic. He couldn't tell in the dark, but it seemed like real money to Benito. And it was certainly far more than the three thousand that Keegan had told Tadeo he was going to get. He dropped it back in the bag, and as he did, the man pulled it away, stepping back and tossing it to the other man that was stood by the door.

"You're just a kid! What idiot uses a kid to swap a brand new Discovery for a bag of cash?!" They laughed and Benito's breathing increased.

The teenager cleared his throat and, speaking slowly with a deep voice, tried to sound threatening. "The kind of man who is waiting outside with a loaded gun and his finger on the trigger, pointed this way and ready to come in here if I'm not out in two minutes."

The two men looked at each other, and the man closest to Benito nodded to the man by the door. He opened a little door beside the larger sliding ones and stood aside, holding out the bag. Benito strolled purposefully towards him, grabbing the holdall and stepping out into the night, just as it slammed and locked behind him.

Benito hurried his pace and turned down the pavement toward the waiting car. He jumped in the back, throwing the bag on the seat beside him.

"Give it here, boy! I want to check it before I leave!" Benito heaved the bag up and over the front seat beside Keegan who zipped it open loudly. Taking a flashlight from the glove compartment, he shone inside and quickly examined his money. A smile spread across his face, then quickly disappeared as he looked back at Benito. "It is a well earned *three thousand pounds*, isn't it, boy?"

Benito knew exactly what he meant and nodded his head firmly. "Yes sir, it is a well earned *three thousand pounds*. There is no doubt about it."

"Good," said Keegan as he zipped up the bag and threw the light back in the compartment. He turned forward, started the car and drove silently back to his house.

When they got back inside, Benito again removed his shoes and put them in the cupboard, then stood waiting for instructions. Keegan tossed the bag on the floor and went in the kitchen to pour himself a drink. When he came back in the living room, he looked at Benito stood by the door. He put his drink on the coffee table and motioned to the teenager to follow him up the stairs. Benito walked silently up the stairs and glanced at the locked door where Marlene was, and wondered if she was okay. They passed another door that was slightly ajar, then Keegan stopped at the next door after that. He stepped to the side and nodded at Benito to go inside. It was a small room, simply furnished with just a single bed and a chest of drawers. The small window had the curtains closed across it. The teenager walked in and sat on the bed, and as he did, Keegan shut the door and Benito heard the lock click.

He got up and pressed his face against the glass, looking out the window which faced the back garden. A faint light from another house just peeked through the trees. It seemed that he had at least a little more comfort than poor Marlene. He wondered about her circumstances – how she came to be with Keegan, and why she stayed with him. She obviously was allowed out sometimes on her own, so why did she come back? She seemed so confident when he first saw her come in the house, flashing her newly polished nails. It was bewildering.

For him, it had been fear of Tadeo at first. Then fear for his mom. Now he was a criminal. He doubted Marlene was a criminal. He wondered what she meant about burning her bridges?

Benito sighed deeply as he walked to the light switch and turned it off. He paused a moment while his eyes adjusted before he walked back across the room and climbed under the covers fully dressed. He stared at the dim light that came through the curtain and thought he would probably be awake all night but the next thing he knew he was sound asleep, back in Louisiana, playing Monopoly with some of his friends in a hurricane.

CHAPTER 6

Thursday 18th August

Toby, Rebeca, Joe and Gwen stepped onto the train into a first class carriage. They put their bags in the luggage rack, then found their seats at a table, where there was a small shuffling of who was going to sit where.

The boys let the girls have the window seats and stood waiting for them to decide which one Gwen wanted. Gwen sat down, but then asked, "Which direction will it go? I have to sit facing forwards, otherwise I get travel sick."

"I think you are facing the right way," said Joe, who sat beside her on the aisle seat. Rebeca sat by the window on the other side of the table with Toby beside her.

Gwen smiled widely at the others: "This is so much more enjoyable than spending time with *Richard*" – she said the name with a groan.

"The very fine man that your parents want you to get together with?" asked Toby, grinning.

Gwen nodded, rolling her eyes. "After three dates, I know everything there is to know about him" – she made a face – "and I am certain he knows *nothing* about me!" Her face suddenly brightened. "However! He had some tickets to the theatre and was annoyed that I was leaving suddenly. So – I suggested he take my friend Katy so the tickets wouldn't be wasted. He wasn't happy, but he was pacified. And Katy thinks I am mad to not be in love with him." Her smile grew wider, "So with any luck, he will soon feel the same about her!"

"If he is so awful, why would your friend Katy want to spend time with him?" asked Rebeca naively.

"Three things: money, status, great looks," answered Gwen simply.

Toby looked at Gwen, surprised at the sound of distaste in her voice as she voiced the last thing. He would have thought she would at least have liked the good looks. After all, she didn't need the money.

"What is 'status'?" asked Rebeca hesitantly, then regretted speaking as they all looked at her with smiles. She was eager to learn new things, but she often felt incredibly naive when her questions invoked humour in others.

"Status, my innocent Rebeca," Gwen began, less patronisingly than she would have when she first met the Nicaraguan girl, "is the importance that others place on you. Richard's family has many businesses."

"And people place importance on these many businesses?" asked Rebeca, daring more friendly teasing.

"Yes, and to people in our circles of friends and business associates, status is almost as highly valued as money." Gwen almost sighed, and again Toby was struck by the disapproval in Gwen's voice.

"If you are in his 'circle of friends', then why do you not value this 'importance'?" Rebeca felt that there was a change in Gwen since they had first met.

Gwen chuckled, "I used to." She looked around at them all. "It's all your fault – you have opened my eyes. You all live in a completely different world from me." Gwen cocked her head at the irony of placing Rebeca in the same category as the boys. "And I am quite enjoying spending time in this world!"

Rebeca thought about Gwen's last statement, and wondered if that meant Gwen would eventually return to 'her world', but decided she did not want to ask any more questions.

Gwen clicked on her phone and turned it towards Rebeca who immediately raised her eyebrows and could not help being appreciative of what she saw. "Oh!" she said involuntarily, as she gazed at the very handsome dark-haired man with designer stubble. "He is one of the most handsome men I have ever seen!" Oblivious of the feelings of jealousy that her innocently spoken words and enthusiasm created in the boys, she just looked up at Gwen, smiling.

Gwen, who was much less innocent of such things, grinned as she nodded her head and took back the phone. "I know, right? What a waste!"

Just then, the conductor came by to check their tickets. "Someone will be by shortly with snacks and drinks."

"Right," said Toby when the conductor had left, not wanting to get onto the handsome Richard subject again, "What else can we do to try and find Benito?"

———⟫●⟪———

Benito smelt it before he was conscious. He opened his eyes to the early morning light and noticed his door was open. He sat up and sniffed. It was definitely bacon. He swung his feet out and flung back the duvet, getting up and stretching his limbs. He tidied the bed then walked across the room, hesitating at the doorway. Just because it was open, didn't mean he was allowed out. He did not know the reptile man well enough to know if he would test him, then punish him for failing a test to which he was not given the rules.

His aching empty stomach pushed him forwards, and he walked slowly out of the room, across the hall and down the steps to find Keegan sat in the living room reading a paper. Marlene was in the kitchen cooking bacon and eggs. They were like a normal couple; it was surreal.

"I wondered when you were going to get up." Keegan looked up from his paper. "Your uncle will be here in half an hour to pick you up. Go and have some breakfast if you want some." He looked back to his paper as Benito tried not to run towards the delicious smell.

Marlene turned her head as the teenager entered the kitchen and sat down at the table where a place mat was set.

"Good morning, sweetheart. Did you sleep well?" She smiled brightly, though her eyes were red and tired. No wonder, thought Benito, wondering if she had managed to sleep at all in 'her room'.

Benito nodded, "I guess so. I don't remember falling asleep and the next thing I knew it was morning." He smiled back at her, wanting to ask if she was all right, but not daring to while Keegan was within earshot.

A few moments later, Marlene had dished out three plates and put them on the table. Benito looked with wonder at the delight before him: bacon, eggs, mushrooms, tomatoes and baked beans. He had not seen such an amazing plate of food since he was in Louisiana, staying at Ellie and Caleb's house with his friends.

Marlene misunderstood Benito's hesitation. "Is it too much? Is there anything you didn't want? I can take it off your plate."

"No!" said Benito as she reached her hand out towards his food. "It just looks so wonderful, I wanted to enjoy looking at it, first."

Marlene smiled appreciatively at his enthusiasm, and Keegan grunted. "That is stupid. It's just breakfast." He sat down, picked up his utensils and began eating while Marlene was still busy getting juice and toast.

Benito silently thanked God for His generous gift, and again asked for protection for Gideon. He then picked up a knife and fork and ate slowly, savouring every mouthful. He was only just finishing when the doorbell rang. Marlene walked over and opened the door, welcoming Tadeo inside.

"Would you like a cup of coffee?" she asked as she shut the door behind him and motioned towards the kitchen.

"Don't mind if I do," replied Tadeo as he kicked off his shoes into the cupboard before walking across to the kitchen and sitting down at the table, opposite Keegan who was just finishing his paper. He folded it up and put it down, looking up at Tadeo.

"How'd it go?" Tadeo asked Keegan.

"Everything went smoothly. I might hire him again sometime." He laughed as he added, "Unless I win him at our next poker game!"

Tadeo laughed as well and Benito felt his stomach turn. As bad as his uncle was, the reptile man was far more sinister. Getting smacked in the head now and again seemed by far, the better of the two options.

Keegan got up and retrieved some money from his cash box, placing the pile of notes in front of Tadeo, who counted them before putting it in his wallet, which he stuffed in his back pocket.

"Pleasure doin' business with you."

Conversation turned to the football game from the previous evening, and some light-hearted disagreement ensued as the men each supported opposite teams. Shortly, Tadeo finished his coffee, and he said to Benito.

"Let's go." He turned to Marlene and gave her a wink. "'Bye, darlin', thanks for the coffee."

Keegan's snake eyes flashed and he slammed his fist on the table: "What'd I tell you about flirting with her?!"

Tadeo glared back at him and he stood up. Neither man said anything as they eye-balled each other for a moment. Finally, Tadeo headed towards the door. Benito glanced at Marlene, smiling sadly at her, and followed his uncle silently out the door.

Benito watched out the window, thinking about Gideon. When they got home, he darted up the stairs, but as he got to the top, Tadeo yelled up at him. "Oi! Get down here, boy! I want the kitchen tidied before you go up to your room!"

Even though he was desperate to see if Gideon was there, he didn't dare disobey his uncle, so Benito walked back down the stairs and into the kitchen. It was a mess. It almost looked like Tadeo had purposefully used extra dishes and pans and strewn them around. There was no other reason for the kitchen to be so untidy after so little time of Benito being away.

Benito started to sigh, then spotted some left-over bacon and scrambled eggs, and half a sausage. He scooped it onto a small plate, then quickly set to washing the dishes and tidying the kitchen.

When everything was washed and dried, and the counters all wiped down, Benito took the little plate of food and stepped out of the kitchen. As he did, Tadeo shouted from the living room.

"Get me a cup of coffee and a couple of biscuits – the chocolate ones!"

Benito spent another five minutes filling and boiling the kettle and putting four biscuits on a plate, then brought it into his uncle. He turned to leave, but Tadeo stopped him.

"How much did he make last night?" Tadeo knew exactly how these things worked. No one told the truth.

Benito stopped, but didn't turn around. "I … uh … I don't know. I just took the bag, I didn't count the money."

"Hmmmm, I'd have thought he would get a lot more for a vehicle like that! You were all right driving it?" Tadeo was guessing, but Benito didn't realise he was being manipulated, and he turned to face his uncle.

91

"Well, I was a bit worried when I passed some cops, as I was sure I didn't look like someone that would be driving a Discovery."

"Hah! So it wasn't a Honda Civic like he told me! Thanks for spilling the beans, boy! I'll let Keegan know how cooperative you were!" Tadeo guffawed and Benito felt sick. "Ha! Ha! Don't look so worried, boy! I don't think his punch is as hard as mine!"

Benito felt sure that not only was Keegan's punch harder, his other punishments were far worse. He didn't want to imagine what Keegan would do to him the next time he saw him.

Suddenly remembering Gideon, he went back into the kitchen for the little dish of leftovers. Tadeo called out as he went past, "What have you got there? I never said you could eat anything!"

Benito stopped dead, his heart pounding against his ribs. "I … uh … thought it would be okay if I ate the leftovers from your breakfast." He held out the little dish and Tadeo laughed.

"Oh, you can eat that!" Tadeo turned his attention back to the television and Benito trotted up the stairs anxiously entering his bedroom.

Gideon was sat on the window ledge, but he jumped down when he saw Benito. The teenager closed the door behind him and brushed the food into the container with his finger. The water bowl was empty, so he took that and quickly filled it from the bathroom sink. He bent down and stroked the soft creature as he ate, and the animal purred loudly in response.

When he finished, Benito shoved the containers back under his bed and propped up his pillow, so he could sit down and lean against it. Gideon promptly jumped on his lap, and as the teenager leaned forward the cat rubbed his head against Benito's face, purring happily. As Gideon settled down on his lap, Benito lay back, enjoying the companionship of the gentle creature.

He had started to drift off when he heard his uncle stomping up the stairs. Benito sat upright, and grabbed the blanket at the bottom of the bed, only just pulling it over him and Gideon as Tadeo burst through the door.

"Why are you wrapped in a blanket?" He scowled at the teenager.

"I ... uh ... I am cold."

Tadeo looked at the window, "Well shut the window then, you idiot!" He walked over and shut the window, then stood beside the bed looking down at his nephew.

"Keegan wants you again – tomorrow. I told him the price would be higher since he lied to me about your last job." He grinned wickedly. "I did reiterate that he was not allowed to break any bones, so don't worry!" He chuckled at his joke and left the room, shutting the door behind him.

Benito sat staring at the door his uncle had just closed, feeling sick. He didn't want to even imagine what Keegan would do to him. A soft 'meow' brought his attention back to the present, as he lifted up the blanket and Gideon looked at him questioningly.

"Sorry, Gideon!" Benito stroked the animal's soft head and was rewarded with a loud purr. It was rather calming, thought Benito. Most of the anxiety dissipated as he cuddled the cat, but he when he realised he was still unsettled, he opened the drawer beside him and pulled out the Bible. He turned to Ephesians and began reading. In Chapter 2, he thought he found what Pastor Frank had told him to look for. At verse eight, he read out loud: "For you are saved by grace through faith, and this is not from yourselves; it is God's gift – not from works, so that no one can boast."

He looked down at the cat who had gone back to sleep on his lap. "There's that word, grace, again, Gideon." He pondered the words he had just read. "I can't save myself. It is a gift.

Grace. God's gift to me." He paused a moment mulling it over and over in his mind. "I think I understand, Gideon! There's nothing I can do to earn my way into Heaven!" His face clouded over. "But if I can't *earn* my way ... if entry into Heaven is a gift ... how do I get the gift??" He blew out through his closed lips, feeling so close, but still so far away from understanding.

———⟫●⟪———

Gwen led the way as the four of them stepped off the train into the busy Birmingham New Street station. Once they got outside onto the bustling street, Gwen headed towards the taxi rank.

"It's only a fifteen minute walk, Gwen," began Joe; then added, "Nothing to do with money, I would just like to stretch my legs." He smiled down at her, but a pout formed on her full lips as she looked down at her wheeled suitcase.

"But my suitcase wheels will get filthy, rolling them on the streets!"

Oblivious, Rebeca queried, "Is that not what the wheels are for – pulling it along?"

"*Inside*, at an airport or station, where they clean the floors, certainly *not* on the streets!" objected Gwen.

Joe shook his head, but he grinned as he offered, "How about I carry your bag?"

"How very chivalrous of you, sweetheart! Thank you."

Toby just rolled his eyes at Rebeca as Joe melted at Gwen's demure smile and picked up her suitcase with his left hand, while he pulled his own small suitcase with his right. The pavement was busy, so they fell into two groups of two, with Joe and Gwen leading the way.

Fifteen minutes later, they arrived at the Hyatt, and Rebeca looked up at the tall building with its glass fronted rooms. "It looks rather fragile, made of glass like that," she commented innocently.

Toby jumped in before Gwen could make fun of her. "Don't worry, Rebeca, the main construction is concrete and steel, there are just floor to ceiling windows in each of the rooms."

Rebeca looked from Joe to Toby dubiously. "That does not sound very safe for you two." Pictures of the two brothers wrestling in a previous hotel came to Rebeca's mind and she imagined them crashing through one of the windows of this hotel.

Joe and Toby laughed in unison and Toby tittered, "Don't worry, they are reinforced, bullet proof, boy proof glass!"

"But why would you need it to be bullet proof?" asked Rebeca nervously, "Are there many people shooting guns in Birmingham?"

Joe smiled and shook his head, "No, It just means it is very strong and there is no need to worry that someone is going to crash through the glass!"

Gwen raised her eyebrows questioningly. Being an only child, she had never witnessed two brothers at play – even as adults. Rebeca did not want to embarrass the two of them – since they nearly broke a lamp at Gwen's parents' expense, so she said no more as they all walked into the grand reception area of the luxury hotel.

Gwen walked up to the desk and the other three sat down in the comfortable chairs, the boys admiring the opulence of the building. Rebeca just looked around curiously, again amazed at how much effort people in America and the UK put into their homes and buildings. Coming from a community in the jungle where homes were made in a matter of days, she wondered at the necessity of putting so much time and money into buildings. There were so many more enjoyable things to be doing – such as fishing. And that did not cost any money in the jungle, either!

Gwen was soon back with two keys, one of which she gave to Joe. "Rebeca and I are on the eighteenth floor. We'll go there first and drop off our bags, then we'll go up to the suite on the twenty second floor where you boys will be staying.

Rebeca glanced nervously at the elevator – another 'western' invention on which she was not keen. Joe caught the look and put his arm around her comfortingly, squeezing her gently.

"Don't worry, Rebeca. I'll protect you from the big bad box! And I will make sure it opens its doors to release you when we reach our floors." He kissed the top of her head, inadvertently closing his eyes and breathing in deeply, completely missing the jealous faces of Toby and Gwen. He grabbed Rebeca's hand tightly and they all walked towards the doors that opened as they approached.

As usual, Rebeca let out a deep breath when the doors opened again on the eighteenth floor and she stepped out into the open. Joe was still holding her hand, unconsciously unwilling to let go of the hope that there could be a relationship between the two of them. Rebeca held on for the comfort it gave her in this unfamiliar situation, unaware of the hope it instilled in the young man.

When Gwen tapped the door handle with the fob she was given, there was a click and she pushed it open. The other three gasped at the large room with the amazing view of the city through the floor to ceiling windows. Rebeca followed Gwen in, squeezing Joe's hand tightly as they walked towards the windows and looked down at the vast city.

Looking over her shoulder at the two beds, she spoke quietly to Gwen, "Would you mind if I had the bed furthest away from the window?"

Annoyed that Joe and Rebeca were still holding hands, Gwen squinted her eyes and smiled mischievously, "Oh, no! I need to have that bed."

Rebeca's face fell, and she leaned closer into Joe who frowned at Gwen, "Gwen! Surely Rebeca can have the bed closer to the door?"

Joe's defence of Rebeca only served to make Gwen grow more obstinate and she dug her heels in. "No, I'm sorry, but I ... have claustrophobia and need to be by the door!"

Having just gone in and out of the elevator without complaint, he knew she was lying but, oblivious of Gwen's jealousy, he thought she was just being mean to Rebeca.

Toby piped up to break the tension, even though he was not happy with Joe's protection of Rebeca, either. "Let's go up and see our room and talk about it later, shall we?"

The girls left their bags and Gwen shut the door loudly behind them. Joe turned to her and Toby, still grasping Rebeca's hand protectively. "We'll walk up the four floors to the suite," he said determinedly, and Rebeca sighed with relief as they walked down the hall to the door that led to the stairs. Gwen started to follow, then changed her mind, pressing the button on the wall firmly. She was not used to having males not trip over themselves to please her, and it unsettled her that the one man that didn't was the same man for whom she had growing feelings.

Toby put his arm around Gwen in defiance of his brother and said, annoyed, "We'll meet you up there!" The two of them entered the elevator, and said nothing as the doors shut and quickly whisked them up the four floors, opening again seconds later.

They turned left out of the lift and walked a few metres before Gwen stopped and tapped the door handle with the other fob. She opened it up and Toby followed her in. "Wow!"

he exclaimed at the large living area with an L-shaped sofa and a table and chairs, with a kitchenette on the right side and the door to the large bedroom on the left. He abandoned his suitcase by the door and strolled over to the vast windows. "It really is a fantastic view!" He looked out at all the buildings and the canal that wound its way through the vast city. "Thanks, Gwen."

Just then, Joe and Rebeca appeared at the door that Gwen had left opened. Rebeca looked around in delight, then, having finally let go of Joe, walked over to Gwen in a conciliatory manner, "It is okay, Gwen, you may have the bed by the door. I do not want to inconvenience you." Gwen smiled, pleased that someone at least, had given in to her. However, her smile faded as Rebeca waved her hand towards the large sofa. "I can sleep on the sofa – it is quite far from the window."

"No!" Gwen replied a little too loudly, causing Joe and Toby to exchange glances. "I was just teasing you, Rebeca. Of course you may have the bed by the door." She forced a smile and sat down on an armchair near the window as she spoke to Joe, "Do you two want to unpack your suitcases? Rebeca and I will go down and unpack ours, then we can go get some lunch."

"Nah," said Joe, depositing his bag just inside the bedroom. "Let's go get some grub."

Rebeca raised her eyebrows. "I did not know they sold grubs in the England. I have not seen any since we got here."

Toby laughed, "That is just slang for food! You certainly won't find any grubs on a menu in the UK!"

"Shall we eat here at the Aria restaurant downstairs or do you want to go out?" asked Gwen.

"Why don't we go to the Canal House? The food looks good, we can eat on the patio that looks out on the canal, and it is only a two-minute walk away!" Toby piped up, looking up from his phone which he had just consulted.

"Sounds good!" said Joe, and Gwen nodded her head, the tension that had arisen earlier all but forgotten.

Rebeca just smiled and said, "I will be happy to go wherever you all have chosen – you know these things better than me."

They were shortly settled in the Canal House at an outside table. It didn't take them long to each find what they wanted, and not long later four different meals were brought to the table. Everyone agreed that the food was indeed delicious, and the weather was perfect for sitting out on the patio. When they had finished eating, the talk turned quiet as they discussed finding Benito and going to the jewellery store. Toby looked at the address and they decided they would need to take a taxi.

Gwen quickly tapped on her phone and looked up. "They'll be here in ten minutes. We may as well make our way to the front."

CHAPTER 7

Shortly, they were out front waiting for the taxi, which pulled up within minutes. Gwen sat in front and the other three climbed in the back. The ride took about a quarter of an hour and when they pulled up in front of the shop, Gwen turned around.

"Do we want him to wait for us?" she asked the others.

The three looked at each other and back and Gwen, each shrugging their shoulders. Joe was going to mention that they did not know how long it would be and that to keep a taxi waiting indefinitely would cost a lot of money, then thought the better of it, so he looked back at Gwen.

Finally she turned to the driver and tapped her phone on his card reader. "We don't know how long we'll be, so perhaps we will just call another taxi when we are ready." The others agreed that this was sensible and they all climbed out of the vehicle.

Toby looked through the glass windows into the busy shop. "I don't think we should all go in." He turned to Rebeca. "Perhaps just you and me?" He was surprised when Rebeca shook her head slowly.

"I would like to look around outside, I think." She looked up and pointed. "What is that?" she asked.

"A security camera," said Joe as he quickly added, "Probably best to put your hand down. They might think we are casing the joint!"

"Casing ... the joint?" asked Rebeca slowly, frowning at him.

"Checking things out so we can come back later and rob the place," clarified Toby, with a smile as a horrified look replaced the frown on her face. He turned to Joe, "Maybe you should come in with me. Two pairs of ears and eyes are best, I think! Both to glean information and to remember it! Plus, being a bit older, they may respect you more!"

Gwen began to pout about being left outside with Rebeca, then decided Joe had seen enough of her bad side, so feigned a happy acceptance as she watched the two of them enter the shop.

Joe and Toby had to wait a few minutes until a member of staff was available, but finally after about ten minutes, one couple blissfully chose an engagement ring and happily left the store, clutching each other in excitement, leaving an elderly gentleman in a grey suit free to assist Joe and Toby. He put the tray of rings away and looked up at them.

"What can I help you two young men with today? One of you getting engaged?" He smiled warmly and Joe and Toby both chuckled and looked at each other.

"No," began Toby, "we are looking for a friend." He paused and cleared his throat, suddenly realising that admitting Benito was a friend, after he had stolen a ring from this very shop, was probably not a good move. He hesitated a moment, then Joe spoke up and the man looked at him, a query in his face.

"Well, I wouldn't call him a friend," began Joe, making a face, then nodding toward Toby, "but my brother here seems to have some kind of soft spot for the weaselly little character."

Toby opened his mouth to protest and the gentleman looked at him confused, but Joe continued: "Toby here seems to think that Benito can't help himself and it is all his uncle's fault. He came in here the other day and stole a ring from yourself." Clarity appeared in the man's face, then clouded again as he became wary of the two young men standing in front of him. Joe gave him his most charming smile as he carried on: "Don't worry, my brother and I are upstanding citizens. We just wanted to help the kid. We doubt he'll turn himself in, so we want to find him, to convince him that handing himself in to the police is the best possible solution to his problems."

"But…" Toby frowned at Joe, who nudged him with his foot.

"Show him a photo, just to make sure we are talking about the same person, Tobs."

Toby pulled out his phone, tapped a couple of times and turned the picture of Benito towards the gentleman.

The man scowled, "That's the scoundrel all right!" he grunted, then looked up at Joe. "But I don't know what I can do to help you."

"Well, did they say anything?"

The man snorted, "Like, 'Here's my address so you can come get the ring I've stolen after we leave'?"

Toby half smiled and raised an eyebrow at his brother, "No, but – I don't know. We aren't cops. To be honest, I don't know that you can tell us anything to help. But Benito really is a lost soul and he really does need help and … perhaps just tell us exactly what happened, anything that was said…" Toby sighed deeply and suddenly realised what a mammoth task finding Benito would be on their own.

The man cocked his head, then spoke compassionately: "Why don't you come in the back with me, and I'll show you the camera footage. The police took the original away, but I made a copy because, well, you never know when one copy might get lost or something!"

"That would be great!" said Joe and Toby in unison as they followed the man into a back room.

He unlocked a drawer, took out a memory card and put it into the surveillance machine, his finger hovering over the keyboard. He looked at Joe and Toby, smiling as he raised an eyebrow pointing to the cameras in the corner of the room.

"And don't try anything funny, because we now have *you two* on camera!"

Outside, Gwen just watched Rebeca, as she gazed back and forth out front of the shop and on the road next to the curb.

"What are you looking for?" she asked curiously.

Rebeca shrugged her shoulders. "I do not know." She breathed deeply as she wondered if pride had again directed her wrongly. Tracking someone in a city was not the same thing as tracking someone in the jungle. How foolish she had been! She said a silent prayer for help, admitting to God that only He would be able to help them find and save Benito. She closed her eyes for a moment and Gwen giggled.

"What – you use 'the force' now?"

Having seen little on the television and nothing at a cinema, Rebeca did not understand the Star Wars reference, but realised from Gwen's intonation that she was making a joke. She tried to imagine Tadeo and Benito coming to the shop and she realised they would not have parked out front if they knew the camera was there. She looked around and saw a quiet little road several feet away. She walked towards it and turned the corner to follow the direction it led.

"They would not have gone far along this road." Rebeca spoke to herself, as Gwen followed her down the lane.

"You mean they would want to be close for a quick 'getaway'!" smiled Gwen.

"Yes," Rebeca said. She looked at the three cars parked perpendicular to the back of a building.

"That looks like some kind of storage building next to the jewellery shop. Perhaps the staff are allowed to park here," commented Gwen, trying to be helpful.

"Hmmm…" said Rebeca as she scanned the ground carefully, "there are some car tyre tracks here."

Gwen looked down to where Rebeca was pointing. "Well, that would be those cars coming in and out."

Rebeca shook her head slowly, "No, these ones here. They look like a car that has just pulled up on the side, facing for a 'quick getaway' as you say. Those ones come in straight, then curve as they pull out onto the road and drive away." She looked up at Gwen. "Will you take a picture? I do not know if they will help us, but you never know what will be important."

Gwen pulled out her phone and duly took several pictures of the car tracks that Rebeca was pointing to. Just then, Rebeca spotted a piece of paper on the other side of the little street. She walked over and picked it up.

"It is – what do you say? – a receipt." She studied it hard. "For some Murray Mints." She frowned, thinking.

Gwen looked at her dubiously. "Not sure a receipt for Murray Mints is going to be very helpful!"

Rebeca glanced over at her and grinned. "Benito likes to eat Murray Mints! He always brings a couple of bags when he comes to Nicaragua." She looked back down at the receipt. "These numbers," she said as she held the muddy piece of paper to Gwen, "Do any of them say what the day was that he bought them?"

Gwen nodded and kept her finger away from the receipt as she pointed, not wanting to touch the dirty paper. "This tells you the date, and this one tells you the time! The name and address at the top is where they were purchased."

Rebeca was amazed. "So much information! Why do they have all that detail on something that just says you have paid?"

Gwen raised her eyebrows and chuckled, "Perhaps so you can track down kidnapped boys?!"

Just then, Joe and Toby came around the corner. "Well, that was almost useless," sighed Toby. "The only definite thing we discovered was that it really was Benito who stole the ring."

"Never mind! The Tracker Queen found something that might help!" Gwen said, with a hint of sarcasm in her voice.

Toby looked at Rebeca, who tried to hide her discomfort at Gwen's dig, behind a forced smile. She handed him the receipt and explained.

"We believe this is a receipt for some mints that Benito purchased."

Toby opened his mouth to query why she felt they were Benito's, then remembered his first day in the jungle, when he dug in Benito's bag and found the bag of Murray Mints. "They were his favourite?"

"Well, I am not sure about that, but he always brought some with him when he came to our village."

Toby looked down at the paper. "Same day of the theft ... AND only about thirty minutes before." He looked from Gwen to Rebeca. "I wonder why the police didn't find this?"

"Well," began Joe, "I'm guessing it wasn't Scotland Yard investigating! Besides, in their eyes, it was probably just a small theft that they weren't that bothered about, when there are so many bigger things to investigate."

"Is there a lot of theft in Birmingham?" queried Rebeca.

"Theft, stabbings, assaults ...".

Rebeca shivered involuntarily as she glanced around her nervously. "I think it is much safer to be in the jungle with the jaguars and coyotes."

Joe chuckled as he strode over to Rebeca and put his arm around her tightly. "Don't you worry! I'll protect you from all the criminals!" He flexed his arm as he added, "No one is going to mess with someone that has muscles like this!"

Toby rolled his eyes and turned to Gwen, "Can you get a taxi here? We'll go to this store and see if they have CCTV to make sure it is Benito. Maybe we can tell which way they approached the shop."

Gwen looked up from her phone. "The taxi will be here in five minutes. We may as well go out front now and wait."

Exactly five minutes later, the taxi pulled up and they all climbed in. Toby scanned the receipt that he still clutched in his hand and, finding the address of the shop where *someone* bought some mints, advised the taxi driver where they wanted to go.

When they pulled up in front of the shop, again they all clambered out and Gwen paid the driver. It was a small shop, so they decided once more that only two of them should go in. This time, Toby opted to take Rebeca inside.

The rotund elderly lady looked up from some paperwork behind the till. "Good afternoon, darlings! How can I help you?" She smiled at them warmly and Toby paused for a moment, deciding what to say.

Once again, the direct approach seemed most sensible, so he said, "We are looking for a friend that ... well, we haven't seen him for a while, and we are trying to find out where he lives."

The woman cocked her head slightly and half smiled as she responded, "Don't all you youngsters keep track of each other on those phones of yours?"

"He used to have a phone but ... but his uncle, whom he lives with, took it away as a punishment."

"I'm surprised your friend didn't leave home!" she chuckled, then became serious when she studied Toby and Rebeca's concerned faces. "Hmmm ... I think I understand." The corners of her mouth turned up and her eyes twinkled kindly at them. "What does he look like?"

Toby clicked on his phone and brought up a picture of Benito and handed it to the woman.

Instant recognition lit up her face and she beamed at them, "Oh, him! Bless him – he's such a lovely, polite lad but always seems a bit nervous and unsure of himself, poor thing." A sad expression spread across her face as she now had an inkling of why. She glanced up at them as she handed the phone back to Toby. "He was in the other day to get some of his Murray Mints."

Rebeca and Toby grew excited and Rebeca burst out, "Does he come in here often?"

The lady slowly shook her head from side to side, "Maybe once a week or so?"

"Can I give you my phone number?" asked Toby eagerly. "And if he comes in again, could you call me?"

The elderly lady nodded and wrote down his number on the sheet in front of her, as Toby dictated it. They were about to leave, when Toby had a thought.

"Do you have CCTV?"

"Yes, right up there." She pointed up to a corner in the ceiling.

"You wouldn't still have the recording of when Benito came in last, would you?"

She nodded her head enthusiastically. "Just give me a minute, I'll ask Tim out back." Her brisk walk was a surprise to Rebeca and Toby, as it did not match her appearance. They heard some muffled voices, and thirty seconds later she came back out with a frown. "I'm very sorry, but Tim is – well, I'm afraid Tim said 'no'." When their expectant faces fell, she tried to encourage them. "But I will keep your number and definitely call you the next time the lad comes in."

"Thank you very much," said Toby and Rebeca in unison, and they left the store.

Outside, they informed Joe and Gwen what the woman had said. "It might have been useful to see what kind of car

Benito got in and which way it was facing," Toby breathed out through his pursed lips. "Oh, well, at least she has our number. Maybe we won't have to wait too long until Benito comes in again."

A demure smile spread across Gwen's face and she tilted her head slightly. "Let me see if I can persuade Tim."

Joe and Toby glanced at each other knowingly as wide smiles spread across their faces. Rebeca pretended not to notice, but fully understood the unspoken conversation between the two brothers.

"Come on, let's give it a go!" Toby motioned to Gwen who followed him towards the shop door. Toby opened it, then stepped back and let her in first. The lady looked up from her paperwork again, surprise on her face as she saw Toby come back in with a different girl.

They greeted the lady, and Toby said sheepishly, "We just wondered if there wasn't anything we could do to persuade Tim to …"

Gwen spotted the security camera and she smiling coyly, as she waved flirtatiously up at the unseen Tim. "Oh, pleeease, Tim! We would soooo appreciate a teensy little look at that recording you have!" Her full lips formed a provocative pout and she winked at the camera. "Please, sweetheart?"

A chair scraped across the floor and the door into the back opened. A medium height, middle aged, plain looking man appeared. He pretended to be annoyed, "Okay, okay," he said frowning as his dilated pupils gave away his succumbing to Gwen's charms. He motioned for Gwen to come into the back room. Toby started to follow, but the man stopped him saying, "The room is really very tiny, only room for one of you."

Toby snickered as he waved Gwen along and she winked at him as she walked passed him in a sultry manner towards the now mesmerised Tim. "Thank you soooo much, hon!" Gwen said as she stopped inches from him, batting her eyes as she looked up at him. She ran her fingers lightly down his bare forearm as she almost breathed out the words slowly, "I do appreciate this!"

Gwen brushed past him lightly as she entered the room and Tim quickly followed, shutting the door firmly behind him.

"Well," said the elderly lady with raised eyebrows, "that's the most excitement Tim will have had in, well ... he may just be in shock for a while." She shook her head, and Toby grinned up at her.

"Gwen is actually a very nice girl." He defended her, suddenly realising he didn't want the lady to think badly of her. "She just knows how to encourage people to do what she wants."

The woman tittered, "You mean, 'how to encourage *men* to do what she wants'."

Toby couldn't help laughing despite himself. "Ya, I guess that's what I mean, all right!" Not wanting to just stand and wait, Toby decided to look around the shop for some chocolate and other snacks that the others might want. By the time he found everything he wanted and paid for his purchases, the back door opened and a glazed eyed Tim stepped out with a grinning Gwen following him.

Gwen paused as she passed him and touching his arm once more said softly, "You have been so helpful, sugar!"

His eyes transfixed on Gwen, the man nodded slowly, "You come back anytime if you need anything else."

"Thank you," she gave him one last demure smile and followed Toby out of the shop, with the woman laughing at Tim who was still standing at the doorway, gazing at Gwen as she and Toby left the store.

Tim suddenly realised the woman was watching him, and he scowled, turning quickly around and shutting the door loudly behind him as he returned to his desk.

Outside, Gwen relayed to the others what she had seen. "Benito arrived and left in a dark blue BMW 3 series. I couldn't quite make out the driver, but it certainly could have been Tadeo. They came from that direction." She pointed up the road, westward.

"Did you see the number plate?" Toby asked eagerly.

"Only the first bit. Not sure how helpful it is," Gwen replied.

"Let's take a walk in the direction they came from, and see if we see any blue BMWs on the way." Joe spotted the bag in Toby's hand. "I'm guessing those are some snacks to help us think?" he asked as he reached in and helped himself to a bar of chocolate.

Toby opened the bag for the girls to choose something, then he took out a Mars Bar for himself. He put the bag in his backpack, and the four of them ambled slowly along as they took note of the vehicles that passed and discussed what else they could do.

After about five minutes, Rebeca spoke up. "That might not be the only shop that Benito went in." The others stopped and looked at her. "If there is another shop he went into, it might help us narrow down the area to look." She pointed across the busy road they were walking along. "If he has been seen in a shop over there, then it would make sense that we narrow our search between here and north. If he was seen in a shop this direction," she paused, pointing in the other direction. "It would make sense to just focus on this side of this busy road." She bit her lip. "Either way, my guess is that we could probably narrow it down between the two shops somewhere."

They all nodded in approval, and Toby took his phone out of his pocket and tapped a couple of times. "There's six shops west of here. Three on the north side of this road, and three on the south. They vary in distance, but the furthest is about half a mile away." He stepped purposefully sideways to stand next to Rebeca. "It will be quicker if we split up. Rebeca and I will take the south side. Joe, you and Gwen take the north."

Joe smirked at Toby's subtle possessiveness of Rebeca, but decided not to argue. "Okay, little brother!" He and Gwen started towards the crossing, then Gwen spoke up.

"I don't have a photo of Benito, do you, Joe?"

He shook his head. "Just send one to my phone, Tobs."

A couple of minutes later, Toby and Rebeca turned down a quiet urban road and left the busy street behind them. They walked in silence for a while, but finally, Rebeca spoke hesitatingly.

"Toby, may I see a picture of a B ... M ... W ... three series, did Gwen say?" As so many times before, Rebeca was hesitant to ask questions of the others about things they all took for granted that everyone knew.

"Sure!" he smiled, and tapped on his phone before handing it to Rebeca. She stared at the photo, trying to memorise as much detail as she could, then handed the phone back to him.

In the first two shops that they tried, the sales clerks had not seen Benito, or at least, did not remember seeing him come into the store.

"Although I only work Mondays to Thursdays," said the young girl in the second shop. "Jane's here Fridays to Sunday. You might want to come back in tomorrow."

Toby and Rebeca thanked her and said that they would. Toby felt slightly disheartened, as Joe had already sent a text saying their first two shops were a dead end. Rebeca smiled and patted his shoulder.

"You get frustrated very quickly. One of the little boys in our village wandered off and we did not find him for a month!"

"Really?!" exclaimed Toby, "How old was he?"

"Six years."

"Wow! How did he survive??" He shook his head disbelievingly.

Rebeca laughed. "You forget, when you grow up in the jungle, you know from a very early age where to find food and how to make a fire!"

Toby raised his eyebrows. "Yes, but it still seems awfully young to be able to last a month on his own."

Rebeca's eyes lit up and giggled as she recalled the incident. "He wanted to start his own tribe, as he decided he wanted to be chief! He had gone about five miles away, following the river. When we found him, he had set up a little camp and was fishing!"

Toby shook his head in wonder. "I bet his mom was sick with worry."

Rebeca tilted her head. "Well, not as worried as a mother from the UK would have been! She knew he could survive on his own. She was more cross that we had had to spend so many days looking for him." She smiled. "My father said that since he did not have a son, if he proved himself worthy, he could be chief when my father was too old!"

"So, how is he doing?" queried Toby.

"He is now ten years old, and he most certainly is the best hunter among the children, and the most responsible and sensible. I do believe that one day he *will* be chief!"

Twenty minutes later, they came to the last shop. A bell dinged as Toby and Rebeca entered. A young man, about Joe's age, covered in tattoos, was serving a girl with Down's syndrome who was buying some chocolate. He noticed that the money she put on the counter was not enough for the treat, but the man took the money and thanked her, putting it in the till as she left the store. When she was gone, he took some change out of his pocket and threw it into the till before looking up at the teenagers. Toby was going to commend him for his actions, but the man seemed embarrassed, so Toby did not say anything about what he saw, but instead just enquired about Benito.

The man looked at the photo on Toby's phone and instant recognition crossed his face. "Oh, yes, I have seen him before. He doesn't come in very often at all, but he was here Monday. Poor kid always looks scared, that's why I remember him." He was suddenly wary, and Toby sought to encourage him.

"He's our friend. We lost contact with him because he lives with an uncle, and the uncle took his phone away."

"Whoah!" His eyes widened. "That's tough!"

Toby frowned, and said vaguely, "Ya, in many ways."

"Give me your number, and if he comes in again, I'll let you know." The man offered helpfully.

Toby duly gave him his number, then they left, nearly tripping on a grey and white cat that was trotting past. Outside, Toby grinned at Rebeca. "I feel like we are getting close!"

The two of them headed back to the first shop on the busy road to wait for Joe and Gwen. Toby decided to wait until he saw them before letting them know what they found. He didn't want them to return before visiting all three shops, in case Rebeca was wrong and Benito had been to a store in a different area.

⸻

As they approached the last store, Gwen stopped and put her hand on Joe's bare arm. A tingle ran through him at her touch, and he tried to keep his cool as he looked down at her questioningly.

"Joe," she began, frowning at him, "what's the matter? You've hardly said a word to me since we split up from Toby and Rebeca."

He could feel the warmth start to creep up his neck, and he paused before speaking, willing his temperature back to normal as he looked down at her from her perfect full rose lips up to her emerald eyes. He closed his eyes and breathed in deeply before he spoke, "I'm sorry, Gwen."

Gwen misunderstood and her eyes looked away, focusing on a squirrel that was scampering along the top of a fence. "It's jung-" she stopped herself, not wanting to make herself appear unkind. "It's Rebeca, isn't it? You're in love with Rebeca."

"Uh … oh!" sputtered Joe. Rebeca had been the farthest thing from his mind, but Gwen's words helped him to focus and he smiled affectionately down at her. "You're right. I do have feelings for Rebeca, but I'm sure you have noticed her loyalty is towards Toby."

Gwen looked up at him questioningly, waiting for him to answer her original question. Surprisingly, the vulnerability in her eyes pushed away his nervousness and he spoke honestly. "You're intimidating, Gwen." He hesitated, not wanting to be too open for fear of embarrassing himself. "I … uh … I've never been alone with you, and you are so beautiful and self-confident that I find it daunting to be alone with you."

She tilted her head as hope glimmered in her eyes, but then she took in what he said about Rebeca. "But your heart is set on Rebeca."

Joe raised an eyebrow at the meaning behind the words and said, "It is no good if *she* is set on Toby!" He laughed and shook his head at the absurdity of the situation, reaching out and stroking her hair gently. Then, changing the conversation, he nodded towards the store, "Come on. Last one. Then we can go find somewhere to eat!"

After another shake of the head, and another 'no, sorry', Joe and Gwen left the shop and headed back to meet up with Toby and Rebeca, hoping they had been more successful.

CHAPTER 8

"Benito!"

Benito's eyes shot open at his uncle's voice bellowing up the stairs. The teenager shook himself. He must have fallen asleep. He stood up and gave a quick glance around the room and saw that his furry friend had left again, then opened the door and stuck his head out to find Tadeo standing at the bottom of the stairs with a deep scowl.

"Yes, Uncle?" He asked, rubbing his eyes as he tried to gain full consciousness.

"I thought I told you to tell me when we were getting low on milk. I want a cup of coffee and there is no milk." He growled. "How difficult is it to tell me when there is half a jug left?!"

"I … uh …", began Benito, but he was interrupted.

"Go to the little shop and pick up some milk. Now." He squinted his eyes at his nephew. "And I'll be deducting the money from your wages – the milk will be twice the price as at the supermarket!"

"Okay, Uncle," Benito came out and shut the door behind him, not bothering to comment on the fact that he didn't *get* any wages. He knew what his uncle meant. He would withhold something from Benito. Quite possibly, not allowing him anything more to eat today.

When he got to the bottom step, Tadeo handed over a couple of coins, and Benito put them in his pocket before bending down and putting on his shoes.

"You have twenty minutes, boy! No funny stuff or … else!" Tadeo enjoyed giving vague threats. He knew the uncertainty would be an added punishment for the boy.

"B-but it will take m-me ten minutes just to get there," stuttered Benito softly, looking down at his feet, not wanting to upset Tadeo by arguing, but desperate to be given a little extra time in case there were a few people ahead of him in the little store.

"Okay, you can have twenty-*five* minutes!" Tadeo snarled at Benito. "I want my coffee by 6:00! That gives you five minutes to make the coffee when you get back."

Benito knew that would be the best he would get, so he said, "Thank you, Uncle!" and scurried out the door, jogging down the street.

⟶⟶●⟵⟵

Toby was just about to message his brother, when he saw Joe and Gwen approach the cross walk across the street. He looked at his watch which read 5:30 and laughed. "What's the betting Joe's first words will be about eating!"

Rebeca smiled and raised an eyebrow, "I am sure that he will not be saying anything that *you* are not thinking!" She knew the boys' appetites ruled their daily schedule.

Joe patted Toby on the back as he and Gwen reached them. "Where shall we eat, buddy?" He rubbed his stomach, while Toby nodded his head, looking at Rebeca and laughing.

"How much did you bet her?" Joe asked Toby and they both chuckled.

"You know Rebeca, she doesn't bet!" replied Toby. "Don't you want to know how we got on?"

Joe sighed, "Go on. By your question, I'm betting you found someone else who knows the little ..." – Rebeca shot Joe a disapproving look and he changed the word he was going to use – "... skinny teenager."

"Yes!" Toby said excitedly, despite his brother's attitude. "Another sales clerk recognised him and took my number." He paused a moment before adding, "So let's go find somewhere to eat, and we can set out a plan of how we will search tomorrow!"

Before he could ask her, Gwen had tapped on her phone and said, "Someone will be here in a few minutes!"

⸻⸻⸻

Benito rounded the last corner to see someone climbing in a taxi already full of people. The vehicle pulled away as he approached the shop. The rest of the curb was clear. "Good," he thought to himself, "that means there shouldn't be anyone in the shop." Most of the people in the area drove everywhere, so few people walked here.

The bell dinged as he walked in and the Maggie looked out from behind one of the aisles, surprised to see Benito in again so soon. The elderly lady gave him a wide smile. "You had some friends in a little while ago, looking for you!"

Benito stopped and stared, breathing heavily from his jog. "F-f-friends?" His first thoughts were which of his uncle's nefarious friends would be looking for him, and how did the lady know it was him? Did some unhinged men have a photo of him? Maybe she meant the police. Benito's heart beat even faster than it had from his run.

Maggie chuckled, "Don't look so scared, love! They looked like some rather nice, *friendly* teenagers." Benito grew puzzled and the woman continued, "A nice young boy that looked rather like you! And a couple of girls."

"Oh!" Benito was shocked, but thrilled at the news.

The woman walked behind the counter and flipped through some papers. The lad gave me his number to call if you came."

The door dinged. Benito and Maggie both looked over and terror filled both of them. Two men wearing balaclavas burst in, one waving a gun and the one behind holding up a knife. Benito and the woman stood still and shot their hands in the air. The first man looked around widely, then shot at the security camera. Benito flinched at the sound, his ears ringing from panic.

"I'll give you all the money in the till!" the frightened woman called out without being asked.

The man behind the mask growled: "I know there ain't much in the till!" He turned towards the door at the back and called out loudly, "You better empty that safe back there and bring it out now!" When the door remained shut, the man with the gun charged towards it and yanked it open. Tim was cowering in the corner. The man with the knife looked from the woman to Benito, waving his weapon at both of them.

"Don't you try nuthin'!" he shouted.

The other man pointed the gun at Tim's head. "Open that safe now!"

The terrified shop owner crawled towards the safe and pressed the buttons, but his shaking hands accidentally pressed the wrong one at the end and the safe remained closed.

"Don't mess with me!" The man shouted and pulled his trigger. Bang! A bullet shot through the chair and Tim covered his ears, curling up into a ball. Maggie could not see Tim from her angle, and she panicked, running towards him. The man with the knife charged at her and plunged his blade in and out of the elderly woman's back. She cried out in agony and collapsed with a thud on the floor.

"I'm s-sssorrrry! I m-mmust have p-pressed the wrong b-bbutton!" Tim looked horrified at Maggie lying on the floor, blood trickling across the floor from her body, but didn't budge from his spot.

The man with the gun looked over his shoulder and when he saw the woman on the floor, he screamed, "Well press the *right* button this time – and NOW!"

Amazingly, Tim managed to press the right buttons and the safe door clicked open, revealing a stack of papers and a bag of the week's cash.

The first man pushed past Tim and grabbed the bag, twirling around and dashing back out, close behind the man with the knife who had darted out ahead of him. The door dinged. Then they were gone.

Still hunched on the floor, Tim pulled his phone out of his pocket, tapping 999. Benito was kneeling beside Maggie. "Is ... is she d-dead?" he asked, but before Benito could respond, the emergency call centre answered. While he gave the details to the woman on the other end, Benito carefully unwound the scarf from the woman's neck, folded it up and pressed it against the wound in her back. There was already a lot of blood on the floor. Benito's eyes welled up. She had always been so kind to him. Like his grandmother.

It seemed like half an hour, as Benito pressed the scarf against the wound that seemed to keep trickling blood through his fingers, but only five minutes later, two police charged into the shop. They quickly assessed the situation, and the woman officer knelt down on the opposite side of Maggie to Benito, while the man went into the back.

The policewoman touched Benito's hand, speaking gently as she saw the tears rolling down his cheeks. "Here, let me take over. You sit down. The ambulance will be here soon, then I'll take your statement, son."

Benito leaned back onto his heels, gladly relinquishing responsibility for Maggie's life to someone who knew what they were doing.

Benito took a deep breath and blew out slowly. As he did, he remembered Maggie's words. His friends were looking for him! Suddenly another thought shot into his mind – Tadeo. Tadeo would still want him back within half an hour; he would never believe Benito. Another thought – would the police know about the jewellery shop and would they recognise him??

Knowing there was no more he could do to help Maggie, he slowly stood and walked casually to the counter. The policewoman said nothing as she attended the elderly woman. Benito racked his brains – how could he get a message to Toby? In a flash, it came to him. He quickly grabbed a piece of blank paper and scribbled out a message. He ripped off a piece of tape from the dispenser beside the till, and casually walked backwards toward the window at the front of the store, keeping the policewoman in view. He didn't want her asking him any questions about what he was doing. Still watching her, he sidled up to the window and taped his message in the window above a 'puppies for sale' notice.

He walked back towards Maggie, then back again to the window, pacing, worrying about Tadeo's response when he returned, worrying about Maggie, worrying that the police would know who he was. Suddenly, the door opened again and two paramedics strode in purposefully, heading straight for the elderly woman and police officer who was attending her. Benito grabbed the door before it shut and, taking advantage of the distraction the paramedics offered, slipped quietly out the door and ran full tilt towards his uncle's house.

⸺⸺⸻⸺

Toby, Rebeca, Joe and Gwen sat around a table in a booth at the back of a Wetherspoon's pub. Joe had a quick look at the menu, but already knew what he wanted. Toby and Gwen soon picked what they wanted as well, but Rebeca, still not completely familiar with the food in the UK, continued to read.

"What is a panini?" She looked up at Toby.

"It's a kind of bread roll."

"What is a wrap?" she asked again hesitantly, realising the others were waiting for her.

"It's like a large thin pancake, and the ingredients are rolled up in it," offered Joe.

Rebeca looked across the menu quickly, not wanting to delay the others' food, but unsure of what to have. Finally, she just picked something.

"Okay," said Rebeca, putting down the menu. I am ready."

Gwen put in their orders, then Toby took out his phone, showing a map of the area he and Rebeca had covered. "This is the shop that sold the Murray Mints." He pointed along the map. "And this is the other one that said they knew Benito." He paused. "I think it would be easier if we drew out a map on a piece of paper."

"Why don't we ask the hotel to print off the map on an A3 sheet? That would make it large enough to see everything well, and then we could mark off where Benito and his uncle would most likely be and divide it up for us each to search," suggested Gwen.

Rebeca was not sure what an A3 sheet was, but decided she did not want to ask any more questions and would just see what it was when the hotel printed it off for them.

While they were waiting for their food, Gwen's phone beeped and she pulled it out. She cringed when she saw the caller ID. Richard.

Gwen looked around the table at the others. "It's Richard. Do you mind if I answer? He's called me three times already today and I keep ignoring him."

They all nodded and Gwen blew out a long breath before clicking 'yes', and forcing a smile at the same time. "Hello Richard!"

The handsome face that she had shown the others the previous day, appeared on her phone. "Hi, gorgeous! I was beginning to think you were ignoring me!" He chuckled at the preposterous thought.

"Of course not," Gwen lied, "we've been really busy. What's up?" She gave him her most charming look.

"Well," he began slowly, like he was going to be the bearer of some exciting news, "you'll be pleased to know I'll be over in London tomorrow!" His wide grin told her he expected her to be thrilled.

"Oh!" Gwen was taken off guard, but quickly recovered. "How lovely!"

Joe, who was sat next to her just out of view for Richard, raised an eyebrow as he grew irritated by this good looking, presumptuous man on Gwen's phone.

"Father has asked me to come over and clinch my first deal for his company!" He raised his eyebrows, clearly anticipating her excitement. "And, of course, you must be with me when we go out for dinner with the CEO and his wife afterwards!"

"Dinner? Tomorrow? But I uh ... what about Katy? I thought you and her got along really well! Surely you would want to take her with you?" Gwen offered.

"Katy?" Richard looked puzzled as though he was trying to remember Gwen's friend, whom Gwen had hitched him up with. "My dear, this is an *important* meeting, I can't have just *anybody* accompany me!"

"But Katy is a lovely girl, I thought you and her ...".

Richard sighed and smiled patronisingly at her, "Oh, baby, you know *you* are the one I want!" He shook his head slowly from side to side 'tsking', "Don't you worry your pretty little head about that!"

"Oh," began Gwen, clearly unsure of how to respond. "But I'm awfully busy here in Birmingham at the moment."

Richard's arrogant smile disappeared and he frowned at her. "Darling! This is very important to me! How could you possibly have anything more pressing than being beside me, and supporting me on my first big deal?"

Gwen glimpsed over at Joe, who's irritation had risen several levels, then back to the screen, unsure of how much to say to Richard, "Well, we need to …".

"And what *is* that racket?" Richard interjected, scowling, plainly unimpressed with her lack of enthusiasm for him. "Where are you?"

Gwen hesitated. "We are … having dinner."

"Darling, it sounds like you are in some *common* eating establishment. Who *are* these people you are with?"

Gwen opened her mouth to retort, but she was interrupted by a chirping on her phone. She glanced at the caller ID. "It's Mummy, Richard, give me a moment, will you?" Without waiting for a reply, Gwen clicked, and in an instant, Richard's disapproving face was replaced by Gwen's stunning mother, who was very similar to Gwen, except for her sapphire eyes.

"Oh sweetheart! I'm so glad I got you!"

"Hello Mummy!" Gwen responded, pleased to escape Richard for a moment. Though her mother's next words crushed her relief.

"Darling, Richard is coming over to London and I want to make sure you are available to have dinner with him and some clients tomorrow." It was a command.

Tears threatened to surface as Gwen spoke quietly, "Yes, Mummy, of course."

Her mother's face spread into a wide grin, "Don't look so sad, sweetheart. He has something very important to ask you, as well! Daddy and I have given our approval. We are absolutely thrilled!"

Gwen tried her best to look pleased, as she suppressed the full blown wail that was growing inside her. "All right, Mummy!"

Her mother blew her a kiss, and was gone. It was all Joe could do to stop himself from grabbing Gwen's phone and breaking it in two. Gwen's bottom lip began to quiver, but within seconds, she had composed herself, and clicked back to Richard's expectant face.

"I'm so sorry about that, Richard! Of course, I'd love to have dinner with you! Please forgive my earlier hesitancy. I don't know what came over me!" Her laugh was shaky, but Richard was easily pacified.

"A peculiar influence from your surroundings, perhaps?" He raised an eyebrow but was obviously smug at her change of attitude. "Never mind, I'll soon rid you of that!" He chuckled, then added, "I'll send you the details." He squinted his eyes and smiled cockily, blowing her a kiss and clicking off without saying goodbye.

Gwen swallowed hard and put her phone down hard on the table, staring at it like it was her enemy. The other three, having moved from distress for their friend to perplexity at her change of attitude, sat in awkward silence.

"Chicken Jalfrezi?" A waitress appeared at their table with several dishes of food.

Toby looked up as he held out his hand, "Uh ... oh! That's mine, thank you."

———⟫●⟪———

Benito burst through the front door and was greeted by his uncle's harsh voice as Tadeo stomped out of the living room towards him.

"Where have you been?! It's twenty past six! And WHY are your hands empty?!!"

Benito stopped dead, paralysed, looking down at his hands as he realised he did not have the milk. Tadeo did not wait for a reply as he lunged at his nephew and knocked him to the ground with the full force of his large right hand. Although dazed, Benito automatically curled up into a ball with his arms around his head.

"I'm sorry, Uncle!" he pleaded desperately, as his head throbbed from the contact with his uncle's fist. "The shop got robbed while I was there!"

Tadeo's left foot stopped mid flow as he aimed it towards Benito's back, surprised by the information, but hesitant about believing his nephew. He wouldn't put it past the kid to make up the story for some reason.

Benito's ears were ringing loudly as he held back the tears so hated by his uncle, "Please, Uncle, it's true!"

Tadeo began to wobble, and he put his foot down. He said nothing for a moment, both to ponder his nephew's claim, and to intimidate him. The large man growled loudly, pointing up the steps, despite his nephew not being able to see his hand gesture. "Get up to your bedroom! I don't want to see your face until tomorrow!"

Benito scrambled to his feet as quickly as he could, and grabbed the railing to steady himself, as he pulled himself up the stairs before wobbling into his bedroom and collapsing carefully on his bed beside his furry friend. Gideon purred comfortingly as he curled around Benito's shoulder and they both listened to the front door slam and Tadeo drive off down the road.

Tadeo drove past the shop and saw the police car and ambulance out front, so he hurried on to the next store to buy his milk before returning to his house ten minutes later. He flicked on the kettle, got out a large piece of cake, made his coffee and settled back on his big arm chair to watch his movie.

As the pain in Benito's head lessened, his empty stomach made itself known and he gave his cat a stroke, worrying about not having anything to feed him. As if in response, Gideon rose to his feet, stretched his legs, gave a big yawn, and jumped up to and out the window, leaving Benito alone with the hunger pains. Soon, his belly hurt worse than his head, and Benito wept silently into his pillow as he slowly drifted off into a fitful sleep, where he was surrounded by mountains of various items of food, each disappearing the moment he reached out to take it.

<hr>

They all began eating their food without speaking, then Rebeca put down her fork and reached out to touch Gwen's hand. "I am sorry, Gwen."

Gwen slowly pulled her hand away, fighting the urge to shake off Rebeca's. She gazed around at the others with a broad smile, the tear filled eyes belying her joy. "What's there to be sorry for? I have a date with the most eligible man in New York state, and tomorrow he is going to ask me to marry him! I'm the happiest girl in the world!"

Joe put his arm around her and squeezed her tightly, speaking softly into her ear "Gwen, it's okay, you're around friends. I'm ... we're here for you."

Gwen closed her eyes, breathing deeply and inhaling the intoxicating subtle scent he wore, melting into Joe's comfort and wishing with all her heart that she felt this way when Richard had his arm around her. A tear trickled down her face and before she could reach in her handbag for a tissue, Joe had gently wiped it away with his thumb.

"You don't have to marry him!" blurted out Toby and Joe shook his head in agreement. Rebeca tilted her head in understanding, surmising the truth.

"I do. Mummy has already decided."

"What about your dad?" queried Toby, "Does he want you to marry Richard?"

Gwen laughed cynically. "Daddy wants to keep Mummy happy. Mummy always gets her way."

"But surely if your dad knows how unhappy …".

"My happiness is not as important as Mummy's happiness. It's just the way it is."

"Couldn't you find someone you and your mom both liked?" queried Toby, still not understanding the way of life from which Gwen came.

"There is no one more *'likeable'* than Richard, in Mummy's eyes," retorted Gwen unhappily.

"Because of his looks and … status, yes?" Rebeca spoke quietly, knowing the answer, but trying to make it clear to the boys. This was the life Gwen lived in. Rebeca, in her own way, understood what that was like.

Gwen nodded, another tear rolling down her face. Joe quickly wiped away that one as well, not knowing what else he could do to help her.

Joe still didn't fully grasp her predicament either. "But couldn't you just say 'no' and find your own husband?"

"And what?? Get a *job*?? And where on earth would I live?!" Gwen almost snarled in response. "My life is all I know. I wouldn't know how to live any other way!"

"Your parents would … cut you off?!" Toby hesitated, not believing the possibility, but Gwen nodded vigorously.

"I would be penniless! And I would be homeless! Mummy would put me straight out of the house." Gwen sniffed. "She would not even let me take any of my things. I would have *nothing*."

Suddenly, all of Gwen's wealth and privilege became meaningless to the boys, and they, along with Rebeca, were overcome with sorrow for their friend's predicament.

Gwen shook herself and half smiled at her friends. "I don't know what has come over me. I was raised for this – this is my life! I knew it would happen. If not with Richard, there would be someone else. Most likely someone I did not care for. That is just the way it is! I'm sure I will grow to ... like him. I don't know why I am being so silly!

Rebeca smiled compassionately and said knowingly, "Perhaps it is these *common* people you are spending time with."

Gwen smirked, enjoying a few last seconds in Joe's arm before she sat forward. "Yes, it is all your fault!" she said, chuckling, looking around the table at the three melancholy faces staring back at her. "Let's just forget it! I want to enjoy my last little time with you ... *all*." Gwen looked meaningfully over at Rebeca, who smiled warmly in return.

So they continued their meal, talking about everything other than Gwen's fate, eating slowly and enjoying a few drinks afterwards, none of them wanting to return too soon to their hotel to go to bed, knowing sleep would bring the morning quickly.

CHAPTER 9

Friday 19th August

Benito woke with a start at 5:00 to the sound of his uncle snoring loudly in the bedroom opposite him. The pain in his stomach had subsided and the ache in his head was now a muted throbbing. He looked around in the dull, pre-dawn light and saw that Gideon had not returned. He turned on his bedside light, sliding open the drawer and taking out his Bible. He opened it up, but a piercing pain entered behind his eyeballs and he closed his eyes, lying back on his pillow and holding the precious Book against his chest. Just holding it gave the teenager comfort and he almost smiled as he held it tightly, breathing in deeply. A sudden thought appeared and Benito almost laughed. He was actually looking forward to going to Keegan's today. At least he fed Benito well!

The teenager tried to go back to sleep, but having drifted off shortly after 6:30 last night, his body had decided it had had enough rest, so finally Benito sat up, slid his Bible back in the drawer, and grabbed some clothes to take with him to the bathroom. He headed out his bedroom and walked silently down the hall to the bathroom, shutting the door as quietly as possible before clicking on the light. He undressed and turned on the shower as hot as he could bear it, just standing with his eyes closed for five minutes, drawing comfort from the warmth that enveloped him, like a glorious hug. Finally, he shampooed his hair and lathered himself, standing for another five minutes to let the water soak over and rinse off every trace of soap down the drain.

Walking back to his room past his uncle's door, he could still hear the steady snoring and he hesitated as he stopped at the landing, hand on own bedroom door, surprised to see it slightly ajar. His heart skipped a beat and he wondered if Tadeo had been in while he was in the shower. His uncle snorted through a snore, then went silent. If Benito was quiet, he might possibly make it downstairs to get something to eat. Benito was just about to put his foot down on the first step when he heard his uncle's bed creak and Tadeo's large feet landed on the wooden floor. How could someone go from waking to snoring and snoring to waking so quickly, he wondered? The teenager bolted into his bedroom and shut the door behind him.

Benito made himself comfortable on his bed with his pillow leaned against the headboard, then grabbed his Bible and opened the front. His friend Ellie, whom he had met in Louisiana, had said that the Bible was split into two parts, the Old Testament and the New Testament. She said the Old Testament was originally written mostly for the Jews, telling them that Jesus was coming, and the New Testament was written for everyone, and talked about when Jesus arrived and showed how people could be saved from hell through His death and resurrection.

Benito ran his finger down the index and found the New Testament. He felt he had read enough about the Israelites' rebellion for a while, and wanted to read about Jesus. Turning to the right page, he sat back and began reading.

Twenty minutes later, Benito's reading was interrupted by his uncle's furious voice.

"Benito! Get! Down! Here! Now!"

Benito squinted at the sharp pain that stabbed the back of his eyes as his heart rate increased and he jumped off his bed, ran out the door and trotted down the stairs. As he turned into the living room, his heart stopped dead and his breathing ceased.

Tadeo stood by his chair holding out his arm. In his hand, he held the scruff of Gideon's neck and the cat dangled helplessly in the large man's hand. Tadeo's other hand held his gun, which rested on the cat's little grey head.

The teenager gasped as his lungs ran out of oxygen. His uncle's eyes were wide with rage and he could hear Tadeo breathe heavily in and out of his nose as the two of them stood for several minutes; Benito too frightened to speak and Tadeo too angry.

Finally, the hand with the gun dropped to his side as Tadeo finally spoke. "The only reason this cat is not dead is because I don't want the neighbours to hear a gunshot!" He paused a moment, then threw the cat at Benito as he shouted, "Get in the car! We are taking this animal for a ride!"

Benito only just managed to catch Gideon as the animal flew through the air towards him, inadvertently scratching the teenager in several places as the creature scrambled to hang on to him. He could feel the little animal's heart beating rapidly as he held him against his chest.

Tadeo put the gun in a drawer, and walked towards Benito, waving him towards the front door.

"But I don't have my shoes …".

"You don't need shoes, boy! Just get. In. The car."

Benito held the terrified cat in one arm while he opened the door with the other. Tadeo followed him out, clicking the car doors open as he shut the front door behind him. Benito climbed in the back, put on his seat belt and hugged Gideon, burying his face in the creature's fur, too frightened even to cry.

Tadeo drove for twenty minutes before he finally pulled into a large car park in front of a huge supermarket. He parked in between two cars, then turned around to Benito.

"Open your door and chuck it out," said Tadeo in a steady voice that was underlaid with pure rage.

Benito's shaking hand opened the car door, and he gently placed Gideon on the tarmac. As soon as his paws felt the ground, the panicked cat darted off, and Benito bid him a silent sorrowful goodbye.

On the journey back, Benito kept looking forward at the rear view mirror and was alarmed at the look in Tadeo's eyes. He had seen him in some rages, but he had never seen his eyes look so completely evil before and the teenager wondered if this would actually be his last day alive.

He prayed silently, "God, I know I can't do anything to get to Heaven. I realise it is a gift. I am sorry that I have not been a good person and have done some terrible things, and that I can't save myself, but I do want that gift. I don't know how I get it, but I do want to go to Heaven! If I die to today, please will you take me in?"

Instantly, he knew. He was still terrified about what his uncle would do to him, but Benito *knew* if his uncle killed him today, he would go to Heaven. The realisation startled him – was that all? He'd said how sorry he was about the wrong things he had done, and he had asked God if he could go into Heaven when he died because of Jesus dying and rising again, not anything Benito did. He had only to be sorry and *ask* God for Jesus' gift?? Wow! Who knew it could be so simple?

Despite his fear, he smiled and thanked God, that whatever on earth he was afraid of, he was now no longer afraid of dying.

"What are you smiling at?" Tadeo growled as he looked in the mirror back at Benito. "I'm not finished with you, yet. I obviously have been too easy on you that you would be brazen enough to disobey me in such a way. You are going to be very, very sorry."

Gwen opened her eyes and looked at her phone on the cupboard by her bed. 8:15. She turned over and saw that Rebeca was dressed and sat on her made bed with her eyes closed.

"Are you all right?" Gwen asked.

Rebeca opened her eyes and looked at Gwen, smiling. "Yes, of course. I was just praying."

"Oh," Gwen said. She was unsure of how to respond. Toby's family were the first people she had seen praying for their meal. She didn't know *anyone* back home who prayed or went to church. Well, except for weddings and things.

Misunderstanding Gwen's hesitancy, Rebeca said, "It is okay, you did not interrupt me. I was just thanking God for various things – but I think I am done for now!" She grinned widely, but then looked at Gwen seriously, "I prayed for you. I did not know what to pray for exactly, so I just asked Him to take care of you and help you with your life."

Gwen felt suddenly tearful again. "Thank you, Rebeca. I don't suppose anyone has ever prayed for me before." She paused a moment when a thought occurred to her. "You understand, don't you? The boys told me you were going to marry someone from another tribe to save Toby and me; but that is the way of things in the jungle, isn't it?" She startled, "I never thanked you for that."

Rebeca tilted her head and smiled knowingly. "You are right. It is our way. My marrying Mundo would also have created a peace between our two tribes."

Gwen's phone beeped and she picked it up. "It's Joe, he wants to know if we are awake and ready to go eat breakfast." She laughed, shaking the sombre mood away. "Those boys are always hungry!" Rebeca grinned and nodded her head as Gwen tapped on her phone. "I've told them we won't be long!

I do so enjoy being away from Mummy – it is so quick to get ready when I don't have to do my makeup!"

By 8:30, they were all sat in the restaurant, deciding what they would have for breakfast. The boys and Rebeca (who decided she did not want to ask questions, so just ordered what they did) all decided to have the full English breakfast, while Gwen chose Eggs Royale – poached eggs and salmon on an English muffins and a hollandaise sauce.

"If you send the map details to my phone, while we are waiting for our food, I'll go to reception and have them print it out on paper, so we can figure out where we want to search today."

Joe and Toby looked at her curiously, "Don't you have to go to London?" Joe asked.

"Not until later. Richard's business dinner is not until 8:00 this evening and he asked me to meet him at his hotel earlier, so we can talk," she tittered. "Actually, he asked me to come later this morning, but I said I really couldn't make it until 7-7:30!" She looked down at her gold watch with diamonds circling the face, mulling it over. "I just need to get a taxi to the airport and Charles will fly me in the jet down to London. I should be able to stay here until 4:30!"

"Isn't that cutting it a bit fine?" asked Toby as he sent the information to her phone.

Gwen waved a dismissive hand in the air. "It will be fine! I can get ready on the jet, so I will be set to go as I walk off the plane in London and get a taxi to his hotel." With that, she stood up and left the others to get the map printed off.

Gwen returned to the table just as their food was served, so she folded the large sheet in half and put it beside her plate while they ate. The boys were quickly finished, and the girls were only half way through their food when Toby spoke up.

"Girls eat sooo slowly!" he complained, as he reached over and took the folded sheet, pushing his dishes to the side and opening the paper in front of him. "Oh! I could do with a pen or pencil."

Gwen put a finger up as she drank her grapefruit juice. She put her glass down on the table and offered, "I have one in my handbag."

It didn't take Toby long to mark out the shops and where he thought they should be looking. "We'll divide into two again." While he was marking the sheets, deciding where they should be looking, his phone chirped. He looked down, grinning and grimacing at the same time as he read the caller ID – T-Rex. He glanced up at the others, "It's Pamela. I gave her the few numbers Gwen got from the BMW registration and asked if it was possible for her dad to get an address over here. Since Tadeo is wanted in America for Gwen's kidnapping, they are keen to exchange information; and although Pamela's dad isn't involved in the case, it seems he has a helpful 'mate' over here who was happy to see what he could find out."

His phone chirped again and he clicked ANSWER. Pamela's broad, braced grin spread across the screen and her blue eyes twinkled happily at Toby.

"Hi there! I bet you didn't expect me to get back to you so quickly! And certainly not so early, 'cause of course, it is five hours earlier here which makes it only 4:00 in the morning, but I couldn't wait any longer because although the information isn't really very helpful, I thought you'd want to know so you could go searching for Benito as soon as possible." She took a breath and continued. "Plus I was all excited because they are having a promotional event at our store and everyone is bringing in their pets – which will mostly be dogs and cats 'cause of course it would be rather hard to bring in a goldfish," she giggled, "and ...".

"Thank you, Pamela!" Toby finally managed to interrupt. "I'm sure it will be a great day for you! So what information *do* you have?"

"I know, right? It will be a great day! So many animals! Of course some people bring in their dogs every day anyway, but there will be *loads* of dogs today and who knows what else?! One customer yesterday said she was going to bring in her pet goat! Can you imagine? A pet …".

"Pamela!" Toby shook his head, smiling, but frustrated, and the others chuckled as they listened.

"Focus, Pamela! What information do you have?"

"Oh of course, sorry! But can you imagine having a …" This time she interrupted herself with a snicker, "Yes, yes, Pamela focus!" Her grin faded slightly. "Well, evidently the few numbers you gave me do match up to a blue BMW, but it is registered to a John Smith – really original, hey? I mean, John Smith, how much more unoriginal can you get? I mean if I was going to make up a name, I'd make up something cool, like George Washington, or Kendrick Abheart or …".

Toby closed his eyes and blew out his breath through closed lips. "Pamela!"

Pamela giggled and covered her mouth. "I'm doing it again, aren't I?"

"Yes," Toby said simply. "Do you have an address?"

Pamela cleared her throat and squinted her eyes, determined to stay on track with the conversation. "The address was mostly right, in that the postcode exists in a little town just north of Birmingham, but the house is a broken down shack that no one seems to know who owns anymore. Sorry." She frowned with her eyes and smiled faintly. The peculiar look she sometimes had, to which Toby had warmed over the few weeks he had known her.

"Right," said Toby before Pamela could go off on a tangent again. "Have a great time at the store today!"

Pamela's face lit up like an excited three year old on Christmas morning. "Sure! I'll send you some photos – especially if I see anything crazy, like a panther!" She laughed and threw her head back at the thought. "Or …".

"Sure, Pamela, that would be great, thanks! We better go get looking now. Thanks for looking into the number for us. 'Bye!"

Toby clicked off before Pamela could say anything more. He slid his phone into his back pocket and breathed out heavily.

Gwen, who had never met Pamela before, raised an eyebrow as she looked around the table. "So that was Pamela." She nodded slightly. "How tiring it must be for her family who live with her."

The boys laughed, but Rebeca tilted her head as she spoke, "Perhaps they are all similar?"

The others had no reply to that, and Toby just shook his head as he focused back on the sheet that lay before him. It wasn't long before he'd marked out what he wanted, and he glanced up at Gwen, "Let's get this photocopied so we can both have copies." About half an hour later, the four climbed in a taxi and headed back to the shop where Benito had bought his Murray Mints. Gwen paid the driver and they all climbed out. Joe grabbed the shop's door handle and was surprised it didn't budge. Rebeca pointed to a note scrawled in large handwriting. SHOP CLOSED FOR A FEW DAYS DUE TO BURGLARY.

"Oh!" said Gwen, "you don't suppose …?"

"Nah," said Toby, "I can't imagine they'd rob their local store – the lady knew Benito."

Joe took the sheet out of his pocket that Toby had given him earlier. He grabbed Gwen's hand. "Come on, Gwen, let's head off."

"Wait!" said Rebeca, who was reading the few notices in the shop window. Look at this. She pointed to a strange notice: Nopuedo! Needs help cooking.

The others looked and Toby read it out loud. That is a weird help wanted ad. Plus, it gives a street name, but not a number. What does Nopuedo mean? Is it someone's name?"

Rebeca grinned at the others. "That is what I used to call Benito – Nopuedo! No puedo means 'I cannot'. Whenever he was at our village with his uncle, I would ask him to help with the fishing or the cooking or other things, and he always replied 'I can't'. He did not seem to think he was capable of anything, so I used to call him Nopuedo!" She frowned, as she remembered. "That was unkind of me."

Toby put his arm around her shoulders. "You were just teasing him!"

Joe curled his mouth on one side. "The kid just asks to be teased. He's so...". His voice trailed off as he saw Rebeca's sad face.

"So we have a street name!" Toby changed the subject. "Why not give a house number as well?"

"I would imagine that he was taking a risk just putting the street name down. If he put the house number as well, and Tadeo saw it, there would be no disguising Benito's request for help!"

They all nodded at this thought and Toby grabbed the sheet from Joe's hand. He looked down and found the street. "It goes in a long U shape. Shall we still split up and start at either end?" suggested Toby. "Or should we start at the same end but just take opposite sides of the street? Oh, Gwen, could you send me the photo you took of the tyre tracks?"

"We could start at either end, but then since there are two of us, we could each focus on either side of the street. That would be the quickest." Joe said, looking at his watch that read 10:15. "We could be finished in time for lunch!" He grinned widely and the girls chuckled.

They all agreed, and split up, with Joe and Gwen heading down the main road to find the farthest end of the street they were to search.

———⟫●⟪———

Tadeo pulled into his drive and got out of the car without saying anything. Benito jumped out and shut the door just as Tadeo clicked the locks on the car. He opened the front door and held it open for Benito, who slid by sideways, expecting a smack as he went by. His uncle glared at him.

"Go up to your bedroom and don't come out until I call you," Tadeo said slowly in a deeper voice than normal.

Benito scurried up the stairs and slipped into his room, shutting the door behind him. He sat down on his bed, shivering from a combination of fear and the cool breeze that blew in his window. A tear rolled down his cheek as he closed his window and he thought of something in the Old Testament that a man name Job had said after all his animals had been stolen and all his children had been killed: "The Lord gave and the Lord has taken away; blessed be the name of the Lord." Another tear rolled down his face, but he thought to himself, if that man could say that after all *his* troubles, Benito could also sat that. He had had Gideon for a short time and the little animal had given him great comfort. At least the furry creature was still alive. Benito felt certain that someone would take in the lovely little animal. "And," thought Benito, "he would probably get fed better and more regularly."

A sad smile crossed Benito's face and he stared out the window at the tree that Gideon climbed to get in, and the teenager felt happier, comforting himself that his little friend would soon find another home – a good home. After all, who could resist such a dear little creature?

His empty stomach began complaining with the pains growing stronger and Benito lay on his bed, hoping to fall asleep to forget about his hunger. When sleep evaded him, he grabbed his Bible, sat up on his bed and began reading.

"Benito!"

Benito sat bolt upright at his uncle's voice, and he rubbed his eyes. His Bible was on the bed beside him. He must have fallen asleep. He looked at the clock on his bedside that read 10:30.

When he heard his uncle's heavy footsteps coming up the stairs, Benito jumped off the bed and headed towards his door, opening it just as Tadeo reached the top.

"Put some clothes in a bag." He spoke slowly and sinisterly. "You are going away for … a while."

Benito began to tremble as he stood motionless, his uncle's face glaring down at him.

"A-away?" Benito finally managed.

"A little holiday … with Uncle Keegan. He's given me an offer I can't refuse." Tadeo leaned forward until Benito could feel his warm coffee breath on his face. "And I've told him that previous restrictions do not apply." He grinned wickedly and Benito's heart began pounding heavily at his chest as the teenager wondered if anyone his age had ever died of a heart failure due to fear.

When Benito didn't move, Tadeo spat as he shouted in his face, "You've got five minutes to pack your bag and get in the car!" Benito spun around and darted back into his room, grabbing what few belongings he had and stuffing them into a small duffel bag and his back pack.

He walked to the window out of longing for his cat and he blinked a couple of times. That looked like … it WAS! Toby and Rebeca! He looked at his watch – four and a half minutes. He had thirty seconds left. Pulling open his drawer, he found a pencil but there was no paper. He looked in the waste bin and found an old receipt. Turning it over, he began to write, but as he did, he heard Tadeo coming up the stairs. Panicking, he shoved the receipt in his pocket and threw the pen in the drawer, shutting it just as Tadeo burst in.

"I said five minutes, not five and a half!" Suspicion entered Tadeo's eyes at the guilty look on his nephew's face. "What were you doing?!"

"I ... uh ... I ... I was ... j-just g-getting my B-bible." Benito stuttered.

A sly grin crossed Tadeo's face as he squinted at Benito and held out his hand. "Give it to me."

Tears threatened to appear and the teenager blinked rapidly, fighting them back valiantly. "B-but Uncle, w-why ... why ...?" The scowl on his uncle's face tightened and his face grew red, causing Benito to drop his bag on his bed, and frantically zip it open, grabbing the precious Book that lay on top of his clothes. His hand shook as he placed it carefully in his uncle's hand.

A guttural, almost animal-like noise escaped from Tadeo as the Bible touched his hand and he swung around, throwing it out the doorway and down the stairs as he virtually screamed, "Never again will you read that *book*!" He almost spat as he said the word. "It is obviously a bad influence on you!" And as Benito stood frozen in horror, Tadeo grew purple with fury as he pointed down towards the front door. "Get out!"

Benito scurried out of his bedroom and tripped on the last stair, crashing into the wall at the bottom. He landed on all fours beside the Bible that had split open when it had impacted the same wall, and his bags fell around him. He reached out to touch the Book, but withdrew his hand quickly at the sound of Tadeo storming down the steps behind him. Benito grabbed his bags and opened the front door, desperately trying to think of how he could leave his unfinished message for his friends.

⟫●⟪

"Look! Over there!" Rebeca exclaimed.

Toby looked ahead to where she was pointing to a blue BMW sat on a drive. Suddenly, he pulled Rebeca behind a hedge and crouched down, motioning her to do the same, as the front door opened. He started to stand as he saw Benito come out, but shot back down again as he saw Tadeo following immediately behind.

Toby poked his head over the hedge and he saw Benito frantically glancing around like he was looking for someone – did he know they were there? Had he seen them coming down the street?

Rebeca looked at him wide eyed, and whispered, "What do we do now?"

Benito walked slowly to the car, trying to stall, but Tadeo came up behind him and smacked him on the back of the head as he opened the back door. "It's open, fool! What are you doing?!"

Reluctantly, Benito tossed in his bags on the seat and sat down beside them. Tadeo slammed the door shut just as his nephew pulled his foot inside. As Benito pulled the seatbelt around him, he opened the door and dropped the receipt on the ground, then quickly shut it as he clipped his belt closed.

Tadeo swung around growling, "What're you doing boy?!!"

"S-s-sorry, Uncle, m-my s-seat belt was s-stuck in the door."

Three seconds later, Tadeo gunned the engine and pulled off the drive, heading toward Keegan's house.

As Toby watched them speed off down the road, he grimaced and swore loudly. Rebeca frowned at him, not entirely sure of the word, but feeling by instinct that it was not something he should be saying. Toby shrugged his shoulders. "We were so close!" As though that excused his language. Quickly, he pulled out his phone and called Joe. "Joe! Tadeo is coming your way – you and Gwen need to hide!"

Toby stood as the car drove off in the opposite direction to them and he shoved his phone back in his pocket. He walked towards the house that Benito and Tadeo had just left, with Rebeca slowly following him. He walked up to the front door and tried the handle, but it was locked. Another curse, and Rebeca, not at all liking the sound of this word, frowned at the back of Toby's head. He whirled around and sat down on the front step, resting his jaw on his hands. Rebeca perched beside him, saying nothing. Several minutes later, Joe and Gwen appeared at the bottom of the drive.

"We just missed him!" Toby moaned.

"Well, you found the house! He'll surely be back," said Joe.

Toby shook his head. "Benito had a couple of bags with him. I doubt they'll be back for a while." Another swear word escaped his lips and Joe laughed, pleased that his brother was no better than him in that area. Rebeca nudged him.

"Why do you keep saying those words?" she asked. "They do not sound nice."

Gwen raised an eyebrow and smiled, "That's because they *aren't* nice."

Toby scowled at her, lost in his disappointment. "If only we had been ten minutes earlier! If you girls had eaten faster ...". His voice trailed off and Rebeca swallowed the hurt welling up inside.

Gwen said cuttingly, "How totally small of you to say such a thing." She laughed, shaking her head. "Anyway! What would you have done if you had come ten minutes earlier – wrestled Tadeo to the ground?"

Toby scowled, but Joe chuckled as he stepped forward, "She's right, little brother! We know where he lives – we can contact the police and they can keep an eye on the place. Whenever they return, they can knock on the door and rescue Benito." He leaned over and ruffled Toby's hair.

"Stop that!" Toby's annoyance with the situation burst into full blown anger at his brother's patronising hair ruffling and he jumped up, pushing an unprepared Joe backwards onto the grass.

"Ooomph!" Joe gasped as the hard ground knocked the wind out of him.

Toby leaned over as if to jump on his brother, and Gwen stepped in front of him. "Enough, Toby, look! How can he defend himself if he can't even breathe?" She turned around and knelt by Joe's side as he gasped for air. Toby, now embarrassed by his behaviour, headed down the drive and stomped off down the street.

Gwen leaned over, her face inches from Joe's. "Need a little mouth to mouth resuscitation?" She smiled coyly and Joe's heart beat heavily in his chest, causing him to gasp more for air.

"I ... ca ... I ... oh ... hurts."

"Are you sure?" She whispered as she placed her lips over his, blowing gently.

"I think that is what Pamela would call P...D...A," said Rebeca, feeling uncomfortable at watching Gwen's flirtation.

Gwen winked at Joe, as she softly breathed out the words, "Nothing wrong with a little public display of affection, is there, hon?"

Joe began coughing and Gwen helped him to sit up, rubbing his back gently. He gasped deeply a couple of times, then began breathing heavily. "I didn't think I'd ever get my breath back!" He paused for a moment, concentrating on his breathing. Feeling rather embarrassed that his little brother had managed to knock him to the ground, he commented, "I didn't realise how much he had grown – he's my height now, and not so skinny!"

Gwen cocked her head knowingly and smiled, "Don't worry! No one is doubting your masculinity. He caught you off guard, that's all."

Joe got on to all fours and Gwen helped him to his feet, reluctant to let go of him when he stood. "You look a little wobbly. I'll hold onto you for a while."

Rebeca raised an eyebrow at Gwen then shook her head, looking down at the ground as she pondered Toby's actions and their next move in rescuing Benito. As she did, a small piece of paper fluttered across her view brushed along by the breeze. Without thinking, she picked it up and a slight gasp escaped her lips as she recognised Benito's handwriting.

"Gone to Worcester C---."

The C-, or was it a G? – trailed off in a scrawl, like Benito had been interrupted or something. Rebeca stared at the paper, face scrunched up and lost in thought.

"What is it?" asked Gwen and Joe in unison as they noticed Rebeca staring at a scrap of paper in her hand. They came closer as she held it out to them and Joe reached out to take it.

"A note. Well, the beginning of a note from Benito. It looks like he was interrupted."

Joe nodded thoughtfully as he showed Gwen, who was determined to hang on to him for as long as possible.

"Do you know what this…" Rebeca hesitated as she tried do sound it out, "Wer…ces…ter is?"

Joe looked at her and smiled. "It's pronounced 'wuster' ."

"That is a very strange way to spell it."

"It is!" Joe agreed, grinning. "And in answer to your question, it's a small city not too far from here. South." He breathed deeply and slowly, relishing the air now filling up his lungs with ease. "I'll give Toby a buzz and let him know."

"What?" A curt reply answered Joe's call.

"You're such a baby!" frowned Joe, "I'm the one who should be angry!" He took another cherished breath. "Where did you storm off to?" When his question was met with silence, he continued, "We found a note from Benito."

"I did not storm off, I just decided to … wait, what? A note?"

"Ya! Where are you?" Joe snickered.

"I'm – oh can't you just tell me?"

"No," Joe said stubbornly. "Where are you? We'll bring it to you."

"Well," began Toby, determined to save face, "I decided to just go back to the original shop and see if I could discover anything else."

"Ya, sure," smirked Joe, though his brother couldn't see him. "What'd'ya find?"

"Nothing." Toby huffed faintly. "Are you coming, or what?" He clicked off without saying goodbye, and Joe put his phone back in his pocket. He looked at the girls as he nodded down the drive. "He's at the shop. Let's go."

Gwen had her arm firmly around Joe's waist and his arm was around her shoulder as they walked along with Rebeca trailing behind. Joe looked back and winked at her, "I could use some support on this side as well!" he said, waving her up with his right hand. "It's a wide enough path for all of us."

Rebeca raised her eyebrows and rolled her eyes, but a small, unbidden gremlin of spite encouraged her forwards, knowing it would annoy Gwen, and she came up beside Joe on the other side. Oblivious to the tension he was creating, Joe contentedly put his arm around Rebeca as well, pretending to lean on her.

CHAPTER 10

Tadeo pressed the buttons on the keypad, and within seconds, the gates opened, allowing the BMW to crunch across the gravel as it rolled up the drive. He stopped a couple of metres from the door and got out, looking expectantly in the car at Benito, who grabbed his two bags and climbed out as well, following his uncle. The solid oak door opened as they reached it and Keegan stepped back, letting the two of them in. His snake eyes flashed nefariously as Benito looked up at him and he inadvertently shrunk back as he walked past into the house, immediately taking off his shoes and placing them neatly beside Tadeo's.

Keegan looked down. "Put yours in the cupboard," he sneered, "you're going to be here a while." Benito complied, bending down, opening the door and tossing then gently inside, then stood up with his two bags in either hand, waiting for direction. "Put them upstairs in the room where you were before," Keegan instructed. Benito nodded silently, wondering where Marlene was as he walked across the cream carpet, through the living room and up the stairs.

As Benito came down the stairs, he heard the two men talking in the kitchen, and he stopped near the bottom to listen.

"I nearly finished him off today! I might cool down in … maybe a week. Plus I need to sort some things for my big job and I don't want to have to be watching him." Tadeo chuckled sinisterly. "I have to go visit his Mama at some point – I think she is getting better, and I can't have that!"

Keegan's evil laugh joined Tadeo's, and Benito's heart rate increased as fear for his mother consumed him. What was Tadeo going to do to her?? How could he stop his uncle from … whatever it was he was going to do??

"So I get 'im for a good price for the week, then, huh? Since I am doing you a favour …?" Keegan bartered.

Tadeo had anticipated his response and had already hiked up the price, so when he brought it back down it would be where he wanted it in the first place. He gave his price.

"You can knock off several hundred and I'll pay you £2,000, since you need my services more than I need yours."

Tadeo pretended to hesitate and grumble, and Keegan pretended he had gotten a good deal. They shook hands. It was all part of the pretence.

Just then, the front door swung open and Marlene breezed in, swapping her outside shoes for her gold ones. Benito held his breath, as he could be seen from her angle, but apart from a sweeping glance in his direction, she gave nothing away as she swayed into the kitchen and greeted Tadeo and Keegan.

"Coffee?" she asked as she walked over to the machine, and Benito took this moment to stand up and walk casually down the stairs and, though extremely difficult, pretended as though he had not heard their conversation.

Marlene placed the cups down in front of the two men sat at the table and she looked up as though startled when Benito walked over. She smiled warmly at him.

"Hello, sweetheart! I didn't realise you were here. Can I get you anything?"

"A glass of water!" said the two men in unison as they laughed at their joke, and Keegan nodded his head towards Tadeo. "The man here said Benito is fasting today. Evidently the kid works best after a fast!" They both chortled at this and Benito nearly burst into tears.

Marlene looked at Benito and back at the men, mouth open, ready to protest. Keegan slammed his fist on the table. Marlene jumped at the sound and Benito was grieved for the woman as well as himself. No food. Until after the job. Benito's stomach growled loudly in response and again the men laughed as though someone had said something hysterically funny.

"Now, what was it you wanted from Marlene, boy?"

Keegan grinned widely and Benito almost expected to see a snake tongue slither out from between his teeth.

"I'll have a glass of water, please, Marlene," Benito said, as he sat on the opposite side of the table to the men.

Marlene brought him a glass of water, and stroked his head as she placed it in front of him. Keegan saw her from the corner of his eye and he yelled.

"Don't you be giving anyone affection but me, babe!" His green/gold eyes flashed at her and she looked at him for a moment, a battle waging in her eyes. Finally, she lowered her head, clicked her way to Keegan, walking up behind him and kissing him on the head, running her fingers across his shoulders.

"Of course not, babe."

He reached his right hand up and grabbed her one hand, squeezing tightly until he heard the whimper. "That's better, baby." Then without saying anything, he slid his chair back, one of the legs landing squarely on Marlene's big toe and she yelped.

"Well, silly woman! What're you doin' standing behind me like that anyway?!"

Marlene hobbled into the living room to sit down while Keegan walked over to the cupboard that held his cash box and he took out an envelope. He returned the box to the cupboard and walked over to Tadeo, slapping the envelope on the table in front of him, neither mentioning the fact that he had had the correct amount of money already counted out and ready in an envelope.

Tadeo opened the envelope and did a cursory count, satisfied that the right amount was in there. However, he wasn't letting Keegan off without a warning.

"If you are short one note, you'll pay triple next time."

The two men laughed, and Tadeo stuffed the money in his jacket pocket, stood up, and walked across the living room. He slid on his shoes and walked out of the door without saying another word.

Benito gulped back his water and wiped his mouth with the back of his shirt sleeve. Keegan grimaced.

"Pigs belong in the shed outback, boy!"

With that, Keegan reached across the table and grabbed him by the ear, pulling the teenager around to his side of the table his eyes squinted shut from the pain. Keegan pulled him over to the front door and shoved him towards the cupboard by the front door.

"Grab your shoes, kid!"

Then Keegan herded him across the living room past the stairs and to the back door, where he slipped on some loafers while Benito put on his own shoes. As they stepped outside into the back, Benito looked around at the high trees lining the garden. Beyond them, he knew was open fields. The one house on the right was several metres away from the fence line. Something Benito only knew from when they pulled up at the front.

Keegan walked towards the far corner where a sturdy shed sat with the full force of the sun beating down on it. Snake man took his key out of his pocket, unlocked it, and shoved Benito inside before heading back into the cool of his house.

Benito stumbled inside the sweltering shed and collapsed into a corner of the near empty building. He curled into a ball and, no longer needing to restrain his emotions, tears erupted and ran freely down his face.

"It's hot!" grumbled Gwen, waving her hand in front of her face. "Let's go back to the hotel and have a swim – before lunch." She winked at Joe who grinned back.

They stood in front of the shop that had been burgled, waiting for a taxi. Toby still had the note in his hand, and was mumbling to himself. "Worcester. Why would they go to Worcester? Is there any point me calling the police now?"

"You may as well," suggested Gwen, "They can keep an eye on the place. Maybe they can break in or something and check it out."

Toby tapped his phone, entering the special number he had been given by Pamela's dad, to report anything they found.

"Detective Brendon O'Reilley," a deep voice answered.

Toby explained who he was, and immediately there was recognition. Toby gave the man the address they had found, and told him about the note that said they were going to Worcester.

"We're going to stay in town for a couple more days, to see if there is anything else we can do," offered Toby.

"Now, don't you kids go messing around. I've been told by Richard Bartley about the trouble you kids got into in Louisiana. You may stay in Birmingham, but you just let the professionals take charge of things. I'll let you know if I need any more information." Detective O'Reilley spoke politely but firmly: "If you get in the way of our investigations, we might have to charge you with interfering with the law."

"Yes sir," said Toby, with no intention of staying 'out of the way'. "Thank you sir. Goodbye." He turned to the others, mimicking the officer, "*You may stay in Birmingham.* Who does he think he is?"

"An officer with authority slap you with an injunction to stay clear of Birmingham if he decides you are in his way?" suggested Gwen with a half smile.

Just then, the taxi pulled up and whisked them away in the stifling vehicle to their air conditioned hotel where they all quickly changed into swimming suits and dashed into the pool where they spent a couple of hours messing around and cooling off, including time out of the pool to have lunch.

<hr />

As Benito's breathing became more laboured, he prayed for relief and thanked God profusely as he saw a sliver of shade begin to slowly creep across the barred window in the side of the shed. Exhaustion overtook him and Benito fell into a heavy sleep where dreams did not venture.

Several hours later, the teenager was awoken by a clicking of the lock on the shed door, and as he heard it creak open, he lay helplessly on the floor looking up at reptile man, and he shivered.

The man actually hissed. "Get up!"

Benito pulled his arms toward him to push his body off the floor, but they were devoid of strength and his face fell forwards, slamming his nose onto the floorboards. Bento flinched at the pain, but he didn't move.

Keegan let out a stream of curse words and, spinning around, he left the door to the shed open as he stamped across the lawn back into his house. A moment later, he came out with a glass of water and a piece of bread and strawberry jam. He knelt down and placed them in front of the semi-conscious teenager.

"I want you in the house in ten minutes." With that, he stood up and returned to his house.

Benito reached out for the water, as he attempted to pour some of it in his mouth while he lay on his side. After a couple of mouthfuls of the refreshing liquid, he reached out for the piece of bread and took a large bite, so hungry that he tried to swallow before chewing it properly and he started choking. He spat out the bread and drank some more water. After a few minutes, he took up the half chewed bread from the dirty wooden floor, and took a smaller bite. Interspersing small bites with gulps of water, he was soon finished and he rested his head back down on his arm as he lay on his side.

After what he was sure was more than ten minutes later, Benito felt slightly strengthened and managed to get to a sitting position. Worried that Keegan was as precise with his times as Tadeo, he willed himself to his feet with the empty glass in his hand, and he slowly wobbled his way to the back door of the large house, tripping on the entryway as he entered, and landing on his knees on the wooden floored entrance. The glass flew from his hand, crashed against the wall opposite him and broke into several pieces.

Keegan ran over cursing and dragged Benito into the house, shutting the door behind him.

"Marlene!" he shouted. The beautiful red-haired woman appeared at the top of the stairs and she started to hurry down towards the boy, then checked herself, slowing as she reached the last few steps.

"Yes Keegan, darling?"

"Clean up this mess." He waved his arm over the shattered glass and Benito himself, sprawled on the floor. "Then get him something to eat." He hissed again. "That Tadeo! The kid is no good to me like this!" He leaned over and gripped her arm firmly. "And don't get all compassionate! I'm gonna have a shower, but I won't be long!" He put his face right up close so his nose touched hers. "Do you understand?"

Marlene managed a feeble smile and nodded her head without saying a word. He trotted up the stairs and left Marlene to deal with the mess at the bottom.

"Don't move, sweetheart, I'm going to clean up the glass first so you don't cut yourself."

Marlene worked quickly in silence, and soon the broken glass was cleaned up, Benito was wiped off, and he was sat quietly at the table slowly eating a ham and cheese sandwich with a large glass of milk. Benito didn't think anything had ever tasted so good. The woman had said nothing the whole time, but Benito could feel in her touch, the kindness and compassion that he wished with all his heart that someone would show to her.

Keegan strolled down the stairs and across the living room into the kitchen, a smell of shampoo and body wash mixed with aftershave floating in along with him. He came up behind Marlene who was at the coffee machine and wrapped his arms around her, nuzzling her neck. He turned her around towards him and kissed her passionately. Benito watched in amazement as she appeared to kiss him just as passionately back.

"Thanks, baby, what would I do without you?" He grinned at her and Benito blinked a couple of times, trying to clear this affectionate lamb from his vision to reveal the evil reptile underneath.

She smiled at the lamb. "Shrivel up and die, sugar!"

He laughed and patted her bottom as he grabbed a coffee and walked over to sit across from Benito who had just finished his food and was washing it all down with the rest of his milk.

"Feeling better, son?" His evil green/gold eyes looked out over his bizarrely transformed, friendly face and broad smile.

Benito looked at him warily, but responded appropriately, "Yes, thank you sir. Much better."

"Ah! Good!" The reptile leaned back in his chair and called over to Marlene. "Get us each a large piece of chocolate cake, and get the boy another glass of milk, babe, will you?"

Benito was certain he could hear a tail swishing back and forth across the floor, and he fought the urge to look under the table as a chill ran up his spine. Marlene placed a large piece of chocolate cake in front of each of them and topped up Benito's glass. She leaned over and kissed Keegan on the cheek.

"Think I'll have a shower as well, now, too, if we're going out. I feel all hot and sticky." Marlene walked around the table and, with her back towards Keegan, smiled and winked at Benito who responded with a blank face so as to not rile up Keegan again. She swayed out of the room, and there was silence as Keegan picked up a paper and began flipping through it.

Each bite of chocolate cake melted in Benito's mouth as he leisurely worked his way through the mammoth piece Marlene had cut for him, and he let the cool milk run slowly down his throat after each couple of bites. All too soon, it was gone, and Benito took the serviette that Marlene had also placed in front of him, and he wiped his mouth before folding it back up neatly and putting it back on the table.

Green/gold eyes appeared over the top of the paper and Benito was certain that very faint trails of smoke drifted out of his nostrils as the reptile grinned at him, putting down his paper.

"Right then, shall I tell you what we are going to be doing?"

Benito stared at the snake eyes, unable to look away as he nodded his head.

"I'm taking my Marlene out for dinner and dancing. Then when we come back, you and I are going to do another vehicle run. You up for that?"

Benito silently nodded his head up and down, unable to look away from the insidious gold orbs, certain that 'yes' was the only answer that would be accepted.

⟢•⟢

Tadeo slowed his BMW as the curve of the road revealed his house. He stopped and backed up until he could only just see a little past his drive. A car was parked up, three houses past his, with two men sat in it. His instincts immediately set off alarm bells. Backing up until the curve of the road hid the car completely, he did a three point turn and drove slowly in the direction from which he had just come.

How had they found him? It must have been that boy! Somehow he had contacted someone. Fury boiled up within him and he made a decision. The kid's mother was now completely fair game.

⟢•⟢

After a refreshing few hours in the pool, the four had dried off, changed and were sat in the living area of the boys' suite. Gwen had had room service send up some cold drinks and snacks.

Toby took a long swig of his coke and put it down on one of the coasters that lay on the dark wood coffee table in front of him. He took out the receipt on which Benito had scrawled his half-finished message.

"Why go to Worcester?" he asked out loud, and before anyone could reply, he continued, "and what was this 'G' the beginning of? – Great? – Gathering? – Gathering what – information? Get? Getting? – Gone to Worcester – Gone for

158

a week??" Toby breathed out a deep sigh at the impossibility of figuring out the rest of Benito's message.

"Did the police not want to see the paper?" asked Rebeca.

Joe snickered. "Like I said before, they probably aren't putting much importance on this! Just one more messed up kid in a bad situation in this city. Too many other things for them to deal with."

"I'll speak to Daddy to see if he can persuade someone to make it important. After all, if they find Benito, they will find Tadeo and can finally put him away for kidnapping me!" She looked at her watch and sighed.

"I better head downstairs to reception. My taxi will be here any minute."

The others looked at her with sympathy, but knew there was nothing they could say to change the situation. Joe stood up as Gwen rose to her feet.

"I'll walk down with you." When they got to the door, he looked at Gwen who only had her handbag. "Don't you need some fancy clothes to go out to this dinner?"

Gwen chuckled, "Mummy has all the jets stocked with emergency supplies! You never know when you might be caught short and need some fancy outfit."

Toby and Rebeca said goodbye and Joe held the door open for Gwen as the two of them headed to the elevator, down to the ground floor and outside to wait for Gwen's ride. They were silent for a few moments, when suddenly, Gwen grabbed Joe's arm and looked up at him earnestly.

"Joe, I ... I know I come off as flirtatious with everyone, but I'm not ... I'm not like *that* ... it's just ... that I don't know anything else, and I'm good at it."

Joe was taken aback, and smiled inwardly at the shrewd analysis of herself. Unsure of how to comment, he let her continue.

"I'm not good at anything else; but I don't mean anything by it. I mean … it gets me things I want in life … but…". Her taxi pulled up and the man called out his window asking if she was his fare. She nodded but turned back to Joe as she spoke softly to him. "It's not going to get me what I *really* want…" she breathed deeply and stood on her tip toes to kiss his cheek, whispering in his ear, "… *who* I really want." And with that, she opened the taxi door and climbed in. Stunned, Joe lifted his hand in a casual wave as the vehicle pulled away from the curb and drove off.

Joe walked out of the elevator in a daze, unable to take in the idea that the most beautiful woman he had ever met, wanted *him*. He stopped as he put his hand on the door knob to the suite and he shook himself when Rebeca's face appeared in his mind and the familiar ache resurfaced in his chest. Life was full of curve balls.

"What's the matter with you?" asked Toby as Joe stepped into the room.

"What do you mean?" Joe asked, flustered.

"You have a weird look on your face — not sure *what* it means!" Toby chuckled.

Joe grabbed a cushion from a chair as he walked by and flung it at his brother who ducked just in time. "I guess it doesn't mean anything then!" And before Toby or Rebeca could say anything else, he said, "Where are we going to eat?"

"Why don't we go to that pub again?" suggested Rebeca who did not feel like trying to decipher a new menu. She could just order what she had last time.

"Sure!" said Toby. "And I thought we could go see a movie afterwards to chill out!" When Rebeca wrinkled her nose, he added mischievously, "There's a good one on, about some guy being the only survivor of a plane crash and he has to survive alone in a jungle!"

Rebeca raised an eyebrow, "Well now, *that* should be interesting!" And the boys laughed.

———————

The same girl was on reception when Tadeo entered the hospital, and he leaned over winking at her. "I know it is nearly finished visiting hours, but please, sweetheart, may I just pop in and see how my baby sister is doin'?" He smiled and tilted his head, raising his eyebrows in a playful manner.

Again the girl succumbed and after a quick call to intensive care, she nodded to Tadeo, who grinned and winked again before sauntering down the hall, humming softly.

Pushing the door open into the intensive care reception, Tadeo became the soft and gentle, greatly worried older brother. The woman on the desk looked up as he came in, and she smiled compassionately at Tadeo.

"Pastor Frank is in there at the moment, but he'll be out in a sec'. He knows you are here to see your sister."

As if on cue, the door opened and Frank came out. He smiled genuinely at Tadeo and offered his hand, which Tadeo shook cordially.

"She'll be pleased to see you!" the pastor said simply, then headed out the door into the hallway.

A nurse duly followed and she asked Tadeo, "Are you Gabriella's brother?"

Tadeo, fully choked up by the emotion of the loving brother, silently nodded his head as he wiped an eye. She turned around and he followed her into the room. She spoke again as he took a seat beside Gabriella.

"Only ten minutes, please, it's not been a good day for her," she said as she turned away and tended to another patient.

Well, thought Tadeo, *Gabriella should be especially pleased to be released from her suffering today, then!*

Tadeo took his sister's hand and stroked it gently. She smiled underneath the oxygen mask, then pulled it down, and in between shallow breaths, she said,

"Tadeo! … Finally you've come … to see me! … I'm so pleased. I've been wanting … to thank you for all the help … you have given Benito … and me." She looked past him, as if hoping to see her son.

He lifted her hand to his lips and kissed it, "Ah, mi princesa! I'm sorry, I have been busy, working hard so I would have some extra money for you and the boy. But it is nothing, if only I can see my baby sister back on her feet, happy and healthy again! The boy's been a big help, as well. I've let him stay at a friend's for a week, to have some time off doing some fun things." He smiled lovingly, but he could see a faint glimmer of doubt in her eyes. *Never mind, what did it matter? She would soon be gone!*

He glanced over to make sure the nurse was preoccupied, then he took a bar of chocolate out of his pocket. He grinned mischievously at his sister and spoke quietly.

"You probably aren't meant have any, but it's your favourite. Surely a couple of squares won't hurt!"

He broke off two squares and placed them in her hand and she smiled at him.

"You are … a good … brother, aren't you?" She strained, almost willing herself to believe, patting his hand. She, too, glanced over at the nurse, knowing she would be scolded, but the chocolate looked so good, and it had been a long time since she had had a treat. She bit off one square and closed her eyes as she sucked the chocolate and caramel, relishing the treat. It was soon gone, and she popped the other one in her mouth just as the nurse looked her way.

"Gabriella!" The nurse chided her softly, swiftly walking towards her, and Tadeo held his breath. "You need to keep the mask on, dear!" She looked at Tadeo, and back at Gabriella, "I'm sure your brother understands."

"Of course, Gabriella! You must wear your mask, we want you to get better! Now rest, little sister, this is only a quick visit to see you. I don't want you making yourself ill." He stood up and kissed her forehead, stroking her head. "You just concentrate on getting well."

Tadeo headed out of intensive care, realising he needed to hurry. He had taken a risk coming here. He wasn't sure how much the authorities knew about him. They would have a description, but he didn't know if they knew his real name and that Gabriella was his sister. But the job was done. He nodded to the lady on reception on his way out, and walked as quickly as he could without being conspicuous, out of the hospital and back to his car.

He drove to the beginning of his road and parked up. He got out and walked just until the curve of the street revealed his house – and the car still parked a few drives down. Tadeo swore. Then swore again. *They must have more than a description of him! How did they find him?!* He'd have to go somewhere for a while.

⸺⸺►●◄⸺⸺

LONDON

Gwen and Richard sat opposite each other at a small table in a quiet corner of the hotel lounge. Richard wore an expensive deep blue trendy wool business suit that matched his eyes and Gwen had chosen the fitted emerald dress she had worn on their first, and what she had hoped would have been their last, date. Richard held her hands as he leaned over the table.

"Darling, you are stunning – as ever!" Gwen smiled a pretend appreciation of his compliment. He let go of her hands, and reached in his breast pocket, pulling out a small dark blue velvet box and placed it in front of her. She looked down at it, willing herself to be thrilled when she opened the box, but she gasped as she pulled it open. A large, pear shaped diamond was surrounded by small emerald stones, in a platinum setting with the band in swirls of the precious metal. It was truly breathtaking. She looked up, stunned at the thoughtfulness in choosing such a beautiful piece of jewellery.

"Richard! It's beautiful!"

He smiled, pleased with her reaction. He reached over and, without asking her, took the ring, slid it on the third finger of her left hand. "I take that as a 'yes'?"

She held her hand out to examine the stunning ring, letting the light refract through the amazing stone. Maybe he *did* care for her. Her smile lit up her face as she looked over at him and he took her hands in his, squeezing them happily.

"It took me a long while to choose it," he drew closer to her, "I wanted it to be as special as you." He looked down, swallowed, then looked up at Gwen again. "I love you, sweetheart," he said, and Gwen tilted her head at the catch in his voice.

"You love me," she said half to herself, and he chuckled.

"Of course I love you! You didn't think I was marrying you just because you were the most beautiful woman in the world, did you?"

Tears came to Gwen's eyes as she wondered if she had misjudged Richard. She felt overwhelmed at the thought of being loved. Richard slid around the table so he was sat next to her and leaned forward, kissing her gently on the lips.

Richard looked over and waved to a waiter. The man hurried over.

"Yes, sir? How may I help you?"

"Two champagnes please."

"Very good, sir. Do you have a preference?"

Richard smiled broadly and held up Gwen's hand, flashing the ring at the man. "Your best! We just got engaged."

The man held out his arms wide, "Oh, how wonderful, sir – and mademoiselle. Congratulations to the two of you! Two glasses of our very best champagne coming up!"

⟫●⟪

Marlene came down the stairs in a sparkly, navy blue fitted sleeveless dress. She wore diamond and sapphire earrings and a matching necklace.

Keegan whistled and walked over to her, taking her hands in his and kissing her cheek. "Give me a moment, and we'll head out." He turned to Benito who was sat on a chair in the living room.

"Come with me."

Benito warily stood up, still unsure of what was going to happen to him while Keegan and Marlene went out for the evening. He followed Keegan up the stairs and the teenager's heart began beating rapidly as he realised the answer. Keegan stopped in front of the little room where he had locked Marlene the last time Benito was there, and opened the door, waving Benito in. A quick glance inside before the door shut and blocked out all light showed him how small it was – merely a cupboard. An empty cupboard with a hard, vinyl floor. Benito huddled on the floor as he heard Keegan click the lock shut. *At least his stomach was full … Thank You, God!* And he smiled to himself at the very satisfying feeling.

"I'm sorry, Joe, but even *I* could see how implausible that scenario was." Toby shook his head as the three of them came out of the cinema and began heading back to their hotel. Rebeca laughed in agreement, but said nothing.

"Oh well," said Joe, rubbing his stomach, "all that implausibility has given me an appetite!"

"Is your stomach ever full, Joe?" Rebeca asked.

"Hmmmm..." Joe smiled and winked at her, "One day, a few years ago. I think it was a Tuesday!"

Rebeca giggled, "Well, I think your favourite restaurant is right up there, that yellow M!"

"I'm game as well!" laughed Toby, and the three headed into the restaurant to get something to eat before they returned to the Hyatt for the night.

CHAPTER 11

The early hours of Saturday 20th August

The lock clicked and a beam of light awoke Benito from his uncomfortable sleeping position. He struggled to his feet as Keegan stepped back, holding the door open for him to step out.

"I'm going to change. Go downstairs and Marlene will fix you something to eat. Then we'll go out to do another evening's work. Pretty much like last time."

Work, is that what he called it? the teenager thought to himself as he walked carefully down the steps, holding onto the rail, stopping a couple of times to stretch out his legs and arms. The delicious smell wafting out of the kitchen drew him in and he sat down at the table to wait for his food. Marlene, who had already changed into pale green tracksuit bottoms with a white t-shirt, was busily heating up some left-over stew she had made a couple of days earlier.

"Hello sweetheart! Are you all right?" she asked him quietly, a look of concern on her face as she empathised with his confinement. Benito smiled faintly and nodded, not wanting Keegan to hear him interact with her and get her in trouble again. The kind woman filled a large bowl of the delicious smelling chicken stew and placed it in front of him with two slices of bread and butter on a plate. She walked to the fridge, quickly poured some milk into a glass and placed it in front of him.

"It's okay, you can eat it now," she said in a reasonably loud voice, then she stood behind him, lent over his shoulder and spoke in a barely audible voice into his ear: "I'll help you. Just do whatever he says over the next couple of days, but I'll help you escape and you won't ever have to go back to Tadeo again." She stood up quickly as she heard Keegan come down the stairs, and walked over to the coffee maker to get him a hot drink.

Keegan sat in one of the soft chairs in the living room and Marlene brought over his coffee. "Extra cream and sugar, babe, just how you like it before you go out." She kissed him on his cheek. "Thank you for a lovely evening."

Keegan took the drink and smiled at her, taking her hand and kissing it. Again, Benito was struck by the appearance of a normal couple interacting. It was all rather bizarre.

"Don't take too long, kid," Keegan called over to Benito in the kitchen. "I want to leave in thirty minutes."

True to his word, thirty minutes later they were driving off in Keegan's black BMW with Benito in the back seat. Soon they were back at Keegan's lock-up. This time, he drove out a Porche Cayenne Turbo GT. Benito wiped his sweaty palms on his jeans and climbed out of the BMW. He didn't think he would ever get used to driving such expensive stolen cars. He wondered about the owners, if they were really wealthy and were just as happy with insurance money. Or were they someone who had to save up to buy such a car – or had it on HP with large monthly payments. He worried that the insurance wouldn't cover their loss.

He only hesitated a moment, but Keegan growled at him and Benito grabbed the key held out to him. The teenager climbed in and slid onto the black leather seat, his hand shaking as he started the car. Again, he wiped his hands on his jeans and he breathed deeply.

Keegan drove off, and Benito put the Porsche into drive, following the man to the garage. This time, Benito did not see any police, but his heart beat fast as he drove along, wondering when he would ever escape this life, and wondering what Marlene meant by saying she would help him. The faint ray of hope was quickly overshadowed by the dark realisation that it didn't really matter. He was a wanted adult criminal now – Tadeo had seen to that. It was either this life or prison. He blinked back the tears at the hopelessness of it all.

As Benito slowed and turned to go into the garage, out of the corner of his eye he thought he saw movement in a car parked down the road, and he automatically became wary. The large doors opened as before, but as he pulled in and turned off the car and the lights went out, he noticed the garage lights were dimmer than the previous time. He looked around and immediately his senses went on high alert as he realised there was a different person by the little pedestrian door.

The man with the bag held it out, as before, waiting for Benito to put the key in his hand, and as he did, Benito was sure he saw another man hovering in the back of the garage in the shadows. The teenager did a quick mental scan of the building and made his plan. He zipped open the bag, pretending to scan through the contents to make sure all the £40,000 was there.

Benito cleared his throat and forced an intensity he did not feel, "Looks like it's all here, but be assured, we'll be back if it isn't."

He swung around, walking purposefully to the door, but just as he reached it, in the same instance as the man standing there leaned over to grab him, Benito threw the bag with full force, knocking him off balance. Propelling himself through the door way, Benito heard the man shouting,

"Police! Stop!"

Benito ran down the drive and glanced down the road, knowing he would see it empty – Keegan was gone. Running full tilt, he ran across the road, dodging the street lights then scampering over a high fence that bordered someone's garden. Adrenalin pumping through him, he tore through the garden into the back and scrambled over that fence. Winding his way through a pathway that went through the housing estate, the night was dark, and if he stayed out of the lights he could remain hidden. Benito darted off the path when he came across another high fence, which he leapt up, scraping his arms and chest as he dragged himself over the top, then landed on his hands and knees on the grass. A shed was in the far corner, and he scooted behind it as he listened to the police shouting and running. Slowly, it became quieter as the officers realised they had lost the teenager. But Benito didn't move even when he could no longer hear them. He slowly let out a breath he did not realise he was holding, and sat down in a more comfortable position.

Where had Keegan gone? Had he gone home? Was the man out looking for him? Benito was tempted to just walk in the opposite direction – but where would he go? For all Benito knew, his friends had given up looking for him. They obviously had seen the sign he put up in the window of the shop, but he hadn't been able to finish his message of where he was going. Tadeo said he was going to be at Keegan's for a week, but would Toby and the others give up by then?

What should I do, God? Where should I go?

Silence.

Benito heard some pigeons cooing nearby, and a couple of cats fighting in the distance. He hadn't really expected God to answer him, but it would have been nice if He *had*. Benito thought for a moment. Actually, he wasn't sure it *would* be nice. No, he decided it would be rather terrifying to hear God speak.

He put his hand down to shift his sitting position and grimaced. The grass was wet. He hadn't thought that the grass might be covered in dew when he had made himself comfortable. Benito stood up and felt his backside – it was not as wet as he figured it would be, but it was still damp. He stretched out his legs and leaned against the fence, still pondering what to do. The cats started fighting again and he heard someone shout out of a window for them to be quiet. He wasn't sure cats listened very well to commands and as they continued, he nodded to himself.

Suddenly one of the windows opened in the house by where he was hiding and he shrunk back further behind the shed, his heart beating quickly. He looked up as a light switched on. It looked like a bathroom window, too small for someone to stick their head out, but Benito decided it was time to go, so he slunk along the fence beside the house and the moonlight guided him to the front gate. He lifted the latch carefully and flinched as it made a loud CLUNK, then flinched again when the gate squeaked loudly as he opened it. Shutting it firmly behind him with just as much noise, he ran down the front path and down the quiet street, trying to stay in the shadows, glad that his trainers did not make a sound other than a soft padding along the pavement as he scurried away.

Benito shortly found himself back on the road that went by the garage and he stopped short. He didn't want to risk the police still being nearby, so he crossed the street and jogged quickly in the opposite direction. As soon as he came across another side road, he took it and carried on running for several metres.

"Hey, ho! Look who's in a hurry to get somewhere!" A young male voice called out from the shadows and Benito's heart doubled its speed as several silhouettes of young men appeared, stopping him in his tracks.

"I don't want any trouble," Benito spoke quietly, putting his hands up to show he had no weapons.

"The speed you were going, looks like you were already in trouble!" laughed one of them, and the others joined him, coming closer in a semicircle around him. Benito saw a couple of knifes as the blades caught the light from the moon that had just appeared from behind a cloud.

"I ... uh ... was just going to the shop for my uncle ... he wasn't feeling well and I was going to get him some flu tablets." Benito stumbled for a plausibly innocent reason to be out so late.

"Speed you were going, he must be close to near death." More laughter as the gang drew nearer. "Anyway! Ain't no shop around here open this time o' night." The leader came up right in front of Benito and the teenager barely breathed as he felt the cold blade against the side of his neck. Benito stood frozen, not wanting the youth to cut him accidentally, and not sure whether or not to say anything else.

The tall youth leaned down into Benito's face and the teenager grimaced at the stench of cigarettes and cheap beer. Benito's eyes strained to see his face, but with the moon at the young man's back, all Benito could see was the outline of the shortly cropped hair and square head.

"You wanna tell me another story?" he growled with the deep voice of a youth that had now gained his manhood.

Before he could decide if it was sensible or not, Benito went for the truth. "I was out with a man sellin' a stolen car, but they'd sold us out to the cops. I only just managed to get away."

The youth slowly slid the back of the blade along Benito's throat as he mulled this information over. "Where?" he asked finally.

"Garage just back there, along that road to the left." Benito carefully lowered his one arm slightly, pointing.

"You in our territory, boy!" He swore and turned to the others, "Ain't he, brothers?" They all mumbled in agreement, nodding their heads and stepping another few feet towards Benito.

Benito's heart was pumping his blood so hard around his body that his ears began to ring. Was this his answer to his prayer? Was this going to be his escape? Death?!

"Hmmmm," said the leader, still breathing his foul breath into Benito's nostrils. "I think a slice across the throat would be too quick. I fancy a bit of fun." He glanced over his shoulder at his friends. "Don't you?"

A raucous laughter ran through the gang as they all agreed in various voices. "A bit o' fun! Ya! It's been boring lately! Ya! I fancy some fun!"

Smack!

Benito's head flew sideways at the impact on his jaw, and he stumbled backwards, only just managing to stay upright.

Smack!

Another hard clip to the other side of his head. Benito held his arms around his head for protection, but then fists began hammering his stomach and his side. He fell to the ground, yelling in agony, but then someone grabbed his hair and shoved something in his mouth.

Please God, help me! Benito silently pleaded as he felt various feet kicking his entire body from his legs to his head. Suddenly they stopped, and Benito, who had had his eyes closed tightly, sensed a light – several lights, and he saw the youths were all standing around him with lighters.

"Have you ever smelt burning flesh?" The leader looked around at the others and they all shook their heads, grinning.

"Let's smell some burning flesh!" one shouted. Then another. "Yah! I want to smell it!"

Benito flinched as the flame touched his bare arm and the muffled scream echoed in his head as tears began rolling down his face at the pain.

Suddenly, two great lights were focused on them all, and the gang scattered like rats into the darkness. Benito coughed as the tears began to block his nose and he struggled to breathe. He heard a car door slam and someone knelt beside him, the lights shining on the man's face.

Tadeo!

The man pulled out the dirty sport sock that had been shoved in Benito's mouth and the teenager gasped in the fresh air, coughing again as he did so.

"What are you doing, you stupid boy?!" shouted Tadeo as he unceremoniously grabbed Benito's arm and pulled him to his feet. "Why didn't you go back to Keegan's?"

Benito winced as Tadeo grabbed exactly where the lighter had burned him, but he tried to hold back further tears. He wasn't sure that Tadeo's reaction to his tears would be any better than what the youths had just done to him. Although, Tadeo would want to keep him well enough to be useful to him.

Tadeo hauled Benito to his car like a naughty child, and the teenager stumbled, trying to keep upright so as to not annoy him further. Tadeo paused as he opened the back passenger door, and he looked at Benito through the dim glow that came from the car's interior light.

Taking a step back, he brushed Benito down roughly with his hand as he grumbled, "You're going to get my car seat dirty!" The large man stood for a moment, scrunching his face, then said,"I think there is an old coat in the boot. Wait a minute."

Benito held onto the car for balance as he tried to gain strength from his beating. His whole body hurt, the ache in his head made him struggle to focus, and the searing pain of the burn pulsated with every beat of his heart.

Tadeo promptly shut down the boot of the car and pushed Benito out of the way. It was all the teenager could do to keep upright as the man spread the large coat onto the back seat. He turned to Benito and motioned him inside.

"Well, get in boy! You have caused me a lot of trouble! The least you could have done was keep the money, you idiot! Now Keegan is going to want payment from me for the loss!"

Benito climbed in and gratefully sat down, wondering how on earth his uncle had expected him to escape the police AND carry the large bag of cash with him. It didn't matter, though. Tadeo's line of reasoning did not always take a logical path.

Tadeo got in the front seat and started the car. Wanting to hurt Benito for all the trouble the man thought the teenager had been the cause of, he spoke sinisterly,

"At least I don't have to be troubled about my outgoings with regard to your mother any more!" He laughed darkly as he slowly turned the vehicle around to face the other way, then out onto the main road heading towards Keegan's place.

The physical pain that Benito had felt dissolved into irrelevant discomfort at Tadeo's cryptic comment. He knew what his uncle meant. What had his uncle done to his mom?! He no longer cared what Tadeo did to him if he saw tears, as he screamed hysterically at his uncle.

"No!" His face fell forward as he sobbed, heartbroken, into his hands.

An evil smile spread across Tadeo's face. For once, he didn't care about the tears. He had broken the boy – he should be no more trouble now, either. So much for Gabriella's God!

———⟫●⟪———

"Joe," whispered Toby, "you awake?"

"How'd you know?" His brother whispered back from the other side of the huge bed.

"Your breathing, mostly. It sounded like 'awake' breathing, rather than 'sleeping' breathing."

"'Awake' breathing?"

"You know, louder and less regular."

"Was there something you wanted, other than to analyse my breathing?" Joe asked, keen to move the conversation away from as to why he was awake.

"I'm sorry."

"That's okay, it's not that big of a deal. It's only my breathing!" Joe chuckled.

"No," said Toby slowly, "I mean for earlier; when I threw you to the ground."

"Okay, let's get one thing straight, you did *not* 'throw' me to the ground. You pushed at me when I wasn't ready, I stumbled back and fell. You're not strong enough to throw me anywhere."

Toby half smiled to himself in the dark at his brother's ego as he continued. "I'm sorry for pushing at you and being the cause of your stumbling backwards and falling. I don't know what got into me. You know I'm not normally short tempered like you are."

Joe took a deep breath and let it out slowly through his nostrils. "Are you just going to keep insulting me? You have a funny way of apologising."

Toby turned over onto his side to face his brother, even though he couldn't see him in the dark. "I'm sorry." He paused before continuing slowly. "I guess I thought we were going to find Benito, and now it looks like we're no closer than we were before. I really want to help him, but ... I also wanted to impress Rebeca. I wanted her to see that I was a man worthy of her affections."

Joe snorted. "Whoah, there, little brother! A *man*? You can't even grow a proper beard yet!"

Toby pulled the pillow from under his head and reached across the expanse to smack his brother across the head with it. Joe responded in kind, and soon they were in a tussle, with Joe's strong arm around Toby's neck. Toby punched his brother hard in the stomach and the two rolled off the bed onto the hardwood floor. Each throwing half hearted punches and trying to wrestle the other into submission, while 'ooompfs! and aghs!' grew louder.

Crash! The sound of shattered glass stopped them dead as the bedside lamp was knocked on the floor and broke into several pieces. For a moment, neither moved as they tried to assess in the dark where the shards of glass were.

"Good job Rebeca isn't next door." Joe said finally and they both chuckled.

"I wonder how expensive that lamp was? Do you think we'll have to pay for it?"

"Put it on the Wentworth's tab," said Joe in an irritated voice as he slowly got to his feet, walking away from where the lamp had landed, and switched on the main light at the wall.

Toby gave him a puzzled look, but was then distracted by the lamp. "I guess we'll have to call down to reception to send someone to clean it up," he said guiltily.

"Go ahead," said Joe, still annoyed, "you started it."

"What do you mean? *You* started it!" Toby stepped towards his brother and swung a right hook at him. Joe easily deflected it and gave Toby a jab in the chest. They both stood glaring at each other, breathing heavily.

A loud knock on the door made them both turn. "Is everything all right in there, gentlemen? We have had a few calls down to reception saying there was a disturbance." A deep male voice spoke from the other side.

"Hang on a second!" Joe called out as he pulled on some shorts, and Toby slipped on his jeans just as Joe opened the door.

A huge, muscular man looked down at Joe authoritatively. He wore a white shirt with the words 'SECURITY' written in navy blue across the left side of his chest. Joe figured he must have been about six foot eight. He gulped involuntarily as he looked up at the man and opened the door wide, waving him in. "I'm so sorry. We … uh … my brother … we had a … disagreement and it got a little out of hand. I'm afraid we knocked over a lamp."

The large security guard stood with his legs slightly apart and his solid arms across his broad chest. "We don't expect that kind of behaviour here at the Hyatt. Certainly our guests expect a quiet stay without trouble. You're not at a third rate hotel, *boys*."

Joe didn't even flinch at the terminology as he spoke quietly, "I know, sir, I'm very sorry."

"Yes, we're very sorry. It won't happen again," Toby nodded fervently in agreement.

The man raised his eyebrow. "I would have thrown you out, but the manager said you were booked in under the Wentworth's name. Is that right?"

"Uh, yes, the Wentworths are paying for this room and the one the girls are in, a few floors down." Joe decided not to mention that Gwen was not there, as that might have influenced the man to chuck them out after all.

He looked each of them over slowly, squinting his eyes. "You don't look like their type of people."

"Uh, no, we … uh … it's a long story."

The security man stared at them intimidatingly a few moments longer before turning to leave. "I'll send maintenance up here, so don't go to sleep."

"No, sir, thank you sir," said Toby, with Joe nodding affirmatively.

The guard shut the door firmly but quietly behind him and the two brothers collapsed into the soft furniture.

"I need a coke!" Joe said as he stood back up and walked over to the fridge, and grabbed a can of pop. "Do you want one?"

Toby nodded, still breathing heavily from the exertion. He took the can from his brother and opened it up, taking a long drink before he spoke. "Do you think they'll tell the Wentworths?"

Joe scrunched up his face. "I don't care."

"What's up with you?"

"Nothin'." Joe glugged down the can and placed it on the coffee table in front of him.

"Come on, you've been acting funny ever since Gwen left." A thought entered his mind as he added, "You're not jealous of Richard are you?" Toby tilted his head. "I thought you were in love with Rebeca." He smirked, "Not that I mind you going after Gwen instead of Rebeca. It helps *me* out." Toby laughed, "But she'd never have you! What can you possibly offer Gwen besides your biceps?"

Joe grabbed the cushion beside him but stopped just before it left his hand to propel it towards Toby. He put it down beside him and he patted it like a dog.

"Looks like I touched a nerve." Toby said carefully.

Joe looked down at his feet. "She said she wanted me."

Toby looked confused. "Who said she wanted you? Rebeca?"

"Gwen. When I walked her down to the taxi. She said she wanted me, but she couldn't have me."

Toby started to laugh, then stopped himself as he saw his brother's struggle. "She said she wanted you?"

Joe leaned back and ran his fingers through his thick dark hair, "Ya, but I don't know why it affected me. Especially when I feel the way I do about Rebeca."

"Well, she *is* hot …", Toby snickered and Joe glared at him, hand ready on the cushion again. "Okay, sorry."

"It's not that." He paused, wanting yet not wanting to talk about his feelings to his brother. "It's just that, spending this time with Gwen, getting to know her, has made me …". Joe's face suddenly changed. The last thing he wanted was to show vulnerability to his brother. "Never mind. It …".

A gentle knock on the door saved Joe from saying more. "Housekeeping," a male voice spoke quietly, and Toby jumped up to let him in. Though not as large as the security guard, this man was still quite beefy. Toby and Joe exchanged glances, realising that the security guard was not ready to trust they would not cause more trouble. The two brothers sat silently as the man cleaned up the lamp, then left with a box full of the broken pieces.

—————⇒●⇐—————

Tadeo pulled onto Keegan's drive and the gate opened. Keegan stuck his head out of the door then stepped back, leaving it slightly ajar. When Tadeo turned off the engine, Benito got out and automatically followed him inside the house, numb from Tadeo's revelation about his mom.

Marlene was stood beside Keegan in a fluffy turquoise housecoat and she gasped as Benito walked in, shutting the door behind him.

"Oh darling! What happened?" She turned to Keegan who was silently analysing Benito and determining his reaction to the boy. "I'll get the first aid kit, all right babe?" She was asking his permission. He finally nodded and she tried not to hurry as she went to fetch what she would need to tend to Benito's wounds.

Tadeo answered the question. "Idiot decided to run off in the opposite direction to here and got caught up with some kids that had some fun with him."

Keegan strode to a cupboard in the living room and opened it up, revealing a collection of alcohol and some crystal glasses. "Whisky?" Tadeo nodded and made himself comfortable in one of the soft, cream coloured chairs. Benito made a movement to do the same, and Keegan nearly dropped the glass in his hand as he growled loudly,

"Not in the state you are in, kid! Get in the kitchen. Marlene will see to you there, then you can go up to your room and get out of those clothes so she can wash 'em."

Keegan handed the generous helping of whisky to Tadeo, then poured himself one of equal size. "I think we both need a large one." He sat in a chair opposite Tadeo, both men silent for a while.

Finally, Tadeo spoke. "I need a place to stay for a few days. Someone's grassed me up and they're watching my place."

Keegan scowled, "So your kid lost all my money *and* my car, and you want me to put you up?"

Tadeo raised an eyebrow, ready to retaliate. "We were both grassed up! The kid couldn't have carried the money out of there, and he couldn't jump back in the car without the keys." He wasn't going to let Keegan make it look like he owed him anything. "Besides," he smiled widely, "I've got something big planned, and I need some help. The guy that was going to assist me has got himself banged up again." He shook his head in disgusted annoyance.

"How big?" Anxious to recoup his losses, Keegan's curiosity was piqued. He wasn't interested in knowing who the other person had been. It was best to keep away from people who ended up in prison regularly; they were too well known to the cops. Anonymity was the key to a successful criminal lifestyle.

"Let's just say," began Tadeo slowly, drawing the other man in, "enough to buy me a big place in the country, away from everyone, where there ain't nobody to bother me or know what I am up to!" It would be far more than that, but Tadeo did not want Keegan expecting higher payment than he was willing to offer.

"What's the deal?" asked Keegan, wanting to know what would be involved.

Tadeo wagged a finger in front of him at Keegan, "I'm still working on the details, but if you want in, I need to know now, 'cause I need to do some organising."

Keegan ran his fingers along the stubble on his chin, making a scratching noise as he squinted at the other man thoughtfully.

"And I want Marlene," grinned Tadeo teasingly.

The gold/green snake eyes went black as he shot to his feet, ready to throttle the other man. Tadeo held up his hands to ward off Keegan, laughing.

"Hold on, there, man! I want Marlene in on the job, is what I mean!"

"I don't normally involve Marlene in my jobs." He glanced over at the woman who was pretending not to listen, as she tended to Benito's wounds. "Not sure she's up to it. She's a bit...", he tapped the side of his head, "simple, you know?"

"She can't be that simple," Tadeo encouraged him, "she was a nurse, after all, when you met her. It's just the fewer people I let in on this, the better, you know? Keep it in the 'family'!" Tadeo chuckled, and Keegan squinted his reptile eyes, deliberating. Finally, he replied,

"Okay, but when you tell me the details, if I think it is going to be too risky in any way, I'm out. Got it?"

Tadeo knocked back the rest of the whisky, exhaling loudly with pleasure, then nodded. "It ain't gonna be too risky, brother. The money will be well worth your efforts. Now, show me to my room, I'm tired."

The two men climbed the stairs, and Marlene took the chance to smile at Benito and stroke his head. "How's that, sweetheart?"

"Much better, thank you, Marlene, you are very kind." Benito smiled sadly. Benito's physical wounds had all been taken care of, but his heart ached for his mom, praying that whatever Tadeo had done to her at the very least, had been quick and she hadn't suffered.

Marlene tilted her red head as she gazed down compassionately at Benito. "What is it, darling? Something else has happened, hasn't it?"

Benito nodded, unable to answer as his eyes filled and he began shaking with silent sobs. Marlene instantly bent down and wrapped her arms around him.

"Oh, sweetheart! It's okay, I'll get you out of this mess." Unaware of Benito's mom, Marlene could only assume that one of the two men had done something to Benito himself.

"Marlene!"

She instantly let go of Benito and stood up, slowly turning around to watch Keegan striding angrily towards her, snake eyes flashing. Through his tear-filled eyes, Benito was once again certain he saw faint trails of smoking flowing out of the evil man's nostrils.

"Obviously you didn't learn your lesson last time the kid was here!"

"I'm sorry, babe! I wasn't doing nothin'! He was just crying and I was comforting him."

"How many times do I have to tell you that you show love only to me?!"

"Baby, I'm so sorry, I don't know what come over me. I'm a sucker for tears …". She started to laugh, as she reached out to Keegan, stroking his face, trying to calm him down as he grabbed her arms, squeezing tightly. "You know it's only you I truly love," she said trying to pacify him as she tilted her head up and kissed him on the lips, despite his painful grip on her. He kissed her back, squeezing her arms tighter. She broke off the kiss, but kept her lips close to his face as she continued, "I love you baby, I do, you know I do. I'm so sorry." She gazed at him pleadingly.

He whispered sinisterly in her ear, "You be quiet now. I don't want Tadeo to know you disrespected me. You make me look bad. You're gonna go in your little room quietly now, ya hear? If you make a noise, you'll be really really sorry."

Marlene nodded silently, as he let go of one arm and remained a tight hold on the other as he pulled her up the stairs to 'her room'. He shoved her inside, then leaned in, taking off her housecoat, leaving her in a thin nightie.

Again, he spoke directly into her ear. I need this to plug up the air coming in from under the door. You obviously enjoy it too much in here – you need to be a bit more uncomfortable!"

"Oh, no, babe, please! It's already dark – I hate it in there, you know I do." She pleaded with him quietly.

He responded by pushing her backwards so she hit her head hard against the wall and she cried out in pain, as she crumpled in a heap, holding her head in her hands weeping silently as the door quietly shut, and the large gap underneath was filled with her fluffy housecoat.

Keegan stood for a moment pondering as to what to do with Benito. As much as Tadeo said he could do what he wanted with the kid, Keegan was not convinced that he would accept someone, other than himself, harming him; certainly not within earshot. In the end, he went downstairs into the kitchen and spoke roughly but quietly to the teenager through gritted teeth.

"It's your fault. Marlene has had to go in her room, and it's your fault. You consistently encourage her to disrespect me. So now I have to discipline her again."

The green/gold eyes pulled Benito into a stare that he could not escape. The teenager's heart beat rapidly as he heard that swish swish on the floor, but he didn't dare look down to see … to see if Keegan did have a tail – too terrified at the thought – the thought of what Keegan was; because it couldn't be true.

"Do you hear me, boy?" Reptile man's eyes flashed along with an inhuman growl.

Still transfixed, Benito could only nod slowly, his eyes glued to Keegan's.

The man nodded towards the stairs. "You know where your room is. Get in there now, and don't come out 'til I say."

Benito couldn't break away from the evil glare, and when he didn't move Keegan made a noise like a deep bark. Benito jumped up, ran across the living room and up the stairs, leaping into the bed and pulling the covers over him, fully dressed, with the irrational realisation that he had not removed his clothes for Marlene to wash.

The distraught teenager closed his eyes and prayed: *Please God, protect Marlene. Be with her in that room. Please protect me. Please welcome my mamma into Your arms.*

Tears flowed freely with his heartfelt prayers, and he imagined God's arms wrapped tightly around him, comforting him. Suddenly, Benito smiled. Keegan couldn't do anything about *that*! And he drifted into a peaceful sleep.

In the little room down the hall, Marlene was shivering in her scant clothing and her head was aching from when it hit the wall. She drifted in and out of consciousness and as the oxygen grew less, her breathing became more laboured. She woke early as she began gasping for breath, trying to remain calm, but the panic grew and insisted that she needed more air. She gulped and strained for every breath until she could take it no more, and she banged on the door with her fists, surprised at how little noise they made. Her arms fell to her side and she collapsed on to her side.

"Keegan!" She tried to shout, but the sound that escaped was barely a whisper. "Keegan!"

Her eyes closed and everything went black as she gasped one last time, "Keegan!"

Keegan looked at the clock by his bed and he jumped up. He didn't want Tadeo to know how he disciplined his woman. He didn't want Tadeo knowing that she *needed* discipline. He trotted quietly into the hall and grabbed the housecoat, retreating to his room and tossing it on his bed before returning and opening the cupboard door.

"Marlene!" Keegan called out loudly as he panicked, seeing the unconscious woman curled up in the fetal position by the door. He knelt down and shook her, "Marlene!"

Tadeo and Benito appeared from opposite directions as Marlene began coughing and gasping in Keegan's arms as he knelt on the floor. Finally she took a deep breath and he held her tightly.

He looked up at Tadeo.

"I don't know what happened. She must have got herself locked in this room somehow! I woke up and she wasn't in bed with me." Marlene took another few deep breaths, coughing in between them, then finally opened her eyes.

Tadeo nodded his head and went back to his room to finish shaving in the private bathroom, not caring in the slightest what Keegan had done to her. Benito, although concerned for the kind woman, took his cue and turned back to his bedroom to change into some fresh clothes.

"You made me look like a fool!" Keegan whispered into Marlene's ears as his panic was replaced by his annoyance that he had shown weakness to Tadeo in his response to finding Marlene collapsed. He struggled to his feet as he pulled her roughly up with him, and dragged her into the bedroom, shutting the door firmly behind them.

Benito finished changing and sat on the edge of the bed, waiting. Shortly, the door to Keegan and Marlene's bedroom opened, and Marlene came out dressed in the green tracksuit bottoms and white t-shirt she had had on the previous evening. Had it only been the previous evening, wondered Benito? It seemed so long ago.

Marlene turned towards the stairs and walked carefully down and into the kitchen. Soon, the smell of frying bacon and brewing coffee drifted up to where Benito was still sitting on the bed, waiting to be told what to do.

Shortly, Tadeo and Keegan came out of their rooms, greeted each other with a smile, and made their way down to the delicious smells. A moment later, Keegan came to the bottom of the stairs and called up to Benito,

"Bring your clothes down, boy, and put them in the laundry room!"

Benito did as he was told, then meekly walked towards the kitchen, wondering if he would be scolded for expecting breakfast. Tadeo said nothing as he and Keegan drank coffee and discussing who had snitched on each of them and discussing what they would do to each, should they ever discover the identity.

Benito quietly pulled out a chair and sat down beside Tadeo. Marlene came over with a glass of juice and smiled at him like nothing had happened.

"Have a good sleep, sweetheart?"

Benito nodded as he drank, but said nothing; waiting silently for his breakfast, surprised at the feeling of hunger alongside the deep ache that permeated him as he wondered again about his mom.

CHAPTER 12

Tap! Tap! Tap!

Silence.

Tap! Tap! Tap! Louder this time.

"Toby! Joe! Are you awake?"

Toby heard the voice from far away, and he struggled to bring himself to consciousness.

"Toby!" It was almost a shout.

Knock! Knock! Knock!

Toby strained to open his eyes and he blinked a couple of times before actually seeing anything.

"Hang on, Rebeca!" he managed to call out, as he rolled over and struggled to a sitting position. He looked over across the vast bed at Joe, who was still snoring, then grabbed his jeans from the floor and pulled them up. He zipped them up as he walked over to the chair and grabbed the t-shirt he had worn the previous day.

Grabbing the phone by his bed, he looked at the time. 9:00! He tossed the phone back and hurried to the door before Rebeca could knock again and draw attention from security.

Toby yanked the door open and spoke abruptly, "Quiet! You'll have security up here ag …".

She looked hurt and confused as he stood back, motioning dramatically for her to come in, and he shut the door firmly behind her as she stepped in the room. Instantly, he was sorry for his harshness and he felt like kicking himself.

"I'm sorry, Rebeca," he sighed deeply. "I … uh … I'm just tired." He was ashamed at the ease with which the lie came, ashamed that he and Joe had nearly got them kicked out of the hotel, ashamed that once again, he was not the 'man' he wanted to be.

She stood in front of him, looking up at him, sadly perplexed. He stepped forward and wrapped his arms around her, pressing his face into her soft hair and breathing deeply of her natural scent. For a moment, she held him back tightly and they stood in a silent embrace, each desiring what seemed unobtainable.

"Ahem …".

Rebeca stepped back, and they both turned to see Joe stood, bare chested with shorts on, leaning against the bedroom doorway, arms folded and, despite feeling saddened at the sight, grinning at them.

"Don't mean to interrupt, but I think it's time for breakfast."

"I think it was time an hour or two ago," smiled Rebeca, blushing slightly from the emotional rush of being in Toby's arms.

"Well, Toby and I worked up a big appetite …" began Joe.

"Because it has been so long since we have eaten," interrupted Toby, glaring at his brother with meaning. Another easy lie.

Joe raised an eyebrow, obviously deliberating whether to go along with Toby; but something spiteful rose up inside him, and he continued, "Tobs and I got into a tussle, broke a lamp, had security come up, and we nearly got chucked out of the hotel." When he saw Toby trying to control his anger, Joe pushed further, "Evidently several of the guests complained as they thought there were hooligans in the hotel."

"You *****!" Toby snarled at Joe.

Joe and Rebeca were shocked at his language, but Joe smiled, inwardly pleased to have goaded Toby down to the level of temperament that he *had* been displaying these days. *It's true*, he thought, *misery does love company*. Within seconds, though, guilt pervaded his conscience and he turned back into the bedroom.

"I'm just going to put a top on and we'll go downstairs."

Unable to look at Rebeca, Toby strode over to the floor-to-ceiling window and pressed his face against the glass, looking out at the vast city, but seeing nothing.

Shortly, Joe came out of the room and they silently headed out of the room. Joe clicked the door shut behind them and, without questioning, they all walked towards the stairwell. They found a table in the corner by a window and the boys picked up the menus. Rebeca already decided to order what she had had the previous morning.

A few minutes later, a waiter came and took their orders, then finally, Rebeca broke the silence.

"What is a 'hoo ... ligan' ?"

Joe and Toby chuckled in unison, and Rebeca smiled at the ease that had finally pervaded the unpleasant atmosphere.

Toby reached over and took her hand, which she squeezed back, then looked at his brother. "Last night, Joe and I were hooligans. How we behaved was 'hooliganish'."

Joe cocked his head, "Not sure that's a word, buddy."

"Does it matter?"

"It does if Rebeca wants to learn proper English!"

Rebeca grinned happily, "That is fine. I believe I understand what a hooligan is now." She paused before changing the subject: "What are we going to do today? When will Gwen be back?"

Joe looked at his phone, already knowing since he had only just checked, but there was no message. He was surprised at how grieved that made him feel. He forced a smile. "She must be having a good time with *Richard* after all."

Toby noted the tone, but said nothing. He had already behaved badly enough to last for several days, if not weeks. Rebeca, too, picked up on his attitude, but remained silent.

"I'd like to go to the Motorcycle museum. I've always wanted to, but for some reason, we never have."

Toby agreed, then glanced over at Rebeca, wondering at her reaction.

"That sounds interesting," she said truthfully. She was keen to learn about all kinds of things she had never encountered before. She added, "I saw a leaflet in my room that talked about a boat ride on the canal that offers live *commentary*."

Joe and Toby looked at each other and grinned. Joe spoke first, "That sounds like a new word for you!"

"Yes," she giggled like a young girl, "I had to look it up in my dictionary. It is a good word, *commentary*." A slight frown passed over her face as she added with furrowed eyebrows, "Though I was unsure what *live* commentary meant. How could you have *dead* commentary?"

Her face was so serious as she tried to understand, that Joe and Toby found it impossible to restrain themselves and they both burst out laughing. Toby leaned over and hugged her with one arm so as to pacify any feelings that might be hurt.

Toby kissed her head as he released her. "The opposite of live commentary, is commentary that is recorded and played back so you can hear it. Like the television, but it is just audio. Often on tours, they give you little devices that you hold and listen to on the tour. Live commentary is when you have a real live person talking."

Rebeca giggled in amusement of her misunderstanding. "Well, *that* definitely makes more sense than anything I was imagining!"

Just then, their breakfasts arrived and they all tucked in eagerly, with even Rebeca now very hungry.

Joe and Toby finished their meals quickly, so they ordered more tea while they sat back and waited for Rebeca to eat hers.

A PING made Joe take out his phone from his pocket. "It's Gwen. She's expecting to be back at the hotel around 5:00 this evening." He tried to hide his disappointment at a text message rather than a call. She says she wants to go to a 'proper' restaurant and has booked a place for 6:00." Despite his disappointment, he tittered as he read her message. "She says that it rather early for a place like that, but she figured it was a compromise to how hungry us boys would be by then!"

Toby and Rebeca laughed in agreement, though Rebeca was slightly unsure why 6:00 would be too early. She hesitated, then decided to brave another question. "Why is 6:00 too early?"

Joe shook his head smiling kindly, "Because it is really expensive and rich people don't go out for dinner until at least seven or eight o'clock!"

"Why is that?" Rebeca asked.

Joe and Toby looked at each other, unable to answer. Finally, Joe spoke up. "I have absolutely no idea!" And all three of them chuckled loudly.

Joe looked at his watch. "Right, shall we go to the motorcycle museum first? Then I wanted to buy a couple of t-shirts. For some reason, I only seem to have packed one in my bag. Then we can go on your canal tour with the live commentary!"

Rebeca grinned mischievously, "You didn't mention lunch?"

Joe laughed, "That goes without saying, of course!"

Tadeo put down his cup of coffee loudly and cursed as he looked at the message on his phone. "It's been moved forward!" Another foul word escaped his mouth and he growled angrily.

Keegan looked up from his breakfast and took a sip of his own coffee. He waited for Tadeo to continue. As far as Keegan was concerned, curiosity showed weakness.

"The gig happens tomorrow." He looked down at his watch and yet another swear word flew out of his mouth. "I gotta go see a man about the paperwork, then I'll be back and explain the details." He shovelled the last of his breakfast in his mouth and gulped back the remainder of his coffee as he slid the chair back and stood up abruptly. He nodded towards Benito. "It all right for the kid to stay here?"

Keegan raised an eyebrow. "Well, you rented him to me for the week anyway, remember?"

Tadeo laughed and nodded, turning and walking out of the kitchen as he threw his last comment back towards the other man, "After tomorrow, you won't be worrying about the boy doin' any jobs for you this week! You can have your money back, then you and Marlene can go on a lovely long holiday!" He laughed and shut the front door behind him. They heard him start the car and back out of the drive.

"That'd be nice, babe," said Marlene as she walked over and snuggled up to Keegan. He moved his chair back and she sat in his lap, wrapping her arms around his neck and kissing his cheek playfully. "We ain't been on a holiday for a long time! Can we babe?"

Benito lowered his eyes and concentrated on his eggs. He could not fathom Marlene ... and yet, in a way, he was no different. He pandered to Tadeo's wants out of fear, to keep the peace. Was that what she was doing? Would he be doing this forever? If his mom was dead, he didn't need to protect her any more. Tears welled up in his eyes and he swallowed hard to stop any more from appearing. But with his face on that camera in the jewellery shop, if he tried to leave Tadeo he would most certainly be picked up by the police and thrown into prison – with grown men. Men as nasty as his uncle and snake man.

"Hey, boy!"

Benito put down his fork and slowly raised his gaze to meet the green/gold eyes. "I need a couple of things from the shop. You know where it is?"

Benito slowly nodded his head, again transfixed by the evil orbs glaring at him.

"Off you get, baby." Keegan pushed Marlene off his lap and he reached in his pocket, pulling out a ten pound note. Then he grabbed a pen and a piece of paper from the edge of the table and scribbled down a few things before sliding the paper across the table, along with the money, towards Benito. "You can have the change." He smiled smugly, "I'm feeling generous!" He bent towards Benito and squinted his eyes as he finished, "Half an hour. I want you gone for half an hour. No more. No less. Marlene and I got some private things to discuss, and I don't want no pryin' ears listenin' in."

Benito took the money and note, and walked across the living room to put on his shoes before checking his watch as he headed out the front door. He had noticed a shop along the way when they came to Keegan's the last time. He figured it would be about ten minutes walking briskly, so he set off at a slow meander.

Glancing down at his watch when he stepped into the little shop, Benito made a face. It had only been nine minutes, even at the slow walk. He took his time as he picked out the few things that Keegan had asked for, including some shaving cream and some milk, and suddenly he was aware of someone close behind him. A man was watching him suspiciously and Benito suddenly felt like a criminal; which was what he must have looked like as he checked his watch and tried to waste time in the shop. He decided to spend some time elsewhere, and went directly to the till where he discovered there was enough left over to buy himself a bag of Murray Mints. He stepped out of the shop and let the door bang shut behind him, the bell above it dinging loudly.

A few minutes later, he spotted a bench, so he sat down and opened the bag of sweets, popping one in his mouth and sucking it slowly, leaning back and watching the traffic go by. A pang pierced his heart again as his thoughts went to his mom. How could Tadeo hurt his own sister? A tear rolled down his cheek and he wiped it away out of habit.

A police car drove by and Benito wondered for the hundredth time what would happen to him. The thought that his friends could help him entered his mind. Could they do anything? Pamela's dad was a cop; in America, but still a cop. Pamela was the kind of person who would do whatever she could to help her friends. Benito wondered if he could somehow get a lesser sentence in a more 'relaxed' prison, since he was 'under duress' when he committed crimes. He had heard about that kind of thing in police dramas. He wondered if it worked in real life.

Benito looked at the time and stood up, walking slowly back to Keegan's place. As he reached the hedge that ran along the front, on either side of the drive, a thought came to him. He hadn't been able to finish his note that he had left Toby and the others, so they probably wouldn't even find the street, but maybe God would guide them. It wouldn't hurt to leave a clue for them as well.

He looked at his watch as he stepped inside Keegan's house. It had been exactly thirty minutes. The living room was empty, but by the time Benito had taken off his shoes and put them in the front hall cupboard, Keegan was walking down the stairs. He walked up to Benito and took the bag of shopping from him.

Unsure of what to do next, Benito walked across the deep carpet and up the stairs to put his Murray Mints on the cupboard by his bed. He sat down, wishing that he had his Bible with him. A picture of the precious Book split open at the bottom of the stairs flashed in his mind and he wondered if Tadeo would leave it there or throw it out.

Just then, Keegan and Marlene's bedroom door opened and Marlene came out. She shut the door firmly, turning in the opposite direction to Benito and walked slowly down the stairs. He waited a few minutes, then followed her.

Marlene was in the kitchen making Keegan a cup of coffee. She looked over her shoulder as Benito walked in. He saw that her eyes were red, but he said nothing. He also noted that she had replaced her t-shirt for a red, long sleeve top.

"Hello, sweetheart, would you like a drink? We are going to watch a movie, if you would like to join us. It is about a man who is the only survivor of a plane crash and has to survive in a jungle."

"Wasn't that just released in the cinemas last week? How ..." Benito's voice trailed off as he realised that for nefarious people like Keegan and Tadeo, getting a newly released movie on your TV was incidental. He continued in a different direction, "Sure. May I have a hot chocolate?"

Marlene glanced at Keegan who nodded, commanding, "Sit down in the living room and she will bring it over to you. I don't want you to spill it."

Obediently, Benito took the chair to the right side of the sofa as he usually did, while Keegan placed his coffee on the table and walked over to open the doors that covered the television. He sat back down and pulled out his phone to connect the movie.

Marlene shortly came over to Benito and handed him his drink, and as she stretched out her hand, he saw the dark red marks on her wrist and he flinched involuntarily. He took the cup carefully.

"Thank you, Marlene."

She smiled weakly and turned to sit by Keegan. As she did, Benito noticed what looked like a wet mark on the back of her t-shirt.

"Marlene!" he called out sharply, not wanting her to get in trouble for staining the back of the sofa. "It looks like you have something wet on your back."

Keegan saw the mark as she started to sit, and pushed her off with both hands on her back. Marlene squealed in pain and Benito realised what the mark was – blood. Benito felt sick as he imagined what Keegan had done to her while he had gone on his errand. Hatred welled up in him, and wanted to launch himself at Keegan, but he knew he was no match for the evil reptile man, so he sat motionless.

"Oh! Baby, that must be where you fell in those rose bushes out front! Let's go upstairs and I'll have a look at the cuts." Keegan put his arm around her shoulder, giving her a kiss on the cheek, then followed her upstairs to the bathroom to 'help' her clean up her wounds.

Benito held the cup of hot chocolate in both hands, staring into the steamy liquid. His stomach rolled around and he put the cup down on a coaster beside him, swallowing hard. He breathed in deeply, trying to think of anything other than his mom or Marlene. Closing his eyes, he imagined he was back in Louisiana playing Monopoly with Pamela and her aunt, along with the others, during the hurricane, and he smiled. They were all such kind people. They would help him, he knew they would. If only they could find him.

"You better not waste that!" Keegan's annoyed voice broke through into Benito's dream and he woke with a start. Keegan was pointing to the drink which no longer had any steam. Benito shook his head and picked it up, carefully drinking down the sweet, lukewarm liquid.

"Put it in the dishwasher," commanded Keegan when Benito went to put the empty cup down on the coaster. Obediently, the teenager stood up and walked into the kitchen immediately.

As he came back into the living room, Marlene reached the bottom of the steps wearing a different long sleeve top. She smiled at Benito as she sat down next to Keegan, snuggling into his arm.

"Thanks, babe." She looked up at him and he smiled down at her.

Benito sat back down, saying nothing. Keegan turned on the movie, and for an hour and forty five minutes, Benito immersed himself in the surviving man's adventures in the jungle.

———⸎———

"I think I would like to learn how to ride a motorcycle," commented Rebeca as they left the museum. "I believe it would be quite enjoyable."

"I've got a bike," said Joe, "I'll give you a ride when we get back home." He took her hand and squeezed it tightly, and she smiled up at him.

"Oh! That would be lovely, thank you!"

Not to be outdone, Toby grabbed her other hand. "But first! I will take you on a boat ride with some live commentary!"

They all laughed, the three of them holding hands as they walked down the road through the car park to where they would meet the taxi that would take them back to the canal.

On the journey back, they decided to be dropped off at the Canal House so they could have some lunch before the boat tour. They chose a table outside and the boys looked at the menus. Rebeca sat back in the chair, stretching out her legs and closing her eyes, enjoying the warm summer sun.

"Are you not ordering anything?" asked Toby as he touched her arm.

Rebeca kept her eyes closed as she said lazily, "Would you choose something for me? I would rather just relax here and let someone else decipher the menu for me!"

Toby laughed softly and smiled at her even though her eyes were shut. It must be tiring to choose meals when you had to continually ask questions about various dishes. He decided on the pork belly curry for himself and the caesar salad with ham for Rebeca, and Joe chose the fish and chips.

While they waited, conversation turned to Benito, and Toby dug into the pocket of his jeans and pulled out the scrap of paper that Benito had left as a clue.

"Gone to Worcester C...", he said out loud. He sighed deeply, squinting his eyes. "Gone to Worcester. Come and rescue me?!" He twisted his mouth. "Or *is* it a G?" He shoved the paper back in his pocked and tapped the table with his fingertips, frustratedly. "If only he had written more. If only ...", his voice trailed off as he wondered if his friend was okay. Benito's uncle was a nasty man and who knew what he was getting Benito to do for him; or what he was doing to Benito.

Their food arrived just then, and as they all began eating hungrily, conversation turned to lighter things. Rebeca was pleased with Toby's choice for her and decided if they came back to eat, she would order the same again.

Soon, they were on the boat, enjoying the relaxing ride along the water and listening to the history of the canals in Birmingham from a live person.

⟶➤●◀⟵

Just as the credits were rising, there was a tap on the door and Tadeo walked in, grinning widely.

"All sorted for tomorrow! Right, let's discuss what is going to happen and what each of you will be doing!"

Tadeo sat in the chair opposite Benito and everyone focused their attention on him.

"Okay. There are three antiques dealers that have gotten together to do an exclusive, invitation only, three-day exhibition, 10:00 to 6:00 each day. They have gotten three owners to lend them some antique jewellery. Although they are all worth a reasonable amount of money, one of the items is priceless: a gold antique necklace set with rubies, white diamonds and one blue diamond." He cleared his throat before continuing. "It was supposed to be displayed on the last day, but they suddenly changed things around and it will now be the one displayed on the first day – presumably the last minute change of plans is to stop anyone from planning to steal it!" He grinned. He held up a thick white envelope, opened it up and pulled out a fancy invitation card written deep golden script, with a QR code on the bottom left hand corner. "I just managed to get the boy and me an invitation to see this exhibition tomorrow."

Benito's heart fell. Tadeo's piercing blue eyes locked on to Benito's gentle brown ones, daring him to defy him. Benito swallowed hard and said nothing, a dark despair pervading his entire being. He felt certain it would land him in the deepest darkest prison for a very long time. The teenager glanced over at Marlene, but her face was emotionless with only her eyes showing the heavy sadness within her.

"Are you listening, boy?!" Tadeo's booming voice brought Benito's attention back to his uncle. "You need to know exactly what is happening. I don't want no mistakes. This is my big break, and if you mess it up, you're finished!"

Benito wondered if that wouldn't be a good thing, but then decided that if Tadeo was going to kill him, it would be a long, slow, painful process. He focused his eyes on his uncle, and listened intently to all the instructions.

<hr />

"I actually enjoyed that!" said Joe, giving Rebeca a one arm hug. "I thought it was going to be boring, but it was really good."

"Ya, me too," said Toby, who grabbed Rebeca's hand and pulled her gently away from Joe. He looked at his watch. "3:30. Why don't we go back to the hotel and have a swim?"

"That sounds nice," said Rebeca, unwilling to let go of Toby's hand, despite herself. "Although I do wish it was not so ... so ... it smells funny." She wrinkled her nose. "It does not smell natural, like the river."

"That'll be the chlorine," laughed Joe. Seeing her perplexed look, he explained, "They add chlorine – a bleach ... a cleaning agent – to kill all the germs. The people in this 'civilised' society don't like to swim in other people's germs." He chuckled, taking her other hand.

"I think this civilised society is rather obsessed with *sanitisation*." She perked up, pleased to finally use the word she had found a few days previously.

"Rebeca, I do believe your vocabulary is better than Joe's!" Toby laughed, and without relinquishing Rebeca's hand, Joe reached over and ruffled Toby's hair vigorously.

When Toby leaned over to retaliate, Rebeca held on to both of them tightly and spread her arms wide. "Enough of that hooliganish behaviour!" She giggled, and the brothers relented, as the three walked hand in hand light-heartedly back to the hotel.

Soon, they were all changed into bathing suits and swimming in the cool water of the pool where they were the only occupants. Wanting to appease Rebeca, the boys kept the splashing and rough-housing to a minimum, relishing the chance to cool down from the hot summer day.

———————>●<———————

Finally, Tadeo finished explaining his plan, and he turned to Keegan. "I need you to come out with me for one last thing." When he saw Keegan looking uncertainly at Marlene and Benito, he added, "We'll only be twenty minutes."

Keegan nodded, and shortly the two men were out the door and Benito heard them get in Tadeo's BMW and drive off down the road.

Marlene and Benito sat in silence for a while. Then suddenly, Marlene stood and walked quickly to the kitchen. "Sweetheart, I have a considerable amount of money saved up from over the past few years. Whenever Keegan has given me money for things, I've kept a little back and hidden it. I want you to have it. You need to leave. Now."

"No! I can't!" He followed her into the kitchen and touched her arm gently as she knelt in front of the cupboard leaning under the kitchen sink. "*You* need to leave Marlene. Please! I don't want him to hurt you any more!"

"It's not enough for me to set up a life for myself," she said sadly, "but it is enough for you to go off and find your friends.

They will help you." She bit her lip. "I don't have any friends any more."

"I'm your friend, Marlene." Benito said quietly, then added pleadingly, "Please, keep saving until you have enough to get away from rept ... Keegan."

Marlene smiled and turned to give him a hug as he knelt beside her. "You're a sweet boy." She breathed out heavily, "I'm a soiled woman. Worthless. My family would never have me back. I have nothing and no one. You have people who love you and will take care of you."

"God loves you, Marlene," Benito insisted.

"A wretched woman like me?" She laughed cynically. "I think God has given up on me as well!"

"While we were still sinners, Christ died for us ..."

Marlene tilted her head: "What does that mean?"

Benito thought for a moment about the things he had read and learned. He said, "Christ took the punishment for our sins. All we have to do is be truly sorry for the things we have done wrong, and trust in Him." He paused, "I wish I had my Bible with me."

Marlene thought for a moment, then turned her attention back to the cleaning products under the sink and methodically moved them out until she found the one she wanted. She had cut a bleach bottle in half, then slid the top back slightly over the bottom so it still looked whole. Taking it out, she pulled it apart and gasped.

"It's gone!" She started trembling. "He must have found it! That's why ... why ...", she burst into tears and Benito hugged her, finishing her sentence.

"Why he beat you so badly today."

She nodded as the tears flowed. Benito struggled to keep back his own tears as he thought of how this poor woman had ended up in Keegan's grip.

"Marlene," Benito said, "Why do you keep saying you love him and showing him affection when he is so awful to you?"

Marlene said nothing for a moment as she looked at Benito sadly. "I pretend. I keep pretending, thinking that if I pretend enough, I will really grow to feel that way and it will all be okay." She bit her lip. "Or ... maybe ... if I keep showing him love ... one day ... he will love me."

Suddenly, Marlene stopped crying and wiped her eyes with the back of her hands. "I better get these things back in the cupboard. You go upstairs. It's best we aren't together when they come back." With shaking hands, she hurriedly began replacing the items as Benito stood up and trotted across the living room and upstairs. He lay on his bed just as he heard the front door open.

"Looking for something, Marlene?" Benito heard Keegan say sarcastically.

"Oh, just a scourer. I thought we had more down here, but I guess I'll have to add it to the shopping list."

Benito came down the stairs and saw Keegan in the kitchen, his arm around Marlene. He kissed her cheek.

"I thought I might do the shopping from now on, baby. I put too much on you. It's not fair."

Marlene said nothing, and lowered her eyes as Keegan leaned in and whispered something into her ear. Benito saw a terrified look cross her face, but then she tilted her head back and gave him a faint smile.

"Make us a coffee, Marlene." Keegan said out loud, as he turned back to the living room and sat down, with Tadeo doing likewise.

She walked over to the coffee maker and filled the machine with water and coffee. "Anything else, Keeg?"

"Get Tadeo and me a slice of that chocolate cake." He glanced at Benito who was standing in the middle of the room.

Tadeo looked over at the numb teenager. "You need to rest, boy. Go up to your room and lie down for a few hours."

"Yes sir," said Benito meekly and obediently returned to his room.

CHAPTER 13

Toby, Rebeca and Joe sat in the boys' room, dried and changed back into their clothes. The boys were watching the ending of the news while they waited for a football game to come on. Rebeca was sat between the two of them on the sofa, reading a newspaper that she had picked up from the lobby.

Rebeca put down the paper when she heard a news flash about a house fire that had killed an entire family.

"How awful!" she commented, watching the report.

"Everyone is devastated in this close-knit community in Gloucester Green." The reporter was saying.

"That is a city south of here, is it not?" Rebeca asked the boys.

"No," began Toby, "Well, Gloucester is a city south of here, but Gloucester Green is a street name in Birming ...".

The three of them looked at each other and shouted in unison, "A street name!"

Both boys began tapping on their phones, but Joe got there first, and the other two leaned over to look at the screen.

"There are two streets with Worcester in the name: Worcester Crescent and Worcester Green."

"Well, it could be either, but at least that has narrowed down the search!" said Toby, and the three of them squeezed enthusiastically into one hug.

"What am I missing?" A voice called out from the door and they all turned to see Gwen walk in the room smiling and in a decidedly happier manner than when she had left the previous day.

"Hello, Gwen!" Toby greeted her with a smile, then frowned, "How did you get in?"

Gwen held up her key card. "They're programmed for both rooms!" She giggled like a school girl and sat down opposite the other three, her hands folded neatly on her lap.

Joe suddenly felt awkward, unsure of what to say after her revelation to him, and then her change of demeanour now.

"We have some new information on Benito's whereabouts!" burst out Toby, jubilantly, realising his brother's discomfort, and he launched into explaining what they had just that moment discovered.

"That's great news!" Gwen agreed, keeping her hands folded in her lap.

Rebeca noticed it first, though she did not automatically link it to an engagement. "That is a very beautiful diamond, Gwen!" And she walked over and sat beside Gwen to look at it closer. "And all those lovely emeralds surrounding it – how pretty they all are together. Did Richard give it to you?"

Gwen laughed, "Yes, we got engaged! We're going to be married after my 21st birthday next year."

Joe and Toby were unsure of what to say, but Rebeca filled the silence as she burst out, "When a man chooses his bride in our villages, he kills a male deer and brings it to her and her family to eat – to show that he can provide for her."

Gwen made a face. "How truly *awful*! Wouldn't you rather have a ring like this?!"

Rebeca let the insult slide over her. "You cannot eat a ring," she said simply, and the boys chuckled as they walked over to dutifully examine Gwen's ring.

"He said he looked absolutely everywhere to find a ring that was as special as me! He loves me. I was wrong about him. He truly loves me." Gwen sighed deeply and gazed out the window, flushed as she remembered her time with Richard.

"That … that is great to hear," said Joe slowly, and when Toby looked at him Joe glared back, silently demanding that

Toby forget everything he had told him about Gwen, and Toby nodded in understanding.

Rebeca watched the exchange between the two brothers and although she didn't know what it was, she sensed the mournfulness in Joe and she felt saddened that something had hurt him. However, she was pleased that things had turned out well for Gwen.

"I'm so pleased for you, Gwen!" She gave her a hesitant hug, which Gwen happily received. Then Rebeca asked, "When will you be twenty-one?"

"The thirtieth of June."

Rebeca frowned, "But that is ten months away! That is a very long time to wait."

Gwen rolled her eyes. "Don't tell me, your people only wait a month?"

Rebeca hesitated but then dove in with her answer, "Actually, when the man brings the deer, if it is accepted by the father of the woman he has chosen, the whole village celebrates by skinning and gutting the deer. Then, while it is cooking over the fire, the chief performs the official union ceremony. After that, there is much eating and drinking and dancing and at the end of the evening, if the man is from another village, the woman leaves with him to his village. If he is from the same village, He goes into his hut and waits for some of the married women to pick up the bride's bed, with her on it, and carry it into her new husband's hut." She paused as they all stared at her, "And then the village continues to celebrate until dawn with much dancing and fermented cassava!" When her explanation was met by complete silence, Rebeca was decidedly thankful that she had left out some of the details.

"Well!" said Gwen finally, making a face, "our weddings are much more detailed! There is so much to plan and things to choose. The wedding dress for one! And all the bridesmaids' dresses and the men's suits. Then there's the venue to choose, the food, the flowers, etc. And of course you have to decide who you will invite, and choose the invitations. Not to mention the honeymoon to plan!" She leaned back in the chair, exhaling in delight, and held her hand up to gaze at the ring, turning it until she could see the light sparkling through it. "Richard says I can choose where we go. I'm thinking maybe a month long Caribbean cruise around all the islands."

"I don't fancy going on one of those huge boats," said Joe, feeling irritable. "Too many people!" He scowled, and Toby nodded in agreement. Not knowing anything about cruises, other than the canal trip they had just taken, Rebeca said nothing.

Gwen looked at them, open-mouthed for a moment, a bewildered look crossing her face. Suddenly she laughed hysterically. "Oh my goodness! Are you kidding me?! You actually think I would go on a cruise liner??" She laughed haughtily and Joe was beginning to wonder what he had actually thought he had seen in her. "Richard's family has a 200-foot yacht!"

A hush fell on the room as the boys and Rebeca digested this information and Gwen again gazed at her ring as she held it up to the light.

"What is a yacht?" asked Rebeca finally.

"A boat with bedrooms and other various rooms on it," explained Joe.

"Oh." Rebeca thought for a moment. "That sounds like a very large boat," said Rebeca simply, frowning as she tried to picture it in her mind.

"Well, it has to be large to hold a swimming pool and a cinema and eight bedrooms and dance hall and gym and … well, everything one *needs* when one goes on holiday!"

"That is terrific," said Toby finally. "I am glad it all worked out for you, Gwen."

"Uh ... ya ... just terrific," said Joe unenthusiastically. "I'm hungry – shall we go get some food?"

Gwen was too lost in her own pleasure to notice Joe's attitude, and just looked out the window smiling. A few seconds later, she turned back to the others who were waiting for her to reply, and she giggled again.

"Of course! Yes!" Suddenly she frowned. "I just realised: you won't have the appropriate clothing to wear. We better leave now and get clothes for each of you." She tapped on her phone and ordered a taxi to take them to a clothing store.

Twenty minutes later, they all walked into a shop that Toby and Joe would never have even stepped foot in before. Again, Rebeca was oblivious to the difference in clothing stores, so she just walked over to some dresses and started looking.

A well-spoken man in his twenties came over immediately to Gwen. "Good evening Miss Wentworth! How may I help you today?" He gave a little bow and she waved her hand out to Joe and Toby. "We are going out to dinner in half an hour, and I'm afraid my friends here ... have ... lost their luggage. Could you please find them something to wear to Carters?"

The man nodded, then looked toward Rebeca, "Shall I get Maria to help with your other friend?"

"Yes, Charles – and myself! I fancy a new dress today – I'm celebrating my engagement!" She held out her hand and the man took it, oohing and ahhhing appropriately as he gazed at her ring.

"How marvellous! Do we know the very fortunate man?"

Gwen shook her head. "Probably not – he's American. He does not spend a lot of time over here. Though that might change as he has just bought his first company over here and is hoping to expand it in the future."

"How wonderful! I look forward to meeting him. One moment, Miss Wentworth while I go and find Maria. I think she took a phone call just before you came in."

Gwen nodded and turned to Rebeca, linking arms with her. "This way, Rebeca, let's have a little browse!"

Joe and Toby turned to the men's clothing and casually looked through them, waiting for Charles to return.

"There aren't any price tags on these," noted Toby.

Joe sneered, "If you have to ask, you can't afford it!"

"This one feels really nice," said Toby, taking out a navy suit that looked like it would fit him.

"That is because it is silk, sir," said Charles, and the brothers turned at his voice. "And a very fine choice, if I may say so." He pointed to the back of the shop. "There is a room over there where you can try it on."

Charles reached into the rack and pulled out a suit with a more fitted style, a slightly different shade of blue, and an almost purple hue to it. "And I think this one, for you, sir. The colour goes well with your skin and hair tone, while the fitting accentuates your solid frame."

Joe raised an eyebrow as he took the suit from the man and Toby, who was still standing nearby, snickered. The man walked over to the rail opposite the suits, and picked out a shirt for each of them. "I believe these will go well with those suits," said Charles as he pointed the way to the dressing room.

Joe stepped forward towards the changing rooms, then stopped and turned to Charles. "We didn't lose our luggage. We are just normal people who don't wear fancy suits. Gwen is just embarrassed because she's a snob."

Toby stood staring with his mouth open, but Charles was trained well. He smiled warmly and replied without hesitation, "We like to take good care of all of our customers, sir, and I will ensure that you all leave happy and well dressed!"

Joe and Toby walked back in the direction that Charles pointed and found two large rooms. The girls had disappeared, and they assumed Maria was taking care of them.

When they were out of earshot of Charles, Toby spoke up, "That was really rude, Joe, even for you!"

"I don't need you lecturing me on manners, Tobs. I won't tolerate being treated so abhorrently, not even by that beautiful cow of a creature, Miss Wentworth."

While the brothers were changing into their suits, Charles slipped some shoes into each of their rooms. Once fully dressed, Joe and Toby came out to look at each other.

"Wow!" Toby spoke first, "You look really smart in that fitted suit over your *solid frame*!" He laughed, even though he meant what he said.

Joe smiled and looked at himself in the mirror, and despite his annoyance he thought the whole outfit made him look quite handsome. He looked over at Toby smiling, "And you look ready to go out and charm the world, as well, little brother!"

Just then, Gwen and Rebeca came around the corner and the brother's jaws dropped. Gwen looked stunning in a deep purple silk dress and Rebeca wore a linen crimson one; both were fitted to accentuate their figures.

"You two look gorgeous!" exclaimed Toby. Joe could only nod his head.

Gwen did a twirl, but Rebeca stood awkwardly with hands to the side, and looked questioningly to Joe and Toby.

"So ...", she started, "are you saying that I have 'scrubbed up well'?"

Toby walked towards her and grabbed her hands, swinging her slowly in a circle, then pulling her close speaking quietly into her ear, making her blush as he said, "You aren't making this 'staying away from you' business easy for me." Out loud, he said, "you look stunning." He looked at Gwen, "You both do!"

Charles reappeared along with a woman – presumably Maria.

"You all look amazing! Is everyone happy?" He smiled with arms opened wide.

"Perfectly, as usual, Charles. And Maria! Thank you very much! Would you get a taxi for us, please?"

Charles nodded and turned swiftly, heading out the door to flag down a taxi. Two minutes later, the four of them were in the cab heading towards Carters of Moseley.

"What about the clothing we left behind?" asked Rebeca practically.

"Maria will send it to our hotel." Gwen suddenly remembered Benito, "So! Tell me what's your plan to find Benito?"

"Well, I was thinking, depending on what time we finish dinner, we could perhaps swing around to Worcester Crescent, as it is the smaller road, and see if we can find anything. If not, after breakfast, we could then tackle Worcester Grove."

They all started talking enthusiastically, wondering if they were finally going to find Benito, but the conversation was cut short as they were soon at the restaurant.

As they entered the restaurant, Joe and Toby suddenly felt out of place and awkward. Rebeca, not understanding the differences between people with money and those with less, was more concerned about deciphering a new menu. Gwen gave her name to the *maître de* and he promptly escorted them to their table, where Rebeca turned to her and said,

"I will have whatever you have, Gwen."

Joe and Toby looked at the menu and found it difficult to not show shock at the prices; and for the first time they too were stumped as to what to order, so Gwen ordered for all of them, along with some wine and a bottle of Peroni lager for each of the boys.

Twenty minutes later, the food arrived, and although it was delicious, Joe and Toby secretly thought there was not enough of it, and Joe whispered quietly to Toby who was next to him, "Think I might need a burger after this!" Toby laughed, but nodded in agreement.

By seven o'clock, they were in another taxi back to the hotel to quickly change before getting in yet another cab to Worcester Crescent.

"Shall we split up like before?" asked Toby to the others, and they agreed that that would be the most efficient way to search. They looked at the map on Toby's phone and soon Joe and Gwen headed off to find the other end of the road to start their search.

After walking for several minutes without speaking, Gwen finally said, "Joe, about what I told you yesterday…"

Joe carried on walking, looking straight ahead, "Don't worry, it didn't mean anything to me. I've already forgotten it."

"Joe!" She touched his arm and he stopped, still looking ahead. "Joe, please. He said he loved me. He *loves* me, Joe." Her voice started to quiver and he looked her in the eyes that were now moist, as she finished, "No one has ever said they loved me before."

"You mean, no one but your parents have ever said they love you," Joe corrected her.

Gwen's face grew even sadder, "I don't remember my parents ever saying that to me."

Joe started to soften, fighting the urge to embrace her. Then, self preservation kicked in and an icy wall shot up around his heart as he spoke coldly, "Well, that's good. I can't imagine why, but least there is one person in the world who feels affection for you!"

Tears freely flowed down her face as she looked at Joe, bewildered and hurt at his unkind words, but Joe's resolve hardened as he frowned at her and, turning back to continue walking along the road, he called over his shoulder,

"Come on, we're losing what light we've got left."

Gwen took out a tissue to wipe her eyes and blow her nose, then swallowed hard before walking briskly to catch up with Joe. They walked along in silence, looking at the houses and the cars out front.

Finally, after ten minutes, Joe's conscience kicked in. Without looking at her he said, "Look, Gwen, I'm sorry. That was mean of me." He took a deep breath. "I'm pleased for you. I …". Joe's eye caught sight of a blue BMW on the next drive. "Oh! I think that's it!"

Gwen excitedly tapped on her phone, then broke the news to Joe. "Sorry, it's the wrong number plate."

"Oh," he said disappointedly, looking into her emerald eyes meaningfully, "looks like I got all excited for nothing … again."

Gwen's heart twisted in understanding, and for a brief moment, she wished her life was simple, as she gazed back up at him. Joe leaned forward and drew her close to him as he wrapped his arms tightly around her, burying his face in her short silky hair. He could feel her soaking up his embrace and he closed his eyes. After a long moment, he released her, looking at her tenderly.

She held his hands tightly, as she said hesitantly, "Joe … I …"

He put two fingers gently on her rose lips and said softly, "Shhh! We'll say no more." Keeping hold of one hand, he began walking, and spoke lightly, "Come on, we may yet find that Benito."

Ten minutes later, they met up with Rebeca and Toby and each revealed their disappointed lack of finds.

"Never mind!" Said Rebeca hopefully, "Maybe we will find him tomorrow!"

"Yes! We'll come back first thing after breakfast!" said Toby.

"Oh!" started Rebeca, "I was hoping to find a church service tomorrow morning to attend. It is Sunday, and I like to go to a service on a Sunday."

Joe tapped on his phone. "I've found an evangelical church that looks good, not so far from the hotel. Service is at 10:30."

"That sounds fine," said Toby, "I don't suppose Benito and Tadeo will be doing anything much on a Sunday!"

———⟫●⟪———

Benito was allowed downstairs later for some chicken and chips that Keegan had purchased from his local chip shop. When they were all nearly finished, a ping drew Keegan's attention to his phone and he squinted thoughtfully.

"Hmmmm, might have a job for Benito tonight that will make up for last night's loss."

"No," replied Tadeo firmly without looking up from his chips.

Keegan frowned and turned angry, "He needs to make up for what I lost."

Tadeo looked up, staring at Keegan across the table, his blue eyes flashing, "I said no!"

Marlene and Benito glanced at each other worriedly as the tension in the kitchen mounted quickly. Benito guessed the men were equally matched physically, with perhaps Tadeo having a slight edge.

"You owe me!" Keegan slammed his fist on the table with a bang and leaned forward trying to intimidate Tadeo.

"I owe you nothing!" seethed Tadeo, "You screwed up yourself – you should have checked your sources better!"

He paused a moment as Keegan deliberated his next move. "I don't want nothin' happenin' to the kid before tomorrow! After that, you can HAVE the kid if you like, and you can do whatever you want with him!"

Benito started coughing as the chicken he was swallowing caught in his throat, and his ears began ringing as panic set in and his heart sent his blood racing through his body at great speed. A worried look passed Marlene's face, but she said nothing. Tadeo leaned over and gave Benito a heavy smack on the back that dislodged the chicken, but unfortunately it ended back up on his plate.

Keegan jumped up in disgust, "Get out of here!" Marlene stood, reaching for Benito's plate as she anticipated his next words, "And get that out of my sight, woman!"

Benito scurried out of the kitchen and headed towards the front door, barefoot but ready to leave as instructed before he was beaten up by snake eyes.

"Stop!" shouted Tadeo, and Benito stopped dead with his hand on the handle, not knowing which man to listen to. He didn't budge as his chest moved in and out rapidly, trying to breathe.

Tadeo's voice calmed slightly as he tried to reason with Keegan, "He ain't goin' nowhere, Keegan. We had a deal. A deal that will make you lots of money. After that …".

"I don't want him here *permanently*, I just want him now and again," began Keegan, calming down slightly as he thought about the amount that Tadeo had offered him. He certainly did not want to lose out on that.

There was silence as both men attempted to keep their dominance. Benito waited, his hand still on the front door, facing away from the men.

"Go up to your room, Benito, and stay there until morning," commanded Tadeo finally, and when there was no rebuttal from Keegan, Benito turned with his head down, and obediently walked up to the bedroom.

Benito shut the door behind him – he wasn't interested in listening to anything else either man had to say. None of it was going to be to his good. He sat heavily on his bed and breathed out so deeply, he had to gasp to breath in again. Tears burned his eyes and his heart ached from the exertion of panic, and from thoughts of what had happened to his mom.

He whispered a prayer that her ending had been painless and that she was now enjoying peace with Jesus. A peace crept into him as he thought about the fact that he would see her again, in a place devoid of evil and where joy abounded.

He pulled open his drawer to get a Murray Mint and was surprised to find a book on top of his sweets. He picked it up and smiled as he realised what it was. A Bible. Marlene must have put it there. He was not sure why there would be a Bible in this house, but he propped himself up on the bed in a comfortable sitting position, opened it up, and began reading where he had left off in the book of Matthew.

———◦◦◦———

Gwen decided to go to the girls' room early and have a soak in a deep bubble bath before bed, so she left Rebeca in the boys' living room watching the television.

The moment the door clicked shut after her, Joe's stomach growled loudly and Toby laughed.

"Me too, brother! Come on, let's go get some real food!" Toby glanced at Rebeca, "How about you?"

Her lips slowly formed a sheepish grin, then giggled as she nodded, "I do believe I could eat something else, as well!"

As they stepped out into the cool evening air, they discussed where they would go. As usual, Rebeca let the boys decide, and they quickly decided on pizza. They began heading towards the nearest restaurant when Joe thought to look at his watch.

"Oh! They'll be closed soon. I better just order a takeaway and have them deliver it here." Toby and Rebeca agreed and when he had placed the order, they went back in the hotel to wait in the lobby.

Soon, they were back in the boys' room with two fourteen-inch pizzas – one Hawaiian and one Fully Loaded. They sat at the table in the kitchenette to eat, since they boys felt they did not want to make any more mess anywhere for maintenance to have to clear up.

"I think," began Rebeca, as she leaned back contentedly in her chair, "I will have to teach my people to make pizza! That is one thing that I have discovered here that I do very much enjoy eating!"

———————

Benito opened his eyes and blinked rapidly at the darkness that greeted him. A sliver of moonlight shone through the window, revealing the silhouettes of the few items in the room. Something was lying heavily on his chest. Gideon??

His hand went up to his chest and he found the Bible resting open and upside down. He must have fallen asleep reading it and he wondered who had turned out his light. A pang shot through him as he thought of his furry friend and asked God to find him a good home where someone loved him.

Closing up the precious Book, he put it back in the drawer on top of the mints, taking one out and popping it in his mouth. He wasn't sure why he found them so comforting. Maybe it was because his dad used to buy them for him. His dad had died while Benito was young, but he retained flashes of memories. Like anytime he was sad, his dad would give him a Murray Mint. He seemed to have an unending supply in a little jar in the kitchen. He never saw his dad put them in, and Benito used to think it was magic, that the mints would just keep filling up the container all by themselves. In fact, Benito thought he remembered his dad telling him that very thing.

Crunching the last little bit, he lay back down and closed his eyes, and very quickly Benito was by the sea of Galilee gathering up a fishing net as Jesus walked up to him and told him to leave his net, and follow Him.

CHAPTER 14

Sunday 21st August

"Get up, boy! We've got a busy day ahead!"

Benito's eye's shot open and he looked across the room to where his uncle was stood in the doorway. Automatically, the teenager sat up in response, rubbing his eyes. He could smell frying onions and his stomach gurgled its pleasure.

Tadeo said nothing, but waited for Benito to start moving towards the door before he headed back downstairs with Benito following closely behind.

Cheese and onion omelettes lay on three plates at the table and Benito wondered who was not eating. Marlene smiled faintly, and silently poured Benito a large glass of juice, then sat down opposite him beside Keegan and began eating some muesli.

The clock on the kitchen wall read 9:00. Benito silently wondered what time they were going to this exhibition. Benito jumped when Tadeo answered his question.

"We leave at 10:30. I want to get this thing done, but I don't want to be there first thing. So I figure if we arrive just after 10:45, that should be just right."

Benito thought that his uncle was giving him lots of time to eat, and was unsure why he had had to get up at that time.

"We need to get our disguises and the plan perfect before we go," Tadeo replied to Benito's unasked question, and again Benito was concerned that his uncle might be able to read his mind.

Benito ate his omelette and toast quickly, and despite the nerves darting about his stomach, he enjoyed his delicious breakfast and thanked Marlene, whom he assumed had made it.

"Actually, it was me," said Keegan and he cast a sideways glance at Marlene, "She can't make an omelette to save her life, poor thing." Marlene responded with a weak smile at Benito who decided it was best to say nothing more.

Soon, Tadeo and Benito were up in Tadeo's ensuite bathroom, with Tadeo working on himself first. The teenager watched in amazement as his uncle was slowly transformed into a pale, old man with a grey moustache, who he hardly recognised. When it was Benito's turn, the teenager was disappointed that he did not look as different as his uncle did, but he said nothing. He didn't realise it was because Tadeo was not worried about Benito being recognised after this job – it wouldn't matter.

When the physical transformation had been completed, Tadeo sat Benito down on his bed, and went through the plan step by step, several times, then they acted it out, several times. Finally, Tadeo was satisfied and he looked at his watch. Perfect timing.

As they walked down the stairs and across the living room to the front door, Benito did not see Keegan and Marlene. When they left, Tadeo clicked the bolt down so it would lock when he closed the door. *They must have gone already*, thought Benito.

Benito's stomach began turning as he climbed into the back seat of Tadeo's car. His hands were sweaty and he rubbed them on his trousers. They weren't as effective as jeans for drying hands. Tadeo had felt that jeans were not appropriate at an exclusive exhibition. Tadeo looked in the rear view mirror when he sat down and heard Benito's heavy stressful breathing. He turned around and his piercing blue eyes squinted at his nephew.

"You better calm yourself now. We can't go in with you looking like you are going to rob the place!" Tadeo growled at Benito.

Benito swallowed hard and closed his eyes, breathing out slowly through his nose; then slowly in and out again, desperately willing his heart to slow down.

"Please, God, help me," flashed through his mind. *What was he thinking?? Was he asking God to help him steal a priceless necklace??* "I don't want to do this, God, but I don't know what to do. I don't want to end up in prison for twenty years, but I ... oh, God, please help me."

He felt calmer after his prayer, but there was no answer to his request. Just silence. Benito opened his eyes and put his hand in his pocket, pulling out one of the three mints he had put there, and popped it in his mouth.

Tadeo watched his nephew and decided he was finally calm enough. "Right, okay, let's go make me a pile of money!" And with that declaration, he turned on the ignition and backed off the drive, then down the road towards the antique show.

There was a large car park at the back of the building, but Tadeo stopped and turned right down a quiet road before he got there. He didn't want his car on any cameras in the parking area, and since he was not going to leave in his car, he certainly didn't want it left there. About fifty metres along the road, he pulled over and parked behind several cars. *Good*, he thought, *no one will notice it.*

When his uncle turned off the car and got out, Benito followed suit and climbed out onto the curb side. He followed close behind, concentrating on his breathing. They turned the corner and walked for several minutes along the road before the building came into view, and Tadeo turned.

"Walk up here beside me, boy! You look awkward trailing along behind me!"

Benito did as he was commanded and trotted a few steps to catch up, then extended his stride to keep up with his uncle.

"And don't look so scared! Look like a bored teenager being dragged along by his father to some exhibition you are not interested in!" ordered Benito through gritted teeth.

Benito concentrated hard and tried to appear bored. He was not sure what that should look like, as boredom was not something he had experienced in his life. Though, he finally decided he could look like a teenager who would rather be anywhere else than where he was at that moment, and his face was transformed as they reached the door.

A well-dressed man was at the entrance, and Tadeo smiled as he handed over his ticket to be scanned. As the man handed it back to Tadeo, he glanced down at Benito and smiled knowingly. He had a couple of teenagers himself.

Tadeo headed in the opposite direction from where several people were gathered around the necklace, and began looking at various other items interestedly. Benito kept his sullen look as his heart threatened to start banging at his rib cage at any moment.

———————————

Gwen had decided to tag along with Toby, Rebeca and Joe, but felt uncomfortable when she did not know any of the songs. The words were on the screen at the front, so she just mouthed them so as to not look like she had never been in a church before. Joe looked down at her and smiled, putting his arm around her and giving her a friendly squeeze. She looked up at him gratefully, and although it made her feel better, she was much happier when they finally sat down and the pastor came to the front to greet them, then to begin his talk by praying. Gwen knew enough to bow her head, and as she folded her hands in front of her she was distracted by her engagement ring.

He said he loves me. She smiled to herself. *After all those things I said about him, he actually cares enough about me to spend all that time looking for a ring as special as me.* She sighed. *Not only does he love me, but he thinks I'm special. No one has ever told me I am special, either.* She imagined all the different shops he would have gone in and all the different rings he looked at, shaking his head and going to another place, until finally – suddenly she was aware that everyone else had leaned back in their seats and were listening to the pastor as he read from Romans 3. She looked sideways at Joe who looked at her quizzically, wondering if she had been deep in prayer. Gwen turned her attention to the man at the front and pretended she was hanging on his every word.

Toby, however, was in fact hanging on the pastor's every word, with certain phrases sticking in his mind: *for all have sinned and fall short of the glory of God … They are justified freely by His grace through the redemption that came by Christ Jesus … Where then is boasting? It is excluded … For we conclude that a man is justified by faith apart from the works of the law.*

Toby's mind was flooded with his sinful words, thoughts and actions that he had been unable or unwilling to prevent and he was convicted of how truly incapable he was of being 'good'. However, he was comforted by the fact that no one was 'good'. Not one.

A great burden fell from his shoulders. There was nothing he could do to save himself from hell. Only Jesus could do that, and it was free.

By the time the service was over, Toby could not stop smiling and Rebeca looked at him questioningly.

"What is it, Toby?"

"I get it, Rebeca. I understand what you were trying to tell me in Louisiana when I got angry with you." He hugged her tightly and whispered in her ear, "I understand."

———⟫●⟪———

Benito was concentrating so hard on calming himself, looking sullen and sticking close to Tadeo, that he was startled when he realised they were finally standing in front of the priceless necklace. Two large security guards were standing on either side of the stand on which it was displayed, while the woman who had organised the exhibition was standing next to it, expounding on the gold chain and each precious stone.

Tadeo opened his mouth to request her to hold it up so they could see it better, but just at that moment, she unsuspectingly obliged him and picked it up carefully, holding it out towards the crowd.

Seconds later, Tadeo let out a cry and fell forward, knocking the necklace out of her hands and falling on top of it as the people gasped. Benito leaned over his uncle, and in the miniscule time it took for the security guards to step forward, the task had been done. The teenager held up the necklace to the man closest to him, and turned back to his uncle, pulling out a phone and tapping as he did so.

"Dad? Dad? Are you all right?" he spoke frantically, then spoke into his phone, "Hello? I ... uh ... I need help, my dad has collapsed! I think he's had a heart attack." He paused a moment pretending to listen, "Yes, he's not long got out of hospital from having a heart attack." Another pause, then he gave their location before adding urgently, "Please hurry!" – pause – "Oh! Thank you!" He placed a hand on Tadeo's back and spoke loudly for the concerned people around them to hear, "It's okay, Dad, they said there's an ambulance just around the corner. Just hang on!" The panic that the people around him heard in his voice was real. Only it was not panic for his father, but for himself, desperate to get out and run far away.

Moments later, a siren was heard outside, and shortly, two paramedics rushed in with a stretcher. The female did most of the speaking as she spoke medical jargon that Benito didn't understand, checking Tadeo's heart beat, his eyes, and other things with various medical implements. Benito's ears began to buzz as all he could think was to run, but he remained where he was, longing for it all to be over.

Finally, they began moving Tadeo out to the ambulance where they said the paramedics could better deal with their patient. Benito gratefully followed them out of the door and onto the ambulance where the man came in the back with them and the woman got behind the wheel to whisk Tadeo away, supposedly, to the hospital.

It wasn't until the doors shut and the ambulance started driving off, that he looked at the man and finally saw the snake eyes. Keegan!

Tadeo laughed and sat up. He grabbed the bag beside him and opened it up, pulling out a change of clothes for himself and Benito.

"Hurry, boy! Take all that off and put these on."

Benito was still in a daze as he complied, and minutes later, they were both transformed into two completely different people that no one would have placed at the scene. Tadeo zipped up the bag and tossed it to the side just as the ambulance stopped.

"Burn it as soon as you get home!" He called out as he opened the back of the door and looked around. There were no houses, just a few warehouses closed up with big wire fences that were locked up well. He jumped out and Keegan gave Benito a nudge to follow. By the time Benito turned around, the ambulance was at the end of the road.

They walked without speaking and Benito stretched his limbs to keep up with Tadeo. The teenager focused on the rhythmic sound of their shoes on the concrete, every now and again their pace going out of sync with each other as Benito slowed up then hurried himself along. The summer sun beat down on them and sweat began to trickle down his back. Tap tap tap went their feet. Tap tap tap – then Benito's mind would wander: *how many years would he spend behind bars – Don't think about that! Focus!* Tap tap tap. Until the two melded together. Tap tap tap – how many years? – Tap tap tap – how many years?

Twenty minutes later, Tadeo and Benito turned up a road into a residential area, and five minutes later, they were at the BMW. Approaching the car, Tadeo glanced at Benito whose head was down, focused on his feet. He clicked the door and got in. Benito climbed in the back, and shut the door firmly. The loud click of the belt fastening snapped him out of his trance and he leaned back and breathed out heavily through his nose, relieved at the silence that entered his brain.

Staring out the window, Benito said nothing as he watched the random houses and people and cars rolling past his view, looking but not seeing, as the images went into his eyes then floated past his brain and out of his head.

He had no idea how long it had been when Tadeo pulled over in a little side street in front of a small shop. Tadeo instructed Benito to come with him as they got out of the car and walked into the store. Benito looked around the small, one-room store. There were shelves full of small household items. Items that looked old and dusty, and probably had been there for years. Items that nobody wanted. Benito wondered if anyone ever came into this shop.

An elderly man sat behind a till reading a paper. Tadeo walked up to him.

"I would like to buy some flowers," he said.

Benito looked around, confused, but the old man nodded and put his hand under the counter. A buzz sounded loudly at the back of the store, and Benito saw a door swing open.

"All of our best flowers are downstairs," the elderly man replied.

Tadeo nodded and walked briskly to the door, with Benito following. A dim light lit a wooden stair case leading down and the two stepped onto the creaking steps as the door shut slowly behind them.

The steps turned twice before they reached the bottom and found another door which was unlocked. Tadeo turned it and they stepped into a small room with a man sat behind a table. His round head was topped with a thick carpet of grey hair that did not look like it belonged to the young face beneath it.

Uncle and nephew sat down in the chairs in front of the table opposite the man, and as they did, Tadeo reached down underneath his thick sweater and pulled the priceless necklace over his head, placing it on the table in front of him, laying it gently on the large soft cloth that was waiting for it. The young, grey-haired man reached out and picked it up carefully, gazing at it through a special glass.

The only sounds were the man as he expressed in various noises his great delight at such a magnificent piece of jewellery and each amazing jewel that adorned it. He scrutinised every millimetre of it, then went over it all again.

Benito was just beginning to understand how being bored felt, when finally, the man laid it delicately back down on the cloth, arranging it as if it was going on display. He stared at it without the glass for a full minute, mesmerised by its breathtaking beauty, then finally looked up at Tadeo.

"She is exactly as I dreamed she would be." A sorrowful look spread across his face. "If only she was mine to keep and behold always." He smiled sadly at Tadeo, "But alas! I can only spend the afternoon with her, and then she must go to her new owner." He reached down beside him, then stood up as he lifted up two briefcases and placed them heavily on the table in front of Tadeo.

Tadeo wasted no time clicking open the brief cases and checking the contents. He took out a little device and flipped through several piles before he was satisfied they were all used and unmarked.

Closing up the suitcases, the large man stood and turned, leaving the room without another word, as Benito yet again followed along behind, up the creaking steps, across the small shop and out the door without a word to the man behind the newspaper at the till.

━━━━➤●◄━━━━

"Right, let's go find Benito!" said Gwen encouragingly as the other three did not appear to be interested in leaving their seats.

Joe gave his brother a hug as they stood up, and finally the four of them left the church and climbed into the taxi that Gwen had waiting to take them to Worcester Green.

As they climbed out of the cab, Joe's stomach growled and he looked at his watch, frowning. "We should have had some lunch first. This is a long road we are checking – we could be a while!" He looked around at the others and asked, "Who is up for getting something to eat first?"

Rebeca and Gwen laughed, but stopped when they saw he was being serious. Toby scowled playfully at his brother and shook his head, but at that moment, his own stomach made some noises and they all chuckled.

Toby patted his stomach and said, "Come on, bro! What's more important, food or finding Benito?" He sighed deeply as he saw contempt in Joe's eyes. "Joe!" he reprimanded him, "You have to stop this! Honestly, Benito did not do anything to you. You terrify the poor kid." Although Toby and Benito were the same age, Benito's personality leaned itself to a much younger person at times and Toby often felt older than him.

Toby locked eyes with Joe who, although at first was unwilling to relent, finally conceded. He opened his mouth to make a rude comment, then shut it. "All right, you win. Let's go save Benito!"

They split up as before and started at opposite ends of the street. Again, Gwen and Joe took the one end, with Toby and Rebeca on the other. Toby grabbed Rebeca's hand and swung it happily as they walked along.

"I feel so free, Rebeca! Like a weight has been lifted that I hadn't realised was there."

Rebeca grinned back at him and squeezed his hand tightly. However, there was something in his manner that made her realise that somehow things were going to be different than she had hoped. Her stomach did a little turn, but she pushed her thoughts away and deciding she was being silly, just revelled in the moment.

"Stop!" called out Rebeca, as she herself stopped walking and turned around. "There was something in that hedge."

"Something in the hedge?" queried Toby, "That doesn't sound very important." He followed her as she walked back a few steps.

"Unless it is an empty packet of mints!" Rebeca's smile reached either side of her face as she reached deep into the hedge, then pulled out the bag that read 'Murray Mints' on the front, and held it up for Toby to see.

"Do you think…?" Toby didn't dare hope.

"How many other people do you suppose there are around here who like these mints that also might stuff them in a hedge?" Suddenly, she dropped her hand by her side and looked over the hedge at the house. Toby's eyes followed.

Rebeca walked up to him and grabbed his hand as the two of them walked on past the house. "Tadeo knows us both," she said unnecessarily, "and Gwen." She thought carefully as they walked. "He didn't see Joe much – I wonder if Tadeo will remember him? Or do you think we should just notify the police?"

Toby was tapping his phone as she spoke. "Joe!" he called out when his brother answered, "I think we found him! Walk quickly to meet up with us." He scrunched his face as he thought of Rebeca's question. "Nah! They might not come straight away. And I don't think he would recognise Joe." He breathed out slowly through his nose. "We didn't really think this through, did we?"

Rebeca raised her eyebrows and shook her head. "Maybe Gwen and Joe have some ideas."

By the time the four reached each other, Joe and Gwen had already begun to form a plan together and they explained it to Toby and Rebeca.

"There's a takeaway not far from here that makes their staff wear silly hats and aprons when they deliver the food. You'd be surprised how just something like that will put people off and they won't recognise people they might have otherwise," Gwen chucked. "My friend did that to me once for a little joke she played on me – and I have known her all my life!"

When the others agreed, Gwen placed an order on the phone for the four of them, and requested it be delivered to a park not far away. Then they headed over to the empty park and sat on a bench by the entrance and waited.

Fifteen minutes later, they saw a moped turn up the road with a delivery box on the back.

"How are you going to get them to hand over their hat and apron?" Asked Rebeca practically. "Are you going to tell them we are playing a joke?"

Gwen shook her head. "They might very well say that they were not allowed to do that." She pulled out her purse and counted four fifty-pound notes, and the others raised their eyebrows at the sight of someone carrying around that much cash. "This, I am sure, will do the trick."

The boy flipped down the stand and opened up his box and took out a bag as Gwen walked up to him.

"Hey there!" Gwen smiled and the boy nearly dropped the bag as he saw her. She winked at him and came up close with the money in her hand. The boy looked down at the money and up at Gwen questioningly. "My friends and I," she nodded over her shoulder at the other three as they sat on the bench watching, "want to play a joke on another friend and we wondered if we could buy your hat and apron." Gwen took the heavy bag of food out of his hand. "Why don't you just go home, and get another hat and apron – I'm sure they give you a few."

The boy stood for a moment, unsure of whether being so close to someone so beautiful or the prospect of a lot of extra cash was the most exciting. He suddenly remembered his box.

"But I have another customer to go to and the food will be cold by the time I get there."

Gwen leaned in closer and spread out the notes so he could count them, then added another two. "Well, now, I'm sure you can just pretend you dropped it and go back and get some more. If they take it out of your wages, this will cover it, I'm sure."

Before Gwen had finished speaking, the apron and hat were in her hands, along with the other bag of food. Moments later, the moped drove off in the direction from which it had come.

"That has killed two birds with one stone," said Gwen as she walked towards them with two bags of food. "We can all have a quick lunch, then Joe can take the other bag and deliver it to Tadeo!"

———»•«———

Marlene came down the stairs after having changed, adrenalin still racing through her body. She had probably sealed her fate by having done this, but now that Keegan knew about the money, she had no choice but to do as he said. *Poor Benito, he is under the same control and has sealed his fate as well. We are both either under the rule of men or the law. What hope is there now but to stop fighting and accept our lot.*

She looked out through the window in the back door and saw Keegan at the burning pile with Tadeo and Benito's clothing. He had decided to keep the paramedic uniforms, as he felt perhaps they might be useful in the future.

Keegan looked up just at that moment and saw Marlene watching him. A sinister smile spread across his face and as he stood behind the dancing flames it looked … Marlene closed her eyes and opened them again, but … it looked like he was one with the flames. Terror raced through her blood stream until it filled her entire being.

Tap, tap, tap.

What was that? It sounded like it was inside the house.

Silence.

She slowly looked around, then looked back at Keegan, but he was standing to the side of the fire, pushing some garden waste onto the flames with a metal fork.

Tap, tap, tap.

Marlene shook herself. The front door! *Who would be at the door? Tadeo and Benito were the only ones who had ever stepped foot inside the house.*

A slightly louder tap, tap, tap, moved her forwards and she walked to the door, but as she started to turn the door handle, she froze. What if it was the police? Would it really be any worse than living the rest of her life with Keegan? A flash of a prison cell and possible cell mates flashed in her eyes.

A muffled male, "Hello?" came from the other side of the thick door. "Freddie's Fry Up – delivery for you!"

Marlene recognised the name of the takeaway. They had collected food from there, but Keegan would never order a takeaway. He would never have anything delivered to the house.

"Benito?" the voice called out questioningly.

Someone had found Benito! Was it the police?

"It's Joe. Toby and Rebeca are waiting down the street!"

Marlene looked behind her quickly, then clicked the lock, jerked the handle down and slowly pulled the door inwards, sticking her head out. A young man dressed in the silly hat and apron stood holding a bag of food. He stared at her for a minute questioningly.

"You're too late!" she whispered, looking over her shoulder, terrified that Keegan would come in, but desperate to help Benito. "You're too late! They stole a priceless necklace and I don't know if I will ever see them again. Tadeo said he was going to get rid of him. You have to help him but I ...".

She looked over her shoulder again.

Suddenly, Joe was struck with guilt for his lack of compassion for Benito, and the urgency of the situation. A crazy idea popped in his head and he pulled out his phone, tapping to unlock it, and placing it firmly in her hand.

"Give this to Benito if you see him again." He paused, looking at the fear in her eyes, "Or you can use it to call someone for help yourself."

Marlene hesitated, but then her fingers curled tightly around the device. She thought a moment, then lifted her top slightly and slid the phone behind the top of her trousers, pulling her loose top down over to hide the bump.

"Who is that?!"

Panic stricken, Marlene slammed the door in Joe's face as Keegan came up behind her. Grabbing her arm, he yanked her angrily away from the door and she stumbled backwards falling into a side table and catching her back on the edge as she went down. Marlene started to call out in pain, but Keegan took a sideways glance at the door and back at Marlene, snake eyes flashing furiously as he hissed a "quiet!" at her between clenched teeth.

Muted tears rolled down Marlene's cheeks as the pain shot through her and she curled up in a ball and rubbed her back to dull the pain in silence.

"You've been told you don't go to the door! I don't want NO ONE to know where we live! Who was it?" Reptile man gurgled angrily.

Marlene took in a deep breath and let it out threw her nostrils as she tried to speak through her anguish. "They were Fr ... Freddy's Fry Ups ... that take away." She took another breath and Keegan kicked the top of her leg sharply and she winced at the added pain.

"We didn't order a takeaway. We NEVER order a takeaway! Why would you open the door to them?" He kicked her again when she didn't answer straight away. "Well? I'm waiting for an answer, *babe*!"

"H … h-heee wouldn't … g-g-go a-away … he kept knocking!" she whimpered.

"If someone is knocking on the door – let them keep knocking! Never. Answer. The door. Again!" Keegan snarled and he bent down, grabbing her by the wrists and dragging her across the carpet. The waistband of her trousers slid down slightly and the carpet burned against her lower back. The furious man turned backwards when he reached the bottom of the steps and pulled her up, banging her back on every step. Marlene could no longer be silent as her body was battered all the way up the stairs and she began wailing.

"Please Keegan! Stop! No!"

But snake eyes dragged her across the landing and into her little room, slamming the door furiously and locking it loudly. He stormed to their bedroom and got her housecoat again, stuffing it underneath the door.

Stomping down the stairs, he went to the cupboard in the living room and poured himself a large whisky, sitting down in a comfortable chair, and leaned back with his eyes closed, slowly sipping the drink to calm himself.

Upstairs, Marlene was huddled in the corner on her side, her crying had subsided slightly and her hand went to the phone that was miraculously still where she had stuffed it. She said a silent thankful prayer to Whoever was up there, that Keegan had not found it. If he had, she probably would not be alive. Tears continued to flow until she became so exhausted, Marlene fell into a fitful sleep dreaming that she was in a metal barrel, bouncing down a never ending hill.

⸺⸻➤●◄⸻⸺

Joe had stood outside the door for a few moments, and he heard the crash inside, guessing that the enraged man had done something to the poor woman. He hesitated, wondering if he should try to get in, but finally decided he had done enough damage for one day. Besides, as fit as Joe was, he was no match for an unhinged madman. Joe slowly walked away, praying for the auburn haired woman, and praying that the man would not find the phone. As he walked, he began worrying that maybe he had put her life in danger, and he breathed out heavily.

Toby stood up and walked towards his brother as he approached the park with his head down, still feeling the urge to go back and do something to help the woman.

"What happened, Joe?" Toby's face grew grave as his brother walked up to him.

Still lost in thought, Joe walked right past Toby and sat down on the bench beside Rebeca, placing the cold bag of food on the ground and resting his head in his hands, an ironic contrast of silliness with his hat and apron, in deep despair. "I don't know if I did something awful or not!" Joe said in despair.

"What, Joe?" asked Rebeca as she put her hand comfortingly on his back. "What happened?"

Finally, Joe spoke, recounting what had happened, as the other three listened with rapt attention. Joe lifted his hands to rub his hair in frustration and when he found the hat, he grabbed it off his head and threw it on the ground, then stood and yanked off the apron. The others said nothing for a moment as they all digested the events in their minds.

"You did the right thing," Toby said finally, "That was really smart. I'm sure if she sees Benito again, she will get the phone to him."

Joe looked up at his brother who was now standing beside him, and he raised an eyebrow. "How do you know this?"

"I'm just saying," began Toby, "that I am sure she will do her best to get it to him."

"If the madman doesn't find it first and kill her...". Again Joe wondered if he had done the right thing. "I just didn't have time to think the idea through."

They were all silent for several minutes, then finally, Joe accepted that he could not change what he had done. "At the very least," he said slowly, smiling slightly, "I can track the phone on the internet, so if she does get it to him, even if he doesn't use it, we can know where he is."

"I wonder if this necklace they stole was more valuable than the rings from the jewellery store?" asked Rebeca, half to herself contemplatively.

"I think we should call the police. Let them know what we found," began Toby. "Maybe if they investigate, they will discover this woman needs help and rescue her."

The others agreed, and Toby immediately tapped on his phone to contact Detective O'Reilley.

The detective answered on the second ring, and Toby launched into their discovery of Benito's latest whereabouts, minus the details of how they got Marlene to answer the door. Brendon O'Reilley was not happy.

"I thought I told you to stay out of this," he said, annoyed.

"Well, we did find out where his last known location was," Toby said slowly, trying not to sound smug.

There was silence, then Detective Brendon said curtly, "Okay, you've told me. My partner and I will go around there and investigate."

"And you'll make sure the woman is all right?"

"Yes."

"Right away?"

Toby crinkled his face as he felt the tension over the phone. The man obviously did not like to be told how to do his job.

"Goodbye, Mr Myers. Thank you for your ... assistance. Now go back home. If you interfere again, I will put an injunction on you so you will not be able to return to Birmingham for some time." A loud silence met Toby's ears. Then finally, "Do I make myself clear?"

Toby made a face to the others as he nodded, "Yes sir, you have made yourself clear." The line went dead, and Toby put his phone back in his pocket. "He's such a pleasant man to speak to!"

The cloud that had been hiding the sun suddenly moved along, and the heat was overwhelming. Joe wiped his brow. "There's nothing else we can do now. Let's go get a beer." The others agreed, and Gwen called a taxi to take them to a pub.

CHAPTER 15

Tadeo drove for nearly half an hour then finally turned down a quiet tree-lined lane that ended in front of an idyllic cottage with purple wisteria growing along the front of it. He parked up and looked at his watch, nodding.

He reached in the glove box and pulled out a cloth bag, then, opening up one of the briefcases, he counted out several notes and put them in the large bag, pulling the string closed tightly. He shut the case, then clicked open the boot of the car. He got out, and going around to grab the briefcases from the passenger side, he put them both in the back under the parcel shelf where they couldn't be seen. Tadeo then sat back in the car and waited.

Benito closed his eyes and pretended he was back home with his mom. A pang shot through him as he thought of her, but he kept his eyes shut and went back to a time when he was at home with her and she was arguing with him to do the dishes. *If only I could go back. I'd happily do the dishes. I would happily do everything she had asked me to do.*

Fifteen minutes later, Benito opened his eyes as he heard the approach of another vehicle, and shortly a silver car pulled up beside the BMW and Phil, the doctor, got out. Tadeo did likewise and they stood in front of the two cars talking quietly. Finally, Tadeo handed over the money and the two men shook hands, before Phil turned away and stepped inside his house, shutting the door firmly behind him.

Tadeo climbed back in the car and looked at his watch again as he tapped on his phone and put it to his ear. Benito heard it ringing, then someone answered. "I'll be there in forty-five minutes," said Tadeo. Benito heard someone, it sounded like Keegan, asking for pizza. Tadeo laughed. "Sure,

I'll bring pizza. I'm hungry too." There was a pause as the man said something muffled. "No," answered Tadeo, "I've got a bed and breakfast I want to get to tonight. I'm going to lay low for a while, until my agent sorts out the house purchase. Then I'll be long gone and I doubt I'll ever be back to this area again. I hate Birmingham." He clicked off without saying goodbye, and Benito wondered if he would be going to the bed and breakfast with him … or the new house."

Benito actually fell asleep on the journey back to Keegan's and he was surprised there were four pizzas on the seat in the front of the car, along with another, smaller cloth bag, when they arrived. He followed Tadeo up to the step and the door opened as they approached, and Keegan took the boxes from his uncle as they entered.

The two removed their shoes and followed Keegan into the kitchen as he placed the pizzas on the table. A very sombre Marlene was placing some dishes on the table. Suddenly, Keegan turned and nodded to Tadeo. "Over here," he said, and the two men walked over to the soft cream sofa. They sat side by side, leaning over their laps so Benito and Marlene could not see as Keegan counted out the money.

Satisfied, Keegan trotted upstairs to lock it in a safe he had hidden in his bedroom. Then, smiling happily, he came back down and they opened up the boxes. The two men had the boxes between them, and they handed Marlene and Benito each a few slices. Conversation was between the two men, as Benito and Marlene ate in silence.

"Everything gotten rid of?" asked Tadeo.

Keegan nodded. "Everything."

"Everything?" scrutinised Tadeo.

"I said everything, didn't I?" Keegan squinted his eyes and the two men silently vied for dominance as they stared at each other while they ate.

Finally, Tadeo stood. "Time to go." He reached his hand out over the table towards Keegan, who looked at him curiously. "It's been ... a pleasure." Tadeo smirked. "I won't be back."

Keegan nodded and shook his hand in a businesslike manner. "It's been a pleasure doing business with you." Keegan grinned as he thought of his stash upstairs. He wouldn't have to work for a long time. If he worked all his plans right, he might not ever have to work again.

Marlene stood abruptly and the others looked at her, startled. "If you're not coming back, perhaps Benito could take the Bible with him that I found on the bookshelf." She looked pleadingly at the two men. "You don't want it, do you babe?"

"A *Bible*?? How did a Bible get on my bookshelf?" Keegan's face slowly turned red.

"I ... I ... don't know ... I just found it there!" Marlene had thought it odd, but she would never question Keegan about anything.

"Go get it! Get it out of my house!" The red pigment was slowly turning purple and Marlene scurried across the living room and up the stairs to the room that Benito had been sleeping in.

Tadeo looked at Benito, deliberating whether he would allow the kid to take the Bible. Benito tried to look uninterested, despite silently pleading with God to allow him this privilege. They walked over to put their shoes back on, and by the time Marlene had come back down the stairs, Tadeo had decided it would be fun to tease the boy, so he said, "Sure, he can have the Bible." And he laughed heartily.

Marlene stood in front of Benito and handed the Bible slowly, with two hands. "I hope you and your uncle are happy," she said as she looked Benito in the eyes meaningfully.

Benito grabbed the Bible, and as he took hold of it, he felt the other item that Marlene had pressed against it underneath. He looked back at her and an understanding flashed across his eyes as he took the precious Book from her.

"Thank you, Marlene," he said in a monotone voice. He turned and thankfully, Tadeo opened the door for the two of them and Keegan shut it behind them without another word.

Benito gripped the book and gift from Marlene tightly with the one hand as he opened the door, placing them on his lap as he belted himself in. And as Tadeo concentrated on manoeuvring off the drive and down the road away from the town centre, Benito looked straight ahead, positioning the phone down the back of his jeans and pulling his shirt over top of it.

<hr />

A firm knock on the door startled them, and Keegan looked at Marlene accusingly. Marlene shrugged her shoulders, frightened. Another firm knock came, then,

"It's the police, we've had report of a disturbance." A loud voice spoke from the other side of the door.

Keegan glared at Marlene. "Look what you've done!" He hissed quietly.

Finally, Keegan stood, deciding it was best to answer to avoid suspicion. As he headed silently across the carpet towards the door, he shot a warning glance over his shoulder at Marlene, who nodded compliantly.

"Hello, officers," Keegan opened the door and smiled his warmest smile at the two large men standing on his doorstep. "How can I help you? Did you say something about a disturbance? I never heard a disturbance." He opened the door so they could see inside, and squinted his reptile eyes back at Marlene, "Did you hear a disturbance, honey?"

Marlene shook her head slowly, smiling faintly at the two policemen. "No, I didn't hear anything."

"May we come in?" asked the same officer.

Keegan nodded and opened the door wide waving them in with his hand. He pointed to the comfortable chairs in the living room and the men sat down on opposite sides.

"What kind of disturbance was this?" Keegan asked frowning, faking concern. "Has something happened to our neighbours?"

"No." The same officer spoke again. "We had a report from someone who tried to deliver a fast food order, that he thought there was some … rough-housing in here." He looked at each of them carefully.

Keegan laughed heartily and put his arm around Marlene as he sat down next to her. "What a laugh, hey sweetheart? You and me 'rough-housing'?"

Marlene put on her best smile, but said nothing, slowly shaking her head from side to side in mock disbelief. The officer wrote something down on his notepad, and his silent partner sat still.

"We've not long been married – we don't even argue yet! Still in the honeymoon period!" Wrinkles formed at the sides of his snake eyes that had been transformed into playful cat eyes. He squeezed Marlene's shoulders playfully and she nodded.

"Yes, indeed! Not a word of disagreement – yet!" She giggled like a besotted bride and looked into Keegan's eyes, seeing beyond the pretence. "Not a word."

"You understand that we have to take these reports seriously. Just in case someone is in trouble. We wouldn't want to be negligent. You understand?" the lead man said.

"Of course," said Keegan.

The officers sat in silence for a full minute, while Keegan and Marlene looked from one to the other, innocently. Finally, the lead officer stood, and spoke to Keegan.

"Can I have a little word with you outside?" He nodded to the front door and Keegan jumped up obligingly, heading out the door with the man right behind him, shutting it behind them.

Inside, the mute officer finally spoke as he looked at Marlene. "It's safe now. You can tell me the truth. If there's a problem, we can help."

Marlene looked at the policeman who spoke kindly in a soft voice. She thought how ironic it was that had they arrived a couple of days earlier, before she had assisted in the theft of a priceless necklace, she would have probably accepted his offer. She knew they would have safe houses, places to help women like her. But now, even with a reduced sentence due to her circumstances – would she not still end up in prison? She couldn't risk it.

"No, I'm fine. Thank you officer, but really, it must have been a misunderstanding. I did make a noise after I told the young man I did not order anything and shut the door, but I walked into that little table over there." She pointed to the table that Keegan had knocked her into. She laughed softly, "My own fault for not looking where I was going!" She smiled broadly and stood, letting him know she was finished. He stood as well and looked at her thoughtfully.

"You're sure?" He tried one last time.

"Yes, yes, everything is just fine!"

The man admitted defeat and stood, giving her a card. "This is a number you can call anytime, day or night."

Marlene tried to refuse it, but he pressed it firmly in her hand. She slid it in her back pocket and walked him to the front door, opening it as soon as she reached it, not wanting to add any fuel to the angry fire that must be burning wildly inside Keegan.

Keegan smiled and the two officers nodded to each other. The lead man said goodbye and apologised for disturbing them as the two policemen got in the car and drove off. Keegan put his arm around Marlene and ushered her inside the house.

"Stupid man thought I was an imbecile. Told me there was some pervert running around the area but didn't want to frighten you. Said he just wanted me to be aware. I know what they were doing." He grabbed her shoulders firmly and squinted his reptile eyes, seething. "See what you've done, answering the door earlier? See the trouble you caused? What did you tell him?"

"Nothing, Keegan, nothing. I said I was fine. I said there was nothing wrong. Honest, babe."

Her bottom lip quivered and frightened tears welled up in her eyes as he squeezed her shoulders ever harder.

All of a sudden, the thought came to him, and he realised what he needed to do – something Tadeo had mentioned gave him the idea – "I think we need to go on a holiday, baby, don't you? Why don't you find somewhere sunny and warm for us to go?"

When Marlene just stared at him, he kissed her cheek and stroke her head, pulling her closely in a tight embrace. Smiling sinisterly to himself, he spoke softly to Marlene, "Somewhere abroad – a seaside holiday."

They sat outside under an umbrella, but the sun still managed to get them as they drank their beers and soft drinks and the four of them grew ever hotter.

"Let's go for a swim," said Joe finally, "it is just way too hot today, and even though this beer is refreshing, a cool dip would really hit the spot." The others agreed and they were soon lolling around in the cool water, with the pool again all to themselves. They played some quiet games with a ball and then eventually they all ended up just floating around lazily in the shallow end.

After an evening meal back at the Canal House, they gathered together in the boys room to discuss Benito and this sad red-headed woman. Finally, Toby tapped on his phone and he breathed in deeply for strength.

"I think we need some help!"

The others looked at him curiously when they saw the seriousness in his face, then they all burst out laughing as the wide braced friendly smile appeared on his screen.

"Hey there Toby! I thought you guys had forgotten me! I mean, I had loads of fun with all those animals that came into the shop and that goat was sooooo cute! Her name was Gertrude!" Pamela giggled, "Gertrude the goat! But she loved me and followed me all through the store – well she didn't follow on her own, of course, because she was on a leash, but the leash was long and the owner was just following aimlessly behind her as she nosed everything, which of *course*, Mr Flatley was annoyed about, but she was really tooo cute for words! And the owner said I could take care of her whenever she went on holidays – isn't that terrific? Of course, I'd have to ask my Mom and Dad first and …".

"Pamela!" Toby burst out when she finally took a breath, "We could do with your help!"

"Oh, great! I'd love to help! Have you found Benito yet? The poor guy – he is so nice and his uncle is so mean! It's like a fairy tale Cinderella, and Benito is a Cinderella, only he's a guy, so of course he'd have to be Cinder Ed, and there isn't a Prince Charming to save him, but I could be Princess Charming if I can help!" She threw her head back laughing and again Toby took his chance to interject into her monologue.

"We found Benito's latest location, but the detective over here we are dealing with seems keener to get rid of us than to find Benito."

Pamela rolled her eyes and nodded her head. "I totally get that! I've met lots of people like that – not just on the force, but in life generally – my brother will NOT be told or advised what to do about ANYTHING! The other day I told him – I actually said the words out loud to him – if you leave your pop in the freezer, it will explode! And what happened? He forgot about it, left it in the freezer, and it exploded and then Mom was mad at him, and mad generally, because she had to defrost the freezer to clean it all up and it went on some fish, so we had to eat fish for dinner and I hate fish and oh! I never told you about the goldfish! You remember I said no one would bring a goldfish into the store? Well someone actually DID can you believe it and it was the biggest …".

Toby rubbed his eyes and hung his head, while Gwen, Rebeca and Joe sat silently watching him, snickering softly.

"Oh! Toby, are you all right?" Pamela's concerned face came up so close to the screen that she became blurry.

He inhaled deeply and breathed out as he spoke, "Pamela, can we please stay focused on the subject to hand?"

Pamela smiled as her eyes frowned – her peculiar look that Toby was now used to. Supposedly it meant she was trying! "Sorry! Yes! I know what you need! You need my Dad. He really is the most tactful person in the world and he can get you to do something without you even knowing it was him instigating it." She bit her bottom lip tightly, presumably to stop it from moving again.

"So he can get this officer over here to properly look for Benito?" Toby asked hopefully. He did a quick recap of the events since they had last spoken, with a special emphasis on today. "Joe can track the phone and he can give you the details to pass on to your Dad, if that would be helpful. He thinks it has to be turned on, but there may be a way that the police can track a phone that's switched off, you know?"

Pamela nodded vigorously, afraid to open her mouth for fear of not being able to stop it again, but still smiled widely.

"Hello Pamela!" Rebeca gave her a wave as she came and sat beside Toby, and Pamela responded with the frantic wave of an excited child.

Toby started laughing as Pamela's face began to look like it was going to explode. "It's okay, Pamela! I've told you everything I want, now. You can speak again!"

"Oh! That hotel you are staying in looks absolutely lush!" she squealed ecstatically, "Show me around!"

Toby first turned the screen around so she could say hello to Joe and Gwen, then took her for a little tour, finishing off looking out the vast windows.

"Wow!" And for a moment, Pamela was speechless with the others responding in silence for a whole minute, then, "Well, I gotta go! I'm actually at work and you caught me on my lunch break and now my break is over and you know Mr Flatley!" – even though none of them did – "One second over your time and he's screaming blue murder!" she tittered. "Well, not blue murder, exactly, because he saves *that* scream for when I am busy chatting to customers and he thinks I am wasting time when I am actually *not* wasting time because I am working on customer relations which we all know is what is really important in a business. Don't you think? Oh! I hear him shouting. Bye!" Pamela clicked off before Toby could reply, and he just shook his head, tossing his phone gently on the seat beside him.

⟶━━●━━⟵

Benito had fallen asleep shortly after they had left Keegan's, and woke up just in time to see the town sign as they entered – TENBY. He remembered Tenby. It was a nice seaside resort – not that he would be able to enjoy it. He remembered his dad taking his mom and him here not long before he died. They were there a week and he remembered it had been sunny and they had spent the whole time on the long sandy beach making sand castles and splashing in the sea when the sun got too hot.

Tadeo pulled into a small car park at the back of a bed and breakfast that looked out onto the sea and what was left of the beach with the high tide. He got out and went around to open the boot of the car as Benito took the Bible that was still resting on his lap, and followed him to the back of the car. There were two bags, a large one for Tadeo and a substantially smaller one for Benito, and as Benito took the bag from his uncle he noticed that the briefcases were gone. They must have stopped somewhere along the way to hide them, and Benito couldn't fathom where on earth Tadeo would have stashed them that would be safe.

Funny, that word 'safe'. Safe from who? thought Benito. *Another criminal? The police?*

Benito silently followed his uncle into the cosy building and a kind looking, rotund woman welcomed them.

"So lovely to see you! Welcome! Welcome! I assume you are Mr Grange and his son." Tadeo nodded and the woman grabbed a key from behind the little desk by the entrance. "My name is Joan. Follow me, dearies! You are up one set of stairs, but you have a lovely view out towards the sea! Just lovely!"

The elderly woman did not move very fast, and it took them a couple of minutes to get up the one flight and into their room, as she puffed her way up. She finally reached it and put the key into the door, turning it and opening the door with bravado. "Isn't it lovely?" Joan breathed out heavily as she turned to the two of them, grinning from ear to ear.

Tadeo just nodded, but Benito said, "It's amazing, ma'am it really is!" And a warm feeling came over him as he felt like he had stepped back in time to the place where he had stayed with his parents. There was a double bed and a single – just like there had been before. "Wonderful!" he said out loud, remembering. Remembering one of the few happy times in his life. Wondering if he would ever experience anything like that again.

"Right then, I'll leave you two to settle in then!" And the woman waddled out of the room to begin her journey back down the stairs.

Tadeo put his bag on the floor then tapped on his phone. "I'm going out for a minute, I'll be back shortly." He glared at Benito and put his face close to his nephew's. "Don't go anywhere!"

Tadeo left without another word, and Benito sat on the single bed, leaning on the head rest as he switched on the TV. He searched through several channels before finally settling on a nature program that today was focusing on mountain goats, then pulled the phone out from behind him, and turned it on.

Just then, there was a tap on the door, and Benito switched off the TV, wondering if he should answer. His heart started beating heavily, wondering if somehow the police had found him. Then he began worrying that the phone would make a noise when it turned on. If it was the police, he didn't want them to know he was there. Panicking, he looked out the window and wondered if he could lower himself out down to the ground.

"Just bringing up the rest of the towels!" the round woman called from the other side of the door. Benito shoved the phone down his back again and jumped off the bed to open up the door, taking the towels out of her hands.

"Now, is there anything else you need?" Joan asked with a friendly smile.

Benito was about to shake his head when suddenly he thought of something. "Do you have some parcel tape?"

She looked at him quizzically. "You want to send a parcel?"

"No … I … uh …". He wasn't sure what to say and just continued stumbling along, "I have something important, that I wanted to keep with me and I was … I … was reading about someone who had taped it onto themselves for safe keeping … I suppose that sounds silly … sorry … never mind!"

"Oh, sweetheart! You are in luck! I have just the thing! I was doing some sorting and I found one of those bags you hold passports and things in, underneath your clothes. Would that be any good?"

"Yes! That would be perfect!"

I'll just go get it for you! The woman began slowly descending the stairs and Benito started to panic. He had no idea how long his uncle would be. The teenager followed the woman down at the painfully slow pace as his heart rate grew ever faster.

Finally, they reached the bottom, and the woman disappeared behind a door marked PRIVATE, and returned amazingly promptly with the promised bag. Benito took it from her, thanking her, and as he turned to leave he paused and said hastily, "Don't tell my Dad you gave me this. He thinks I am silly and it irritates him."

The woman smiled kindly and nodded, tapping her lips with her finger, "Mum's the word, sweetheart! Don't you worry!"

Benito smiled gratefully and trotted up the stairs, terrified that his uncle would be back any second. He shut the door behind him and quickly jumped on the bed, his heart racing. He heard the front door open and close, then someone walk up the creaking stairs, past his door, and up the next flight.

He waited until it was silent again, then he took the bag and fitted it around himself, clipping it tightly. He put the phone in it and pulled his shirt over it. He looked down. *Good*, he thought. You could only tell there was something there if you were purposefully looking.

He leaned back and took the phone out again, tapping the screen. It was on silent. He scrolled through a few things, then he saw the ID – Joe Myers. How had Marlene gotten Joe's phone?

The front door opened and banged shut. Benito shoved the phone into its pocket and pulled his shirt down just as Tadeo put the key in the door and strode in with a plastic bag in his hand. He looked at the television and back at Benito.

"You have to actually turn it on to watch it," he sneered suspiciously, feeling that his nephew had been up to something.

"I ... uh ... I was ... just looking out the window watching the sea." Tadeo continued to look at him, analysing him. "Dad, Mom and I came here when I was little." He looked at Tadeo. "I ... was ... just remembering."

Tadeo deliberated for a further minute, then decided to drop the subject. He picked up the remote that was beside Toby on the little cupboard between the two beds, and switched it on. Mountain goats began scrambling up a jagged cliff across the screen, and Benito was instantly mesmerised by how agile they were, climbing up rocks that someone with hands would find difficult.

However, Tadeo clicked the buttons and switched channels until he found an old movie he wanted to watch, then opened a packet of snacks before cracking open a beer. Benito glanced hungrily at him, but he turned away quickly when Tadeo caught him out of the side of his eye.

The teenager lay down, facing away from his uncle, and stared out the window as he drifted off. Soon he was with his parents sitting on the sand, making castles and laughing with his dad as the sun beat down on them, turning their skin a burnt umber.

———⟫●⟪———

Toby's phone beeped and he picked it off the sofa where he had left it. He smiled excitedly as he saw the caller ID.

"Hello?"

"Mr Myers, this is detective O'Reilley."

"Yes, hi! Have you got any news?" Toby was unsure why he had to introduce himself and wondered if the man really was that thick that he didn't know Toby could see on his phone who was calling.

"Yes and no. We went to the address that you gave us and spoke to the lady; Marlene is her name. She assured us that there must be some mistake and that she was in no danger and everything was fine. She had no idea who Benito was." He sighed. "I don't know what your brother was on, but he obviously got the wrong end of the stick."

"But did you speak to her without the man around?" queried Toby, ignoring the man's swipe at his brother.

The man inhaled deeply, then exhaled loudly and slowly, saying nothing for a moment. Toby wondered if he had hung up and was about to call out to him when the detective finally answered. "Listen, son, don't tell me how to do my job. I know how to deal with domestic situations and everything was just fine there. Stay away from them and go home. Do you understand me?"

"Yes, I understand you," said Toby, deciding it wasn't a lie, since he perfectly understood the man, he just wasn't going to obey him. Then decided to add for effect, even though he didn't feel like it, "Thank you for going there."

The detective clicked off without saying goodbye and Toby looked around at the others, dismayed. The guy is a total loser. How did he ever become a cop? He said...".

"He was talking pretty loudly," said Joe, "we heard the whole conversation. Including that he thought I was on drugs or something. What a jerk." He paused for a moment, then said, "Give me your phone, Tobs. I'll check my tracker and see if the phone has moved. If that stupid cop says this Marlene was still there and the phone isn't, then we know she managed to give it to Benito."

"Either that, or the man found it, and got rid of it," said Gwen.

"Unlikely," mused Toby. "If he had found it, I doubt very much the woman would have been in any fit state to speak to a policeman and pass off as a perfectly happy woman. He would have beat her up good and proper."

Joe cringed at his brother's words and hung his head. "Please, Toby, don't rub it in."

"Sorry," said Toby, then passed the phone to Joe. "Go on, let's see where the phone is."

Joe took a few minutes to get into his account on Toby's phone and they all waited anxiously to see where it would be.

A wide grin spread across Joe's face, "He *must* have it! It's in Tenby!"

"Where is Tenby?" asked Rebeca.

"On the south west coast of Wales," said Gwen as she began swiping on her own phone.

"I guess we need to head to Tenby tomorrow, first thing, then!" said Toby as he put his arm around Rebeca and squeezed her shoulders happily. "I feel like we are getting close!" He paused a moment then added, "We better look for somewhere to stay! At a nice beach-side town like that, people probably book way ahead."

"Sorted!" said Gwen, smiling as she looked up from her phone. "We are booked into the Heywood Spa Hotel for a week. We can always cancel if we find him sooner! Or stay for some fun at the beach!"

"Okay, then," chuckled Toby. "What about train times?"

Gwen frowned and shook her head. "No thank you! Too long with a couple of changes. I'll hire us a car." She cocked her head, looking at Joe and grinned: "What do you fancy driving, Joe?"

Joe opened his mouth to speak, but remembering the sports car Joe had chosen in Florida, Toby interrupted his brother's thoughts with, "Not a sports car! You can choose something that strokes your ego, but it has to be roomy!"

Gwen nodded, "Of course! How about a Porsche Cayenne?"

"Uh ... sure!" grinned Joe.

Within seconds, Gwen was speaking to someone at a car rental. "Hello, this is Gwen Wentworth – I want to rent a car for a week – do you have a Porsche Cayenne? – I think the SUV would be better – that's fine – yes. I'd like it delivered to the Hyatt Regency ... Oh, one moment!" – she turned to the others, "What time shall we leave?"

"I think we should get moving early," said Toby, "what about 6:00?"

"Are you kidding me?? No, it has to be no earlier than 8:00!" Joe made a face and Gwen frowned, nodding her head to agree with Joe.

"7:00, then," conceded Toby, "no later!"

"I need to be awake to drive," Joe squinted his eyes at Toby.

"I'll drive then!" said Toby, annoyed.

"You have to be twenty-three," said Gwen, smirking, "I think 7:30 would be a fine compromise, don't you, Joe?"

Both brothers blew out between closed mouths, staring at each other, each irritated that he wasn't getting his own way, yet satisfied that the other brother wasn't either.

"Well," said Gwen standing up, "I, for one, need to get to bed now if I am going to be able to get up early enough to get some breakfast before we go."

Rebeca stood as well, though she was usually awake by 6:00 anyway. The two girls said their goodbyes, then left the boys to go down to their room.

"Me too," said Joe as he yawned and stretched his arms above his head before standing up and heading to the bathroom to brush his teeth.

Toby's thoughts wandered to the sermon that morning and he pulled out his phone to find the Bible translation the pastor had used – the Christian Standard Bible – and started reading ... *In the beginning, God created the heavens and the earth* ...

———⟫●⟪———

Benito was woken by the gentle flapping of the curtain as a cool breeze blew off the sea and through the open window. It was dark and his uncle was snoring in the bed next to him. The teenager pulled off his shoes, then stripped down to his boxers and slid under the duvet, pulling it up to his neck as he snuggled down onto the soft pillow.

For a while, he listened to the mix of night sounds that one hears at a seaside town like Tenby. The faint swooshing of the sea as the waves rolled onto the shore, an owl hooting in the distance and a couple of gulls 'huoh huoh'ed loudly as they argued over a prized perching spot on a building on the other side of the narrow street. Then some girls giggled hysterically as they passed underneath Benito's window, making their way back to their own rooms, while at the far end of the street, two men talked loudly about whose football team was better as they staggered out of the pub and in the opposite direction to the B&B.

Although noisy, the normalcy of the sounds comforted Benito, whose life was anything but normal, and he wondered what it would be like to hang out with other teenagers; go to the pub and argue about football teams like it was the most important thing in the world. He wondered what it would be like to walk down the street with his friends, calling out to the girls, laughing and generally, just doing what teenagers did.

Benito slowly drifted off and was just entering a pleasant world with other teenagers, walking down a street laughing, when his stomach began growling, keeping him just conscious enough so that he could only enjoy the dream as a bystander instead of joining in with the fun.

CHAPTER 16

Monday 22nd August

The alarm clock beeped loudly beside Joe and he woke up to turn it off, noting the time, 6:15. He turned over and saw that the other side of the bed was empty. Surely Toby was not up already! Joe flung off the duvet and swung down his feet, tapping the floor a few times to try and wake himself. He stood up, and as he headed to the bathroom he saw his brother unconscious on the sofa, dressed as he had been the night before.

"Hey, Toby!" called out Joe as he strode quickly over and shook his brother, "You all right?"

Toby's eyes shot open in a panic and he blinked a few times, disorientated. He looked out the window at the sunshine, then up at Joe, slightly confused. "What time is it?"

"6:15, buddy! You sleep there all night?" Joe snorted happily, shaking his head, but pleased his brother was okay.

"Umm ... no ... I mean ya ... I mean I was here all night, but I don't know how much sleep I got!" He sat up properly and looked around, finally finding his phone on the floor beside him. "I was reading."

"Must have been good!" chuckled Joe as he walked towards the bathroom, anxious to get in the shower before he had to argue with Toby about who was going first.

"It was, I was reading ...". Joe had slammed the bathroom door behind him while Toby was still speaking, but Toby continued to himself, "... and I learned so much! I can't believe what I thought I knew that I really didn't." He clicked the button on the side and saw his phone was out of battery, so he went into the bedroom to find his charger and plugged it in. He lay back on the bed with his hands behind his head and while he waited for Joe to finish, he thought about what he had read. He had read the Bible before – not the whole thing, but enough. Well, he had thought it was enough, but now, it was like he was reading with a completely new understanding and he was keen to be able to find some time soon to continue.

When Joe came out of the bathroom, Toby was anxious to share some of his newly found information. "Do you know, in Genesis 1, it actually says: evening morning day one, evening morning day two, evening morning day three? I mean how more clear can God get that He made the world in six actual days – not the millions of years we were taught in school?"

Joe looked at his brother, tilting his head and analysing his newly acquired enthusiasm for God and the Bible. "What about all the fossils in all the rock layers?"

"I know, I asked myself that, and then I thought, well *that's* stupid in itself, because if a herd of cattle dropped down and died in the middle of the field, how much of their remains would still be there in ten years, let alone long enough to be covered with soil or whatever? It just wouldn't happen. So I looked it up on a website I found earlier, Answers in Genesis[1], and they talk about Noah's flood as a catastrophic flood – not just rain for forty days, but the entire oceans of the deep breaking apart and volcanoes and the one continent, Pangea, breaking apart with rapid plate tectonics; all of which would cause tsunami after tsunami, bringing gigantic layers of ash and other things over the land, covering the animals that were trying to escape."

"But how did the water cover over every high mountain?" persisted Joe.

"Well, the mountains only got that high with the rapid movement of the earth's plates. That's why you can find marine fossils on the top of mountains."

"Okay," continued Joe, "how come the fossils look like they go up the layers in progression of complexity of animal?"

"That's easy. The first tsunamis would have gone over the marine and smaller things first, then as they increased they would cover more and more able animals until the biggest and fastest animals had gone as far as they could away and finally got covered themselves."

Joe looked at his brother thoughtfully, then spoke suddenly, "You better get ready! We need to go down to breakfast soon!"

Toby checked the charge in his phone before gathering his things to have a wash and get dressed in the bathroom. Joe pondered his brother's words as he got dressed. Funny how he had never really thought about it all. Maybe that was the heart of his own problem. At some point, he had stopped listening to God and His Word, and had just listened unquestioningly to people – people who did not want to know God, people who did not want to be accountable to God and therefore wanted to disprove His existence.

Soon, both boys were ready and heading down the stairs to pick the girls up on their way to breakfast. They chattered excitedly as they ate, and by 7:20, they were all ready, waiting in the lobby for the car which turned up promptly at 7:29.

They put their bags in the back, and as Joe took the key from the man who delivered it, he said to Joe. "Be careful. There's been a couple of these stolen in the city in the last few days."

Joe nodded. "We won't be in Birmingham, we're heading to Tenby."

The others climbed in, and Joe slipped behind the steering wheel and buckled up, adjusting the seat and the mirror, familiarising himself with all the controls and grinning like a kid on Christmas morning. He tapped the satnav with the address that Gwen gave him, then pulled away from the kerb, pleased that it would take a few hours to get there so he could enjoy the drive.

Benito opened his eyes and squinted at the bright sunshine that shone through the window. He wondered what time it was. Joan had said breakfast was between 8:00 and 9:00 and he didn't want to miss it. That was, if Tadeo was going to let him eat.

Just then, he heard the church clock chime eight times. That gave him a bit of time. Benito decided to get up, have a wash, and get dressed. Maybe that would wake his uncle.

When Benito came out of the bathroom ten minutes later, his uncle was sat up and he grumbled at him, "What took you so long, boy?!"

Benito opened his mouth to speak, but decided that anything he said would just annoy his uncle further, so he remained silent as he passed Tadeo to make his way to his own bed to sit and wait for – hopefully – breakfast. After a long while, the door opened and Tadeo appeared, dressed, and sat back on his bed and clicked on the TV remote, bringing up a news channel.

Benito decided his uncle was probably just asserting the power he had over him. Unbeknown to Benito, that was exactly what Tadeo was doing. He was a narcissist and he enjoyed controlling every aspect of his nephew's life.

The church clock chimed again – 8:30, and Tadeo glanced sideways at his nephew who was looking out the window. Tadeo knew Benito was hungry, so he decided to wait another ten minutes before heading down the stairs to breakfast. It was like an addiction to Tadeo, manipulating and controlling another person, and he wondered if he should go through with his plan. After all, when Benito was gone, who would he have power over? A picture flashed in his mind of the pretty young woman he had recently met and taken out for a meal when Benito was at Keegan's place. Emily was her name. She was a lot younger than him, probably only mid-twenties, but she was gullible. He thought of Marlene. Tadeo knew what was going on with Keegan and Marlene, but he didn't care. In fact, he figured he could have the same thing with Emily. It was just a case of manipulation. Getting her to see her family and friends as less important as Tadeo grew more important; that in fact, Tadeo was all that she wanted; making her realise that he could give her all she wanted or dreamed of. Then the clincher – get her to do something that she could never admit to her family and friends to having done – and hey presto! She was committed to him for life!

He smiled to himself. No, he'd stick to the plan to deal with Benito. Emily was a new challenge to look forward to, but he knew he could make it happen. She would certainly be a lot more enjoyable to live with than Benito.

But first, thought Tadeo, he needed to have a little fun with Benito. He couldn't resist it. The kid just asked for his mind to be messed with.

"Right, let's go have some breakfast." He turned off the television and Benito, who did not need to be told twice, followed close behind down to the dining room.

Joan greeted them as they entered the room, smiling broadly. "Oh! I was wondering if you two were going to have some breakfast!" She pointed them to a table by the window, and they sat down. A young couple with two young boys were just finishing up and the mother smiled at Benito.

"What can I get you?" asked Joan.

"I'll have the works," smiled Tadeo congenially and the woman nodded happily.

"How would you like your eggs?" Joan was a woman who loved to please.

"Scrambled, please." Tadeo was in a good mood now that everything had been decided in his mind. He was looking forward to it all.

Joan turned to Benito, "How about you, son?"

Benito's stomach growled loudly and the woman smiled, "Sounds like you need the works, as well!"

The teenager nodded and said 'scrambled' just as Joan opened her mouth to ask, and she laughed heartily, turning away and trundling slowly to the kitchen to let her husband, the cook, know there would be two more breakfasts required.

Tadeo squinted his eyes and looked at Benito, smiling. "I thought we'd take a boat ride around Caldey Island, son, what do you think?"

Benito stared back at Tadeo wondering what he was doing. Maybe he was just pretending to be a normal family to those watching.

"Oh! We did that yesterday," said the woman, "didn't we boys? It was fun, wasn't it?"

The two boys nodded their heads vigorously and the one shouted out excitedly, "We saw some dolphins! They were really close to the boat! It was cool!"

His father smiled down at him and ruffled his hair lovingly. "We sure did son – and it *was* cool!"

"Well," said Tadeo tilting his head at Benito, acting the doting father, "that settles it! We must go see those dolphins!" He looked at the man and added, "Thanks for the word of advice!"

Benito, sitting with his back towards the family and looking confused at Tadeo, still said nothing. Tadeo chuckled and said to the family, "Teenagers! Nothing excites them!" The couple smiled back at him.

By the time Joan came back in with Tadeo and Benito's breakfasts, the young family had finished and were leaving the dining room. As they passed Tadeo and Benito, the woman spoke to the teenager kindly.

"There is a fast boat, a Rib ride – you would enjoy that, I'm sure! And you can still see the seals and possibly dolphins." She smiled at him, then followed her husband who was ushering out the two boys who had started to punch each other playfully.

Benito smiled, even though the woman had already turned away from him. How nice to be a part of a normal family. Joe and Toby play fought together still, even at their age. Benito wished he had had a brother. He pushed the thoughts of family out of his mind as he tucked into the delicious food that had been placed in front of him, he and his uncle eating in silence.

⟶⟶●⟵⟵

"How far a drive is it to Tenby?" asked Toby, as he leaned forward behind Joe.

"We'll be there about 11:00," answered Gwen, who was sat in front with Joe. She turned around and smiled, "Isn't this more comfortable than the train?" Joe turned on the radio and she faced back towards the front to grin at Joe who had begun singing off-key to a popular tune.

Toby leaned back in the comfortable leather seat and reached out to take Rebeca's hand. He squeezed it firmly and smiled at her. "I read the Bible for hours last night. It was like I had never read it before – like I was understanding the words for the first time! Oh, Rebeca, it was amazing. It IS amazing. I just wanted to keep reading and reading and not stop!"

"I can see it in your face, Toby."

"I want to learn all I can."

Rebeca said nothing as she looked at the earnestness in his face. Sorrow was mixed with her joy, and she felt ashamed and selfish. She felt like a jealous girl that did not want to share him. And yet she knew, ultimately, it was right.

He grabbed her other hand and held both tightly in his. He leaned forward and whispered so only she could hear. "I love you, Rebeca. You know that?"

She nodded, and a tear trickled down her cheek. He wiped the tear gently with his thumb and leaned closer speaking in a whisper, "I still want you with my whole heart. I just need time. Time to learn what this all means to me: what *God* means to me and how I go forward with what is going on in me." His lips met hers and he lingered, wanting her to know. He sighed. "I do love you, but I need you to wait."

"Hey! No PDA in the car!" Joe looked at them in the rear view mirror and Gwen glanced over her shoulder grinning.

"Let them alone, Joe! If they want to make out in the back, let them!"

"We're not 'making out', Gwen! I just gave Rebeca a kiss." Toby frowned and was struck with the importance of defending Rebeca's honour. The importance of him being honourable to her. He spoke quietly again so only Rebeca could hear: "I need to pursue my relationship with Christ before I pursue my relationship with you. Only then can our relationship be what it should be." He chuckled, then added, "Does that sound corny?"

Rebeca half smiled with a light laughter in her voice. "You sound like a pastor!"

He grinned and patted the seat between them. Quickly, she unbelted and moved to the middle seat and belted up again. He put his arm around her and she leaned into him, sighing deeply. She had to trust God for their future. For *her* future. Even if it was without Toby.

———————⊷●⊶———————

"I've booked us on an 10:00 Rib Ride, how about that?" Tadeo looked up from his phone and grinned to Benito sat on the other bed. Benito stared at him, but said nothing. He didn't know what Tadeo was up to. Benito's heart rate increased as various thoughts ran through his mind – none of them good. Tadeo's smile widened and he winked at Benito, "Come on, we better get going if we are going to get there on time!"

He smiled at Benito and again Benito's pulse rate quickened. *What was his uncle up to??*

Benito put on his shoes and followed his uncle out of the room and down the stairs into the sunshine. Many people were walking up and down the streets and a couple passed them with large ice cream cones.

"That looks good. How about an ice cream, son?" Tadeo looked down at his watch. "We have just enough time to get an ice cream!" He smiled happily down at Benito who nodded slowly. An ice cream did sound good, but Benito was growing more and more wary.

"I'll have a mocha chocolate." Tadeo turned to Benito as they stood inside the ice cream shop. "What would you like, Benny?"

Warning bells rang wildly in his head, but Benito managed to say quietly, "Double chocolate, please."

"How many scoops?" The young girl behind the counter grinned happily at them as though selling ice cream was the best job in the world.

"Oh, hmmm, what do you say, Benny? Think you can handle three?"

Benito just looked at his uncle oddly as he nodded his head slowly up and down. They took their ice creams and as they walked out of the shop, Tadeo patted Benito softly on the back. "These look great!" Then added, "And that boat ride is going to be fun!"

They reached the boat launch just as they finished their ice creams, and joined the people on the sandy beach queuing up to get on. A few minutes later, everyone started moving forward toward the loading dock and down the wooden planks where they climbed on board the boat.

They had a quick safety message as they all put on their life jackets, and soon the boat was moving out into the water towards Caldey Island. Once they got through the other boats and the people who were swimming close to the shore, the boat picked up speed and Benito reached his hand out to the spray from the sea.

━━━━━➤●◅━━━━━

"Oh! I will be glad to get out of this car. I need to stretch my legs," said Rebeca. "I do not know how people ride in these all the time."

Joe had just pulled up into the car park of the Heywood Spa Hotel. They all agreed that it would be good to get out and walk around. As they were getting their luggage out of the car, Gwen looked down at her large case and up at Joe. He smiled and picked it up in his left hand, since he had already taken his bag out with his right. Not to be outdone, Toby reached for Rebeca's small bag, but she grabbed it first.

"That's fine, Toby, I can mange it," she grinned, and added, "But thank you for your chivalry!"

"Don't tell me – the new word!"

Rebeca giggled, I found it this morning and knew it wouldn't be long before I could use it! They went inside and booked into their rooms, then Joe quickly tapped on his phone to see where Benito was.

"Looks like they are out at sea," he said, frowning. "Why would they be out at sea?"

"On a boat ride?" Gwen raised her eyebrows questioningly. "Isn't that what people do when they go to the seaside?"

"Tourists go on boat rides – Tadeo and Benito aren't tourists," said Toby, worriedly.

"Not being funny, but it is still sending out a signal, so that must mean he is all right," Gwen commented.

"I think we should walk to the beach and see if we can find them when they come back on land," said Rebeca. "I could do with a walk." She grinned as she added, "And we can find something for you boys to eat! It's been a while since breakfast."

They all agreed, and were soon heading down the street towards the beach, stopping at a fish and chip shop along the way. After making enquiries, they found the place from where the tourist boats launched. Joe checked the location, and found the signal was on the far side of Caldey Island.

"Let's go a bit further along the shore and find a place to sit and eat our food. We don't want to be standing right here when they get back."

So they walked about thirty metres along and found a place to eat while they waited for Tadeo and Benito's return. There were lots of people on the beach, so there was no risk of Tadeo spotting them.

"What are we going to do when we see them?" asked Rebeca sensibly.

Toby sighed. "I don't know, yet. We can't very well call officer O'Reilley – he'll probably ban us from Tenby as well!

Maybe if we follow them for a bit, we can wait for a chance to get Benito alone. There's got to be a time when Tadeo isn't right there by his side."

"Like perhaps if they go to a restaurant and Tadeo has to take a leak?"

Rebeca frowned. "'Take a leak?'" she asked, but understanding crossed her face the moment she asked the question. "Ah, yes, I think I understand."

———

Benito almost forgot he was with Tadeo, as he grew mesmerised by the seals sunning themselves on the rocks and a few more daring ones swimming out to the boat as the captain slowed down until they were barely moving. People got out their phones and began excitedly taking pictures.

They moved along the coast of Caldey Island and found another herd of seals sunbathing on rocks and floating relaxed in the water, with a few curious youngsters coming up close.

Finally, the boat moved away and picked up speed as it went out to sea a little further in search of dolphins. They were soon rewarded by a pod of the playful creatures as they swam and played in the water. Unfortunately, they did not come very close, so for most of the passengers with poorer cameras, the animals were not big enough to see well on their screens. But nonetheless, all the passengers were thrilled at being able to see the animals in real life as the captain of the rib boat slowed it right down so they could enjoy the view.

As the dolphins headed back out to sea, the rib boat speeded up, following them for a while before heading back to the dock. As they got out, everyone talked happily about the trip and Tadeo turned to Benito. "I think I'd like to have a little walk around Caldey Island – what do you say?"

Again, Benito just stared at him oddly, and Tadeo chuckled as he turned to a girl who was selling tickets for the boat to Caldey Island. "That one is just about to leave, the boat on the other side of the dock." She pointed as she gave Tadeo the tickets.

Four pairs of eyes watched from the distance as the pair got off the one boat, then spoke to the girl and turned around to head back down the dock to another.

Tadeo and Benito trotted down the planks of wood as a man waved at them to hurry along. They jumped in, and found a seat. There was no need for life jackets on this boat, as it was slow and at a low risk of capsizing.

Benito enjoyed the ride, letting his hand dangle down into the water as the boat cruised at a gentle speed. The sun made him sleepy, and he closed his eyes, pretending he was on the boat with his friends instead of his uncle.

The next thing he knew, Tadeo was tapping his shoulder. He opened his eyes to find they were docked at the Island. They all climbed out and walked up the paved road towards the Abbey which was home to a small community of Cistercian monks. The abbey was a large, attractive building painted bright white with red clay roof tiles. A smaller, similar coloured building, which looked like it was housing, ran along the front of it. Along the way, they stopped at a gift shop and Tadeo looked around while Benito stood hesitantly by the entrance. Eventually, he walked in a few steps and looked at a stand of bookmarks. He found one that said BEN, with a picture of the lighthouse and a couple of birds that inhabited the island.

"Would you like that, son?" Tadeo stood behind him and Benito jumped.

Without waiting for an answer, Tadeo took the bookmark from his nephew's hand and paid for it, along with a couple of other things he had purchased. He handed the bookmark to

Benito who mumbled a quiet 'thank you' and put it carefully in his back pocket.

They followed the paved road south as it rose towards the white lighthouse that looked like it was encased in a large house. They were both disappointed to find that they could not actually climb the building as it was private, so Tadeo led them westward along the cliff path.

The sun was beating down on them as they walked along, taking in the beautiful view like a father and son on a holiday together. A breeze blew up from the sea, but only cooled them slightly. As they started off they were quite far from the edge of the cliff, blocked off by a large selection of gorse bushes, but as they walked along they got closer to the edge, and the gorse gave way to grass.

"Let's go right to the edge, Benny! I want to have a look down!" Tadeo's wide grin was disconcerting and Benito hesitated.

"That's okay, I'll wait here for you," said Benito quietly.

"I want you to see it with me, Ben," said Tadeo firmly, and Benito followed him obediently to the edge. A sign warned them of the dangers of cliffs, but Tadeo took no notice as he stood right on the edge, with Benito a few feet behind him.

"Come stand beside me," commanded Tadeo and Benito slowly moved forward until he was right next to his uncle. The breeze was stronger as it blew up the cliff from the sea and Benito's heart rate sky rocketed as his uncle put a large hand on his shoulder.

"I wonder if anyone has fallen to their death at this very spot," whispered Tadeo insidiously, his hand pressing heavier on Benito who had to plant his feet firmer in the ground to not wobble.

"How long do you think it would take before you were dashed against the rocks? Would you have time to ponder your death?" he whispered in Benito's ear as his hand grew ever weightier.

"You two are braver than us!" a woman's cheerful voice jerked Tadeo's head back and he hid his scowl with a friendly grin as he saw the middle age woman and, presumably, her husband reading a signboard that talked of the view and what they might see if they looked out.

Annoyed, but still smiling, Tadeo stepped back and pulled a shaky Benito with him. "It is most exhilarating standing on the edge, isn't it son?" Then added as they passed the couple to continue on the path he added in a meaningful voice, "You two should try it." Benito gave the couple a half smile and trotted eagerly away from the cliff to a safer section of the path.

After the walk, they had a little look around the island, examining the small St David's church and walking the little woodland circular walk which Tadeo declared as boring, but Benito thoroughly enjoyed. It was a safe walk, in the shade, and he almost felt relaxed.

Finally, Tadeo took the road back to the dock and they only waited five minutes before another boat taxi arrived with passengers from Tenby. When they had disembarked, Tadeo and Benito stepped on, along with a couple other people. The captain waited a few minutes for anyone else who might turn up, before turning on the engine, and cruising slowly back to the mainland.

❧

"Another one of those slower boats is coming back!" Rebeca pointed to a taxi boat that was moving slowly along the water towards shore. Just before it reached the waters busy with people and boats, it slowed down even further, and coasted gently to the dock.

Someone jumped off and moored it to a couple of posts. The people climbed out and four pairs of eyes scanned the group carefully as they walked along the dock and stepped onto the sand.

Toby saw them first – the large man and the skinny teenager. "There they are, right in the middle of the people!" As they stepped onto the beach, Toby squinted his eyes. "Tadeo looks like he is smiling! Not an evil smile. Just a 'that was quite fun' smile. Weird." Toby scrunched his face. "What is Tadeo doing? Why did he bring Benito here? For a holiday?? It doesn't make sense."

"That woman said they had stolen a really expensive necklace. Maybe Tadeo is just lying low for a bit. The police aren't going to suspect that he is holidaying in Tenby!"

Gwen stood and brushed the sand off her capris and shook her sandalled feet. "I do so hate sand! It gets everywhere! Shall we follow them?"

"Yes," said Toby, and the rest of the group stood and followed a good distance behind, though it was highly unlikely that Tadeo would have spotted them through the crowd had he happened to turn around. "We don't need to get too close, since we can track Benito's phone, but we want to be close enough so we can see if they go somewhere that Benito might be separated from Tadeo for a moment. That's all we need – a moment. Long enough to let Benito know we are here to rescue him."

"Why not just send a text?" asked Rebeca, pleased that she now knew a little bit about the technology that the others used so easily and frequently.

"Um…", Joe began and his face fell. The others looked at him questioningly. "I don't know if it was on silent when I gave it to the woman. All I know was that it was fully charged and if he doesn't use it for anything, it should last about five days."

"That's okay," said Toby "we can wait until they are surrounded closely by people. If the phone does make a noise, Tadeo won't know where it came from." He tapped on his phone. "Right, I'm ready for the opportune moment to press SEND."

A few moments later, he saw his chance when a rowdy group of young teenagers stopped and blocked the street for a few minutes as a couple of them argued. Tadeo and Benito waited a minute for them to get out of their way, but Tadeo decided not to wait and he did an about-turn and began heading right towards Toby and the others.

"Quick! In here!" Toby ducked into a clothing store with Joe and the girls close behind. They walked quickly to the middle and Toby pretended to look at a shirt as he watched the door. He panicked when he saw Tadeo and Benito through the glass windows and hesitate by the entrance. "Hide!" He hissed at the others and they crouched behind a display. A couple of women looking at dresses eyed the group suspiciously.

The door opened and Benito and his uncle walked into the store. Toby, Joe and the girls huddled together as they heard Tadeo's deep voice.

"I'm sure there will be a hat for you in here, son. Let's have a look!" Tadeo and his nephew turned as a clerk approached them. "The hats are over here, sir."

Toby felt a tap on his shoulder, then Rebeca whispered in his ear. "There's a back entrance to this store, see?" She pointed back past several racks of clothing.

Toby nodded. "On my signal." The others waited. Just then, Tadeo turned his back to them and Toby put up his hand, "Now!" he whispered, and the others quickly walked towards the back.

Toby stopped and turned around. Benito was facing in his direction. Toby just about motioned to him, but at the last second decided against it. Benito was sure to give him away in surprise. He'd have to wait to see if the kid got his text. Quickly and quietly, he followed the three out the rear entrance of the store.

"Oh!" cried Rebeca as they stepped outside onto the busy walkway.

"What?" asked Toby as his pulse quickened. He looked in the direction she was pointing and began laughing. It was an ice cream shop. He gave her a hug as Joe chuckled. Gwen did not understand the joke and she looked curiously at Joe.

"Rebeca has a thing for ice cream – they don't get it in the jungle!"

Gwen raised her eyebrows, but nodded smiling, "I would quite like an ice cream myself!"

"What do you want, Toby? We'll get the ice creams – you better keep an eagle eye on the phone to make sure they aren't heading this way."

"Pecan, pistachio and double chocolate," he said, grinning.

"I don't think that is a thing," frowned Joe.

"Not all in one, but I'll have three scoops, please!"

Joe smirked and shook his head. "Come on, girls," and he put his arms around each of them as they crossed the street side by side to get their frozen treats.

They soon exited with Joe carrying two cones that each looked like they were going to topple over. Toby quickly rescued one of them from him, and he nodded down the road. "Let's get a little distance between us while we see what they are going to do and where they are going." They walked quickly at first, then slowed down as Toby glanced at the flashing icon on the screen. "We can take it easy now, they've left the store and are carrying on in the direction they were going originally.

The four of them sat on a low wall and began devouring their ice creams. Within minutes, the boys had consumed their three scoops and cones. Gwen and Rebeca, who had only had two scoops each, were still working on their second.

Joe, who was sat next to Gwen, put his face close to hers. "Need some help with that?"

"Certainly not!" she tittered, and placed the palm of her hand firmly on his nose, pushing him away.

"Oh! They've gone into a Chinese restaurant!" said Toby, looking at his phone. "You girls can wait here and finish, if you like. Joe and I will go have a look. It might be easier to avoid Tadeo seeing us if there are only two."

Gwen and Rebeca were happy to be left to their ice cream cones in peace and nodded agreement as Toby and Joe scurried off down the street and around the corner. They slowed up as they got closer to the restaurant and stopped when they saw the entrance. Tadeo and Benito were at the take-away counter.

Toby cursed as he realised the two were not going in to sit down. "Oops!" He looked guiltily at Joe when the word escaped his lips. "Thought that would stop." He frowned at Joe's smirking, "Not sure why, since being a Christian hasn't helped *you!*"

Joe cocked his head and scowled at his brother. "Okay, now add being mean to your brother onto your list of sins!"

Toby laughed, "I guess I thought …".

"That you would be better at it than me?" Joe raised an eyebrow, looking snidely at him. "You don't instantly stop sinning," he began, then thought of Caleb, the man he had met in Louisiana who had had a bad temper when he was younger and was changed instantly when he became a Christian and no longer struggled with that. "Though, sometimes people are instantly cured of some sins. Mostly you are just aware of them more, and are better at stopping yourself." His thoughts drifted to his own temper he still struggled with. "Then again, sometimes you are left with ...".

"Come on! They're moving again!" Toby interrupted and walked in the direction that Tadeo and Benito were headed. Soon they stopped outside Seaview Bed and Breakfast, and Tadeo unlocked the door and the two of them disappeared.

"Well, we know where they are staying, now. Think they'll stay there the rest of the day?"

Tadeo and Benito did stay in the B&B for the afternoon, causing Toby, Joe and the girls to come to the conclusion that after the initial rush of excitement, surveillance work was decidedly quite boring.

As the afternoon dragged on, the sun disappeared and dark clouds began rolling in off the sea and the girls began to shiver as the wind picked up and the temperature dropped. People around them began packing up their things as the tide rolled in as quickly as the clouds.

"Let's go back to our hotel. They have a hot tub that I want to warm up in!" Gwen suggested, and stood up from where they were sitting on the beach and headed off in that direction before anyone had the chance to disagree. "Besides," she added over her shoulder, "where are they going to go in this?"

Joe and Rebeca stood to follow, and Toby reluctantly joined them. "Okay, but what if Tadeo leaves Benito in the B&B and goes out somewhere?"

"Then he will call you on my phone," said Joe who, while he was not cold, was rather bored of just sitting and waiting, and felt a soak in the hot tub would be a diversion, if nothing else. "Besides, the girls want to change into something warmer; and I might grab a jacket in case it rains. We'll come back as soon as we've had a dip and changed. It will be time for us to eat again, and we can sit down somewhere more comfortable!"

After relaxing in the hot tub, discussing all the scenarios of how they were going to rescue Benito, since they were the only ones in the tub, they were soon dressed for possible rain and walking back towards Tadeo and Benito's B&B. Tadeo and Benito had not moved. Well, Benito had not moved, and they felt certain had Tadeo gone out, Benito would have texted, if not called.

Toby looked up at the sky, "Looks like we didn't need these rain jackets after all, the clouds are disappearing."

"And it is getting warmer," complained Joe, who took off his jacket and slung it over his arm.

"They're coming out!" said Rebeca quietly, although they were far enough away not to be heard.

Joe's stomach growled loudly. "Let's hope they are going somewhere to eat — because that is exactly what I need to do before I collapse!"

Gwen squeezed his hand and laughed, "You're such a drama queen, Joe!"

Fortunately, the restaurant that Tadeo and Benito entered to sit down in was directly opposite another restaurant that Toby and the others entered.

They were immediately greeted by a waitress with some menus in her hand. "Table for four?" She smiled animatedly at Joe and he grinned charmingly back, winking at her in a friendly manner.

"Yes, please," he said, answering for them.

"Near the window," piped up Toby, interrupting the flirting between the two of them.

"Sure!" the girl said, still gazing at Joe. "Follow me."

She took them to a table for four that looked out through the window at the restaurant opposite. "My name is

Alexandra, and I'll be your waitress for your meal." She placed the menus on the table in front of them, then with one last glance at Joe, turned back towards the door to greet a couple that had just entered.

CHAPTER 17

Tadeo sat with his back to the window and Benito was opposite. He tried not to appear like he was looking for someone as he gazed out the window. When they had gotten back to the B&B, Tadeo had gone downstairs to speak to Joan and Benito had taken the opportunity to see if he could possibly send a quick text to Toby. He unzipped the pocket and pulled out the phone, thrilled to see the message from him – *they were in Tenby*! He was just about to text back when he heard his uncle's heavy feet on the stairs and only just managed to put the phone away before the door opened.

There they were! It was all Benito could do to keep a straight face as he watched the four friends enter the restaurant opposite.

"Have you decided what you want?" asked Tadeo as he looked up to see Benito gazing out the window.

"Uh ... oh! Yes!" He looked down at the menu that he had not yet opened. "I mean, no."

Tadeo looked at his nephew, squinting his eyes and rubbing his temples, wishing that he could just smack the kid across the side of the head. He really was tiring. *Never mind, not long now.*

"I ... uh ... thought I did, but I'm not sure." He opened the menu and looked down at the list, choosing something quickly so as to not annoy his uncle further.

⸺⬥⬥⬥⸺

"Well," said Joe, leaning back and patting his stomach, "that was very satisfying!"

"Oh!" said Gwen as her phone chirped. "It's Mummy. I better answer."

The three said nothing, and Joe moved over slightly so when Gwen clicked ANSWER, her mom could not see him. He wasn't sure she approved of Gwen spending so much time with them.

"Hello, Mummy! I've been meaning to Face Time you. I wanted to tell you about Richard and my engagement, and show you the amazing ring that Richard gave me!" She held up her hand to the screen.

"Oh, darling! I *chose* the ring – I know what it looks like!" Her mother laughed softly.

Gwen's three friends felt sick for her at her mother's words, as Gwen failed to hide the devastation at the revelation.

"*You* chose it?" Tears threatened and Gwen swallowed hard.

"Of course, darling! You didn't think I was going to let Richard choose it for you! It had to be a stunning ring – I couldn't take the chance that he would choose wrong!"

"But he ... he said ...".

"That he looked everywhere for something perfect?"

"Something ... like that ... ".

"Oh darling! Isn't he just wonderful? Just like your father: he knows exactly the right things to say!"

"But it's not true. He lied."

"Gwen, darling, husbands lie. Wives lie. That's how a good marriage works! Knowing the right things to say to make you feel good."

"But not if it's not true," persisted Gwen.

Lady Wentworth frowned at her daughter. "Sweetheart, I think those *friends* of yours have had a bad influence on you. You need to come home. Very soon." Her voice was firm.

"I ...".

"They're leaving the restaurant!" Toby stood up and headed towards the door. Joe and Rebeca stood to follow as Gwen said good-bye to her mom.

"I've got to go, Mummy. I'll call you later."

"I'm going to speak to Charles to make sure he has the plane ready to return on Wednesday." Gwen's mother spoke authoritatively. "Goodbye, darling." She blew her daughter a kiss and Gwen clicked off the phone without further comment.

Rebeca hurried to follow Toby, but Joe waited for Gwen as she put her phone away and got up slowly. Her emerald eyes were moist and she bit her lip as she looked everywhere but at Joe.

"We better go or we will lose them," she said, her voice just a whisper.

Joe had no idea what to say, so he took her hand and squeezed it gently. She pulled away from him, and suddenly her head shot up and she jutted out her jaw defiantly.

"Please Joe, don't. I'm fine. Let's go."

Rebeca and Toby were stood at the corner of a building, both peering around, and Joe chuckled at them. "Like you two don't look like you are following someone!"

Toby turned around and made a face at his brother, then looked compassionately at Gwen. "Gwen, I ...".

"I'm fine, Toby." She looked at Rebeca who had a sorrowful face, but said nothing. Rebeca was not always sure how to respond to Gwen. They weren't the closest of friends. "Can we just tend to the matter at hand?" she said, desperate to think of something else for the moment. "I have to go home on Wednesday, so we need to get Benito and wrap this up soon," she said coolly.

Toby nodded and peeked around the corner again. "Okay, they are far enough ahead now. Looks like they are going to the docks."

The four of them followed slowly at a distance, wondering what Tadeo was going to do. He went down the wooden planks and followed a little dock jutting out to the right where several small boats were moored. The four looked at each other.

"Do you think one of those is Tadeo's?" said Joe.

"Hmmm...," began Toby, "is there somewhere to hire a boat so we can follow them?"

Joe pointed to a sign above a small shop that read 'Tim's Rentals'. "I'm guessing they rent out boats."

Rebeca looked at Tadeo and Benito as they stopped by an old twelve-foot wooden clinker day-boat, and Tadeo looked around.

"I think we are a bit close," commented Rebeca. "Why don't we wait for them to leave and we can go in after to make enquiries in the shop?"

"I could do with some more sunscreen," commented Gwen as she looked at the shop they were stood beside, and went inside to find some. The others followed to have a look around while they were waiting.

By the time Gwen had found her sunscreen and Joe had gathered his necessary 'surveillance' snacks, Toby could see that Benito was again on the move. The small boat had been untied and Tadeo was guiding it slowly through the other moored crafts and people who were swimming where they shouldn't be.

"Surely they are not going out to sea *now*? This cannot be good."

The four friends hurried down the road and into Tim's Rentals. "We want to hire a boat!" said Toby hastily, and the man laughed.

"You sound like you are in a hurry!" He looked at the four of them, shaking his head. "Unfortunately, I rented out the last one fifteen minutes ago. The others went out earlier in the day and they aren't back yet."

"Is there another place that rents out boats?" asked Toby anxiously. He was certain that Tadeo was not taking Benito out on a leisure cruise.

"I'm afraid I am the only one that does smaller boats. If you give me your number, I can give you a call should any of them come back shortly. Otherwise, it will be too late for tonight and you'll have to book one for the morning."

"We have to go tonight," Toby said, frustrated, and the man raised an eyebrow.

"I'm afraid that's the best I can do," he said firmly.

Toby blew out through pursed lips and gave the man his number, then turned around to face the others in the small shop. "Let's go," he said defeatedly and they slowly stepped outside.

"What now?" asked Gwen, as they meandered towards the dock.

"We wait for someone to come back with a boat," said Toby before adding, "and pray that one returns soon!"

They wandered towards the dock, and when they reached the end, they sat down with their legs dangling, watching the activities of the boats and swimmers in the evening sun.

Clouds again began to form on the horizon, and soon they grew thick and menacing, covering the sun completely. A cool stiff breeze drifted off the sea and the girls put on their jackets.

⸺➤●◄⸺

The small craft bounced on the light waves as Tadeo steered the vessel out to sea, and Benito's heart began pumping his blood around his body at a rapid pace. Tadeo looked at him and smiled.

"How do you like my boat? I bought it a few months ago and someone has been keeping an eye on it for me." His voice was raised above the sound of the motor. When Benito remained silent, he continued, "I thought you would enjoy a private ride out on the sea. Are you enjoying the ride, Benny?"

Benito shivered involuntarily and zipped up his warm hoodie as the cool spray splashed his face. There was no enjoyment of the sea this evening as Benito grew more and more frightened of what his uncle was up to. He looked back at the shore and was dismayed to see how far they had gone already. He had a life jacket on but it gave him little comfort.

"I think Keegan might take your friend on a little boating trip somewhere. When I mentioned my buying a boat, and going for a trip in it, he seemed interested in taking Marlene on a trip to the sea somewhere. Though he prefers the sunshine. Not like me. I love a good rain storm." He gazed out at the dark clouds hovering over the open sea. "No, he said he would like to take Marlene abroad somewhere where the sun shines a lot. Somewhere foreign where people don't take any notice of you or what you are doing; whether there is two of you one day or one of you another day. No one cares. No one notices. I do like a place where no one notices you. Don't you?"

Benito was processing his meanings and the terrified sick feeling inside him increased to encompass his new friend. *Please God, protect her, even though she doesn't know You. Give her a chance to get to know You. Help her find a life away from Keegan.*

"How far shall we go, Benny?" The friendly façade was waning and Benito sensed the evil again in his uncle's voice like the electricity that fills the air just before a lightning strike.

Tadeo looked off in the distance for a moment, then looked directly at Benito. "You shouldn't have encouraged her.

She had a lot of freedom before you came along. I imagine you filled her head with a lot of nonsense about God and a 'better' life! Well, she *had* a good life, Benny boy. She came and went as she pleased with all the money she wanted and you took that away from her with your silly ideas. Anything that happens to her now will be *your* fault."

Benito remained silent. There was no point in explaining that it was Marlene who had tried to help him. It would make no difference to Tadeo. Still, he did wonder if he had not met Marlene if she would have been happier. She *had* been more free.

Tadeo looked out at the angry clouds that were building quickly and breathed deeply into the cool breeze. "I do love a good storm. Don't you, Benny?"

Benito's heart was pounding quickly and his ears were ringing from his racing blood as the boat slowly started bouncing ever so harder and higher with the increasing size of the waves.

Just then, a particularly large wave made the boat jump up higher. "Doesn't this just get your adrenalin going, Benny?" He had to speak loudly above the sound of the engine and the wind as it grew increasingly frantic.

Benito began wincing every time his uncle called him 'Benny'. He felt like his uncle was smacking him lightly as a preliminary for whatever was the true motive for going out. He still had that confidence he had discovered a few days ago, that he was going to Heaven, but the comfort that brought was overshadowed by the possible journey of getting there. Drowning was not the way he had hoped he would go.

The temperature began dropping and Benito shivered in his light hoodie. His uncle looked at him and cocked his head, smiling. He took off his jacket and handed it out to Benito. Benito just stared at it for a moment, then as he felt it grow another few degrees colder, he took the offering and put the large jacket around him. Its huge size made him look like a toddler and he shivered again.

"You should have seen your mom, Benny, when I gave her the chocolate." He sneered in remembrance and a pang shot through Benito's heart. Tadeo looked off across the horizon, thinking about the visit. "So trusting she was, Benny."

Benito flinched at the past tense and silently he pleaded with God that her death had been quick and painless. He was thankful that she had not known what kind of man her brother had turned out to be.

"Ya, she took that chocolate and actually thanked me!" He looked at his nephew through his squinted, piercing blue eyes. "Silly cow thanked me for killing her." He threw his head back and laughed heartily.

The realisation hit Benito and he lashed out at his uncle angrily, "You poisoned her chocolate?! You evil wicked man!" He stood up fiercely, then wobbled and fell back down on the bench as the vessel bounced along.

This only made Tadeo laugh harder. "She thought her God was going to heal her from her sickness! Ha! Her God couldn't even save her from my poison! She took it eagerly, stupid cow!"

"She is not a stupid cow!" Benito defended his mom angrily, this time not moving.

"She *was* not a stupid cow!" Tadeo corrected him, guffawing loudly into the wind. "And where is she now, Benito? Huh? Where is she now? You have some silly notion she is sat at the feet of some loving God in Heaven??"

Tears filled Benito's eyes and he pulled the jacket around him closer as the whistling wind threatened to remove it from him, his lips quivering from fear, from anger, and from the cold air whipping at his face.

"Let me tell you something, Benny boy! There is no Heaven! There is no God! When you die, that is it! You are dead and your body rots in the ground and gets eaten by maggots! Your mother is being eaten by maggots, Benny, do you hear me??!" His snide laughter was buffeted by the storm.

Benito looked behind him, but he could no longer see the shore as the light grew ever dimmer from the heavy blanket of black clouds that now covered the entire sky. Lightning flashed in the sky several miles away, and Benito automatically counted in his mind until the thunder: one, two, three, four, five, six – then a quiet rumble.

Tadeo cut the engine and scowled at his nephew who was now clinging to the side of the boat as it rocked wildly on the waves. "I want my jacket back!" He thrust his hand across and Benito reluctantly gave it to him.

Great drops of rain began to fall one at a time like a giant dripping tap in the sky, and Benito tried to cross his arms across his chest to warm himself, while still holding onto the side with one hand.

"And take off your life jacket. You don't need it."

"B-b-b-but … I … can't swim very well …," Benito stammered. "What if … what if … I fall overboard?"

His uncle laughed hysterically, "You stupid boy! You are as stupid as your stupid mother! You both have a great *stupid* gene!" He put his face close to Benito's and growled, "You both are so stupid you think your dad died from a random mugging!"

Benito's heart began banging at his chest. "No!" He screamed. "No!"

"Yes! Benny boy! Yes! He was stupid too! He found out about my 'activities' and threatened to go to the police! Ha! I stopped him! Of course I didn't do it myself – there are plenty of people who will do that kind of thing for a bit of cash!" He chuckled loudly and rubbed his chin, sneering at Benito, then leaned back again. "Do you want to know how much your dad's life was worth, Benny? Do you?"

Benito closed his eyes and covered his ears, howling, "No! No! No!"

His uncle pulled Benito's hands away and shouted at him as he laughed, "Two hundred pounds, Benny! Your dad's stinking life was worth no more than two hundred pounds! I probably could have got the kid to do it for cheaper, but I was feeling generous! Two hundred pounds!"

"Come to think of it, your mom's life was worth even less! The chocolate and poison together only cost me fifty pounds! And what a show that was! She was in such pain! She writhed and cried like a baby, foaming at the mouth – she was in agony for hours, Benny! Hours!"

"No!" cried Benito, "You're lying! She was in the hospital! You wouldn't have stayed after you gave it to her!"

Tadeo cocked his head and smirked, "You're right, Benny, and you know why I didn't stay?" He stretched out his arm to the side and swung it over hard against the side of Benito's head with a loud SMACK! "Because! I'm not *stupid*!"

Benito let go the side of the boat as he grasped his head with both hands, his ears ringing from the pain. The boat jumped and Benito fell to the floor of the boat at Tadeo's feet. Tadeo grabbed the life jacket, untied it and yanked it off, tossing it into the angry black waves.

⸻

Toby's phone pinged and he answered it anxiously. "Yes?" He paused as he listened, then said, "Okay, we'll be there now." He hung up and swung his feet up on the deck, pushing himself to a standing position. "A boat has come back, but we can only have it for an hour, because a storm is coming in."

The others followed suit and Joe piped up, "Ya think?"

Toby picked up speed and began jogging towards the rental shop, rushing in and talking as he entered.

"Right, we're here, how much is it?" he huffed out.

The man held up his hand, "Whoah! Hang on now, I just looked at the weather forecast, and I can't let you rent a boat at the moment. The storm is coming in a lot faster than I thought. You can come back tomorrow, and get one first thing."

"We need it now!" Toby leaned over the counter almost shouting in his panic, and the man stepped back, as Joe put his hand on his brother's shoulder to calm him.

"Toby, calm down. The man has a point! The storm is getting bad!"

"All the more reason to get out there now! We have to find Benito!" cried Toby, fearful for his friend.

"Hang on," said the clerk, "If someone needs help out there, you should call the coastguard. They're equipped for this. How do you know this Benito needs help?"

"Because ... oh ... because ... we don't have time for this! The coastguard might not go out if we don't have proof!"

"Proof of what?" the man frowned.

Toby spun around and pushed past Joe as he stormed out of the shop. "We need a boat!" He said frantically.

Gwen held up her purse and smiled, "I might have enough in here for a private rental."

<hr/>

"Yes!" shouted Toby, excited, "Let's go!"

The four friends hurried down the dock and turned down where it jutted out to moor the smaller boats. A few people were milling about, with a couple of people still seeing to their crafts, and making sure they were safe from the coming storm.

"We need a boat!" Toby called out and several heads turned to look at the hysterical teenager.

"There's a rental shop just over there," an elderly man pointed in the direction of Tim's Rentals.

Toby shook his head, "He won't rent us one now because of the storm coming." As if on cue, a gust of wind raced across the dock, whipping some sails loudly. The bemused people looked up at the dark clouds and out to sea at the menacing waves.

The elderly man smiled nodding, "That would make sense. There's always tomorrow, son. You seem keen to go for a ride."

"But you don't get it! We need to go out and find our friend *now*!"

"Well, then, if someone is in trouble, you need the coast ...".

"Guard, I know!" interrupted Toby. He turned to Gwen. "How much have you got?"

"Three hundred," she said without looking in her purse.

"Okay!" Toby turned back to the group, "Who of you has a boat they'll lend us for three hundred pounds?"

The people stared warily back at Toby, but no one took up the offer.

"But I can get another thousand out of the bank," offered Gwen urgently.

A dark-haired wiry man with a weathered face stepped forward, a cigarette hanging out the side of his mouth. "I think I might be able to oblige you," he said slowly.

"Great!" said Toby excitedly. "Gwen! Go get the money now."

As Gwen hurried off to the nearest bank, the elderly man spoke up again. "I don't know if you want to take out Ed's boat in this weather." The group around him laughed. "It's a bit rough."

"Like Ed!" laughed a woman, and the group chuckled, nodding.

"As long as it floats!" said Toby.

"Aye! She floats all right! And don't you go listening to these folk! They just are jealous they don't have such a fine craft as mine!" Ed held out his arm and motioned Toby, Joe and Rebeca to follow him to his boat.

He stopped in front of an eighteen foot craft that was in need of some paint. Toby thought it did look rather decrepit, but there was no other option, so he nodded to Ed. "It looks fine."

"Now, I take it you know how to handle a boat?" Ed asked, raising an eyebrow.

"Um …". Toby turned to Rebeca, "Have you ever handled a boat with a motor?"

Rebeca smiled and nodded as she grabbed her hair that was waving wildly in the stormy air. "I have some relatives in another village who acquired a boat with an engine in it. I did drive it a couple of times. Though, I do prefer oars! It is more relaxing." As she said the words, she frowned at her frivolous talk of relaxing when their friend's life was very possibly in danger.

"Now the only trouble, of course, is fuel. I only got a quarter o' tank left. It could take ya a reasonable way, but I don't normally go out with anythin' less than half a tank." He scrunched his face as he looked across the harbour to a boat filling station. "Bill's closed down for the night, so I don't know what we're gonna do 'bout that."

Toby's heart fell as anxiousness for his friend threatened to overwhelm him. The man scratched his head then turned to his friends that were still milling about and shouted, "Hey Danny! You got some spare fuel these kids can have?"

A tough looking, well-muscled man smiled and nodded, "Aye, ya! But it'll cost ya!" He laughed as he walked off down the pier to find the spare container of fuel he always kept on board his own boat.

Just then, Gwen appeared in the distance and hurried down the wooden planks toward them. When she reached Ed, she handed him the thousand pounds that she had just collected from the bank, then opened her purse to get the other three hundred. A wide grin spread across his face as he took the money and stuffed it in his shirt pocket.

Danny walked up with the container of fuel and put his hand out to Gwen who looked at Toby and shrugged her shoulders. "That's all I have. I can only get a thousand pounds a day from the machine."

Still grinning, Ed patted her shoulder and laughed, "That's all right, Missy. I'll give Danny a bit of this." His hand touched his bulging pocket as his other took the container from his friend. "I'll show you how to fuel 'er up, son." Ed walked back towards his boat where Toby and the others were standing, and leaned over to put the fuel on the hull before stepping in himself.

But Toby looked at the little beeping icon on his phone which seemed to have stopped moving and grabbed the man's arm. "We don't have time! We have to go." He spoke loudly as the wind whistled across the bay, picking up speed.

A look of concern passed across Ed's face as he looked at the sky and then looked around at the group of friends stood waiting to get into his boat. "I'm not so sure this is a sensible thing." He hesitated as panic started racing through Toby's bloodstream. "Are you sure you lot wanna go out in this? I mean, I feel kinda responsible, as it's my boat."

Rebeca stepped forward and touched the man's arm kindly, smiling encouragingly. "It is all right, you need not worry. I have been in storms like this – I am from a place in Nicaragua where we travel a lot by boat. We will be fine."

Toby jumped lightly down into the boat and grabbed the sides as it moved around on the choppy water. Joe followed suit, glancing up at Gwen.

"Well," said Ed, his conscience mildly mollified, "at least put the life jackets on – they're piled in that cupboard in the bow."

"Thank you!" said Rebeca and she bent down to untie the vessel while Gwen stood watching from the pier, deliberating whether or not to join her friends.

"It's okay, Gwen, you've done more than enough, coughing up the money. You go back to the hotel and have a relax in the hot tub. We'll be back in no time!" Toby encouraged her.

Suddenly, determination swept across her face and she carefully put a foot down into the boat. Joe reached out and grabbed her, helping her in. Rebeca finished untying the craft and expertly jumped in as she pushed the boat away from the dock. She then quickly made her way to the controls and started up the boat, standing as she guided it slowly backwards until she was clear of the boats on either side, and could then turn it to head forwards slowly out into the harbour, bouncing lightly over the waves.

She called over her shoulder, "Toby, come up beside me, so I can see what direction we need to go." Her hair whipped wildly around her head and Gwen called out,

"Rebeca, would you like a hair band?" Rebeca nodded, but Gwen just gave the item to Joe, so he could wobble his way to the front where Rebeca was. She quickly tied up her hair, then sat down behind the wheel, pushing the lever forward to increase their speed, just as a streak of lightning lit the sky in front of them.

The rain was falling heavier now, and Benito pulled his hoodie tighter around him, even though it was useless to stop him from getting wet. Tadeo zipped up his own waterproof jacket and leaned his head back laughing.

"Isn't it exhilarating being out on the sea in a storm?!" He shouted loudly as another flash of lightning lit up the sky.

This time, Benito only got to the count of five. It was coming closer. He slid off the bench seat and crouched on the hull of the craft, clinging to the oars that were locked in a brace beside him.

Please God! I don't want to drown! Please help me! Benito pleaded silently as he wiped his wet face with the back of his hand, while he held tightly with his other.

His uncle looked completely unhinged as he laughed dementedly, holding his arms wide as though he was embracing the storm. He bounced on the seat as the craft danced on the ever higher waves. "Glorious!" Tadeo shouted and his eyes almost disappeared upward like he was in some kind of spiritual trance. Although Benito was certain it was not any spirits that *he* wanted to experience.

The temperature dropped suddenly again as the angry storm whipped its way across the sea and the rain pelted Benito as he uselessly covered his head, crouching into an ever tighter ball. A large jump up from the boat unbalanced Benito and he put his hand down to steady himself, distressed to find a layer of water flowing by his feet. The wind danced itself into a frenzy and had become gale force, slamming against the side of the craft furiously, knocking it sideways as the ferocious waves attempted to toss them ever higher.

Benito crouched down even further, sitting in the frigid water that rolled around the hull, wondering if his uncle would forget he was even there as the deranged man continued calling out to the storm as though he was worshipping it.

"Yes! Yes! The power! The power of the storm! Oh how I want power like that! Yes!" His voice grew ever louder and more piercing like he was possessed and Benito shivered even more from the terror of watching his crazed uncle who appeared to be almost joined with the storm itself. Benito was unsure of whether that was even more frightening than the storm and the thought of being tossed into the frantic cold waves and floating down to the depths.

Abruptly, Tadeo shot to his feet and almost screeched, "It is time!" A deafening, inhuman howl from the depths of his soul erupted from his mouth then disappeared out into the storm like a wild creature returning home.

Benito crouched still tighter, but Tadeo stepped forward and grabbed Benito's arm tightly, calling out, "A sacrifice! A sacrifice to this glorious storm!"

And with that, Tadeo reached out his other arm, grabbing Benito's and raising him effortlessly above his head, screaming his deep voice into the gale, "Tonight! Tonight all my enemies will be gone! And I will be free! FREE!!!"

Gwen huddled next to Joe as he held her closely with his arm around her shivering shoulders. He took off his jacket that he had slung over himself after he had put on the life jacket, and wrapped it around her.

Rebeca shouted to Toby, "I believe you can pull that tarpaulin over the bars to give us some cover from the rain!"

So Toby fumbled with the heavy fabric and Joe stood to help him, with their task hindered by the boat jumping along the waves. Soon, between the two of them, they had it over the front third of the boat and were at the very least, sheltered from the rain.

"Can't you go any faster?" said Toby.

Just then, the boat jumped and Toby scrambled to keep himself upright. Rebeca looked at him and raised an eyebrow.

"I think this is as fast as we can safely go." She spoke loudly. "We are no good to Benito if we are capsized!"

"And I think Ed will want more money if we don't return his boat in one piece!" called out Gwen as she snuggled deeper into Joe, holding onto him tightly as they bounced across the angry waves.

She looked up at Joe and sniggered in a childlike defiance: "My mother would kill me if she knew what I was doing!"

Joe cocked his head, torn between compassion for Gwen's predicament and scorn for her acceptance of it. "Gwen," he began, looking deep into her emerald eyes.

She reached up and put her manicured fingertips onto his lips. "Shhh! Don't let's spoil this moment. This is so exhilarating! I feel completely free! I have to go back Wednesday where I'll be under the control of Mummy again." She sighed deeply. "Probably even more since she's afraid of your ...". She shook her head. "It doesn't matter. I'll *never* be this free again. Let me enjoy this time – even if it is saving Benito from his evil uncle!" Gwen lay her head on the chest of Joe's life-jacket. He buried his face into her thick, soft, cropped hair and kissed her head. He closed his eyes, breathing in deeply, inhaling her scent and locking it into his memory.

"Is there a way of connecting your phone to the navigation system on this boat?" asked Rebeca. She was always amazed at what the devices were capable of, and felt certain this was one thing it should be able to do.

Toby shrugged his shoulders. "I'll try. It would be easier with a cable, but I'll try the bluetooth."

Rebeca had no idea what a blue tooth was, but she moved over slightly, so Toby could stand directly in front of the system on the dash, while she held tightly to the wheel, continuing to direct the boat to where Toby had last indicated.

It took him several minutes to figure it out, but finally, he got it hooked up. "Got it!" He smiled at Rebeca. "I wasn't sure an old boat like this would be able to connect, but it looks like he has updated this navigation system, if nothing else!"

"They were heading south-west when they first went out, but it looks like …". Toby squinted at the screen and looked carefully at all the readings. "This can't be good!"

"That they are heading directly south now?" asked Rebeca.

Toby looked at her, and for the hundredth time, was amazed at her navigation and tracking abilities. He chuckled and kissed her cheek, holding out his phone: "Shall I just turn this off?"

She cocked her head and half smiled, "I may know what direction we are going, but I do not know where Benito and his uncle are."

"Use your tracking abilities!" Toby teased.

"Ha. Ha." Rebeca shook her head and grabbed the wheel tighter as they were buffeted by some extra high waves. She pushed forward slightly on the throttle and began snaking the boat back and forth so they were not heading directly into the waves.

"How come you can handle such waves and wind? Surely even in a big storm, the water doesn't get like this on that river by you!" said Toby, keeping an eye on the bleep on the screen.

"My father's brother took my father and me for a journey down the river out into the open sea when he got his motorized boat. A ferocious storm blew up and we were caught out in it for a few hours. It was smaller than this – so actually, this is a little easier to handle!" She added, "What I mean is, it is easier for the boat to handle." She frowned as she thought of Benito. "But not as small as that boat that Benito and Tadeo went out on."

Toby grabbed her hand and pointed to the beeping on the screen. "It is still beeping, so that the phone is still out of the water." He looked out into the storm then said quietly, *"Please God, protect Benito. Keep him safe."*

Another bounce jolted the four a couple of inches in the air and Gwen squealed. "I think you need to ask God to keep *us* safe as well! I may be marrying a jerk, but I don't want to die!"

"We're gaining on them!" called out Toby excitedly, desperate to reach his friend before Tadeo hurt him – or worse! He traced his finger across the screen, trying to familiarise himself with the information it gave. "I think it says we are a mile away. They are still moving but…".

"They are only moving as fast as the wind is," finished Rebeca.

"Which means that they are moving very very slowly, or…", Toby continued.

"Tadeo has cut his engine for some reason." Again Rebeca finished for him.

"Or it is stalled." Toby twisted his face. "Maybe I was wrong. Maybe they *were* just going for a ride and they ran into trouble."

"Either way, Benito – and maybe Tadeo – needs help," said Rebeca.

"That man deserves…".

"No, Toby," Rebeca interrupted him, "do not wish bad on anyone – even your enemy. Otherwise you are no better than him."

Toby scowled and gritted his teeth. "I'm sorry, Rebeca, but I think he deserves to be struck – down – dead!"

CHAPTER 18

"ACK!!" Tadeo cried out as a stabbing pain pierced his heart like a lightning bolt.

THUD!

Benito suddenly found himself battered and bruised on the hull of the boat with Tadeo's heavy body lying on top of him.

Gasping, Benito clawed his way out from under his uncle and across the hull that was now a couple inches deep in water, rolling over on his back and taking in several deep breaths as he finally escaped Tadeo's hefty frame. He lay there in the shallow water, thankful he was still alive. He rolled sideways back and forth with the pool in the boat sloshing over him as the boat bounced erratically on the water. He shivered uncontrollably as the cold rain pelted his aching body, wondering if this was still the end; if he was going to float out to sea and die in this little boat as it slowly made its way further and further from civilisation.

Benito jolted as a hand grabbed his ankle. "Oh ... no ... you ... don't!" A gravelly voice struggled, the grip on his ankle belying any lack of strength from his uncle.

His head bumped along through the water across the wooden planks, and scraped his back as his uncle slowly pulled him towards where he was now in a slumped sitting position. Benito strained to regain some semblance of strength to fight Tadeo and he lashed out, kicking and flailing.

"You're going over, boy!" The gravelly voice found the last of his energy in the recesses of his evil being.

Benito clawed at his uncle's face desperately, trying to get him to let go, but his uncle pulled him closer to him and manoeuvred him in his arms so he was up by his chest. Tadeo was breathing heavily, the pain in his chest unbearable, but seething at the thought of the possibility that his nephew could survive.

"You ..." Tadeo hefted him higher, "are ..." and higher, gasping at the effort as he fought against the agonising pain that spread across his chest, "going ..." higher he lifted him, "over!"

The next thing Benito knew, he was in the air, then the freezing waters opened their arms to grab him and hold him tightly as he thrashed about in the waves, gasping for air as he clawed at nothing to keep his head above the water.

A great flash lit up the sky and Benito saw his uncle screaming into the storm as he pulled out his gun and released the whole round into the hull. A huge wave crashed over the small craft then threw it into the air, throwing his uncle into the sea where he disappeared into the depths. The boat landed on top of the next wave and broke in half, flinging pieces of wood in all directions.

"Please God, help me!" Benito called out into the storm as he strained to tread water in the relentless waves as they bashed him and tried to push him underneath their arms. He felt the weight of his clothes as they soaked up the water, so he held his breath and just kicked his legs as he removed his thick hoodie, then pulled off his shoes. He did feel slightly lighter, but his jeans were lead weights on his legs. He gasped, then held his breath again as he let the waves push him along while he fumbled with the button and zipper. He was thankful they weren't skinny jeans, as once he had finally undone them, they were still a struggle to peel off his legs. He kicked free and pushed himself back above the water, treading water in his t-shirt and boxers.

He jumped as something hit his back, and he reached out to find a large chunk of the boat floating past him. He grabbed it, and struggled to find a couple of places that his hands could grip as he dragged himself onto the several planks of wood that were miraculously still fixed together.

———⋙●⋘———

Beep! Beep! Beep! The signal on Toby's phone flashed on the screen as Rebeca and the others slowly grew closer. Then ...

Nothing. The signal suddenly disappeared.

"Oh, please God, no!" Toby cried as he tapped the screen with his fingers. "No!" He shouted louder, "No!" He smacked the screen hard with his hand and Rebeca took one hand of the wheel, squeezing his hand firmly.

"It just means his phone is not contacting us anymore. It could mean anything. Maybe Tadeo found it and threw it in the sea," she shouted through the storm, trying to encourage Toby as she focused on the sea in front of her. "We'll just head to the last known location, and I am sure we can find him from there."

Rebeca let go of his hand to hold onto the wheel as she struggled to keep the boat at the best angle and speed to safely reach their friend, silently praying that God would help them find him.

Sheet lightning lit up the sky and a few seconds later, a loud BANG filled the air, making the four of them jump.

"Is it safe being on the sea in a small boat in a lightning storm?" shouted Gwen.

Joe turned to her with a slight smile. "I don't think it safe to be on the sea in a small boat in *any* storm."

———⋙●⋘———

The rain pelted the windows and she could hear the water pouring from the gutters into the water butt at the back of the house and Marlene pulled her cardigan around her. It wasn't cold in the house but it was a comforting action and brought a flash of memory into her head as she thought of a storm when she was a child. She had run and jumped in her mom's lap and her mom had wrapped her arms tightly around her and she revelled in how protected that had made her feel.

Marlene continued to tap on her laptop, then looked up at Keegan who was sat on the sofa across from her, watching a football game. "I found a two-week holiday in Greece for a great price," she looked at the screen then wrinkled her face. "Oh, we'd have to leave on Wednesday." Her fingers hovered over the keyboard then moved to click off the site, but Keegan grabbed her hand.

He winked at her. "We can be ready by Wednesday. Book it!"

"Are you sure?" she queried. He wasn't usually one for rushing things.

"Yes, babe, book it." He bent his head and lifted her chin gently with his fingers so her lips would meet his and, for one brief moment, Marlene was content. It would be a lovely holiday. She turned back to the laptop and continued the booking.

She closed the computer and stood up. "I better go have a look at my clothes and see what I want to pack!" she smiled down at him.

"I'll take you shopping and buy you some new things. I want to make sure you look beautiful on our trip." He picked up the remote and clicked OFF. "Come on, let's go. We'll get your nails done and a facial – the works! You'll be the hottest babe on the beach!"

Contentment vanished at his words. He called the shots. She was his possession to control. A prize to be shown off.

To make him feel good. He was incapable of caring about someone other than himself. He hated too much to ever love.

She forced her smile back on. She had to play the part. For her own sanity she would pretend. He might control her, but she could pretend that she let him; that really, it was her decisions. After all, wasn't it? Didn't she choose to stay with him? There wasn't a lock on the front door. She wasn't a prisoner; was she?

She suddenly realised he was stood at the front door, holding out her jacket like a gentleman. Holding her head high, she swayed towards him and turned to slip her arms in before turning back around and giving him a peck on the cheek.

"Thanks, babe, you're a sweetheart!"

———⟶⟵———

Benito slowly grew aware of the discomfort of lying on something and suddenly realised the bag with the phone was still attached to him. It was now filled with water which most certainly rendered the devise useless. He tightened his grip with his left hand before letting go with his right, and turning slightly to his side so he could unbuckle the bag and pull it from around his stomach. Immediately, he grabbed hold with his other hand again, just before another wave pushed into him and raised him high in the air. He closed his eyes and prayed for the hundredth time for God to save him.

The next thing he knew, he was on a swing in the park not far from his childhood home. His father was pushing him and they were both laughing. Grey clouds filled the sky and the wind was picking up, but he could still feel the warmth from the earlier sun as he held tightly to the thick ropes.

"Higher, Daddy! Higher! I want to go as high as the sky!"

His dad pushed him hard and Benito reached his toes out to the clouds, sure that if he could only stretch a little farther, he could touch them. Another push and Benito reached out his hands to touch them. At first there was exhilaration as he flew towards the clouds, then panic as he realised he was falling towards the hard ground.

But his dad was ready. He was tall and strong and grabbed Benito from out of the air and held him tightly, squeezing him lovingly, pressing his face against Benito's cheek.

"I got you, son, I got you!"

Benito wrapped his terrified limbs around his dad more tightly than he thought possible and it wasn't until his dad had walked into their house that he loosened his grip enough to look his dad in the eyes.

"You saved me, Daddy! You saved me!"

His dad had given him a wide smile and kissed his forehead firmly: "I love you, son!"

His dad had never reprimanded him. He had never told him what a stupid thing he had done. They both knew it was. It was a mad moment that he had never repeated, and his dad knew he wouldn't. Benito was cautious and thoughtful after that. Quiet. Always weighing the risks to the irritation of his friends at school. To the point where he became bullied. Still, he never took chances and did what his dad told him to do.

Until that day. When his mom told him his dad wasn't coming home any more. That he would have to spend some time with his uncle Tadeo while she found a job to pay the bills. She worked extra hours at first, so he had lived with his uncle for a few months. After a while, when she had paid for the funeral, he came back home, and only went to Tadeo's after school. But by then, he had already been exposed to his uncle's lifestyle. The life that would become his. The life that he didn't want, but couldn't escape.

The next thing he knew, he was in his uncle's back garden. He had done something wrong but he couldn't remember what it was. Tadeo grabbed a bucket of dirty, soapy water that Benito had just used to wash the floor and threw the contents on Benito's head.

Icy cold water brought Benito back to consciousness and he choked and coughed out the water he had inhaled as he felt himself sliding into the sea. Clawing at the wood, he had to use every last ounce of strength to pull himself back up so he was once more lying on top of the planks.

Benito became aware that he was no longer shivering and wondered if it was getting warmer. Then he realised he could no longer feel his hands and feet, but his ears felt like ice. He wondered if this was what hypothermia felt like.

Light flashed across the sky and two seconds later Benito jumped at the BOOM! and let go of the wood again. His heart pounded at the sound ringing in his ears, but he felt sleepy. He was so tired. He didn't remember ever being so tired. He felt his body slide slowly back into the water. It didn't feel so cold now. It was almost comforting. Maybe drowning would not be so bad after all.

⟶►◄⟵

"What's that?!" Toby had found a powerful flashlight in the hold where the life-jackets had been and shone it out into the water. "Stop!"

Rebeca pulled the throttle all the way back and the boat slowed. She held onto the wheel and looked where Toby was pointing. Joe leaned over the edge.

"A little my way, Rebeca!"

Rebeca tried her best to move the boat in the direction he wanted, but the waves kept beating her back. Finally, he reached it and pulled it into the boat.

An orange life-jacket.

"No!" screamed Toby. Then he shone the light outwards across the sea, waving it back and forth, calling as loudly as his lungs would allow him, "Benito! Benito!" But the gale just threw his voice back to him and he pounded the side of the boat with his hand.

The boat rocked violently and Toby crashed sideways, nearly dropping the light. He reached out and grabbed the side as he was nearly thrown over into the mounting waves. He fell to his knees and shone the light out into the dark, waving it back and forth again, shouting, "Benito! Benito!"

His light caught something bobbing on the surface of a wave which threw it closer to them. He nearly cried as he saw what it was. A large section of a boat. A boat that had been broken into pieces.

Rebeca opened up the throttle slightly and steered as slowly as she could, into the pieces that had been widely dispersed from the relentless waves.

A light shone on Benito's face and he opened his eyes. Was it the sun? Had the storm passed? It was gone as quickly as it had appeared, but Benito shook his head and took a deep breath, the desire to live calling him, urging him to drag himself back onto the debris.

There it was again! A flash of light in the dark. Benito looked up but the rain pelted his eyes and he squeezed them shut. He thought he heard his name, but he must be dreaming! No one knew he was out here. A gust of wind turned him away from the light and a large wave rushed at him, pushing him back into the darkness.

Something brushed against his leg. Then again. Could it be a shark?! Were there sharks in these waters? Benito was suddenly wide awake at the thought of being attacked by a shark, and he pulled himself further up the planks of wood, pulling his knees up under him so his feet were out of the water.

He felt it before he saw it. The crackling electricity filled the air around him and his hair stood on end. The sky lit up like it was day and a second later BANG! Benito closed his eyes and clung to the boat debris, once more praying that he would somehow make it back to the shore alive.

———◦◦◦◦———

"Keep circling!" called out Toby as he frantically swept the light back and forth, trying his hardest to be methodical so he didn't miss anything. However, as the boat rose and then dipped on the waves, and the debris floated farther and farther apart, Rebeca was finding it nearly impossible to do as requested.

"There! What's that? Over there, Rebeca!" Rebeca struggled to steer the boat in the direction Toby requested, but finally managed as a wave lifted them up high, then brought them down low.

Toby tried to keep the light steady as she drew closer to the large section of boat bobbing wildly in the water. Then she saw him – someone clinging on – it had to be Benito! She carefully steered the boat towards him, but every time she got close, a wave pushed him away.

"Come on, Rebeca!" cried Toby as they all watched in horror as two large waves came together upending Benito's raft and tossing him into the dark waters.

Suddenly, Joe shot to his feet, kicked off his shoes and launched himself in the direction they had last seen their friend.

"Joe!" Gwen screamed as she leaned over, straining to see him as he fought the water to reach the planks.

Toby tried desperately to maintain the direction on of the light as he shone it to guide his brother. Then, blackness! Toby let out a stream of curses as he banged the light with his hand bringing it momentarily back to life again before it died completely. He shook it and shook it, then threw it to the floor as he collapsed on his knees with his head in his hands.

"Please God! Help them! Don't let them die!"

Rebeca did her best to hold the craft in the same place as it jumped and got tossed back and forth, praying Joe would be guided by the red and green lights at the front of the boat and be strong enough to make it back with Benito.

Panic had sent Joe into the water, but as he adjusted to the frigid temperature, a calmness came over him and he focused on the wood. When the light went out, he took a deep breath and strained his eyes to see the silhouette floating on the waves. He swam steady, going with the waves and letting them take him closer. Finally, he reached the planks, and just as he did, a head burst out of the water gasping and hands shot up, scrabbling to reach the planks.

Joe reached out to him and Benito panicked as he felt the hand and he fought him, not knowing what or who was grabbing him. Was it Tadeo trying to pull him back down??

"Benito!" he shouted, "It's Joe!"

Suddenly, Benito stopped thrashing, but as he did, he started to sink back down and he began to panic. Joe grabbed him from behind and put his arms around his chest. "Lean back onto me, Ben." Benito relaxed slightly and leaned back into the saving arms. "That's it, Ben, I've got you!" Joe said in his ear.

He could see the coloured lights of the boat, as it bobbed up and down, and he strained against the waves to pull them both towards it while Rebeca turned the craft and headed at a snail's pace back towards them.

"I can see them!" she called out to Toby as she got closer. She strained to see them in the lights from the boat that only shone weakly out into the water, but she kept the boat facing towards them as she moved along slowly. It wouldn't be easy to come alongside them close enough for them to reach the boat without going over top of them.

Toby leaned over as Rebeca drew near, but just as he touched Benito, a wave grabbed them and pulled them away. Rebeca moved forward and fought her way back as she turned around to come at them again.

Toby moved to the other side, arms down as far as he could reach, when Gwen came along beside him, a rope in her hand.

"I found this at the back! Here!"

Toby quickly tied a large loop and hung it over the edge, waiting for Rebeca to get closer. He couldn't see around the front and waited for Rebeca to ...

"I'm alongside them now!" she called out over her shoulder, keeping her eye on where she last saw the two.

Just then, the moon shone out through a small break in the clouds, and Toby threw the rope out and shouted to Joe, "I've thrown a rope out in a loop Joe, can you see it?!"

Joe let go with one arm and reached out, stretching back and forth to find the life-saving item. Finally, he yelled, "I've got it! Hang on a minute!" He fumbled with the loop as he wrapped it around Benito.

"Pull Benito up, then throw it in again for me!" called out Joe.

"No!" shouted back Toby, "We might lose you and not be able to get back to you! Gwen and I can pull you both up!" He looked over at Gwen who was fumbling with the other end of the long rope.

"Here! I'll tie the middle up to this bar here, then we won't lose the rope!" She quickly wrapped the rope around the bar on the side of the boat, then tossed the other end out to Joe, but it was not far enough.

Rebeca pulled back the throttle to STOP and rushed over to help Toby and Gwen. She grabbed onto the end that was tied to Benito and Toby quickly brought the other end back into the boat, then tossed it out again, where it landed just by Joe. He slipped the loop around him, while still holding to Benito to keep his head above water.

"Okay!" Joe shouted, "Pull Benito in first!"

Rebeca drew the rope in until Benito was touching the boat, then Toby leaned over to grab his hand.

"Come on, Benito!" Rebeca pulled on the rope while Toby heaved Benito in by his arms. Gwen bent over to grab his legs, and together, they rolled him over the side and carefully laid him on the hull before quickly turning back to retrieve Joe. Between the three of them, they manoeuvred the exhausted Joe over the edge, finally sliding his feet over the side as he fell beside Benito who was crying with his face onto the hull.

Joe lay on his back, straining to replace the oxygen in his body that had been depleted by battling the raging waters to rescue Benito. He groaned as Gwen threw herself on him and held him tightly.

"Oh, Joe! I thought you were gone!" Tears flowed freely and Joe turned to kiss a salty cheek before he fell back again, exhausted.

"Is Ben all right?" Joe gasped loudly to his brother.

Benito coughed and wept as he cried out, "Joe! I owe you my life! Thank you Joe!"

Suddenly Toby said, "Where's Tadeo?"

Benito's sobbing subsided slightly as he answered, "I think he had a heart attack." He breathed deeply then spoke slowly as he described to the others what happened.

"Take us back to shore, Rebeca," said Toby as Benito finished his story.

"Certainly!" Rebeca smiled and stood to start up the boat and pointed it towards shore as Toby sat beside Benito who was lying on his back with his knees up, on one side, and Joe lying closely on the other, with Gwen kneeling beside him.

Rebeca pushed open the throttle as she snaked her way along the waves back to the shoreline and they all began breathing sighs of relief as they moved closer.

A mile from shore, however, the engine coughed and sputtered, then sputtered again before dying completely.

"I'm afraid we are out of fuel," called out Rebeca. "I thought we would make it! We were so close!"

"We've got the spare jerry can we can use!" piped up Toby, but Rebeca shook her head, shouting back to him,

"We'll never manage it in this storm! We'll have to wait for it to subside!" Rebeca sat down beside Toby on the seat with the other three still lying on the bottom of the boat by their feet.

The rain began falling heavier in a deafening deluge and the wind whipped across the sea, lifting the waves even higher, tossing the boat like a toy. A bolt of lightning shot through the sky and a second later there was a loud BOOM!

"We're like sitting ducks, out here on the water," shouted Rebeca, snuggling closer to Toby.

"Oh! What's that?" asked Gwen, as she pointed to a bobbing light sweeping across the waves. They all turned as she stood up and pointed.

Just then, the boat tilted precariously as a huge wave slammed the side, throwing them against the side and propelling Gwen screaming, into the icy waters.

"Gwen!" Joe shouted as he scrambled to his knees to see over the edge. He couldn't see her.

A deep voice called out through a mega phone as the light grew closer, "It's the coastguard! Are you in trouble?"

They all shouted at once, "Help! Help!"

"Someone's just gone overboard!" Joe shouted, terrified that Gwen would be swept out to sea.

They heard the boat chugging louder as they got closer, then slowed the engines as the friends kept shouting at them to find Gwen.

Slowly, the large craft made its way around the smaller one, the strong light shining like the sun into the water, searching for Gwen. Joe was on his feet now, hanging on tightly as he watched and nearly jumped in when Gwen appeared at the edge of the light as it swept past her. Someone jumped in with a life preserver and swam over to Gwen. Even though she was wearing a life jacket, she still fit into the hole and held on with her rescuer grabbing the rope. The two of them were pulled in carefully to the large craft, then it turned to face Toby and the others.

A short while later, the small craft was being slowly towed back to the shore with the three friends lying down in their boat and Gwen on the rescue craft.

When they reached the docks, two men jumped out of the rescue boat and tied the smaller craft to the pier, then helped the four out onto dry land. An ambulance was waiting, and a couple of paramedics attended Benito, Gwen and Joe.

"How did you know to come and look for us?" Toby asked one of his rescuers.

"I felt guilty for letting you youngsters take my boat out in this weather!" a voice called out in the darkness.

Toby and Rebeca turned to see Ed walking towards them, a strained smile on his face.

"When the time passed along, I got worried. I knew you'd run out of fuel and you wouldn't be able to fill it up in this weather. I don't know what I was thinking. I'm sorry. I'm so glad you are all right!"

"Gotta go, just got another call!" One of the men patted Toby on the back, and the two of them trotted down the planks to their boat.

"Thank you!" shouted out Toby and Rebeca to their backs, and they each raised a hand in acknowledgment.

Toby faced back to Ed. "Well, we're glad you did lend it to us! We found our friend over there, on pieces of his boat that had broken up."

"I think I need a beer!" said Ed, relieved that they were all all right.

"Me too!" called out Joe from the back of the ambulance.

The paramedics were happy to release Joe and Gwen, but wanted to take Benito into the local hospital to monitor him overnight. Gwen had already ordered a taxi to take them back to their hotel.

Soon, they were back at their hotel, where Joe and Gwen happily got into some dry clothes. Toby tapped on his phone, making a face as he did.

"Detective Brendon isn't going to be happy."

He got the answering machine, so left a short message saying that they had found Benito in Tenby, but Tadeo was missing. Two minutes later, Toby's phone rang and a very angry voice shouted down the line.

"I thought I told you to go back home! You said that was where you were going!"

Toby sighed deeply, and decided it was best if he didn't correct the man that that was not exactly what he had said to him ...

"Right, I'll speak to the police in Tenby and get a couple of officers around there shortly to take your and Benito's statements." The man actually sounded like he was growling as he added, "Just stay there and they will come and deal with you!"

Toby smiled as he clicked off. "I think he was trying to frighten me."

Rebeca chuckled, "Hopefully the officers he sends over will be more friendly!" Then she added, "We better go down to the bar and join Ed!"

Ed had just finished a beer as he sat chatting at the bar with the bartender who happened to be a cousin. Joe ordered their drinks, then they all sat down at a table talking animatedly about their frightening adventure, and wondering how Benito was doing.

Half an hour later, two police officers walked in the bar, a man and a woman, and Toby waved them over to their table.

"Are you Toby?" the woman asked him as they walked up. He nodded, and introduced everyone at the table. "We'd like to speak to you first, please," she said to him as she motioned to a table in the corner away from the various people who were in the bar.

Toby followed her over and sat down with the two of them. They were quite friendly, and the woman spoke kindly and compassionately to Toby as she asked him to go over all the details. Detective Brendon had told her the background up to where he had last spoken to them in Birmingham, but she wanted Toby to go through everything himself.

The officers spent twenty minutes asking Toby questions and writing things down, then had each of the others sit at the table with them by themselves to give a short statement. Finally, after about an hour, they were satisfied that they had gotten everything and said they were heading over to the hospital to speak to Benito. The policewoman took Toby's number and said she would call him with an update the next day, and possibly for more information if required.

Gwen anxiously asked that they not contact her parents, but as she was over eighteen and her parents were not involved with the case, the policewoman assured her that they wouldn't be notified.

"Mummy would be awfully upset," Gwen said as she sat close to Joe.

"I don't think our mom and dad will be very excited, either!" said Joe, grinning down at her. "It's probably best we tell them all about it when we get back home, eh Toby?" He glanced over at his brother, smiling widely.

"We have lots to tell them when we get back home – bad *and* good!" Toby grinned wearily and put his arm around Rebeca, squeezing her happily.

"I'm so glad I had that navigation system put in," said Ed. My friends laughed at me because of the age of my boat and all, but it was a gift from my wife. She knows how I love gadgets! It was for my sixtieth birthday last month. She said she couldn't afford a new boat for me, but she could afford to give it a little updating!"

Joe felt Gwen's head slowly growing heavier on his shoulder and he chuckled when he looked down and saw her asleep. The others smiled.

"I think we could all do with getting some sleep!" commented Rebeca, as she stood. Toby followed, and Joe gently touched Gwen's cheek to wake her.

Ed stood as well, but he said, "The night's early! I'll have another couple with Freddie." He nodded to his cousin who was busy serving a customer.

"Thanks again!" Toby and the others said meaningfully.

"Glad to oblige!" Ed beamed as he added, "And also glad it all turned out well!"

CHAPTER 19

Tuesday 23rd August

Toby woke to his phone vibrating on the wooden cupboard by his bed. Groggily, he rolled over on his back, picked it up and answered quietly, "Hello?"

"Hello, Toby, this is Detective Burrows." Toby recognised the policewoman's voice from the previous night.

"Uh-huh?" Toby said sleepily.

She tittered as she said, "Sorry, did I wake you?"

Tobby nodded, "Ya, but that's okay. What news do you have?"

Her voice became serious as she said, "I'm afraid a body was washed up on shore early this morning. It meets the description of your friend's uncle, so we will need Benito to identify him. I thought I would collect you first, then go over and pick Benito up from the hospital. I called, and he is ready to be discharged. I thought you might want to be with him when...".

"Of course!" said Toby firmly. "I'll get dressed and be ready to go in ten minutes." He clicked off, and looked over at the other bed to see Joe deep in sleep. Toby got up quietly and had a quick wash and was dressed in five minutes. He found some paper and a pen in one of the drawers and scribbled out a note for his brother.

Quietly, he opened the door and jumped as Rebeca's beaming face stared back at him, right hand raised to tap on the door. "Oh!" he said in a loud whisper, as he stepped out and shut the door behind him. He looked at his watch. "Wow! You slept in, Rebeca! It's 9:15!" He kissed her lightly on the lips, then pulled her to him, wrapping his arms around her and breathing in deeply.

They stood for several minutes, enjoying the closeness. Content to say nothing, but just relishing being together.

Finally, Toby spoke, "They found Tadeo's body. Well, what they *think* is Tadeo's body. The police are picking me up on their way to collect Benito so he can identify it."

Rebeca stepped back and looked up frowning. "May I come as well?"

"I don't see why not," said Toby. "We'll ask when the officers arrive. I was going to wait in the lobby for them." He took Rebeca's hand and they walked in silence to the front entrance where a police car pulled up just as they walked out the door. An officer stepped out of the passenger side and opened the back door for Toby and Rebeca.

When they arrived at the hospital, Rebeca waited in the car with the female officer while Toby and her partner went in to break the news to Benito.

Toby and the officer walked briskly down the hall and found Benito's room. They greeted Benito solemnly, then the officer broke the news to Benito about finding his uncle's body.

Benito said nothing for a moment, as he sat on the side of his bed with his feet dangling down. His clothes had been dried and he was dressed, waiting to be collected. Finally, he spoke, and looked sadly at Toby.

"I suppose I should be upset," he began slowly, "I mean, he was my uncle, after all." He stared off across the room while Toby and the officer stood silently. "But I just feel ... relief." He let out a long slow breath. "I feel ... free." He paused before adding, "If only this happened before he ...". Benito couldn't bear to say out loud what Tadeo had done to his mom. He looked up at Toby and then over at the officer. "Do those thoughts make me a bad person?"

Toby put his hand on his friend's shoulder, but the policeman spoke. "After what you have been put through, it is totally understandable, son. Are you up to seeing him?"

Benito nodded and glanced at Toby, "If you'll come with me."

"Of course! Rebeca is outside, too. She wanted to be with you, as well."

Benito smiled, "You are good friends." Toby smiled back at him and gave him a one armed hug.

The policeman waited a moment, then said, "Right, are you ready?"

Benito slid off the bed to his feet. "Ready as I'll ever be."

Twenty minutes later, Benito stood by the white sheet, with Toby and Rebeca close behind him. He took a deep breath, then nodded to the coroner, who slowly slid the sheet down just below the man's chin.

Benito let out a little gasp at the sight, then nodded, and turned to his friends who wrapped him in a group hug. "It's really him. He's really gone. He's gone."

They walked out of the building with Rebeca and Toby on either side of Benito, and climbed back in the police car. The policewoman drove to the B&B that Benito had been at with his uncle, and went in with him to speak to Joan and get Benito and Tadeo's things.

Joan was distraught when she was given a brief explanation, and she gave Benito a hug, "Oh, you poor boy! I hope it all goes well for you!"

Benito gathered his few items, and the policewoman took Tadeo's things. "We need to have a look to see if anything is evidence, but we'll give the items back to you when we are finished."

"I don't think there is anything I want," said Benito, "but thank you."

The three were soon dropped back at the hotel, where they found Joe and Gwen in the restaurant having breakfast. They both stood and gave Benito a hug and then motioned to the buffet table. Toby and Rebeca eagerly piled their plates and Benito followed behind, guilt nagging him as his stomach begged him to fill his plate. It didn't seem right that he should be hungry when his uncle was dead; and his mom ... Slowly, he chose various items until there was no more room on the dish, then made his way to where the others were now seated and tucking hungrily into their breakfasts.

Toby updated Joe and Gwen and they both nodded solemnly. Benito, Toby and Joe went back for seconds while Rebeca and Gwen finished theirs. Gwen grinned at Rebeca happily.

"I've booked us in for a full body massage!" When Rebeca looked at her slightly confused, Gwen flicked up her hand and laughed, "You'll love it!"

They booked Benito into a room of his own, where he decided to take some of the pills that the hospital had prescribed him and lie down. Toby and Joe decided to go for a soak in the hot tub while the girls had their massage.

Rebeca was grinning from ear to ear when she and Gwen met up with the boys. "How wonderful that was!" She turned to Gwen, "Thank you very much! That was most enjoyable!"

"I think we need to go to the town, now," suggested Gwen. "I'd like to look around."

"Great idea!" said Joe who turned to Toby, "We better bring back some Tenby rock for the girls!"

"I'll go check on Benito, first," said Toby, concerned for his friend. The others sat down on some chairs outside while they waited.

Toby tapped on the door, and when he didn't get an answer he used the spare key that he had gotten for himself. "Benito! Are you okay?" He called out as he entered.

Benito groaned quietly as he rolled on his side to look up at his friend through squinted eyes. "I'm so tired, Toby, and this bed is so comfortable. I just want to sleep!"

Toby chuckled and patted Benito's shoulder. "We're going to town. We may stop there for lunch."

"That's fine," said Benito softly, closing his eyes again. "Wake me when you get back in time for tea."

Before Toby shut the door behind him, he could hear Benito making soft snoring noises and he smiled happily to himself. Benito was going to be okay.

They walked into town, and at the first shop they went into, they found some Tenby rock. Rebeca smiled as she looked at the round, eight-inch long, hard sweets with the word TENBY that went all the way through as you ate them.

"I thought you were buying rocks!" she giggled. "I'm sure they would like those much better!"

They stopped for lunch in a pub, after which they meandered slowly around the town, then discussed going to the beach, which Gwen protested.

"I will only walk on the beach to get on a boat!" she moaned with a smile on her face. Despite her complaints, she was thoroughly enjoying the last day with her friends who had grown to mean so much to her. "Shall we go on a ride?"

They all agreed that this would be a fun idea, and ended up on the same boat that Tadeo and Benito had been on the previous day. They all took pleasure in being on a fast boat in the sunshine with a professional at the helm. The seals were all out, to the delight of the group; and on their circle around the island, the dolphins came in quite close and everyone chattered excitedly.

Around 5:00, Joe and Toby's stomachs rumbled and the girls shook their heads. Rebeca laughed as she said, "I do not think you two need a watch – your stomachs tell you exactly what time it is!"

They went to their rooms to freshen up for the evening meal, and Toby knocked on Benito's door to see if he was ready. Benito's face still looked groggy, but there was a relaxed look in his eyes that Toby had never before seen.

"Give me five minutes to splash some water on and put on some clothes," Benito said with a lazy smile.

Shortly they were all seated in the restaurant waiting for their food. Talk quickly turned back to their adventures and they all chattered excitedly, no one wanting to mention Gwen's predicament.

"So what are you going to do now?" Joe asked Benito.

"I don't – oh!" he interrupted himself. "Marlene!" Everyone looked at him confused; he continued, "Tadeo said he figured Keegan was keen on copying him on a ride out to sea! He said he thought Keegan would take her abroad to where it was sunny!"

"Well, maybe he has decided to do something nice for her," said Toby, not grasping Benito's meaning.

"No! You don't understand! Tadeo said Keegan wanted to go somewhere where no one noticed him. Where they wouldn't notice if one day there were two of you and the next day there was one! Keegan's going to take Marlene on a seaside holiday on the continent and get rid of her on a boat trip – like Uncle Tadeo tried to do to me!"

"Do you think Detective O'Reilley would assign someone to keep an eye on them?" asked Gwen, knowing the probable answer. "What else can we do?"

Toby got out his phone and tapped. "There's only one person who can help!" He looked down at his watch. "If I got it right, she should be on her lunch break!"

Benito pulled his chair closer to Toby's so he could see the screen. The screen flashed CALLING for ten seconds, and Toby was just about to give up when a huge braced grin flashed on the screen.

"Hey there!" She waved fervently like a toddler. "Oh, Benito! They found you! Oh fantastic! I'll have to let my dad know – he did contact someone he knew in the Birmingham police – did they help you? Or maybe not, since he only managed to speak to someone this morning! But I guess it doesn't matter because you are safe and sound – well you *look* safe and sound! Are you?" Benito opened his mouth to respond but Pamela continued, "I do wish I could be there! You guys are having such adventures! You must tell me about them, so I can feel like I am part of it all! Oh! You'll never guess!" And before anyone could guess, she told them, "I'm going into the police academy! I'm going to live with Aunty Ellie and Uncle Caleb because you have to be nineteen to enter in Florida, but only eighteen in Louisiana! Oh, it's too bad I'm not a cop now or I could help you myself – though it doesn't look like you need helping, since Benito is alive and well right there before my very eyes!" She took a deep breath and Benito dove in.

"We need your help with something else, now; and it is very urgent." Benito continued to talk for fear of Pamela getting sidetracked before they actually got off the starting blocks: "We need you to get your dad to find someone to check on a woman." He quickly gave her a shortened version of Keegan and Marlene, then asked anxiously, "Can you get your dad to help? Can he get someone to watch their house or something? I'm really worried and I feel certain that Keegan is going to do something to her!" Now it was Benito's time to take a breath and let Pamela speak again. However, she just stared at Toby and him, squinting her eyes and pressing her finger firmly on her lips.

Toby misunderstood and spoke out, "You can speak, Pamela, its okay! We need to know if you can help!"

Pamela smiled thoughtfully and giggled, "I have an idea! Give me the address, and I'll get back to you!"

"Thank you, Pamela, that's terrific!" said Benito, feeling slightly relieved that she might be able to help his friend. "You'll get back to us straight away?"

"It might take a little time, but I will do all I can to help!" She looked up at a clock that Toby and Benito could not see. "Oh darn! I gotta go! Listen, I promise I'll get back to you ASAP! Bye!" She clicked off before Toby and Benito could reply.

"Oh, I do hope she can help Marlene," said Benito. "She saved my life, giving me that phone." His thankful gaze went around the table and rested on Joe, "You all saved me – especially you, Joe. I'll never forget it."

Joe shrugged off his thanks, "Look, it was the least I could do for being so horrible to you since I met you." Silently, he was amazed at how the bitter hatred towards the teenager had dissipated and was thankful for the peace that now filled him. God did change something in him after all. Hopefully it wouldn't be the only thing.

"What shall we do now?" Toby asked the others. "I don't want to go back into Tenby, and I don't feel like watching the television."

"Shall we play cards?" asked Rebeca eagerly. Toby had taught her to play cards when they were in America looking for Emmie, Toby's little capuchin friend.

"Sure! I'll go get my cards and we'll meet in the lounge – there's a table there."

"I think I'll pass. I'm not keen on cards," said Gwen, "Besides, I want to get a manicure and a facial before I head back tomorrow – I'm going to a dinner party with Richard on Thursday to meet some friends and family." She flashed a forced smile at them before she made her way out of the restaurant to the treatment rooms.

"Is Richard her boyfriend?" asked Benito as he walked with Joe and Rebeca to the lounge.

"Her fiancé," corrected Joe, shaking his head.

"You don't like him?" asked Benito curiously. "Have you met him?"

"No, we have not," said Rebeca, "but I think there are some qualities he has that are not very pleasant."

"So why is she marrying him?" Benito looked at her, confused.

"Her parents found him for her. It is the way Gwen's people do things."

Benito accepted the explanation without further question as they sat down at the table and good-naturedly argued about what game they would play.

After several rounds of a simple card game with Benito doing very poorly, he leaned back in his chair with a huge grin on his face.

"This is great!"

The others looked at him, confused. Toby asked, "You don't like winning?"

"It's not that." He looked from one to the other, "It's just great to do a normal things with friends. Just hanging out!"

Joe cocked his head and looked at Benito thoughtfully. He had never truly taken into consideration the truly awful life that Benito had had with his uncle. No friends. No fun. No 'hanging out' and doing something simple like playing cards. "It must have been very lonely for you," Joe said, again surprised at the compassion that threatened to overwhelm him. "I'm so sorry that he got to your mom before he died."

Benito's smile faded, "Ya, she trusted him. She thought he had been led a little astray by some 'unpleasant characters', she used to say, but she had no idea what he was up to." A faint smile crossed his face as he looked off into the distance, "But I know she is in heaven now, and she is happy."

"We can ask our pastor if anyone in the church can help you – give you a place to live until you can get a job and fend for yourself," offered Joe.

"That would be great, thanks," said Benito through a huge yawn. That set them all off, and they decided that they had still not recovered from the previous night, so an early night would be welcome by them all.

Gwen was in their room when Rebeca entered, and she flashed her nails at her. "What do you think? I've gone for a bold red for a change!"

Rebeca looked closely. "They look lovely, Gwen." Then she added, "Gwen, I am glad we have become friends." Looking at her pensively, she added without the pity that she knew Gwen would have hated, "If there is anything I can do, just let me know."

Gwen laughed, "You never know, I might have to come and visit you in your jungle sometime, just to get away from it all." Then frowned, "*Are* you going back? You and Toby seemed to …".

"Yes, I am going back. I miss my family and my home. I have had some amazing adventures, but I know that is where I belong." She took a slow breath and exhaled just as slowly, "I don't know what Toby is going to do." She cocked her head and smiled, truly thankful for her new friend, "But I will happily accept whatever God has planned for me."

"You really believe that, don't you?" Gwen asked, curious at this faith of her friends that she did not understand. "My life is planned by my mother …," she said cynically. When she realised Rebeca might try to continue a conversation in which Gwen had no desire to participate, she grabbed her pyjamas, and headed into the bathroom.

CHAPTER 20

Wednesday 24th August

This time it was Toby who knocked at Rebeca and Gwen's door early the next morning. Gwen slept through the soft knocking, as Rebeca climbed out of bed and answered the door in her t-shirt and pyjama shorts.

"We need to go to Birmingham! I think we can find Marlene for Benito and save her!" Toby burst out before Rebeca could say a word. She stepped out into the hallway, pulling the door nearly closed behind her, putting a finger to her mouth.

"Shhh, Gwen is sleeping."

Toby suddenly frowned, looking at her clothing. "You are out here in your pyjamas!"

Rebeca took a deep breath before speaking. "Toby, how many times do I have to question your fear of being in a certain type of clothing when it covers the same amount as another type of clothing? In fact, this is covering more than my bathing suit yesterday, and you didn't complain about that!" She raised an eyebrow at him and he grinned sheepishly.

"No, I didn't. You did look … amazing!" He cocked his head at he looked at her in her pyjamas. "Come to think of it, you look amazing in that, as well!" He shook himself, "But its …" he interrupted himself. "Okay, okay! Anyway, Pamela left me a message last night, or I guess early this morning. She's smart! I think she is going to make a great detective."

"Well, what was the message?"

"She decided to get her Dad to get his friend over here to do some digging, and they found the names that are on the house purchase where they are living. Obviously the names listed are not their real ones, Keegan and Marlene; they're Tom and Brenda Johnson. She also asked him to check if there were a couple in the same name booked on a flight going out of Birmingham to somewhere sunny in the next day or so, and hey presto! They are booked on a flight for Greece at 4:00 this afternoon!"

"Great! So will the police stop them before they get to the airport?"

Toby made a face. "No, they said they had no reason to prevent the couple from getting on the plane and going on a holiday. There is no evidence – other than what Keegan told Tadeo who told Benito what Keegan was planning on doing."

"Well, when you put it like that, it does sound not very convincing," replied Rebeca. "So what did you have in mind? That we stop them from going to the airport?"

"I doubt that we could stop them from going to the airport, but if we find them at the airport before they get on the plane, and somehow get Marlene away from him out in public …".

"I should think he will be keeping a very keen eye on her; how do you plan on doing that?"

Toby grinned mischievously, "That is where Gwen comes into the plan! Pamela thought of that as well! So, we'll leave after breakfast which we will go for in … half an hour?"

Toby leaned down to kiss her, then stood up straight. "I can't kiss you in your pyjamas. It's not … right …".

Rebeca rolled her eyes and chuckled as she turned around, slipping back into the room to change into some 'appropriate' clothes and wake up Gwen. Soon, they were all in the restaurant, tucking into the delicious buffet breakfast, with all three boys filling their plates twice.

There was time for a quick dip in the hot tub before they returned to their rooms to pack up their belongings to get ready to go. Benito had a tiny pack, compared to the others, and Joe made a silent note to himself to make sure the poor kid got some more clothes.

By 10:00, they were all in the Porsche with Joe happily at the wheel, eager to spend another three and a half enjoyable hours driving a vehicle he would never be able to afford to own. The time passed quickly as they chatted animatedly about various things, including the plan to get Marlene away from Keegan.

"Oh! The pastor just got back to me," said Toby, looking at his phone, "He said there is a family that would be happy to take you in. They have some older kids who have left home, and one teenage son still in high school, so they have plenty of room. Their names are Don and Gina Peterson."

"That's great," grinned Benito, "A real family! I've always dreamed of having a brother!"

"I don't know, Ben," said Joe, without taking his eyes of the road, "Having a brother isn't all its cracked up to be!" Toby leaned forward and gave him a friendly smack on the head. "See what I mean, Ben? Nothing but abuse!" he chuckled.

"We can drop the car off at the rentals at the airport, and I'll have Charles meet us there to take my luggage. We're flying home at 5:30, so I'll stay here after we get this Marlene lady! I assume you all will be heading home on the train?" Gwen spoke, forcing herself to be positive about her return home as she turned to Joe with a closed-mouthed smile. He squeezed her hand gently and nodded with a quick glance in her direction as he followed the signs for the airport.

It was quite busy at the car rental depot, so Gwen gave Charles the key to the Porsche, as well as her luggage, with a promise to meet him at the private jet hangar by 4:30. The others just had rucksacks, so they carried them on their backs as they all hurried to the airport departures to look for Keegan and Marlene.

Joe looked at Gwen, who had chosen clothes suitable for her part in the plan, and he smiled at her admiringly. There was no way she could fail. His heart skipped a beat and he swallowed hard. It was useless to think of it – for so many reasons! He was glad she would be heading back to the States. He was growing fond of her.

They entered through the doors and Joe noted there only seemed to be one airline leaving from that departure area.

"You're sure which one they are taking?" he asked.

Toby nodded and pointed down the airport, "The next section is arrivals, then after that is the rest of the departures. Maybe we should split up, in case they come in down there where the other departures are. It's a bit of a weird set up, and if they've not been here before, they might possibly come in down there." He looked at his watch. "They should be here by now, dropping off their luggage. Certainly not much later!"

"Gwen and I, and Benito if he likes, can head towards the other departure entrances. You and Rebeca can go to the airline check-in section. Since only two of us have phones, we can only break into two groups," said Joe.

"Benito will have to come with us," said Toby. "Only you and he know what Marlene looks like."

"Oh ya! I hadn't thought of that!" Joe grabbed Gwen's hand and the two of them headed towards the entrances.

"So, you're still going through with it?" Joe spoke as he scanned the airport, looking for the attractive auburn-haired woman with a man.

Gwen glanced up at him, but saw he was looking around the airport. She sighed heavily, relishing the feel of her hand in his. "I have no choice, Joe. We've been through this."

"Because of the money?" Joe asked curtly, still holding on to her soft, manicured hand.

"No, not just the money. I told you. It's all I know. I don't know how to live any other way. Plus, even though my parents have never told me they loved me, I don't think I could cope with being shunned by them."

"You *really* think they would shun you?" Joe's tone softened and he glanced down at the stunning young woman. Even with her thick blond hair hacked to a very short hair style when she had been in the jungle, it didn't detract from her beauty. In fact, he thought it added to it. A pang shot through him.

She caught his glance and smiled softly up at him, nodding. "Daddy wouldn't be keen, but he does do whatever Mummy tells him to. I have a few aunts, uncles and cousins, but my mom is a formidable force – I am sure they would follow suit. I'd have nobody."

"What about friends?" Joe persisted. "What about Katy?"

"Oh, she'd be happy, of course! It would pave the way for her and Richard to possibly get together. But then, of course, she couldn't then remain friends with me."

"Surely this doesn't actually happen in the twenty-first century?" insisted Joe.

"In my world, it …".

"Oh! I think that is them!" Joe interrupted as he pointed to a couple just entering the airport. An auburn woman with a tall, dark haired man headed towards the luggage drop off area. Joe and Gwen quickened their pace and Gwen psyched herself up for her performance.

"Aren't they heading to the wrong airline drop off?" Gwen queried.

"Uh … oh … maybe Toby got the airline wrong."

Twenty metres from the couple, Joe was just about to step away from Gwen, then he stopped dead and pulled Gwen back.

"It's not them."

They carried on walking past the unaware couple who laughed happily. Joe intensified his gaze trying desperately to look at each person in the airport, as they walked along. They had nearly reached the far end of the airport, when Gwen's phone buzzed. It was Toby.

"They're here." Toby explained where they were and Gwen turned around as he spoke, with Joe following, both walking briskly. "They are joining the queue! Hurry!"

By the time Joe and Gwen reached the other three, Keegan and Marlene were in the middle of a queue. Toby looked at them crossly, "What took you so long? We'll have to wait again. Gwen can't do her thing while they are in the middle of the queue."

"Sorry, Tobs, we were right at the far end of the airport," Joe apologised. Though he felt it unnecessary, he could see that Benito was looking a little frantic, and realised that Toby must be feeling his friend's anxiousness for the woman's safety.

Just then, Benito spun around and whispered loudly, "Keegan is looking this way. I think I am going to have to go off for a bit. You all know what they look like. You can play the parts, and I will watch from a distance over there." He pointed to a seating area. The others nodded, and Benito tried his best to saunter casually over to the chairs.

"We can't just stand here watching them," said Toby. "We look a little odd – especially with no luggage."

"We have our back packs," spoke up Rebeca, "Maybe we are going for only a short journey somewhere?"

"Hello, there! You all look a little lost. Can I help you with anything?" They turned at the friendly voice. A short, female airport worker with a CAN I HELP YOU? vest grinned broadly at them.

"Oh! That is so kind! Thank you very much, but we are looking for someone – to say goodbye to them. They are going on a long trip away," Gwen smiled back.

"I can have them paged, if you like," said the dark-haired woman as she took out her radio.

"Oh! No! Thank you again, that really is kind, but we want it to be a surprise!" Her smile widened as she raised her eyebrows and the woman nodded.

"Sure! I hope you find your friend!" The woman waved as she turned and headed quickly in the direction of a crying child who appeared to be on his own.

Fortunately, the line moved quickly, and ten minutes later Keegan and Marlene were at the front, dropping off their luggage. Toby, Joe and Rebeca watched, as Gwen made her move, and began trotting carefully in her high heels towards the couple.

The group held their breath as they followed Gwen several metres behind. Keegan and Marlene were walking ever closer to the security check, but the crowds had waned slightly. Gwen drew closer, but still waited.

"I don't think it's going to work!" said Toby helplessly. "There aren't enough people around!"

Benito watched at a distance, and panicking, stood and began to follow his friends, praying that God would help them.

Suddenly, a large tour group burst through the doors and into the airport, right where Keegan and Marlene were walking.

"Oh!"

Keegan felt a pull on his arm and he turned, annoyed and ready to get cross with the person who had grabbed him amongst the crowd that had appeared out of nowhere. He took a sudden intake of breath when he saw her face. He had never seen someone so naturally stunning. He had always thought Marlene was beautiful, but she had nothing on this woman. She was on her knees looking up at him with amazing emerald eyes that took Keegan's breath away. For a moment, he said nothing.

"Oh!" she said again in a pained voice. "I'm so sorry! My heel gave way and I've hurt my ankle!" She hit him with her most alluring, vulnerable look and he was hooked.

Keegan looked down her perfectly shaped legs as she stretched out the right one, showing the heel dangling off her shoe. She offered one of her perfectly feminine, perfectly manicured hands as she pleaded with the most desirable rose coloured pouting lips oozing out seduction,

"Would you please be so kind as to help me to one of those chairs over there?"

Keegan didn't need to be asked twice. He took the hand and helped her up to her one foot. "Here, lean on me and I will take you over, sweetheart."

———»•«———

"Oh no! It's little Miss Helpful!" Joe whispered as the CAN I HELP YOU woman headed in Gwen's direction. He called out as she passed, "Oh, Miss?"

She stopped immediately and turned around, smiling when she recognised Joe and the others from earlier. "Yes?"

"You know," he spoke slowly as he watched Gwen's progress, pacing his conversation with her to match. "My friends and I, we were thinking …". A quick glance in Gwen's direction, then, "Maybe you could call our friend after all. We don't want to miss him."

"So, you want me to page him for you?" She grinned, happy to bring the friends together.

"Yes … but…". Another glance at Gwen, "Could you ask him to come to Customer Information over there, and say there is something wrong with his passport?"

The woman's smile faded slightly as she said hesitantly, "Oh, I'm not sure I would be allowed to do that…".

"Please?" This time it was Rebeca.

The woman looked at the three pairs of pleading eyes. "I'll go over and have a quiet word with Tammy, but I'm not promising anything."

"That's fine," said Joe, smiling charmingly at her, and Little Miss Helpful headed in the direction of the help desk at the far end of the airport.

"Now!" Said Toby, and as the group moved forward, Benito saw them from his vantage point and headed over.

<hr>

When the woman fell onto Keegan, Marlene just waited, expecting Keegan to brush her off. Although the woman was stunning, Marlene didn't anticipate her effect on Keegan and was surprised at his rapt attention. She reached out to tap him on the shoulder, when someone tapped on hers first and she spun around. She frowned at the familiar face, trying to grasp where she had seen it before.

"Come with us Marlene!" he whispered, "Benito sent us." When she just stood and stared at him, Joe panicked and he took her arm gently, pulling her away from Keegan and Gwen. She took a couple of steps and a few of the tourists from the large group invaded the gap between her and Keegan as the tourists talked excitedly.

Benito reached them just then, and he said a little too loudly, "He's planning on killing you, Marlene!"

The others looked at him and around them, but no one else had heard. She looked at Benito confused and still didn't move. Rebeca moved along side her and gently took her arm, pulling her forward, and something about her convinced Marlene to move in step with them. Toby took off his hoodie and put it around Marlene as they walked, and Rebeca encouraged her to zip it up. Joe grabbed her carry-on luggage that she was dragging behind her as he pulled out a baseball cap and Rebeca said just loud enough for her to hear:

"Put up your hair, and hide it in the hat."

Marlene did as Rebeca instructed, and grabbed her hair, wound it up in a knot on the top of her head, and as she did, Joe put on the cap. As he did, he glanced over his shoulder to see Keegan was examining Gwen's faulty shoe. They kept up the pace until they were lost in the crowd, then headed out the furthest doors where they finally slowed their pace.

<hr />

They reached the chair, and Keegan took the opportunity to put his arm around Gwen and move in a little closer as he helped her to sit down. Just then a tall, dark haired, solidly built man approached from the other side.

"Darling! I've been looking everywhere for you!"

Gwen smiled up at him, "Oh, Charles love, this man has been *so* kind to me."

Keegan stepped back, glanced up at the man, then took another step back as his eyes had to go up another few inches to look at the man in the eyes. "I was just helping your ... uh ... this young lady to a chair, as she hurt her ankle," he justified himself.

The man squinted his eyes at Keegan and crossed his arms across his solid chest intimidatingly. Keegan took yet another step back.

"I'll just leave her ... you ... the two of you ... I can see she no longer needs my help, so I'll just go back to my ...", he suddenly remembered Marlene and he looked over where he had left her. She was gone.

Without another word to Gwen and Charles, Keegan walked briskly to where Gwen had interrupted them, scanning the airport for Marlene. He looked frantically back and forth, looking for her red hair and the bright blue top she was wearing, holding himself back from shouting her name.

Where was she?!!

He broke into a trot as he pushed his way through the crowded airport, all the while desperately twisting his head, first right, then left, then right again, like a terrified parent that has lost his child. A few people spoke angrily to him as he barged through, but he didn't stop until he reached the end, then he turned around again and headed back the other direction, annoying some of the same people.

He slowed his pace, breathing heavily. *What could have happened to her?? She would never have had the courage to just leave him!* Keegan swore under his breath.

Then he heard over the tannoy, "Would a Mr Tom Johnson please come to customer information. There is a very minor problem with your passport. Please come to customer information before entering security."

Keegan stopped dead. No way. His heart started racing. A stream of obscenities flew out of his mouth. One more wide gaze around the airport, and he made his way quickly to the door and outside. A taxi pulled up, and Keegan jumped in.

CHAPTER 21

"Oh Charles, you really are a sweetheart!" She smiled coyly at him and batted her eyes.

"Now Miss Wentworth, you know that doesn't work on me." He grinned down at her and she pretended to pout. "I am old enough to be your father."

"That's okay! I do like an older man!" She turned her rose lips into a seductive kiss and blew it into the air at him.

Charles cocked his head, reached out with his hand and pretended to grab it from the air before it reached him. She gave him her best 'offended' look and he chuckled as he reached down and grabbed the shoes that he had dropped beside her when he walked up to confront Keegan.

"You asked me to bring some shoes, miss?"

"What would I do without you, Charlie?" She touched his hand meaningfully as she took the shoes from him and swapped them for what she had on.

"That's why I get paid the big money, Miss Wentworth."

"Oh Charlie, you don't do it just for the money, do you?" Gwen looked at him, a hint of hurt in her voice.

"You know I don't. I've been with your family a long time, and I've grown quite fond of you."

Gwen raised an eyebrow at him mischievously. "Yes?"

"You're like a daughter to me, Gwen."

Gwen huffed and Charles snickered kindly at her as he picked up the broken shoes, waiting for her to put on the others.

"It worked, Gwen!" Toby appeared from nowhere and gave her a big hug. "Thanks! Benito says a big thank you as well. He and Marlene called the policeman who had originally offered her help when they came to her and Keegan's house. We saw Keegan get in a taxi, but Benito and Marlene didn't want to risk the chance of him coming back while they just waited outside for the officer, so they are waiting inside at security."

"This is my hero," – she put her arm around Charles, hugging him firmly – "as well as my pilot."

"I thought he was staying with the plane to wait for you?" asked Toby.

"I realised I would need some shoes I could walk in, after I broke the heel on these ones, so I texted him that I would explain when he got here, but to please bring me a pair of shoes and when he saw me, pretend to be my husband to save me from an obnoxious man!" She gave him another hug. "He's the best!"

Charles cleared his throat, then spoke politely and authoritatively, "We need to make a move, Miss Wentworth."

"Give me a minute to say my goodbyes, Charlie."

He nodded, and stepped aside. She gave Toby a firm hug, then moved on to Rebeca, hugging her happily. "Thank you for being my friends! You must all come and visit some time." She turned to Joe, and, taking his hand, led him several metres away so she could say goodbye privately.

"Goodbye Gwen," Joe said simply, hugging her.

She gripped him tightly then as she released him, she said, "Kiss me?"

He leaned over and gave her a friendly peck on the cheek and she frowned at him.

"Kiss me properly, Joe," she pleaded, tears welling up and her bottom lip quivered.

"I can't," Joe said in a pained voice. "You're promised to someone else. It would be wrong."

She leaned forward, embracing him, tears wetting his t-shirt as she rubbed her face into his chest.

"I lov…".

"Stop, Gwen," Joe spoke firmly as he gently pulled away from her, holding onto her shoulders at arms length.

She took a tissue from her bag and wiped her eyes. Then she reached in her bag and pulled out a small box, handing it out to Joe.

He looked down as he took the box. His eyes widened as he saw what it was. "It's the latest iPhone! That must have cost ... sorry, I know I know, it's crass to talk about money." He started to hand the box back. "I can't, Gwen."

Gwen pushed it towards him again, "I want to make sure you stay in touch with me, please." Her eyes implored him and he sucked in his breath.

"I am not going to be your 'bit on the side', Gwen. You are marrying this guy, and in God's sight, that bond is unbreakable."

"But I don't believe in God," she persisted.

Joe closed his eyes and breathed out slowly, fighting his emotions, "Yet another, and unarguably the most crucial reason, that we could never be together."

Gwen scrunched up her face incredulously. "Even if you passed my mother's test of money and prestige?"

"Yes."

"God means that much to you?" she queried, trying to comprehend.

"He's a part of me." Joe struggled to explain, "It's like ... He's in my DNA – I am who I am because of God."

Gwen frowned, still not understanding. Undaunted, she pushed the box firmly in his hand, "You are a good friend, Joe. I'll take what I can get. I won't ask for anything more than that. Please take it."

Joe reluctantly took the phone and looking over at Toby and Rebeca, he reminded her, "We are *all* your friends."

"But you're my *best* friend," Gwen had the last word as she stood on her tip toes and started to kiss his cheek, but then at the last second, slid sideways and stole a kiss from his mouth. Then she turned and made her way back to Charles, who was looking her way and tapping his watch.

The pair hurried out of the airport and left Joe, Toby and Rebeca waving them off. Toby looked in Joe's hand. "What have you got there?" he asked nosily.

"A new phone." He cleared his throat and said casually, "She wanted to make sure we all stayed in touch."

Toby winked at him and offered, "You mean she wanted to make sure *you* stayed in touch?"

Joe frowned seriously at his brother, "She's getting married, Toby. Let's just move on from that subject, okay?"

"Shall we go find Benito?" interjected Rebeca, wanting to keep the peace between the two of them.

The boys nodded and shortly they arrived at the security desk where Benito and Marlene were still waiting. Marlene still wore the hoodie and the cap that they had put on her and she looked like a tall, lost child, sad but relieved to be rescued.

"Thank you." She looked at them all, and although she had already said it several times, glanced at Benito as well. "I told the officer about the necklace. He seemed to think I wouldn't do any jail time ... because of the circumstances." She nodded to Benito, "I mean, *we* wouldn't do any jail time."

A few minutes later, the police officer that had visited Marlene a few days earlier came to the security desk. He had a woman officer with him. Marlene smiled gratefully at him, but said nothing.

"I'm so glad you changed your mind, Miss ...".

"Marlene, please call me Marlene."

"This is PCW Eleanor Waters." He introduced the accompanying officer who smiled warmly at Marlene and shook her hand as she spoke to Marlene.

"We'd like to take you to the station first, to get a statement from you. Then we will take you to the shelter and settle you in there. They will help you with all the things you need, including helping you get back in touch with family."

Marlene frowned and she hung her head, "My family won't want to get back in touch with me. I ...".

PCW Waters shook her head gently and touched Marlene's arm, "It doesn't matter what you have done or what you think you have done. I've been in domestic for over ten years, and I have never seen a family that weren't keen on welcoming back their loved ones."

A faint glimmer of hope entered Marlene's watery eyes and she queried in a whisper, "Really?"

"Really," the officer assured her, before glancing at the others and back at her partner.

"We could do with more information from yourselves, as well," the officer looked at Benito then the others. "I'll call another car to take you to the station."

They said their goodbyes to Marlene who walked off in a daze at the prospect of finally being free from Keegan and eventually back with her family.

Another car and officer arrived for the others and took them to the station to get more information from all of them. They took statements from each of them regarding what they knew about Marlene and Keegan, which was rather limited with Joe, Toby and Rebeca.

Benito gave detailed accounts of what he witnessed in Keegan's house, and then the officers enquired more regarding the necklace. Benito thought he remembered the name of a street near to where they dropped off the necklace, so after the interview, the police took Benito and his friends in two cars to the street to see if he could locate the building. When Benito pointed it out, the two officers who interviewed him said he could leave with his friends in the other car that would take them to the train station.

Although the police said they would probably want to speak to him again, and they had not yet decided if they would be charging Benito with anything, they decided he was low risk of running, so just took Toby's number and address for future questions and possible witness for Marlene.

The four were relieved to finally get on the train and find some seats together in a regular class coach, where they all duly fell asleep until the train arrived at their home town. Joe woke as the train pulled up, and they all scurried off to find their mom who was waiting to take them home.

The twins greeted them excitedly, each holding onto either of Rebeca's hands and pleading with her to take them hunting rabbits. She laughed and said they would perhaps go out the next day.

The next morning, Toby got a call from one of the police who had interviewed them the previous day. He asked to speak to Benito, so Toby went down the stairs to find Benito and Rebeca at the kitchen table eating breakfast. A worried look passed over his face when Toby told him who it was.

"Do you think they decided to charge me?" Without waiting for a reply, he continued nervously, "Please will you sit down here and put it on speaker phone?"

Toby nodded and informed the officer what he was doing, so he could be a support for Benito. He pressed the button and held out the phone across the table.

"We got a call from the hospital, who said your mom has been asking for you. She's been worried as she didn't know how to contact you."

Benito looked confused and said nothing for a moment. Finally he spoke in a shaky voice with tear filled eyes, "M-m-my mom? But she's ... Tadeo said he killed her."

The policeman said compassionately, "Oh son, I'm sorry about that! He may have thought he had, but they managed to pump her stomach from the poison he had given her, and she's feeling a lot better."

"Are you serious?!" Benito burst out with a broad smile and the officer confirmed that his mom was indeed alive and well.

"Yes, she's out of ICU and they said she can go home, as long as there is someone to care for her for the first few days." He paused. "Although, that is some bad news, in that her flat tenancy was cancelled due to non-payment of rent. So, you'll have to find another place to live."

Benito, Toby and Rebeca grinned happily at the news of Benito's mom, and Rebeca gave him a big hug. Finally, Benito said to the officer. "What about the house that my uncle had? I think he owned it."

The policeman said he needed to check it out and put Benito on hold. Several minutes went by, then finally he came back to Benito, "I'm afraid that even if he did own it, there is nothing to say that it should be passed to you and your mother. Plus, the house may have to be sold to pay for your uncle's criminal activities. However, there is a shelter that takes families, so we can probably get you and your mom in there for a bit, until you get back on your feet."

"It's somewhere to go, for now! And I can get a job," Benito said enthusiastically, and the others nodded happily with him.

"I'll give the shelter a call to see when you can go there, then you can phone the hospital and let them know when you will be picking her up."

While they waited for the officer to call back, Toby contacted the Petersons to say Benito wouldn't be going to their house after all, but the generous couple insisted that Benito's mom stay with them as well.

Toby contacted the officer straight away to say the shelter wouldn't be needed, then Joe suggested they take Benito to town to pick up some clothing and any other items he would need. Joe had a little bit of savings left over from university, and he had spoken to the Petersons, and between them they had put together a little fund to pay for whatever Benito would need.

The four friends spent the day laughing and generally enjoying what Benito called 'normal hanging out with friends'. They all tried on clothes and helped Benito pick some things out, and of course, stopped for lunch at the boys' favourite restaurant.

Early the next morning, Toby knocked on Benito's door and was startled that it opened instantly, with Benito fully dressed.

"The Petersons are coming over after breakfast and will take you and me up to Birmingham – and, if the police say so, we can collect your things from your uncle's house, then come back down and get you and your mom settled in your new home!"

Although Benito was extremely excited, he still managed a huge breakfast, and even Joe was amazed at the amount of pancakes and bacon the teenager consumed. The Petersons arrived shortly after they finished to take Benito and Toby up to the hospital, where there was a tearful reunion between mother and son.

They then drove to Tadeo's house, where Gabriella waited in the car with the Petersons while Toby and Benito walked up the drive to the house. Benito went around the side and came back holding a key that Tadeo kept hidden outside in a safe spot.

Unlocking the door, the first thing Benito spotted was his Bible, still split open and lying on the floor. He picked it up carefully and put it in his backpack before making his way slowly up the stairs, half expecting his uncle to call out at him from the living room to get him a cup of tea and some cake.

Toby followed close behind and entered the bedroom after Benito. Benito took out a large bag from the wardrobe and gathered what few belongings he had as Toby wandered slowly around the room imagining what it had been like for his friend to live here with his evil uncle. Toby strolled over to the window and opened it up. He leaned out and immediately jumped back as a grey cat launched itself through the opening and jumped on Benito's bed meowing frantically.

"Gideon!" Benito swept the creature up in his arms and held him tightly. The next minute, he bent down and, reaching under his bed, grabbed the water dish and rushed to the bathroom to fill it as he carried Gideon in one arm. He carried the water and Gideon back to his room and put them both on the floor by his bed. He knelt beside the animal, stroking him as he drank thirstily.

Toby smiled, but queried, "Tadeo let you have a pet?"

Benito shook his head, "Uncle didn't know." He paused a moment, frowning at the horrific memory of Tadeo discovering Gideon. He could not bear to voice out loud what his uncle had done, so continued with a brief explanation. "Well, not at first. Then he dumped Gideon in a car park several miles away." His grin returned as he looked down at the gentle creature. "I can't believe he found his way back!"

"You better finish packing, the Peterson's are waiting." Toby hated to rush his friend, but he looked outside and saw everyone waiting patiently for them to gather Benito's belongings."

Benito gave the creature one last stroke before he shoved the rest of his things into a second bag. He put on the now heavy backpack, then gathered Gideon up in his arms as he turned to Toby. "Can you bring the other bag?"

Toby picked up the second bag, but silently wondered what the Petersons would say when Benito came out with a cat.

They made their way down the stairs and out the front door with Toby shutting it behind them. Benito repositioned Gideon in his one arm as he took off his backpack, holding it with the empty hand.

Mr Peterson climbed out of the car and walked over to Benito, putting a kind hand on the teenager's shoulder when he reached him. "Is he yours, son?"

Benito was so overwhelmed at finding his little friend when he never expected to see him again, that he could only nod as he snuggled the comforting creature tightly.

"You can bring him, if you like. We already have one cat; what's one more?" Mr Peterson smiled widely as he took the backpack from Benito and put it in the open boot. Benito looked at the man, grateful tears filling his eyes.

Benito turned to Toby, "Will you lock the door?" And before Toby could reply, Benito climbed in beside his mom who gave Gideon a little stroke as he curled up happily on her son's lap. Toby wasn't long, and he quickly returned after locking the front door and putting the key back from where Benito had taken it. Toby put the bag in the back, and climbed in beside Benito and his mom.

"I just need to make one stop," said Mr Peterson as he signalled to drive off and headed down the road. A few minutes later, he pulled up in front of the shop that Benito used to go, where the robbery was.

"Oh!" called out Benito, leaning over the seat as Mr Peterson opened the door to get out. "Please will you ask how Maggie is? She got stabbed in a robbery … where …" – Benito suddenly realised he hadn't told the police that he had been there, and they might be looking for him. He swallowed hard. "Two men robbed the place when I was there, and I … ran off … I was afraid Tadeo would be angry with me for being late." He scowled at the memory, feeling guilty for running away. "I guess I have something else to tell the police."

Mr Peterson nodded in understanding and made his way into the shop. Shortly, he came out with a few things in his hands, and broad smile on his face. "She is doing well!" he said as he climbed in the vehicle and passed his items over to his wife. "She is out of hospital, and resting at home. They said she should be back in next week." He looked thoughtfully at Benito.

"We'll make a quick stop at the police station where you can speak to the officer assigned to your case … I'm sure it will be fine. You were only a witness that time, after all. If they catch the two culprits, they may want you to testify."

It only added another half an hour onto their journey home, and Mr Peterson went in with Benito as he spoke to the officer about Maggie. As they left the station and climbed back in the car, a worried look passed over Benito's face and he shook his head slowly,

"I think I might be involved in too many things," he said quietly.

Mr Peterson looked over at his wife who nodded, then offered, "We can be with you any time you need to speak to the police, if you like, son." Then added, "And if you have to go to court to testify about anything, we will go with you."

Benito rubbed his eyes with his left hand as his right hand rubbed Gideon's soft head. He whispered just loud enough for Mr Peterson to hear, "Thank you, sir. That is very kind of you both. Thank you."

CHAPTER 22

Three weeks later
in the Nicaraguan jungle

Rebeca giggled as she lay back against the bow of the little boat gazing up at Toby pulling at the oars. "Are you sure you do not want me to row?"

Toby cocked his head and smiled, "I am fine, thanks! I had a great teacher. Don't you think I row well, now?"

The sun shone brightly in the clear blue sky, and Rebeca let a hand trail along the water, relishing the coolness against her skin. A sad look spread across her face. "Do you think Gwen will be all right?"

"You heard her yourself. Despite everything, she would rather spend the rest of her life with this Richard than living without money and being rejected by her family and friends." He squinted his eyes, thanking God for Rebeca's love for him. He still couldn't believe that he hadn't seen what an incredible girl she was straight away. He thought of Gwen and felt a combination of compassion and cynicism. "Besides, she has all that money to keep her happy."

Rebeca frowned, "I will pray for her. I think she is so starved of love that she is desperate to take anything; and she is so used to wealth, she has no idea how to live without it. How very sad it is."

"And we have nothing in comparison!" laughed Toby.

"Speak for yourself!" replied Rebeca in teasing haughtiness. "I have all this." She waved an arm, gazing around her at the clear river water and the huge variety of trees and plant life. She closed her eyes and listened to the sounds of the jungle that she appreciated so much more, now that she had been in what she called the human jungle. Brightly coloured birds cawed and cooed and cried, while some monkeys in the distance squealed at each other.

"And what about me?" queried Toby in mock hurt.

"Let us not talk about that," said Rebeca quietly. "Not now." She moved carefully forward and leaned against his knees as he rowed.

Toby suddenly stopped rowing and listened to the shouting in the distance. "What is that?"

Rebeca opened her eyes and looked in the direction of the noise, concentrating. A wide grin spread across her face and she said, "The men are back from hunting and they have caught a very large deer. We will be feasting tonight! Hurry! We must go back and help with the preparations!"

Toby spent the afternoon helping the men prepare and set the deer on the fire to cook; while Rebeca and the women gathered vegetables and prepared them to go in the large pot as Rebeca's grandmother oversaw the operation.

As the dark settled, the food was shared out amongst the men first, then the women and children. Everyone had plenty and there was much laughter and chatter, though Toby did not understand any of what they were saying. Rebeca began translating, but he stopped her, with a relaxed gaze and a shake of his head.

"I can still enjoy this all, even if I don't understand."

"Do you think you will enjoy the ritual tomorrow – to become a man in our village?"

Toby nodded. He knew some of it would be difficult, even painful, but he knew it was something he wanted to do for her; and himself.

When everyone had consumed all that they wanted, the fire was fed until it danced brightly and the villagers encircled it. A couple of drums and a few strange instruments were brought out as people began to play, sing and dance.

Toby and Rebeca danced around the fire, laughing for what seemed to Toby, to be hours. His eyes watched her continuously, taking in everything about her from the fire shining on her dark hair and in her dark eyes, to her smooth skin and feminine curves all the way to her feet that danced barefoot. Suddenly, he was overwhelmed, and he grabbed her hand, leading her away from the fire into the seclusion of the trees.

For a long while, they said nothing as they stood together. Toby wrapped Rebeca tightly in his arms, and she slipped her arms around his waist, breathing in each other's scents as they listened to the celebrating around the fire.

Finally, Rebeca spoke, her voice shaking, "Three years is a long time."

Toby buried his face in her soft hair and inhaled deeply. "I know. It wasn't what I had planned, but when my parents told our pastor about my newly acquired faith, he spoke to the elders at our church about some money that the church had put aside. They immediately all felt I should have it to go to theological college … and when they spoke to me, I just knew …".

"That it was right," finished Rebeca.

"I will come and visit you once a year," Toby offered tenuously.

"No," said Rebeca firmly, "that would make it too difficult." She pulled away slightly and looked up at him, a myriad of emotions racing through her. "You can send me letters at the school. I will still be going there regularly when I finish my education. My teacher said I could be her assistant." She forced a pretend contented smile up at him.

Toby breathed out heavily through his nose. "I suppose you are right. Plus, I don't imagine I will have enough money to fly down here once a year. This was the last trip, courtesy of the Wentworths." He grinned, remembering what it was like to just do anything and go anywhere without thinking about money. "It was fun while it lasted."

"I am happy to be back home," said Rebeca thoughtfully.

Toby smiled down at her, "Don't tell me you won't miss ice cream!"

She laughed and said teasingly, "Oh, of course! I may miss it more than I miss you!"

Toby drew her back close to him and she nestled against his chest with tears in her eyes. Toby swallowed hard. "I *will* come back, Rebeca." A tear fell from his eye and landed on her dark hair. "And when I do, I will come for you – with the biggest deer you have ever seen."

———————

THE END

ENDNOTE

1. https://answersingenesis.org

Printed in Great Britain
by Amazon

32373375R00205